Mr Tumnal

T E SHEPHERD

Mr Tumnal

shepline

First Published in Great Britain in 2015 by Shepline Words, Bicester, Oxfordshire

words.shepline.com

2 4 6 8 10 9 7 5 3

British Library Cataloguing-in-Publication Data
A catalogue record for this book is available from the British Library.

ISBN 978-0-9571756-7-9
E-BOOK ISBN 978-0-9571756-6-2

Edited by Zedolus Proofreading & Author Services, Bath, England
Twitter: @ZedolusProof

Typeset in Goudy Old Style by Shepline Creative, Oxfordshire
creative.shepline.com

FOR
imaginary friends
everywhere

'Of course it is happening inside your head, Harry, but why on earth should that mean that it is not real?'

Harry Potter and the Deathly Hallows, 2007

'And if they're fictional, it is entirely acceptable to cheat on fictional men with other fictional men.'

Jane Rawson, August 2009

'Wouldn't it be weird to discover you were related to someone fictional? You'd start to doubt your own existence.'

David Mitchell, QI, January 2010

'Memory is a wonderful thing if you don't have to deal with the past ... yeah, a memory's never finished, if you really think about it.'

Richard Linklater, Before Sunset, 2003

PART ONE

Summers School

andante scherzando

1

The notes echoed in Louis' mind, a tune that had been carried with him all his life. All his life? No, for the last few years the notes had been strangely absent. In fact, thinking about it, he couldn't now remember the last time that he had heard them. Still, he heard the tune and it was instantly familiar. Louis searched through his fragmented memories for the time when he first heard the tune – a haunting flute melody. The soundtrack to his childhood.

He pursed his lips and whistled, and the tune sang out. The room was filled with the music, and outside of his own mind he could hear the tune again. But where, when, did he first learn the notes? And why had he blocked all memories of it from his mind?

Once more the tune remained lodged in his head. Later that night, as he stood before the bathroom mirror and brushed his teeth, the music kept on playing. It was there as he lay with his head on the pillow and wished for sleep, and it was there in the morning from the moment he first woke up.

And still it was a mystery as to where the tune came from. Louis Tumnal almost made himself late for work by scouring through his music collection for some clue, leaving piles of CDs, cassettes, and vinyl around the hi-fi. He left the flat wearing his corduroy jacket, pushing his twenty-year old bicycle out the gate for the short cycle across town to his school.

The bell was ringing for morning registration when Louis arrived for work, and he hurried in after the last few children with his leather satchel tucked under his arm. He knew that he was late, but he thought he might just get away with it; until, that is, he heard the unmistakable click of stiletto heels on the hallway floor behind him, and the curt, clipped voice that followed them. He turned and faced Miss Leroy.

Miss Leroy was a force to be reckoned with at school, feared by both pupils and staff alike. Louis Tumnal could not focus on what Miss Leroy was telling him now, as her presence in front of him at that moment stirred other deeper memories.

The first time Louis heard the tune was also the first time that he encountered Miss Leroy. She was then head of music at Wren Hoe County School. He recalled the exact moment: it was his eleventh birthday and he was sprawled on the playground in the heavy drizzle, with his trousers ripped and his knees grazed, clutching his new flute to his chest, and choking on tears. She swept out of the music block in her floral dress and stiletto heels, as his assailants scarpered down the lane in the direction of the bicycle sheds.

She scooped him up and led him back to her office, to clean him up and dry his eyes. He remembered squinting through his cracked glasses as she worked to repair the flute, a present to him only that morning. When she lifted the flute to her lips and played that first tune, it was like magic.

Through pursed lips and with nimble fingers, the song sung through him, and gone was the throbbing pain of his wounds. She'd handed him the flute, and with careful instruction, taught him how to get his first note. At first he struggled; his hands were too small to hold the instrument, his fingers slipping off the keys. The only noise was the splattering of air and spit.

Miss Leroy wouldn't let him give up though, and when the bell sounded for afternoon lessons she sent word to his form teacher. For the rest of the afternoon, Louis sat in Miss Leroy's office and learnt to play the flute. After what seemed like hours of trying, a note – which he later learnt to be G – escaped his lips. Of course he couldn't repeat the note straight away, and fumbled through an octave of miss-blows and spittle whilst his teacher encouraged him. Then he got the note again, and by playing with the keys, another. There was no turning back.

His first lesson went past the end of school, with him playing his way through *Three Blind Mice* as students poured out of their classrooms, surging across the playground to funnel their way out of the school grounds. Over the next half hour the last stragglers left, and the cleaners began patrolling the corridors with rotawashers. By five o'clock, Louis realised how late it had gotten, and after panicking about it, Miss Leroy bundled him into her Morris Traveller and drove him home.

That was how it began, weekly lessons and daily practices for the next seven years. Louis never considered that he became what he would call an exceptionally fine player, but he joined the school orchestra and passed his grades. Miss Leroy always pushed him further and encouraged him when he did well; and she always made time for him, even when she became Miss Leroy, Headmistress.

From that moment on Miss Leroy had become part of his life, guiding his future and helping him attain his goals. Louis smiled. One day, Miss Leroy stopped being a teacher and became his friend.

Louis came round from his daydream to find Miss Leroy still in front of him, and still waiting. He mumbled something in response to what she might have asked. It was enough to satisfy her, and she clipped off back down the hallway as he made his way to class.

'What are you smiling about?' Sarah's words came as a surprise to Lewis, and he sat up briskly, suddenly alert again.

'Dad? Why are you acting so – weird?'

Lewis looked to his side, and to his eleven-year old daughter sitting next to him; staring up at her father with those big, round, searching eyes, and that coy, enchanting expression on her face.

'It's just strange for me,' said Lewis. 'I don't know if I'll ever get used to parents' evening like this.'

'You're being ridiculous,' Sarah countered. 'You conduct parent's evenings all the time.'

'Not as a parent! Not with my little troublemaker at my side!'

'Dad–'

Sarah reached over and gave her father a reassuring hug. He settled back down in his chair, twitching his fingers nervously, and staring with a fixed gaze at the name plate to Miss Leroy's office door.

Miss Leroy. How old was Miss Leroy? Was she ever married? All through school, as a pupil and even, Lewis had since discovered, in the staffroom, the talk was the same. Some people thought she was younger than she looked, some that she was older. Truth was she never said. He remembered the scandal that went around the school when someone thought they had seen her 'stepping out' with a man. Then there were the writings on the toilet doors – Lesbian Leroy, as she was known.

All that Lewis knew, or cared, was that she had saved him when he had been bullied, and she had taught him about music. He learnt early on, during those first, private music lessons, that she lived in a big house in the Park Town area. Her family obviously came from some wealth; indeed, she was principle sponsor of the City Orchestra.

The office door in front of them opened, and Dr and Mrs Ashbury stepped out with their floppy-haired son Alexander in tow. Lewis faked a smile at the family; he had always thought there was something odd about Alexander, and when he had then met his mum and dad at last year's parents' evening, he remembered realising why.

The door to Miss Leroy's office opened again, and her secretary summoned Lewis and Sarah in. Minutes later, although it could have been hours, Lewis was sitting alongside his daughter on one side of Miss Leroy's desk. The office was in the original red-brick Victorian part of the school, with a view over the playground and the 1960s extension. Her desk was neatly arranged with a selection of books and pencil pots; on one corner of the desk was a gilt-framed picture of a young man in a formal suit, which Lewis could not remember seeing before. Opposite Lewis and Sarah, Miss Leroy sat, in her usual pristine elegance, her long black hair fastened in a bun; she was reading the school report through her horn-rimmed reading glasses. Eventually she closed the report book and looked from father to daughter.

'Well,' Miss Leroy began. She looked first to Sarah and then to Lewis, and that was all that Lewis heard of his daughter's music report. The song was in his head again; a haunting flute melody that silenced the world outside.

Occasional snatches of Miss Leroy's voice echoed through into his head; a report on Sarah's involvement in the school production. Lewis remembered his own part in the winter concert, aged thirteen and standing at the front of the stage playing that same flute melody. Through child's eyes he scanned the audience, seeking out his parents who of course were not there. Did they ever come and hear him play? From the front row Lewis could see the tall, stately shape of Miss Leroy with eyes fixed on him, willing him to play just as she had taught him.

When Miss Leroy looked up now, it was with those same eyes that she looked at Lewis; almost, Lewis thought, as if she was reaffirming that, like his playing of the flute under her tutorship, he should bring up Sarah in the correct and proper way.

Later that evening, Lewis Tumnal walked home with Sarah. The late July evening was still light, but with a slight chill to the air and the last of the spring blossom lay in the gutter. Lewis' bike released a regular, rhythmic squeak as he pushed it along.

'Dad?'

Sarah's voice, following the silence of the night, startled Lewis out of his day-dreaming.

Lewis glanced down at the girl who was walking next to him, and gazing up at her father through large, appealing eyes. She had that look about her that a question was coming.

'Why do you wear your wedding ring around your neck?'

Lewis felt the gold ring between his fingers. He hadn't been aware, but all the way down the road he had been fingering the ring where it hung. He pulled his hand away self-consciously, unsure of what to do with it instead.

'It doesn't fit. It never has.'

Later, he sat in the lounge opposite his daughter and unlocked the chain. He slipped the ring off and turned it over in his fingers, before passing it to Sarah.

'It was my grandfather's, you see,' explained Lewis 'We always meant to have it resized. We never did.'

'It's unusual.'

'I guess.'

Lewis looked at the gold band, set with a stone of obsidian.

'It's not the usual band of yellow gold.'

Sarah turned the ring over in her hands before passing it back to Lewis.

'Night, Dad.'

She planted a kiss onto his cheek, hastened from the room, and bounded up the stairs.

*

Louis continued to sit in the lounge, turning his grandfather's wedding ring over in his hands. Slowly he threaded the ring back onto the chain and fastened it round his neck. The tune echoed through his mind again, growing louder and more relentless as it pounded his brain; Louis clutched at his head, pressing his fingertips to his temples.

He picked himself up from the sofa and staggered out of the lounge. Pausing in the hall, he leant on the protrusion of banister that jutted out from the wall. He stopped and stared at it; a reminder from the days long past, from when this flat was part of a much larger house.

2

A sparrow flipped and flapped on the ledge outside the window, doing a little dance amongst the last of the spring blossom and the faded, curled seed heads. Louis blinked himself awake, and realised how transfixed he had become by the little bird. He glanced back down at the pile of marking in front of him, and let out a long, resigned sigh.

The afternoon sun slanted through the tall school windows onto the rows of desks stacked with chairs. He looked up again, and a shaft of sunlight hit him on the face, blasting him with summer heat and blinding light. Rising from his desk at the head of the class, he moved to the window and lowered one of the blinds. As he returned to his desk he eased his corduroy jacket off and onto the back of the chair, before fingering inside his collar and flicking back the top button. He loosened his tie and lifted his pen to another exercise book, flipping it open to another scrawl of almost total illegibility. Briefly he pondered why they couldn't teach children to write properly these days, before remembering that he was the English teacher, and this was the bottom set in the year; any effort he tried to put in was, frankly, wasted. He read through the opening paragraph, vaguely reminiscent of something he had once read on Wikipedia, were it not for the lamentable spelling and poor sentence structure. He frowned, and began striking through the errors.

Exercise book followed exercise book, and essay followed essay; the clock ticked loudly in the otherwise mausolean classroom, with every movement of the second hand seeming to reverberate around the room. Louis continued to mark papers until just after five-thirty, the sky cast in the rich, warm glow of evening.

Louis had long since ceased to hear the endlessly ticking clock, when he was startled back into life by a knocking at the door. He glanced up to see Beth peering through the wired glass. She clicked the door open and popped her head round.

'You coming then?'

Louis glanced down at the pile of marking still in front of him, and winced at the thought of it still being there tomorrow.

'Okay, why not? I'll see you out the front in, what – ten minutes – five, maybe?'

Beth nodded, and was gone. Louis began to gather up his marking, placing it in ordered piles on his desk and dropping his pencils and pens back into his old, much-loved, suede pencil case.

For a moment Louis paused, staring down the length of desks and the rows of chairs, before gathering up his jacket and satchel. Flicking down the line of light switches, he let the classroom door swing shut behind him as he walked the length of corridor through the middle of the 1950s red-brick school. Far off at the end, a cleaner was silhouetted against the window with a rotawasher. Walking past the courtyards of the old H-block, he looked out at the school allotment filled with rows of potatoes, runner beans and tomato plants.

At the staffroom he lingered for a moment to check his pigeon hole, before cutting through to the bike sheds.

Beth was already waiting out the front of the school when Louis free-wheeled round the side of the school. He dismounted in front of where she was chatting with Tom and Polly in their Lycra shorts, straddled across their expensive bikes. Further off, some children were grouped around a small play area opposite.

'Alright, Louis?' Tom greeted his friend.

Louis nodded, and lifted his hand in recognition. Tom was tall and thin, and walked in a way that stooped his round colourless head between his shoulders. Louis smiled as he remembered Polly's description of him, just before she first introduced him to the group of friends as a very tall, thin, tortoise. Louis wished that he could engage Tom in conversation more, but he couldn't. He used to think that it was the intense cycle fitness regime, that he had now got Polly in on too, that separated them, or Tom's success at being the lead cellist in the Wren Hoe Symphony Orchestra.

He glanced at Polly, considering how she had always liked the creative side to her men. He remembered how, when they were both at university – over a decade ago now – he had once thought that he might have had a shot at a relationship with her.

'Louis!'

Louis snapped out of his day dream.

'Are you coming then?' Beth asked, obviously for the second time. 'To the pub?'

Louis returned Beth's gaze, vacantly at first; then he brightened up and smiled.

'Of course.'

Tom and Polly walked ahead, wheeling their bikes next to them, with Louis a few steps behind Beth with his bike. They left the school grounds and turned the corner, with Tom already going off on one about a conveyancing job he was involved in;

musician he might be, but it did nothing to shift Louis' opinion of solicitors – Tom's day job.

Louis looked up and across the road as he turned the corner. From a park opposite where children played, Louis' eyes met with those of a ten-year old girl, staring back at him from big, searching eyes that picked him out from behind her fair fringe.

He looked away, at the road ahead beyond the handlebars of Polly's bicycle. Behind him, the girl's friend called out.

'Sarah!' We're going round Stacy's now—'

The words were carried with Louis down the road; those eyes teased out Louis' memories. He reached up and fingered the ring on the chain around his neck.

A man sat with a pint of beer and a laptop at a table; across the room a girl was messaging on her phone. Next to him his friends chatted away. Louis sat with his pint of Guinness in front of him, and fiddled again with the ring around his neck.

'Hey Louis,' said Beth. 'What's on your mind?'

Louis shrugged, woken from his day dream. He shook his head.

'I was just remembering when this place used be all wheat sheaves and scythes. A proper pub.'

'Trace the origins of the public house, my friend,' Tom said, with a laughable American accent. 'Was ever thus. The Plough, The Old Plough, now The Downloader.'

'Free Wi-Fi with every pint,' added Polly.

Louis laughed.

'Some of us still have dial-up.'

He placed his mobile phone on the table; a clunking handset next to Beth's iPhone.

'As a musician, I should have a totally ambivalent attitude to this place,' declared Tom, placing his pint of Old Shires firmly down on the table.

'How so?' Beth asked.

'I know as a music venue it's never likely to play host to the Dumas Quartet, but did you know that if the record industry really wanted an end to digital piracy, they could do worse than order the closure of The Downloader.'

Tom lifted his glass and supped more ale.

'Don't you think it's actually more likely that the free Wi-Fi is used by us teachers on a Friday night, checking our email and updating our Facebook statuses?'

Polly leaned across the table.

'Ignore him, Louis. Tom's just having his weekly rant.'

Beth finished checking something on her phone, and placed it down on the table to retrieve her drink, before turning to Louis and nudging him playfully in the ribs.

'Anyway Louis, it's not like you can really take a pop at technology,' started Beth, 'How much was that fancy new digital camera?'

'Fair point.'

Louis grinned.

'Though I do still happen to prefer my photographs printed on bromide than reduced to the indignity of 72 pixels of a flickr page.'

He sipped again at his drink as he watched for the next reaction from his friends round the table.

'You're looking forward to the summer, then?' returned Beth.

Polly leant forward.

'Oh yeah, I forgot, Louis. Photography – summer school. Is this the second year?'

Louis nodded, and slowly relaxed into the evening.

'You really can't get enough of teaching, can you?'

Later that night, Louis pushed his bicycle along the pavement towards his house in the north end of town. Headlights flashed by from the passing cars, as he stood and unlocked the blue, peeling door in the high stone wall of Cotswold stone, stained with the grime of years of being next to the tram-route. He pushed the bike through into the garden beyond, and let the door swing shut behind him.

Leaning the bicycle up against a rose bush that rambled its way up the side of the large Edwardian house, Louis moved towards the front door. He paused for a moment, distracted by the stars beginning to show themselves in the dusty blue-grey sky. Within the walled garden, the traffic was a forgotten background to the crickets that chirped in the bushes. He found himself lost in the night sky, following every dot-to-dot pattern of the twinkling stars, until he staggered backwards and almost fell.

Louis woke himself, and crossing to the front door, he let himself in. Standing in the hallway, there was a door to the left of him into the lounge, the filled-in remains of what would have once been a grand staircase to the next floor, and a corridor along the side of the apartment. He swung his satchel off his shoulder, dumped it against the wall, and moved forward into the kitchen.

Louis crossed the floor of the kitchen and pulled a glass from a drainer. He filled it with water from the tap and drank.

Two beers, it was only two beers.

He refilled the glass.

3

'Lewis!'

With his glass still raised to his mouth, Lewis turned. Across the room from him, Amanda stood in the doorway to the kitchen in her dressing gown, arms folded.

'Amanda, love.'

He set the glass down and moved to approach, arms open.

'I'm sorry, did I wake you?'

Amanda raised her hands against Lewis' approach.

'No, I wasn't asleep.'

'I lost track of time. I'm sorry.'

Lewis stepped forward.

'Don't touch me,' Amanda said, pushing her husband away. 'You forgot about me, about Sarah. Just like you always do.'

'I went to the pub after work,' explained Lewis. 'We're three days from the end of term—'

'It's 10 o'clock at night, Lewis!'

Lewis stepped back. Amanda was right. He'd been stupid. He should have realised.

'Now that I know that you aren't lying face down in a gutter somewhere, I'm going to bed,' Amanda said sternly. 'Are you coming?'

Lewis raised his head, watching his wife at the door. He nodded.

'In a minute. You go on up, I won't be long.'

Amanda turned and left. Watching her go, he could see her cross the hall and round the newel post at the foot of the stairs. It was a few minutes before Lewis finally tuned back to the sink and refilled his glass.

The haunting melody re-entered his mind; the same few bars that had been torturing him these last few days. Louis grabbed a pen and the back of a utility bill and sat at the table. He wrote the tune furiously as it played in his head; scratching out mistakes and trying to hear the notes in his mind until he was happy. He felt sure that, for whatever reason, he had to identify what the tune was.

The following day he was no closer to identifying it. He scoured the music library at school, to no avail. He still heard the tune as he marked books at the end of the day.

Louis closed the last of the exercise books and put it on the pile on the corner of his desk. He looked at it; the last of the marking for this term. Lifting his head, he gazed out at the window where the little wren was back, shaking a grub about in its beak. He got up, and slowly approaching the bird he was able to get within a foot of the window before it froze, returned Louis' stare, and then flew off.

Louis crossed the room again to his desk, and began to return his pens and books to his satchel. As he did so, his eyes fell upon the scrap of paper on which he had scribbled down the tune. He fetched it out and looked at it; the hurried collection of notes sketchily placed onto a stave.

Slowly he shook his head.

'No idea, mate,' Tom said, passing the scrap of paper back to Louis. 'Could be anything, or nothing.'

Louis took the piece of paper back and stared at it, the tune still as unrecognisable to him as before. He sighed and carefully folded the square of paper, before slipping it back into his jacket pocket.

Opposite him, at the table in the quiet far corner of The Downloader, Tom lifted Louis' almost empty beer glass and waved it in front of him.

'Same again, Louis?'

Louis waved the question away.

'It's okay, I need to be going now—'

He repeated the excuse to Beth and Polly a few minutes later, when they returned to take their seats.

'Yeah, I know,' Louis excused. 'A million and one things to do tonight though...'

'The photography course?' asked Beth. 'You shouldn't be doing it if it's going to cause you this much stress.'

'Beth, it's not...' Louis began. 'I mean, I—'

'You enjoy it, I know.'

Beth smiled.

'Best get a move on, hadn't you?'

She nudged her friend gently in the ribs.

Louis left the pub and briskly set off in the direction of home, only to stop sharply after a few hundred yards. He turned and looked back down the road, where he could still clearly see the iconic sign of The Downloader – a silhouette of a girl dancing with iPod against a seventies-style blaze of colour – swaying in the wind.

What was he doing? He had friends back there who wanted to spend time with him; he was having fun too; and here he was walking away. Why? To what? Louis wavered over the idea of going back.

He couldn't go back; by which, of course, he meant that he could go back. It would be all too easy to go back now; to take his seat at their table and re-join the conversation. Except, that is, that he couldn't do that. To go back into the pub now would be to admit that he didn't have plans, and that his life wasn't as full as he pretended. No, he would continue now, as planned, and maybe, on the next session at the pub, stay longer; go for the meal that would inevitably follow on that evening. But not tonight.

Louis turned and continued down the narrow lane, the high Cotswold stone wall on one side, and the allotments on the other. Continuing to dwell on his hesitancy, he played out how the evening could have gone, had he had the confidence to stay.

As he let himself in to the flat, his brain was turning over ideas for stories. Ignoring the pile of mail on the mat, he rushed straight through to the lounge, dumped his satchel next to his desk, threw his jacket onto the armchair, and set to writing. He pulled out his Moleskine notebook and fountain pen as he was sitting down, opened it to a clean page, and let his mind go, writing the snatch of story.

At some point during that period of furious writing, the lamp at Louis' desk was switched on, bathing his work in a pool of light within the darkening evening. Eventually Louis replaced the cap to his pen, clicked it home, and sat back to look at what he had written.

A door banged upstairs somewhere; Louis raised an eyebrow, before sitting forward again to write. As he wrote; snatches of scenes that cut together; conversations half-completed in themselves, but which built upon each subsequent scene; it came together, crescendoing into a meaning. He remembered one of his all-time favourite films; a guy and a girl meeting on a train, talking; spending the night in Vienna walking, and talking; always talking.

He stopped. Suddenly Louis became aware of someone behind him. He turned.

Sarah.

From her face, he could tell that she was waiting for an answer. Louis fumbled and stuttered; his mouth twisting over words of excuse and uncertainty.

'You're rubbish, Dad,' Sarah said, as she threw down her bag and slumped onto the sofa, crossing her arms defiantly.

Lewis approached his daughter.

'Maybe a clue?'

'Did you even know I was here?'

Sarah's reply was clipped and confident.

'Of course. No – I had these words, these ideas that I needed to get down on paper.'

Sarah lifted her head and stared.

'Oh, the curse of the writer. Woe that the words shouldn't be allowed to speak!'

'Sarah–'

'What's for dinner?'

Lewis' face twisted, trying to unravel the series of questions, each on the heels of the last.

'Dinner? You know, the third meal of the day? You're on duty remember, because Mum's got a management meeting. You know that.'

Lewis glanced back at his desk. He retrieved his watch, which he had since laid out next to his notebook; then he returned his focus to Sarah.

'Yes,' he said.

But she was already gone.

Later that evening Louis cooked himself dinner, serving up a bowl of pasta shells and sundried tomato and olive sauce. He sat at the small fold-down table in the kitchen and ate the food in silence, as the couple from the flat above argued and fought. It was a regular exchange in the evening, and ended, as always, with the doors slamming, followed shortly after by the low growling of a car turning, and the scrunching of the gravel driveway.

And then there was silence; silence in which Louis sunk further into his thoughts, and into his own imagination.

4

The end of term did, eventually, come; a hot July day that made Louis pleased to be on lunchtime monitor duty as he patrolled the playing fields behind the school, although to some extent he missed the humour-filled staffroom banter to which he never really contributed. Laughter was too large a statement to make about one's personality, and it was the best that Louis could usually do to offer up a wry smile. By contrast, as lunch monitor he got to wander alone, quietly contemplating his own thoughts.

Louis worked his way along the steep grassy bank that flanked the playing fields, where children were lounging around eating, laughing and joking, and watching the more energetic kids playing football on the cricket pitch. In time he found himself down at the far end of the fields where the school grounds backed onto The Dell – an old quarry that had long ago become overgrown and taken over by wildlife.

On the school side of the boundary, the playing fields sloped down through a small copse of trees to a series of ponds and drainage ditches. It had been a hot, dry summer this year, and the ponds were all but empty, their muddy bottoms fractured with deep fissures. Louis stood and stared at the pools. Why, he wondered, did the children of this school no longer gather down here, as he remembered himself to have done? But then, he considered, even during his time as a pupil of Wren Hoe County School, the popularity of the place had waned over the years; and yet he had still continued to come down here...

Suddenly, Louis became aware that he was not alone. Standing slightly further back, still in the sun, and tall and upright in her floral dress, was Miss Leroy. Louis felt her gaze on him as if he was thirteen again.

Louis stepped towards the headmistress hesitantly.

'I thought I saw a couple of students down here,' said Louis. 'Karen Wilcox and Jules McPhaddon, you know.'

Louis left the pools behind him and climbed the slope. Ahead of him, Miss Leroy said nothing, but remained staring straight ahead.

'It's been a long old term, hasn't it?' continued Louis. 'I expect you will be pleased more than anyone once this afternoon is finally over.'

As he emerged from the dappled shade of the copse, Louis' vision was blinded by the sun. He blinked his eyes shut, and when he opened them again seconds later, Miss Leroy was gone.

Louis shrugged and continued on his way, this time taking the direct route back across the field, stopping only a couple of times to sort out a bit of play fighting and to sign an autograph book for one of this year's leavers.

As the clock above the main entrance ticked closer towards afternoon school, Louis headed for the lobby outside of the staffroom to check his pigeonhole for the last time that year. Whilst sifting through the school announcements and the 'Back to School' circulars, Beth arrived at his side.

'Almost there, Louis,' she said cheerfully. 'Two more hours and we never have to set eyes on Year 11 again.'

'Except for when they come back next year for Sixth Form—' added Louis.

Beth frowned at Louis' pedantry.

'But at least next year they should at least have chosen to come to school,' Louis added, by way of apology.

'Yes,' said Beth, and sighed.

Louis pushed the unwanted papers back into his pigeonhole, but remained there next to Beth.

'You are coming next week?' asked Beth. 'To my birthday party?'

Louis turned and looked at her.

'Of course I am,' he said.

She smiled, patted him on the shoulder, gathered up her things, and left, ducking out the door and hurrying down the corridor. Louis turned away and looked blankly at the pigeonholes. Shit. He considered the last party he had attended; a swathe of friends all filling the upstairs room at The Downloader, all laughing and joking and dancing; and he himself, on the edge of things, wanting so much to get up and dance, but not being able to.

The afternoon passed soon enough, and at three-thirty the bell rang for the end of school. His class clamoured to leave, as Louis finished off packing up his desk. Slowly he became aware that not everyone had left. Looking up, he saw Sarah.

'Yes?' asked Louis.

'I—' the girl stammered, 'I — you—'

'Sarah, what's wrong?'

'I can't tell you.'

She stepped away, suddenly unsure of herself. Louis reached out to stop her, but stayed his hand in time.

'What?'

He stared at the girl.

'I don't understand.'

'No. You never do,' Sarah threw back at him. 'Maybe you never will.'

And with that, Sarah turned and marched out of the room, leaving Louis left standing in the empty classroom. *What did she mean? What had she been trying to say?* Once more the music entered his mind, haunting his thoughts with its melody.

'Is everything okay?'

It was the unmistakable voice of Miss Leroy. Louis looked up as she left the doorway, and stepped further into the room.

'You seem troubled, Lewis,' said Miss Leroy, with her familiar clipped pronunciation. 'I don't like to see my...' she hesitated. 'My staff troubled.'

'It's nothing, ma'am.'

Whatever the staff called their Head in private, Lewis knew of no-one who called her anything other than ma'am to her face.

'Just the end of term. I need a rest, you know how it is?'

'Of course.'

Miss Leroy smiled thinly; Lewis returned to his packing up, slowed down by the knowledge of the headmistress watching him. He looked again at her, and was about to speak—

'You must come to dinner,' Miss Leroy announced suddenly. 'It's too long a time since we've really conversed. And you must bring your charming wife, I can't remember the last time I saw her.'

Lewis stopped.

'She's very busy,' he answered.

'No doubt, but still you must come, soon.'

Miss Leroy underlined the last word with her tone, fixing her gaze directly upon Lewis, before turning and sweeping from the room, leaving Lewis listening to the clip of her heels down the corridor.

The prospect of dinner at the Leroy house was not something that he relished. He could remember his time as a boy, when there was nothing he liked better than to be invited to tea with Miss Leroy; but that was when he was learning to play the flute, and when that was all that he had in his life.

Now Lewis tried to ease himself out of Miss Leroy's watchful eye. He accepted that she had done much for him over the years; from saving him from bullies to allowing him to excel at music, through to giving him a job back at his old school. But did he really need a mentor now? He had his life, his work, his friends...

'You ready to go?' came Beth's voice.

Louis looked up. Beth was hanging off the doorframe, holding up her car keys. He nodded.

Louis didn't own a car, so when it came to the end of term Beth would load everything of his into the back of her Ford Fiesta and meet him back at his house, while he would cycle.

Beth slammed the boot of her car shut, while Louis stood by with the last box in his arms.

'So,' Beth said.

'You want a coffee or a tea before you get off?' offered Louis.

Beth smiled.

'Sure, why not?'

They made their way through the door in the stone wall, into a garden that was a jungle of plants and flowers tangled amongst each other. Summer sun filtered down through a spider web of overhanging branches; birds sang, and flipped and flapped above them in the canopy.

'I love your house,' Beth sighed. 'It's like *The Secret Garden* – don't you ever just imagine that all this is yours?'

'What? Instead of just a small, ground floor flat?'

'It's hardly small Louis!' exclaimed Beth.

Louis shook his head.

They arrived at the front porch and entered into the little lobby, with the different alarm buzzers and post boxes for the flats, continuing through to Louis' apartment.

Beth waited in the lounge while Louis clattered about in the kitchen making tea. Beth wandered, stooping to examine the range of books on the shelves, and looking at the pictures. There was one print, Monet's water lilies, but other than that they were all photographs. Beth recognised them all as being Louis' own work, and they were exquisitely framed. As she looked, she became particularly struck by one large colour print of a small bird pulling a grub from the ground.

'You like it?'

Beth jumped. She had become so lost in the picture she hadn't noticed Louis re-enter the room.

'It's amazing,' Beth said. 'You are clever Louis, to have captured that bird.'

'You should see the number of missed, blurred, and out-of-focus shots!'

'And modest with it.'

Beth smiled. She took the mug of tea from Louis, and carefully cupped her hands around it. She stepped back, looking for a place to sit. Louis wasn't forthcoming, and so in the end, she perched on the end of the sofa. Louis took a seat in the Ikea chair, which rocked gently.

'So, the end of term at last—' Beth said.

'Not long until your birthday—' began Louis at the same time.

They both stopped and laughed. Neither statement seemed enough to start a conversation though, and it fell into an awkward silence.

Beth drank her tea and fetched a photography magazine from the coffee table to browse. Occasionally she looked up at Louis where he sat. Eventually, seeing Beth engrossed in a magazine, Louis relaxed and fetched out his book to read.

Beth dipped in and out of the magazine for the next half an hour, wanting to start a conversation, but not when Louis was so obviously content in his book. Eventually he looked up and closed the book, returning it to the neat pile on the coffee table.

'I guess I should be thinking about dinner.'

'No really,' Beth said, hastily putting back the magazine. 'I should be going.'

In the hall, Beth gathered her belongings and said goodbye. She told him she would see him next at the party, and she hoped he enjoyed the summer school next week. And then she left.

Louis stood at the door and watched her go, allowing his hand to slowly push the door closed, waiting for the reassuring click as the latch fastened. He stepped back from the door.

'Beth's nice isn't she?' Amanda said.

Lewis nodded and smiled.

'She is, yes. We've always been good friends.'

He stood for a moment, remembering the first day back at Wren Hoe County School, now as a teacher. It was also Beth's first day.

'Come on, my love,' Amanda continued. 'Let's get dinner on.'

Later that evening, the dirty risotto bowls remained on the coffee table as an idle reminder to a good meal. Amanda was curled, legs tucked beneath her, on one end of the sofa watching television; Lewis sat at the other end with his laptop, working through the exercise sheets for Monday's photography course.

Amanda laughed along with the television, and Lewis offered up the occasional punctuated, sardonic retorts to the programme; Amanda laughed at those as well. The programme finished, and Amanda muted the sound when some annoying announcer began to witter over the opening titles. She shifted in her seat and leaned in closer to Lewis; slipping her arm around his shoulders, she began to fondle his hair.

'You're so hard-working Lewis,' Amanda whispered.

'Am I?'

'Yes,' said Amanda. 'During term time you're marking or doing lesson plans, and in the holidays you're preparing for summer school. When I get home from work it's as much as I can do to make dinner.'

'It has to be done,' Lewis shrugged. 'I can't not...'

He carried on typing and rearranging text.

'I'd be too knackered.'

Lewis looked up.

'It's my thing, I guess.'

He returned his focus to the computer screen, with its multiple windows and high pixel resolution.

'Lewis!'

Lewis looked round. Amanda's face was closer than ever now. He had time to see her smile, before she pressed a kiss to his lips.

'I love you.'

5

Louis woke sharply, the morning sun slanting in between a crack in the curtains. His dream was still vivid in his head. *But was it a dream or the real-life of yesterday?* He propped himself up on his pillow and looked to his left, at the untouched pillow next to him. It had been, like always, so vivid; so life-like.

Downstairs he made himself breakfast and ate it at the table, with the summer sun bathing him through the windows, and to a chorus of birdsong. Idly chasing muesli through a bowl of milk with his spoon, he read about the latest sub-professional digital camera, and dreamed quietly to himself of being able to hold one in his own hands and play with the new ultra-sensitive chip-set.

After a leisurely start to the day, Louis headed out to the shops, stocking up on food for the week; taking delight in the many varied stalls of the covered market, each eschewing its own particular, seductive aroma. Back home for a late lunch, he read for most of the afternoon and an early dinner before he headed out again, this time with satchel and photography bag, cycling his way across town.

Louis arrived at the Civic Centre a little after seven o'clock. A 1970's building of concrete and glass, which did hold some architectural details that some understanding designer had added with a nod to its place in the historic town; now it seemed to exist only to slowly degrade, becoming with each advancing year much more of a sorry reminder of the hope and prosperity with which it had been built.

Louis locked his bike to the railings and headed inside, past the scruffy interior, down a few steps to a back corridor, and the stairs to the basement.

The lower floor was a subterranean maze of corridors and studios. Art in all its forms spilled out of their allotted spaces, onto the gloss painted concrete floors and block-work walls. Louis made his way directly to the grandly named 'Photography Lab', in reality a classroom lined with computers, with a further collection of desks in the centre also installed with computers.

He found a free terminal at the head of the central table, and began to get out his notebooks and camera equipment. This year's course book was already on every desk, and Louis sat back in his chair to peruse its contents. As he sat reading, a girl maybe a few years younger than him entered the room.

She remained at the entrance to the room for a few agonising moments longer, before Brian – a tall, older man with a mass of curly white, almost albino hair – greeted her. Eventually more new students arrived, and Brian released Kathryn from his conversation to welcome them with the same jovial enthusiasm. Kathryn stepped further into the room, and took the desk and computer immediately to the left of Louis.

Louis, suddenly aware of how much he had been staring at the girl, flinched and looked away, hurriedly returning to the introductory pages of the course book, and re-reading them for the sixth time without taking in any more of it.

From the corner of his vision, Louis continued to snatch occasional glances at Kathryn.

'Hi, I'm Kathryn.'

Louis looked up. She was beautiful.

'Louis,' he answered diffidently.

Kathryn sat at the work station, clutching her bag to her and jiggling her leg nervously.

'I've never done anything like this before,' she said.

Louis nodded.

'And you?' Kathryn asked.

'Last year,' replied Louis. 'It was good.'

Kathryn smiled, and pushed Louis for more conversation.

'I won a photography competition last year – in the local paper. Made me want to learn more, you know? And a friend and I, we went down to London last year to the Wildlife Photographer of the Year exhibition – at the Natural History museum. Abso-bloody-lutely amazing; I'd die to be that good.'

'You'd like to do it professionally then?'

'Yeah, that'd be so cool.'

Kathryn grinned.

'Not that I'll ever be able afford to make the break from the day job.'

'Which is...?' Louis probed.

'I work at the University Press; Production Editor for some deadly dull society journals.'

Louis nodded.

'And you?' asked Kathryn.

Louis' attention was fixed on Kathryn and her wide blue eyes and golden locks. He glanced round the room as the desks filled up, mentally working through pairs or trios of places to calculate if he would end up working with her, however the class was divided up.

'What do you do, um... Louis, was it?'

Louis was jolted out of his daydreaming by the pronouncement of his name.

'I'm a teacher. English and Creative Writing at Wren Hoe County.'

Kathryn was about to respond, when Brian called the class to order. He launched into an animated introduction and talked through the course book.

Louis sat back in his chair, keeping half an eye on Brian as he leafed through this year's workbook. Already his mind played through ideas for photographic projects, and he began to picture them; forming them in his mind, like the emergence of the image from the clean white piece of bromide paper in the developing tray.

'That was brill,' exclaimed Kathryn, at the end of the two hours, 'I just want to get out there and start work on the project.'

'I know what you mean,' added Louis. He returned his belongings to the bag, half an eye on Kathryn's packing to try and synchronise the activity and thus, he considered, they could coincidentally leave at the same time and continue to chat. Not that he was good at 'chat'.

Kathryn deliberated over her project book.

'Just had a thought,' she said, and moved to Brian, asking for further clarification.

Damn. Louis fiddled with the straps of his satchel. He only had his camera itself left to be packed away; he could wait, but wouldn't that seem too obvious? He lingered a bit longer, but felt insanely uncomfortable. Slowly, Louis began to edge towards the door, but Kathryn was immersed in Brian's conversation.

'Louis. Good to see you.'

The loud, course voice was suddenly in his ear. Louis cringed, before turning to face the tall, broad-shouldered man who was eager to shake his hand.

'Colin, hello...' returned Louis. He pinched a smile.

'I wondered if you'd be back this year,' said Colin. Before Louis could answer, Colin was continuing. 'I've got a great photo collection from the summer. I took myself on a bit of a tour; the Trans-Siberian railway.'

Louis opened his mouth to speak, to excuse himself from the conversation, but Colin already had his album ready; a lavish, larger-than-A4, photo book. A glance across the room confirmed to Louis that Kathryn was still receiving an explanation from an enthused Brian; he felt that he could give a small amount of time to one of Colin's projects.

Louis stepped up to where Colin had laid out his work and began studying the photographs. Technically they were amazing, but it seemed to Louis that they lacked passion: soft-focused ordinary objects, with little explanation as to why. In the background, Colin gave a rambling narration to each and every image in excruciating detail.

'So what do you think?' asked Colin eventually.

Louis stammered, unsure of what to say; of how to enunciate his thoughts.

'They're good,' he answered. Not quite a lie.

'When I think of where I was a year ago, this is just so, so vibrant,' Colin said, with passion.

Louis glanced round. Across the far side of the room, Brian was packing up his things. Kathryn was gone. Louis' heart sank.

'Sorry Colin, I've just remembered. I've got to go.'

Louis slung his satchel over his shoulder, and was halfway across the classroom before Colin replied.

'Sure thing. See you next week, Louis.'

Louis raised a hand in confirmation, left the room, and quickened his pace. He hastened down the maze of corridors and took the stairs two at a time. Arriving outside the front entrance, he was in time to see Kathryn board a tram which pulled out and trundled off down the road.

Louis raised his eyes to the stars and sighed deeply. He made his way to his bike, and went through the careful and intricate procedure of releasing the various locks and chains.

Back home, Louis let himself into his empty flat, running over tonight's conversations in his head. Regret seeped into his mind as he remembered the moments of conversation with Kathryn where he had failed to respond. He remembered her smile, her offer of coffee which he had refused. He remembered – and cursed – how he had made up an appointment in his diary, and then how he had missed out on arranging a drinks evening.

Are you on Facebook? Louis heard Kathryn's question even now. He also heard himself rejecting the fad of social networking, much as he had done countless times after work in *The Downloader*, to the ritual mocking from Beth and Polly.

Louis lifted the lid of his computer now, and tapped 'Facebook' into the search engine; minutes later, and he was in the midst of setting up his profile. His finger hovered over the mouse button, as he deliberated over his relationship status; eventually he clicked past it, and the other options too, skipping through to begin searching for friends. Very quickly he discovered that he didn't even know Kathryn's surname, and that there were dozens of Kathryn's in Wren Hoe, not counting the many million elsewhere in the world.

He left the computer with his half-completed profile left up on the screen, and moved to the sofa. He slouched back into the cushions and pulled his camera out of its bag; he began to fiddle with it and play with the settings. He was a good photographer, he knew that, he knew how to compose a shot and tell a story; that said, there was so much that he still didn't know about how his camera worked.

He heard Kathryn's voice again, talking her way through her camera. It was only an E400, but she knew every setting and function. He recalled her explaining how she had forced herself to sit down properly with the instruction manual on day one and learn it, instead of diving straight in, pre-judging the rules and using intuition to figure it out. Much like he was doing here and now.

Louis pushed the camera back into its case and pushed it to one side. Tomorrow, he decided he would do just that. He would teach himself how to use his camera properly. Just like Kathryn.

6

Dreams rattled through Lewis' mind, in much the same way that the trams clanked past, with a whining hum of wheels and the hiss of electricity along the cables, beyond the high stone wall outside his bedroom window. Brakes squeaked, and then there were voices and footsteps on the pavement, disappearing into the darkness.

Lewis, then fifteen, was one of the last to leave orchestra that night. He walked the silent after-school corridors, listening to his own footsteps on the polished floor. He left the school grounds, comforted by the sight of Amanda Jones where she waited at the gate. As he approached her, Amanda's eyes were wide and gazing back brightly. She moved to give him a kiss, but he just took her hand and they began to walk home.

Amanda was lead oboist in the school orchestra, and she understood Lewis' confusing and complicated ways perfectly. She did not question his need to leave orchestra separately, meeting up only after everyone else had gone home; his shyness was part of his charm.

Now, as they walked, they talked; Lewis deconstructed the rehearsal that had just been, running his mind back over the difficult bits and where he had gone wrong or fluffed up. Amanda listened. She was very good at listening; not once did she force the conversation into a direction with which Lewis was uncomfortable. She was his perfect companion.

At Longwall Street they were in time to board one of the city trams as it rattled into its stop. Lewis loved riding the trams around his city. Often though, when he was with Amanda, he preferred to walk, as walking meant that he could talk more easily. And it wasn't as if it was more than a couple of stops up the Woodstock Road until they reached his house, a large Edwardian building on the corner of two streets, and set back from the road behind a tall, stone wall.

Lewis had not yet allowed Amanda into the house, or even through the wooden door in the garden wall; this was again something that Amanda had understood perfectly and unquestionably. She stood before him now, prepared to say goodbye. She saw the distant approach of a tram that she would catch after they had parted.

'Till tomorrow then.'

Lewis remained silent, as he looked back at Amanda, entranced by the blue of her eyes.

He pulled back the sleeve of his coat and checked the time. Both his parents were working late tonight, before going to some work meal at the old castle. He chewed at his bottom lip.

'Amanda,' he began, tentatively.

She smiled coyly, reaching out her hand to reassure him.

'Yes, Lewis?'

'I don't suppose – I mean you don't have to, I won't mind if – but...'

'Lewis. Just say it.' Amanda said, with a grin.

'Would you like to see the garden?'

There, it was said; it was probably the lamest chat-up line ever, but at least it was said. Lewis felt relief and fear churning through him; shaking with nerves, he tried gripping his hands together to stop himself, but it only made the shaking worse.

'Hey, don't be scared,' said Amanda, 'Of course. I'd love to.'

Lewis opened his mouth to speak, but Amanda beat him to it.

'And don't worry, I won't stay long. It'll be fine.'

Lewis pulled his keys from his pocket, and slipping the key into the Yale lock, he pushed the thickset, heavy wooden door with its flaking blue paint open. He stepped through, and turned to offer a hand to Amanda. Pushing the door shut with a reassuring clunk, suddenly the outside world was gone; and Lewis was left alone with Amanda in the garden oasis of his parent's house.

It was a warm, sunny evening of late spring, and the garden was draped in greenery and pungent blooms. Birds sung from the treetops, and flapped and fought around the bird feeder; butterflies flitted from flower to flower.

'It's beautiful, Lewis,' Amanda said, as she pushed back her hand. She stretched out her arms to either side, and closed her eyes into the sun.

Lewis edged closer to Amanda, little by little, until the back of his hand brushed against her bare forearm.

She dropped her head and turned to face him; the suddenness surprised him, and he wobbled on his feet. Amanda grabbed him and held him in front of her.

'I've been wanting to show you this for ages.'

'Why didn't you?'

'I–I don't know,' Lewis stammered, 'Never the right moment I guess.'

Never brave enough, is what he knew she was thinking.

'Silly!'

Amanda smiled; Lewis grinned, if tentatively, and shuffled from foot to foot. She held out her hand.

'Shall we walk?'

Lewis wavered for a moment, but when Amanda offered her hand again, he took it. As their fingers interlocked, Lewis felt a rush of emotions at such a simple pleasure. He had long dreamed of this moment, wondered what it would feel like; it was better than he could ever have imagined.

They walked slowly about the garden, hand in hand. Lewis was able to point out the names of all the plants in Latin; every one was at its peak, thanks to the loving care by his mother. At one point Lewis stopped them both and pointed. In hushed tones, he pointed out the little wren having a wash in the stone birdbath.

Amanda turned to face Lewis again. They found their faces close to one another.

'It's beautiful here,' Amanda said again. 'Thank you for sharing it with me.'

'It's okay.' Lewis said, as hesitant as ever.

Amanda reached up and brushed his cheek with her hand.

'You are really special, Lewis. You do realise that, don't you?'

She smiled again, pulling him in with her gaze. Lewis stuttered to respond, but no words came out.

'Don't speak,' Amanda breathed.

She leaned closer to him, and somehow, without warning, they kissed. Lewis had to force himself to breathe again. He blinked, and blushed, then kissed her again, this time longer and slower.

With the sky cast orange in the last light of the setting sun, Lewis sat with Amanda on the double swing under the hazel tree, their arms and fingers interlocked. They sat, in silence, listening to the evensong of the garden before dusk.

'Amanda—' began Lewis.

She turned and looked at him.

'Yes, Lewis?'

'Does, does this mean…' he said, with difficulty. 'Are we … going out now?'

Silence. Amanda squeezed his hand tightly in hers. She smiled in response, then they returned to sitting in silence.

'I've never had a girlfriend, before now.'

'Doesn't matter,' answered Amanda.

*

Across the wall came the screeching of brakes, the hiss of electricity along cables, and the whine of wheels. The adult Lewis woke in his bed, with the early morning sun slanting in through a gap in the curtains. He blinked his eyes open, and he reached out to put his arm around Amanda.

He smiled as he remembered his dream, loving how his memories, still vivid, continued to come back to him, unfolding in his mind like a story. He propped himself up on his arm and gazed upon Amanda; slowly, he stroked his fingers through her soft hair.

He was so lucky to have found Amanda. She understood him perfectly; so perfectly, even, that Lewis sometimes thought she understood him more than he understood himself. Thinking back now, he could not remember Amanda before they were together. It sounded like a crazy thing to think, now that he considered it, but it was true. Other friends he could remember being around, and being the friend of other people before he knew them. But not Amanda.

If Amanda had moved into town during the year of his eleventh birthday, then this lack of knowing her would be obvious to the point of needing no explanation; Amanda Jones, though, was as local to Wren Hoe as himself. Both her parents were professors at the university, and her father was even a widely celebrated academic on the more cerebral BBC programmes.

She had been to the same school as him, and in most of the same classes for his whole childhood. Why was it, then, that he had no memory of her existence before that day when they had first met on the front row of orchestra?

He looked down at Amanda, where she lay, asleep. Why did it matter so much? He leant down, and carefully kissed the top of her head.

7

Lewis sat at his desk, staring at the computer screen and the confusing array of options and menus, getting increasingly annoyed and frustrated by the inability of the darn machine to do what he wanted.

'What's the problem, Dad?'

Lewis looked over his shoulder at where Sarah had broken away from her reading to look up towards him.

'Just Photoshop. I can see in my mind what I want it to look like, and I know it's possible because I've seen it in magazines, but can I get the damn thing to do it?'

'Can't it wait 'til your next college night?' Sarah asked.

'At this rate it's going to have to.'

'Just that with all your flapping and your strops, you really are putting me off my book.'

Sarah grinned.

'Thanks for your concern,' Lewis responded.

'My pleasure,' Sarah said simply.

Sarah smirked and returned to her book, T.S. Eliot's Four Quartets; she lapped up the imagery with unbridled delight, through metaphor and grammar. Across the room, her father went back to cursing his computer. Occasionally she looked up and smirked.

Lewis clicked and dragged on the mouse, tapping the keyboard through repeated undoes. He shook his head, and muttered more fervently.

The telephone rang; a tingle of bells from an analogue phone that cut the silence. Louis pushed back his chair and crossed the lounge into the hall, where the receiver sat in its cradle on the sideboard.

'Hello?' answered Louis. 'Oh hi, Beth, how are you?'

As he listened, his face changed; his expression dropped, and his smile soured.

'Is she going to be okay?'

Louis shuffled from foot to foot and ambled around the room, not sure what to do with himself.

'No, of course. Yes sure, I can visit with you.'

Lewis found his hand on the banister, his palm clammy on the wood beneath.

'Shit. This is awful, Beth.'

And then after a few moments:

'Yeah, I'll see you in – what – half an hour? See you. Thanks, Beth...'

He stared at the receiver for a few moments more before dropping it back into the cradle, and continued to stare blankly at the telephone. He flinched sharply and shook his head clear of thoughts, to ascend the stairs at a fast pace, rounding the top of the landing and headed towards his bedroom.

'Amanda! That was Beth on the phone. Apparently it's Miss Leroy; she had a stroke yesterday, and is at the Morton Morris now—'

He stopped upon discovering that the bedroom was empty.

'Amanda?' Louis was puzzled. Not only was Amanda not where he thought she was, but there was also no sign of her ever having occupied the room. He panicked and threw open the wardrobe doors: just rails of his shirts and jackets, neatly hung. He turned on his heels and all but ran from the room, almost colliding into the wall where once had been the top of the stairs. Dazed, he navigated his way back down the corridor to the lounge.

'Sarah! Do you know where your Mum is?'

The lounge, too, was empty. Curiously, lying on the sofa, next to the cushion where Sarah had been sitting, was a copy of *Four Quartets*. He picked it up, frowned, and replaced it to the top of the pile on the coffee table.

Louis felt sick as his insides churned with worry. He sank onto the sofa, and was still sitting in the same spot half an hour later, when there came a rap at the door and the chimes of the doorbell. He stirred from his thoughts. Beth, he realised, and leapt to his feet.

A few minutes later, Louis and Beth were leaving the house and making their way through the overgrown wilderness of the garden, past a double swing hanging from an old and overgrown hazel tree, its seat flaked of paintwork and discoloured with moss and algae. Upon seeing it, Louis stopped for a moment and remembered. Beth called him on, and he followed her out onto the street to her car.

For the first few minutes of the journey across town, Louis sat in silence as Beth drove. At a set of traffic lights, Beth finally broke the silence.

'So, how's summer school?'

'It's good,' replied Louis emptily.

'Anyone from last year back again?'

Louis sighed and threw his gaze aloft.

'Colin, would you believe—'

Beth gasped.

'No! Wasn't he the really old guy, with more money than artistic sense?'

'Yeah. And he's fixed himself on being my friend too.'

Beth shook her head in sympathy, and accelerated away from the junction.

'There's a new girl though,' Louis added. 'Kathryn. She seems to be ... you know, more normal.'

'Yeah?'

Beth's interest had been piqued.

She has a half decent camera,' continued Louis. 'But boy, does she know how to use it. A good eye—'

'And?' said Beth, expecting more.

Louis' response was a quizzical, twisted face of confusion. Beth grinned.

'So you like her.'

'I'm hoping that we might be able to work on some projects together; anything not to work with Colin again.'

'Is that the only reason?' asked Beth, disappointment laced through her voice.

Louis shrugged.

'She seems to talk my language – I think. Beth, what are you getting at?'

Beth laughed.

'Just looking for some holiday gossip, Louis. Until now, mine has involved helping my mother choose new curtains.'

Louis nodded. He tried to answer, but could not find the words.

'So what does Kathryn do?' Beth asked, pushing the conversation again. 'When she's not capturing the moment on the camera?'

'Works for the University Press – editor or something. Seems to have a healthy attitude towards work.'

'She sounds cool.'

Beth pulled into the car park entrance at the foot of the modern, block-like hospital, fiddled with the machine to get her ticket, and waited for the barrier to rise. Soon they were both striking across the forecourt to find Miss Leroy's ward.

They headed past the queues and crowded wards of the NHS part of the hospital to a private wing at the top of the hospital, which opened out onto a cloistered roof garden.

Beth moved tentatively with Louis to Miss Leroy's private room, and entered quietly. They found her sat up in bed in a hospital gown, and looking like a pale reflection of the stern headmistress of Wren Hoe County School. As they stepped up to her bedside, she looked up and her face brightened.

'Louis,' she said, smiling. 'And Beth too. It's good of you to visit your Head.'

'Don't be silly,' said Louis. 'We couldn't not come.'

Miss Leroy smiled thinly. In the absence of conversation, Louis and Beth found chairs to bring over; as Beth stooped to take her seat, Miss Leroy looked up again.

'Beth love,' Miss Leroy croaked. 'Would you be so kind as to warm my wheat pillow?'

She gestured to the side unit.

'Two minutes. I think there's a microwave in the lounge on the floor below.'

Beth forced a smile.

'Of course.'

After Beth had left the ward, Miss Leroy propped herself up further, and adjusted her spectacles.

'Now, Lewis. Come, sit closer. She patted the side of her bed.
Lewis moved his chair accordingly.
'Tell me,' Miss Leroy said with a smile. 'How is Amanda?'

Lewis startled himself awake.

'Huh? She's fine, miss. Same as ever.'

How did Miss Leroy know about Amanda?

'Good. It's just... I've heard things, Lewis. Things that concern me. You are happy at home?'

Lewis nodded slightly, uncommitted.

'You must look out for the dear girl. She's your saviour, Lewis.'

'I don't understand.' Lewis said, twitching with confusion. 'Why are you telling me this? Why now?'

Miss Leroy remained silent to the question, choosing instead to continue to hold Lewis in her gaze.

'You shouldn't be worrying about me.'

Lewis pushed his chair slightly further away.

'You're in hospital, ma'am. You should be making sure you get better.'

Miss Leroy smiled.

'Oh, Lewis, you don't need to worry about me. I very much intend to make a full recovery.'

Lewis nodded. That, he could very well believe. He tried to remember how many times over the course of his life he had seen Miss Leroy ill.

'Bring your charming wife with you next time, Lewis.'

Miss Leroy fixed him again in her gaze. Lewis nodded, and quietly agreed in a non-committal way. A silence descended over the conversation. Lewis looked around the hospital room, his gaze drawn to posters and signage displayed boldly against primary colours. He looked again at Miss Leroy, who it seemed, was regarding him too.

'Miss Leroy?'

'Yes, Lewis?'

'Do you remember the tune that you taught me? The day you first taught me to play the flute?'

'What of it, Lewis?'

'I just wondered – I can remember it, but–'

Lewis was hesitant.

'What is it? What's it from?'

Miss Leroy considered the question. Eventually, she lifted her head from the pillow and directed her full gaze on Lewis.

'That is not important.'

Lewis looked, and looked again at the headmistress. He wanted to protest, to argue; but knew that it was pointless.

8

'Weird,' Beth said, as she slouched into the driver's seat of her car and sighed heavily. She glanced up, and saw Louis looking back at her, puzzled.

'Unbelievable,' she added. 'I get the call from the ward sister – Miss Leroy has been admitted – a stroke and all and that she's asking for me – and you – and we come rushing over and—'

Beth slapped the steering wheel.

'She didn't even want to see me. What's that all about?'

Louis shook his head slowly, and stared blankly into the distance.

'Did she say anything to you?'

'Not really.'

Louis thought back on the visit, tussling with his mind about what to say, and even before he's really thought it through—

'She asked me, next time, to bring my wife.'

He turned and looked at Beth. She laughed; the kind of laughter that kept on coming.

'That's good. Very good.'

Beth forced herself to stop laughing.

'At least now we know that she *has* had a stroke! She's cracked!'

'Beth!'

'Yeah, sorry, that was insensitive of me. But still, it made it worth my while coming. Fetching wheat pillows? I ask you…'

Beth coaxed the car to life, and began the drive home, still smiling and chuckling at what she had heard.

'I suppose you could take Kathryn with you?' suggested Beth. 'That would fox her!'

'That'd hardly be the best first date,' Louis commented. 'Not that I'm a huge expert.'

'Good point,' agreed Beth. 'Hey, my name's Louis, you want to visit my demon of a headmistress in hospital? Maybe not.'

She laughed again.

'You should bring her along to my birthday party though,' said Beth. 'If you like?'

'Beth, she's just a friend,' said Louis. 'Not even a friend yet, if I'm being honest.'

'Well, the offer's there, Louis. Or if not Kathryn, bring someone else; the more the merrier. Really…'

A tram rattled past as they queued round the northern bypass; Louis watched the people pass, jammed into the yellow carriages. For a moment, he thought he saw Kathryn.

That afternoon, Louis stood in the bay window of his lounge, hands cupped round a mug of tea. Looking out into the garden, birds flitted from tree to ground, and from feed to tree. Beyond the birds and the bushes, he could see the double-swing in its sorry, neglected state. The swing had been a huge part of his childhood growing up in this house. He had a distinct memory of sitting on it as a boy, but not one single memory of being pushed by his father or mother.

Half an hour later, Louis found himself out in the garden, scrubbing the swing down with a wire brush and hot, soapy water. Gradually, bit by bit, he revealed the swing from his memories, if in a faded, distressed guise.

Taking secateurs and tenon saw to the ash tree, he hacked and butchered it back to free the ropes and create room to swing. As he worked, he thought of what Beth had said, and wondered if Kathryn would like to go to a party. He always imagined that an event would be an easy thing to arrange, to see someone outside of the normal setting. And it needn't be a date, as such, did it?

Louis tried to imagine how the conversation would go. He pictured Kathryn as she had been the other night, first accepting the offer gladly and mentioning how she had been thinking that they ought to meet up outside of class; but secondly, he pictured her politely excusing herself and fleeing from him. In this vision, subsequent scenes showed her working at opposite sides of the class, and he was left to work alone, or worse, with Colin.

'She might even already have a boyfriend,' he said out loud, and disturbed a few birds preparing to roost. Then Louis heard Beth's voice giving encouragement.

What if she doesn't?

Louis sat forward on the sofa, leafing through his course notes and project outlines, sketching out his ideas. At seven o'clock he slipped all the files and books into his satchel, scooped it up along with his camera bag, grabbed a carton of juice and a cereal bar from the kitchen, and headed out of the flat.

As he moved to retrieve his bicycle, he stopped, and instead ventured out onto the street to board the next city centre-bound tram. At St Giles, Louis rounded the corner into George Street, to board a waiting trolley bus for the last bit of the journey down to college.

When he arrived in the basement photography lab, Kathryn was already there. She was standing at the front of the room, drinking coffee and chatting with Brian and Colin. He spotted her bag at one of the workstations, and went to deposit his at the neighbouring one before joining the others.

'Evening all,' Louis announced brightly.

'Louis,' Brian said with a nod.

Already, Louis could see Colin edging towards him with a file of photographs. He was pleased when Kathryn spoke up.

'Louis, hi,' Kathryn said.

'Hi.'

Louis glanced over at where he had left his satchel.

'Hope you don't mind?'

'Of course not,' Kathryn answered. 'To be honest, it's nice that I've remembered some faces. Normally I'm terrible.'

'Same here. Names, fine; faces, fine; but try and get me to put the two together...'

'You remembered mine,' Kathryn said, smiling.

Was she flirting with him? Louis wished that he was better at reading the signs.

'Louis, if you've got a moment.'

Colin was pushing his photography file between Louis and Kathryn.

'Vertigo, yeah? My nephew has a plane, flies it from the airfield; I thought if I went up with him, then I could get some brilliant images.'

'Sounds good,' Louis said, turning back to Kathryn. 'I think I favour looking more into how vertigo makes you feel, myself.'

'Me too,' agreed Kathryn. 'Well, that and I don't think publishing wages will stretch to aircraft.'

'I could arrange a trip up for you too, Katy—'

Katy? Louis stared in disbelief at Colin. Surely he wasn't angling for a date with Kathryn? He must be old enough to be her grandfather.

'Grrr, can you believe that man?' Kathryn hissed to Louis, when Colin had left the room. They were busy working through some exercises to teach them how to handle RAW file processing, and had decided to work together.

'What? Colin?'

Louis decided to be charitable.

'I think he's harmless, mostly.'

'Really? I have a horrible feeling he was hitting on me!'

'He did sound a bit forward,' said Louis. 'I'm sure it was nothing.'

Kathryn frowned. She read the same paragraph again in the course book, and looked up to stare at the screen.

'You know, it's not the subject that scares me. It's the having to do it all in RAW format.'

Kathryn knocked away the mouse.

'Plus, I don't reckon my poor computer is going to be able to cope.'

'I think we can book slots here. Maybe we could arrange to book the same time and help each other out?'

Kathryn's face brightened.

'That's actually a really cool idea, Louis. Definitely we should.'

Louis felt a warmth of confidence grow within him. Ask her, he heard him tell himself. Just ask her.

Following class, Louis and Kathryn packed up their gear and walked through the warren of corridors to the main entrance. Louis was about to head to his tram with Kathryn, when he realised that she had stopped by the railings. He turned and looked at her in silence. Slowly, and simultaneously, they each held up their hands; in Louis' was a bus ticket, and in Kathryn's a bike lock. They each commented on the other's chosen transport at the same time, and both laughed.

'What are the chances?' Louis said rhetorically, damning himself for not cycling tonight.

Kathryn stood again, fastening the lock around the rack on the back of her bike. 'Well anyway, we've got each other's mobiles now. I'll be in touch when I know what I'm doing at the weekend, and we'll arrange to hunt all things vertigo.

Louis nodded. It was on the tip of his tongue to ask her. *Ask her*, damn it. Kathryn wheeled her bike round and mounted it. *Just ask her, Louis*. He fumbled in his mind for the right choice of words.

'Sure, yeah,' answered Louis.

Say it. His mind began buzzing, with the pain of the pressure of not being able to find the right words.

'Bye Louis. See you later.'

Kathryn cycled off on her journey home, leaving Louis standing on the street outside the college, alone. He rammed his face into the palm of his hand, and tried to press out the frustration.

9

A new day. Lewis finished his breakfast and headed out into the garden. Ever since he had remembered how the garden had been that spring day fifteen years ago, when he had first kissed Amanda, he had been looking at the overgrown, shambolic reminder to his mother's work with embarrassment and regret.

He went round the side of the house to the old rickety garden shed, with the bowed wooden door and the ivy that reached in through knot holes and split timbers. Inside he found that the ivy had worked its way around his childhood bike. In a box at the back, he found a selection of his father's old tools to begin his assault on the garden. He hacked back the longer grass and undergrowth with a sickle, before fetching out a cylinder mower. In the late summer it was hot work pushing the mower up and down the lawn. He stopped and fetched a long glass of water from inside, splashing some onto his forehead and pouring the rest down his throat. As he went back to the lawn, he spied Sarah sitting with a friend on the sunny patio outside the lounge. They were laughing and joking, and discussing things from the magazines that they were flicking through.

'Anytime you want to help!'

Sarah looked up and shrugged an answer to her Dad.

'You're doing a great job!' she called out.

Lewis grinned, and continued to push the mower backwards and forwards across the lawn. With every push, clippings spewed out of the back, showering over his feet and disappearing between his toes. The sun blazed down on him and the birds sung, and the memories came sweeping back.

Years before, Lewis had lain out on the lawn with Amanda, their school revision books in front of them; testing each other about the laws of momentum, the conditions of equilibrium, and the reasons behind Hamlet's madness. After a particularly poor round of questions, Amanda flopped onto her front, flattened her copy of Tom Duncan's Physics for Today and Tomorrow, propped herself up on her elbows, and read. Lewis read too, but his mind was filled with all manner of other thoughts, and after the sixth attempt at reading the same paragraph, he gave up, turned onto his side, and watched Amanda.

He had dreamed, and wished for days like these, for forever. Often he had gone for walks or cycled through the university parks, and seen the young couples lying with each other in the grass, imagining himself as one of them. In the oasis of beauty that his mother had created here in her garden, this was his own private park.

Snip, snip, snip. The slicing sound of metal shearing against metal came to the fore of his mind...

'Lewis! Have you got a minute?'

The sound of his mother's voice cut through the silence, just at the moment when he was about to reach out and stroke Amanda's hair where it lay across her bare shoulders. He looked up to see his mother across the other side of the garden, reaching high into a bush with her secateurs and garden twine.

Lewis tied back the rose bush to the cast iron frame of the arch, just as he had done for his mother all those years before. Of course, the bush now was nothing but a skeleton of the rose that his mother had tended. He wondered how it could have gotten like this. How could he not have

Across the garden, Sarah and her friend left the patio where they had been sitting and headed round the house to go inside. Louis tried to remember. Sarah was the daughter of the family who had moved into the flat upstairs. They seemed to be a nice family, although he hadn't seen much of the parents. Still, that would no doubt change when he came to teach the daughter next year, and they attended the next parents' evening.

Eventually the pruning was done, and he headed indoors for a refreshing glass of juice from the fridge. The secateurs lay on the kitchen table. On the far side of the room, Louis stood in front of a large cardboard box on the counter, with his arms delving inside of it. A small, satisfied grunt passed his lips as he brought out his flute case. Wiping away thick layers of dust, he brought it to the kitchen table and opened it, much as you would open a jewel case. His flute was just as he had left it the last time he had played it, with a packet of Rizlas, and the stub of a 3B pencil.

He slid the barrel of the flute together, and found his fingers automatically finding their way onto the keys. In his head he heard the tune, melodic beats of trilling sibilance. Tentatively, he lifted the flute to his lips, took in a deep diaphragmatic breath, and let the instrument speak. He finished the phrase and smiled. It must be almost ten years since he had played, and his fingers knew exactly where to go.

'Lewis?'

Lewis, flute in hand, swung round on his heels. Amanda stood at the kitchen door.

'You haven't played for ages.'

'I know,' said Lewis. 'This song, it's been bugging me for weeks – always in my head.'

'It's good. I always liked it when you played,' said Amanda. 'I should get my instrument out, too.'

'That would be good.'

Lewis remembered the days and evenings of years gone past, playing themselves into fits of giggles as they wrestled with the latest orchestra arrangement.

'Maybe tonight.'

Amanda returned this with a look of withering incredulousness.

'No,' she said firmly. 'Some of us are not as talented as my darling husband. I need to get back in. The poor oboe might even need a service.'

Lewis couldn't help himself. His mouth took a little downward turn at the corners.

'Don't pout,' she told him. 'Doesn't suit you.'

Lewis looked down at his flute again. He fiddled with the keys, running them through silent trills and soundless arpeggios. Amanda left the room and Lewis lifted the instrument again to his lips. The song, as familiar as always, sang out clear and haunting.

Louis stopped abruptly. The house was thick with silence. A draught blew from somewhere. Louis put down his flute and slowly moved to investigate. As he entered the hall the front door banged shut, rebounding off the mortise block where it struck the frame. On the doormat lay the local newspaper. He stepped out into the garden, but there was nothing and no-one untoward. Returning to the flat he scooped up the newspaper, closed the door properly, slipping the deadlock, and carried the paper through to the kitchen.

Miss Leroy's face looked back at Lewis from the front page of the Wren Post, alongside the thick-type headline and article about the health of the local headmistress and city personage.

He read through the article, subdued by the reminder of Miss Leroy's health. He frowned at the inaccuracies of the reporting, and wondered how they could get away with telling lies about the person that he had only ever had support, and advice - even love - from. In the years since their first meeting, Miss Leroy had been like a mother to him. He saw her now, in front of the whole school, clipping up and down the front of the school hall in her stiletto heels, her flowery dress swishing at every turn. He pictured her next to him at the desk, first helping the schoolboy Louis through his homework, and then again as a student teacher, advising him on lesson plans.

Lewis was fifteen years old again, in the garden of his home, and helping his mother tie back a rose bush. Amanda was across the garden, the beauty that she was; but when he turned to look at his mum, the face was a blank. How did his mother carry her hair? What was the shape of her nose? The curve of her mouth? He couldn't picture any of it. He looked again at the newspaper. That, in front of him – the face of Miss Leroy – was the face of his mother.

10

Kathryn hurried from the colonnaded main entrance of the University Press, calling out goodbye to the cheerfully friendly porter in the lodge as she left. She rushed to cross the road, to board the tram moments before it rattled and clanked its way along Walton Street, on the rails that that were carved through cobbles, broken bitumen, and flooded potholes. Clinging to one of the loops of leather that hung from the ceiling, Kathryn kept her shoulder bag, camera case and the bundle of canvas and cane clutched close to her, as the tram lurched around the corner into Worcester Place.

She jumped down from the carriage, and strode off down the short walk from the canal basin to the mainline railway station. Passing the business school, she made her way through the landscaped gardens to the grand and imposing palatial station with its large, central dome directly over the Botley Road. She dodged commuters and entered the main hall. Having fumbled with the change and auto-ticket booth, she made her way up the marble staircase to the waiting room.

Situated across the tracks, beneath the main dome, it was a vast and airy waiting room, with wood panelling, lavish drapes, portraits on the wall, and comfy leather sofas. It seemed more like the lounge of a posh hotel than the waiting room of a mainline railway station.

Kathryn stopped and scanned the faces in the crowd. There, over on the left, she spied Louis, who spotted her as she approached.

'Thanks for coming.'

Kathryn found it hard to hold onto all her bags, as she was barged by suited professionals in a hurry. Louis was quick to take the camera bag from her.

'Thanks. We should probably be on our way.'

The train breezed into the station as Kathryn and Louis rushed down the staircase, Louis trailing his hand on the brass rail. The train was packed, and they were pushed away from each other to separate parts of the carriage. Kathryn stood in the aisle halfway down the carriage, between two old ladies bickering over the top of their shopping bags and a young man with gelled back hair, shiny suit and salmon pink shirt, boasting loudly into his iPhone about how fit various girls he knew were, and how much they all must love him. She glanced down the length of the carriage, shrugging when she caught Louis' eye.

Eventually the train pulled into Wantage station and they squeezed their way out onto the platform, able once more to breathe fresh air and to leave the commuters and gossiping old grannies behind. Louis and Kathryn made their way out onto the road to catch the rural bus service out along the ridgeway.

The road twisted and turned into the late-afternoon sun; light flickering through the trees and hedgerows, dancing from side to side of the bus with every bend in the road. Kathryn sat between the window and Louis, her bags on her lap, clutching the bundle of kite wings to her.

'I'm still not sure if I get it—' said Louis. He reached out a hand and ran his fingers down the kite, the canvas between his thumb and forefinger.

'I still don't know if it's going to work!' Kathryn laughed. 'It's just from this dream I had – a classic flying one – but there was this hillside and a kite, and I was following it and getting these weird views, and it just made me feel so sick. It was like how vertigo makes you feel.'

'So you want me to fly the kite while you take the photos?'

Kathryn nodded.

'Well, I'll try. I was always useless at kite flying myself.'

Leaving the bus at the edge of the village, Kathryn and Louis lost no time in crossing the road and striking out across a small field with a couple of ponies; from there they made their way up an ancient sunken lane, framed by the dark, twisted trunks and branches of an old, coppiced hedgerow.

Halfway up the hill, they turned off the track and crossed a stile into a summer meadow, swathed in grasses and wild flowers, and flitted over by bees and butterflies. They walked the field on a path of flattened grass, rounding the top of a rise beneath which the white horse was marked out in chalk.

Kathryn stopped, slung down her shoulder bag into the grass, and laid her camera bag down next to it.

'Here then,' said Louis. He glanced up, and Kathryn smiled and nodded. She was busy unfurling the canvas wings and slotting the rods into place.

'It was my grandfather's you know. He made it. I have got a modern one – you know, a Chinese dragon thing – but I thought this one might be better.'

She grinned.

'And, to be honest, it may look prehistoric; but it flies brilliantly.

Kathryn snapped, lying on her back in the meadow, focusing on the foreground grasses; her camera held above her, as Louis pulled on the kite strings. She flung herself over and rolled onto her front, still snapping. She paused, flicked the controls onto rapid fire, and lifted the viewfinder to her eye once more. Exhilaration burned within her; this was feeling good.

Above her the kite swooped and soared, arcing through the sky. When it was high she just tracked it through the viewfinder, but when it was low she was playing with the focal length; shooting from within the grass, tilting the camera, and making abstracts from the scene.

Louis kept hold of the wooden handles and tugged on the strings, guiding the canvas as it brushed the sky. At first, he was completely aware of Kathryn, leaping and rolling around the meadow a short distance away. Then, he became lost in the kite's flight. He stepped back, and followed the kite forward, watching it silhouetted against the sky.

He heard Kathryn call his name. He glanced away from the kite and its momentum faltered. In a rustling of wind through canvas, it dived ungracefully out of the sky and thumped to the ground. Kathryn picked herself up and ran to retrieve it. As she made ready to set it off again, she looked up towards Louis.

'Can you fly it lower?' she called. 'I want to try and get some shots with the kite and the horse in frame together!'

Louis nodded, and called back his understanding. The kite was launched and he pulled back on the strings, wrapping the cords back and around, shortening the length. He glanced round and saw the horse stretched out on the hillside beneath him, etched in the chalk.

Gradually Louis settled into the rhythm of the flight, and he controlled the path of the kite. He lost track of time as he followed the trail across the sky, becoming mesmerised by it.

Time slipped by, imperceptibly; seconds into minutes, and minutes into hours—

Kathryn lay on her front in the meadow grass, propped up on her elbows and reviewed the pictures on her camera. Louis was next to her, facing towards her with his notebook spread out in front of him, and a fountain pen resting on the open pages. He wasn't writing, but idly playing with the leather page-marker, rolling the end between his fingers.

She thumbed through the shots, flicking backwards and forwards in constant comparison, and occasionally deleting one that was blurred, or which failed so completely even on the three-inch LCD screen.

'Is that your journal?' asked Kathryn, reviewing her photographs. 'What do you write about?'

'No. My novel.'

'Really?'

She looked up.

'Have you published anything?'

'Not yet,' Louis said, frowning. 'I've had a few poems published in magazines. And my last novel is currently out there being ignored by an editor—'

Louis stopped himself short as he remembered Kathryn's job.

'Sorry.'

'It's fine. I'm not exactly the same kind of editing.'

Louis relaxed after his inadvertent choice of words.

'So what's it about? Your novel?' Kathryn asked, setting her camera down.

Louis opened his mouth to answer, and clammed up. The question always led to this, and he didn't know how to answer. He feared to answer in case the novel – his novel – was ridiculous; he wished the story was easier to explain, or at least that he was better at explaining it.

Kathryn reached out and patted Louis' arm.

'It's okay, you don't have to tell me. I understand if it's a secret.'

Louis smiled weakly. He turned and gazed off into the distance; somewhere, far off across the meadow, a man and woman in their forties walked arm in arm while their dog chased butterflies, and further off a couple of young lovers lay together in the grass.

Louis laid back in the grass and shut his eyes. What a perfect afternoon this was. He reached out his arm and ran his fingers through the grass, enjoying the tickling sensation on his skin.

'Thanks for coming today.'

Kathryn's voice drifted over him where he lay, eyes closed against the sun.

'No problem. It's been fun.'

'I wasn't sure if my idea was going to work,' she added. 'You know when you imagine something so completely clearly? I get it all the time when I picture something in my mind – usually at the most inconvenient times – and then when I have time to get my pens out, I just draw rubbish.'

'I think I understand...'

Lewis continued to lie amongst the grasses, his eyes squeezed shut against the sun, with Amanda sitting alongside him. Although he couldn't see her, he pictured her there, looking through the images on her camera, just as she had been before he laid back his head. He began to reconstruct Amanda's appearance, her actions and her expressions as she spoke. The way she hooked back her hair, and smiled in that coy way that Lewis had first noticed the day at band when they had first met.

He reached out with one hand, catching the back of his fingers on her arm. Lewis felt the heat of the afternoon sun on his face, and remembered the days in the park. He rolled over and threw his arm over. His head brushed past her hair, and he blinked his eyes open.

'Lewis?'

He kissed her on the forehead.

'What are you doing?' Kathryn asked, pulling away from him. Louis blinked and refocused. Out of the haze of his imagination he now saw Kathryn. He retreated, both physically and vocally.

'I'm so, so sorry,' he spluttered, his pulse now racing. 'I was – it was a dream. I'm so sorry.'

'You were dreaming of kissing me?'

Kathryn wasn't surprised.

'Yes. No, I mean – it wasn't you. Not that you – no, err—'

'Louis.'

Kathryn fixed him with a firm stare, and Louis was silenced.

'You're jibbering,' she said, and grinned.

11

Kathryn sat at her desk in her office pod, transferring author corrections onto a clean set of proofs. Occasionally she lifted her head, to click through emails and files. She reached across the desk for her thumbed copy of Hart's Rules, and in passing she caught a teasing expression from Charlotte across the desk divide.

She returned to the paper, peering to inspect the faxed and indecipherable author's scrawl. She let out a sigh of frustration, looked away and then back, refocusing on the words, and attempted to solve the puzzle, letter by letter. Flagging a reminder to herself with a Post-it note, she moved on. She glanced up again, to find Charlotte watching her.

'What?' asked Kathryn.

Charlotte leaned forward.

'So— what?'

Kathryn drew out the question, knowing full well to what Charlotte was referring.

'So, yesterday afternoon? How did it go?'

Kathryn laid down her red pen and turned to face her friend.

'It was good. Project's going well.'

'You so know I wasn't asking about the project.'

'Or at least not the photo project,' Eleanor chipped in, from her desk on the furthest side of the pod.

Kathryn blushed.

'I only said he was nice.'

Kathryn saw how Charlotte was looking at her.

'Okay, so he's kind of cute, unassuming; that doesn't mean...'

'Kath.'

Eleanor leaned forward from around the computer monitor.

'You're as bad as my brother Ben when he met the girl he was going to fall in love with.'

Kathryn was caught wide-eyed and open-mouthed by Eleanor's words.

'I said he was cute and an interesting person to talk to. That's some leap from saying I'm going to fall in love!' she laughed.

Gradually, Kathryn's co-workers went back to work. Kathryn sat still for a while longer, thinking and chewing on the end of her red pen.

'He did kiss me,' Kathryn said abruptly.

Silence. Work stopped. Charlotte and Eleanor looked up, staring back at their friend.

'On the forehead, I mean,' Kathryn said, blushing. 'Not the lips or anything.'

'And you didn't think this was important enough to mention before?'

'It wasn't anything, though. It was hot, there was the sun; he was dreaming—'

'Kath, he *kissed* you!' Charlotte exclaimed.

Kathryn reflected on this for a moment, smiling.

'He was really embarrassed.'

'Well, if you didn't encourage it I'm not surprised,' Charlotte said, her words almost a chastisement.

'I can't believe you just said that,' said Kathryn. 'Besides, I don't even know if he's seeing anyone. He couldn't hang around after we got back to Wren Hoe.'

Charlotte grinned.

'Sounds to me like you know what you've got to ask him next. When are you next meeting up?'

Kathryn retreated into quietness and coyness. Eleanor looked again round the edge of her monitor.

'Kathryn...?'

'Umm... this evening,' Kathryn admitted. 'We are meeting up in the computer lab...'

Louis sat in the upstairs room of the coffee shop overlooking the Broad, his hand poised with his fountain pen over his leather notebook as he deliberated over the words. He read back the last few lines, heard the voice in his head, and placed the nib of the pen to the paper. And stopped. Again he lifted the pen. The thought, the words – they just didn't fit.

He lifted his head and gazed off into the middle distance. Around him, people sat at tables, chatting into the background hum of conversation. He blinked and turned his gaze to the view from the window into the bustling street below.

'Penny for your thoughts?'

Louis looked up as Beth approached the table with the coffees. He shrugged.

'Just trying to work out what happens next.'

He clipped the lid back onto his pen, and laid it down in the spine of his open book.

'I know what the next big scene is in the story. I just don't know what happens to get there.'

'Sounds like my life to me!' Beth laughed, and took a seat across the table from him. Louis nodded slowly and frowned.

'How's the new girlfriend?'

Louis stared at Beth, confused.

'I don't have a girlfriend.'

'Whatever—' Beth joked. 'Kathryn, then? You invited her to my birthday party yet?'

'She's okay, we're meeting up later to work on our college assignments. Two heads are better, you know, to grapple with RAW file format conversions.'

Beth reached over and poked Louis in the arm.

'You're doing that thing again.'

'We had a productive afternoon yesterday too,' continued Louis. 'We went out to the White Horse so Kathryn could do her photo shoot. Yeah, it went well. And I've got some things I did the other day, so we've got plenty to work with.'

'You've not asked her, have you?'

Louis chose to ignore the question, instead looking again at the half-completed page of his novel. He shook his head at the sentence with nowhere to go.

'Have you heard any more about Miss Leroy?' he asked.

'I phoned the hospital this morning. She took a bit of a downturn yesterday evening, but that seemed to have passed by this morning.'

Beth frowned.

'I feel a bit bad about it to be honest. I should care more really, but—'

'It's hard to believe that Miss Leroy could ever need help or saving,' said Louis. 'She's always so strong.'

Beth nodded her head vigorously, pleased to find some agreement with her that she wasn't being cruel. Louis reflected again on the pages of his novel. Decisively, he took up the pen and added one last sentence to the chapter, before turning the page and writing the header to the next chapter, and closed the book. Slowly and deliberately, he wrapped the leather tie around the cover, slipping it back through twice over to fasten it shut. Lastly, he slipped his fountain pen between the tie and the cover, hooking it carefully into place.

Louis sat forward to the table, and set the notebook down squarely in front of him. He checked the coffee mug, and drained the last of its contents.

'So, are we off then?' he asked.

Louis and Beth left the tall, narrow and charmingly wonky coffee shop on Broad Street. They chatted away as, under Beth's direction, they turned left and walked towards town.

'I do appreciate this, Louis.'

Beth's words were lost to Louis as he became caught up with something else he glimpsed in the street. He turned his head to watch as a girl and her mother walked past and entered the coffee shop. A memory stirred within him. His gaze became locked with that of the blond haired, blue-eyed girl, as she looked back at him over her shoulder. Sarah.

Louis forced himself to blink and look away.

'Sorry, Beth – I didn't – what was it you said?'

'I was just saying thanks. Polly was going to help me, but Tom hadn't told her they were going off to some art fair in the Cotswolds. I don't know...'

'I just hope I can help.'

'You'll be fine,' Beth said brightly.

They continued on down the street, chatting casually with one another. From the coffee shop doorway, Sarah watched them go until her mother called her inside.

12

Louis was sat at the workstation in the basement computer lab. He checked the time on his watch as the second hand ticked past 5:20 pm, then he sighed and sat forward to browse some of the BBC News website.

Kathryn burst through the doorway and skidded to a halt, with her bags swinging forward around her. She threw her gaze around the room to hunt out and find Louis before making straight for him.

'Sorry I'm late,' she garbled breathlessly. 'Heck of a day.'

Louis nodded, waiting impatiently while Kathryn fumbled and fought with her bags. Occasionally she glanced up at Louis, offering him withering expressions, and sighing after the return of nothing more than an uncertain shrug.

'I've got Photoshop all set up,' said Louis.

'Brilliant.'

Kathryn collapsed exhausted into the seat, and reached for her drinks bottle. She sighed.

'So. How have you been?'

'Not bad. I finished off my photo shoot this morning. Met up with Beth – she's a friend from work – for coffee, had a write of my novel, bite to eat, came here.'

'Very nice. Wish my day was as relaxed.'

Kathryn shook her head.

'Got home yesterday – only had an electricity bill waiting for me. £850! How am I supposed to pay £850?'

Louis shrugged, and fiddled with his course notes.

'So I was on the phone for forty-five minutes this morning, most of which was spent listening to the synthesised *Four Seasons* – and when I did finally get through I had to argue my way past some jobsworth ignoramus—'

Kathryn paused barely long enough to take breath.

'Not that I had time to be sorting out someone else's mistake. The rest of the day was spent trying to get an issue makeup off, which is not made any easier when I have to deal with egotistical authors who haven't read the style guide.'

Louis looked down and leafed through the pages, struggling to think of something to say.

'I wish I had time to sit in coffee shops and write my novel.'

Louis looked up.

'You're writing a novel too?' he said excitedly.

Kathryn glared at him, relenting after a few moments into a smile.

'Hardly. In that way, I am definitely not creatively inspired.

Louis grinned.

'I'm sorry you've had a rubbish day. If it's any consolation, this afternoon wasn't exactly easy.'

'No?'

'My friend, Beth. She had me off, helping her choose dresses. What do I know about dresses... ?'

Kathryn's face dropped with disbelief.

'Louis, tact? Have you ever heard of it? I've just said what an awful day I've had, and you try and sympathise by telling me about your shopping trip?'

Louis was silent. Defeated and confused, he sat inspecting his own thoughts. He tried to speak but could not get the words to come out. Again he tried, and again he stopped.

Kathryn picked up on Louis' discomfort and relented, reaching out a calming hand to take the course notes from him and to make peace.

'I'm sorry,' she said, 'Just – tough day. You know?'

Louis nodded quickly, and managed a smile.

'So what was this friend's dress for?'

'Beth? She's hosting a birthday party for herself; thirtieth. I think we found one.'

'Cool.'

Louis smiled, glancing back at the computer screen and the empty instance of Photoshop.

'Yeah, of course,' said Kathryn, 'Where are we up to.'

As she spoke she fiddled with the straps of her camera bag, and extracted the memory card from its slot.

'You got your card reader?' Kathryn asked.

Louis and Kathryn walked from the glazed college entrance, illuminated in electric brilliance, and out into the now dusky dark of late summer evening. They were laughing and joking, deconstructing the successes and failures of their session in the computer lab.

'I'm still not convinced it's worth all the effort.'

'You don't think? Once we got the hang of what we were doing, the quality was so much better. I'm half-tempted to take the CD to a late-night photo booth now; I want to see what they come out like on proper paper.'

'I guess,' Louis said. 'But don't you find it's the quality of the lens? Get yourself a decent camera and fit it with a proper lens, and JPEG's fine.'

'For real?'

Kathryn shook her head.

'Louis, that might be the case for party photos that you shoot off on an own brand roll of 35mm, albeit with your top-notch camera, which you then get developed at Boots. Then, yes, maybe it's comparable.'

'You were just talking about going to the photo booth,' quipped Louis.

Kathryn continued unabated.

'Handling the RAW file, didn't you feel like you were back in the darkroom; dodging and burning, playing with filters? You just have so much more control.'

'Sure, give me a dark room any day. I'm just not convinced myself that I can translate what I can do in a darkened room to a computer.'

'You're doing the course!' pursued Kathryn. 'Surely you're not frightened of computers?'

Kathryn's words trailed into the silence that followed. Kathryn realised that she may have somehow stung Louis' feelings, and reached out to reassuringly squeeze his arm.

'Look, I need to get food. You want to come for a drink?'

Kathryn fixed her gazed solely on Louis, and offered him a warm, rich smile. Louis glanced quickly at his watch, shuffled his feet, and agreed.

'Big Bang?' asked Kathryn.

Louis grinned.

'Cool. Who doesn't like sausage and mash?'

Louis sat opposite Kathryn, tracing his fingers through the condensation on the surface of his glass. He felt awkward sitting there with the room behind him, his back to the door, and it didn't even make a difference that he could see Walton Street outside, with the lights of the passing trams streaked across the glass behind Kathryn's back.

The waiter seemed to duck round from behind Louis, appearing to suddenly be at the table with their food, and was gone again without so much as a surly word.

'Looks good,' said Louis, as he took up his knife and fork.

'So when's the party?'

'Huh?'

'The thirtieth birthday, that you were dress shopping for?' Kathryn prompted.

Louis blushed, and ducked his head in an attempt to hide the reddening of his face.

'Oh, the party? Saturday.'

Louis cut into his sausages, and forked them up with the mash and onion gravy.

'Do you carry your notebook everywhere you go?'

Kathryn nodded towards the leather-bound book alongside Louis' place setting.

Louis swallowed his mouthful and glanced first to Kathryn, then to the book.

'It's a condition, I'm afraid. I can't be parted from it.'

Kathryn laughed.

'The man and his notebook. An *avant garde* film if ever there was one.'

'Or nouvelle vague?' Louis said, with a grin.

Kathryn smiled with amusement. Their meal fell to silence again. Occasionally – at every opportunity – Louis glanced up at Kathryn. Sometimes he would catch her eye, and he would hurriedly bury his gaze in his dinner. He had to ask her; he could hear Beth's voice inside of his head telling him that he must ask her. But he couldn't. There was the fear, the uncertainty, the unknown. He ate more of his food and looked at Kathryn's left hand, the empty ring finger. Did that mean she was single? He looked away, and pushed another forkful of food into his mouth.

'Did you know there was a band called Nouvelle Vague?' Kathryn began again. 'They're French – named themselves after the film movement – and they play covers of old classics, but in a funky kind of *bossa nova* style.'

'Uh-huh.'

'So what kind of music do you like?'

Louis stopped mid-chew; then slowly carried on, clearing his mouth. This was just the kind of question he had feared.

'I don't know really.'

He felt himself blush, and stumbled over his words.

'I always hate that question. Like when someone comes to visit, and they start inspecting your record collection.'

'Oh, I know! Like if you pass someone your iPod to see something in particular, and then they start looking through everything.'

'I'm afraid my musical taste is woefully eclectic,' said Louis. 'It doesn't help that I'm a teacher, so I'm exposed to all kind of music I really ought to not give the time of day; but for whatever reason, I actually end up quite liking.'

'I promise I won't go looking through your CD collection.'

Louis smiled, slightly more at ease by Kathryn's reassurance. He wasn't sure, but he felt now that this might be someone who he wouldn't mind looking through his music collection.

'So what are you up to Saturday?' Louis asked abruptly. Kathryn thought for a moment, then shrugged.

'Nothing, I think. Pizza and telly, probably.'

'Because I was wondering? That party I was telling you about – I was wondering – if you were interested—'

Louis garbled out the last of the words in a nervous rush. Before Kathryn could answer he added more in haste.

'Beth, you know, she asked me if I knew anyone. She wants as many people there as possible; and there's going to be this cover band playing – they're really good. I mean, not a date obviously, but if you wanted to go – as a friend...'

Kathryn smiled coyly. She sat forward and fixed her gaze from her bright blue, almost iridescent eyes. She chewed slowly on her lip. Louis suddenly remembered something Beth had told him, and sat forward too, mirroring Kathryn's posture. His heart raced at the prospect of her answer.

13

Amanda stood in the kitchen, clipping back her potted plants; snipping off the dead and dying, and tidying up the straggly ends. She moved from room to room and from bookshelf to windowsill; from plant to plant, offering out water and collecting up off-cuts of greenery in return. She stopped at the lounge window, with the sun blazing in through the small, glazed panes, and began to reshape a Busy Lizzie. Through the open window she could hear Sarah with a friend in the garden, talking.

'Yeah, it's the friend of my sister's,' Caz said to Sarah. 'Should be cool.'

'Saturday you say? You want to meet here? Mum and Dad are going out.'

Caz nodded enthusiastically, and pulled out her phone to read a text.

Back in the room, Amanda moved off with her pruning scissors and off-cuts of plants. In the kitchen, as she deposited the debris in the waste bin, she found Lewis at the counter, preparing supper. As she approached, he glanced over his shoulder.

'Hi...'

Amanda nodded.

'Lewis, where are we going on Saturday?'

Lewis jumped, startled.

'Saturday?'

'I heard Sarah talking just now. Something about us going out on Saturday.'

'Yeah...'

He nodded.

'To Beth's party – you know, for her birthday? I told you about it back at the end of last term.'

'Did you?'

Amanda shrugged.

'Guess I must have forgotten.'

Lewis plunged a handful of spaghetti into the pan, and proceeded in pressing it down into softened strings.

'Her band is going to play,' he said. 'I think it should be good.'

As Lewis continued preparing dinner, Amanda shuffled through the post, sifting about half into the recycling before heading out of the room to file the rest. As Lewis put the oil in the pan to heat, he reached across and flicked on Radio 4. He also fetched over a copy of Photographer's Monthly to have on the side next to him.

Ten or fifteen minutes later, as the rousing theme music of Bartlet Green ushered in another dose of *The Archers*, Louis carried his bowl of spaghetti carbonara to the kitchen table. He settled himself down in front of his dinner, with a fork in one hand and his magazine on his other side.

Lewis entered the lounge, carrying his novel. In the armchair and sofa were Amanda and Sarah, already watching something on television.

'Particularly good dinner tonight, Dad,'

'It was, you know,' agreed Amanda.

Lewis hesitated and blushed awkwardly. They were right of course. That spaghetti carbonara was one of his best. It was weird actually, when he thought about it.

'I don't know why,' Lewis said, with a shrug. 'I never do anything different; but sometimes they are really nice, and sometimes they are a bit meh – same old, same old.'

He sat down on the sofa at the far end from Sarah, curling a leg under him, and began to unwind the tie from his book.

'So what are we watching?'

Sarah glanced round at her father, and offered him a what-does-it-look-like glare.

'Fair point,' replied Lewis. He settled back into the squidginess of the sofa and ignored the drama playing out on the television. He fetched out his pen and flicked through the pages to where he had got to last, read back a few lines a couple of times, sat staring at the words for a while longer, and then pulled out a photography magazine from the pile on the coffee table.

Lewis hugged his daughter goodnight on the landing and pressed a kiss to her forehead, which she took with a certain amount of grudging forbearance before retreating to her bedroom. Lewis smiled gladly and returned to his own bedroom, where Amanda, in her nightie, was just finishing getting ready for bed, in front of the 1950s dressing table that was Lewis' mother's.

Lewis climbed into bed, plumped up the pillows behind him, and retrieved a large hardback digital photography handbook which he propped open on his knees. He read until he was halfway into an article about histograms and post-camera processing, and just about keeping with the subject matter, when his eyes started to droop, and he caught himself snorting awake for the second time; he decided it was time to go to sleep.

Louis snuggled down into his pillow on the left side of the bed, looking across his bedside table as he flicked off the lamp. A few minutes later he turned, changing sides; and stretching an arm and a leg out across to the empty right side of the bed, slid gently into sleep.

Soon, dreams and memories began to wash over him; back and forth, they cycled through his mind. His mother and father were standing in the hall; faceless figures, seeing him off to a school disco that he never went to. Omnisciently, he looked down on his fifteen-year old self standing outside the school window, with the disco lights flooding his face in an ever-changing array of colour.

Another night in his dream, and another party, saw Louis walking along the road outside the school, averting his eyes from his classmates as they piled out, laughing and joking, boy and girl in each other's arms. The dream ebbed away, and landed him back at university, and standing outside halls. The music thudded beyond the walls of the common room, to where Louis stood in the yard behind the bins at the back of the bar, trying to pluck up the courage to go inside. His fingers tightened around the cold neck of the cider bottle.

A couple of students, his hand down around her bum, staggered through the night in front of him and entered the halls. Lewis pushed himself, and willed himself to go in, but his feet were rooted to the ground.

Amanda slipped her hand into his, her fingers interlocking with his, and he felt the rush of her warmth and comfort.

'It's okay. We don't have to go,' Amanda reassured him. 'If you don't want to.'

Lewis looked to his side; suddenly, he was no longer alone. He smiled and apologised as they walked off.

The dreaming Louis watched them go; Beth too, hanging out of the door to the halls, watched Louis walk away into the night, alone. She shook her head, sad and uncomprehending, for her friend. Slowly she stepped back, and let the door swing slowly shut and click into place in front of her face. It was only then that she saw him – or was it her – a silhouette of a person standing way across the field, also watching Louis.

Miss Leroy's face jumped into the forefront of Louis' dreaming mind; her face, the lines of which swirled into his dream; and his mind filled with questions. What had she been doing standing in that field, watching him leave a party he had never attended? His hand closed around Amanda's, holding tight to all that was real.

The dream drifted away, and Louis turned over in his bed and drifted into deeper, sounder sleep.

Across town, in the private room of the Morton-Leroy Hospital, Miss Leroy sat up in her bed. Oblivious to the comings and goings of the hospital, she looked at the book in front of her – a diary. She traced the words on the page, and fixed the picture of the boy, Tumnal, with her steely gaze. She closed the book and returned it to her locker, before switching off the light and plunging the room into a half-light of security lighting and blinking instruments.

Saturday came, and Lewis paced the hall, stopping occasionally in front of the mirror. He hated seeing his own reflection normally, but tonight he felt strangely compelled to tweak his collar of his shirt, or adjust the cuffs.

Again he paced the floor, glancing at the time, agitated. Finally, he heard a creak of floorboards, and turned to look as Amanda came slowly down the stairs, fixing her earrings as she went. He stopped and looked again. He could never quite believe how gorgeous his Amanda looked. Her auburn hair reflected the light with a subtle radiance.

'Amanda,' he stuttered. 'You look beautiful.'

Amanda smiled and blushed.

'Really? You always say that, Lewis.'

Lewis returned his wife's gaze dolefully. It was true, though; she was beautiful. He stepped up to her, and slipped his arms around her waist while she still stood on the bottom step. Lewis pulled Amanda into an embrace and kissed her. This was just like old times. He was suddenly the shy little boy from the garden again, kissing his new and unexpected girlfriend.

Amanda pulled back, laughing.

'Come on Louis, we're going to be late.'

They were half-way out the door before Lewis stopped again. Louis? She hadn't called him Louis for, how long...?

'What did you call me?' he asked her hesitantly.

Amanda laughed kindly, and tugged him by the arm, slipping hers around his.

'Sorry, Lewis,' she said. 'I keep forgetting.'

They slipped their coats on and left the house. Amanda stepped across the garden towards the gate while Lewis locked the door. He turned and stood on the threshold to the tiled porch for a moment. In the garden Sarah and Caz were sitting on the swings, giggling amongst themselves.

As Lewis made his way down the path, Caz looked up and called out.

'Have a good evening, Mr Tumnal.'

Lewis looked up.

'Alright, Caz, Sarah.'

He offered them a wave. Caz and Sarah fell about laughing, as Lewis followed Amanda out through the gate.

A tram slid in past where Lewis' taxi sat in a queue of traffic, and arrived at the next stop. The traffic moved again, and he passed Kathryn as she disembarked from the tram and began to walk down the street. Lewis' taxi turned in to the gravelled entrance of the University Sports and Social Club. Lewis followed Amanda out of the black cab, and returned to the driver's window to settle the fare. Then, as the *cab moved off and turned to exit onto the road again, Lewis moved to embrace his wife, and ushered them both into the brown brick 1960's pavilion building.*

From across the car park, Kathryn stood, staring over at where Louis entered the social club alone.

The inside of the sports and social club was dimly lit, and not helped by the same uninspiring brown brick as the outside. The memorabilia from the University of Wren's rugby team's past sporting glories did nothing to brighten up the interior. In one corner, the band were setting up while a disco rocked out of the sound system.

Kathryn stood nervously in the entrance, wondering what she thought she was doing here. She scanned the room; picking out faces, searching tables and the bar for Louis. On the third pass around the room, she spotted the tweed jacket on the back of a chair and, now she looked closer, the back of Louis' head.

Louis sat at the table with Beth and Tom and Polly, listening to some anecdote of Tom's. Kathryn approached the table from behind Louis' back and wavered, pondering the moment of interruption.

'Louis,' said Tom, after a break in conversation. He nodded his balding head over Louis' shoulder at Kathryn. 'I think there's someone...'

Louis turned, at first both curious and worried, before relaxing at the sight of Kathryn. He jumped to his feet immediately, and ushered her to somewhere more private.

'Louis?'

'Kathryn, hi,' he said. 'Good to see you.'

'I thought we arranged to meet outside?'

Louis hesitated in front of Kathryn. He couldn't believe how beautiful she was.

'Did we? We did...' he stuttered. 'Let me introduce you.'

Kathryn rolled her eyes at this. How did she come to be dating – was this a date – this man? She stepped up alongside Louis as he turned to face the people around his table, and hooked her hand partly around his arm, as if claiming possession.

Louis introduced Kathryn first, and then Beth, Polly and Tom, with much diffidence and hesitation. Kathryn waited patiently while Louis stood behind his chair, his hands fidgeting with the jacket slung across the back of it. Eventually she nudged closer to Louis.

'Shall we?' she said, nodding in the direction of the bar. 'Drinks?'

'Of course, yes. Let's,' agreed Louis.

He ushered Kathryn away from the table and towards the bar, remarkably more at ease when he was alone with her. They jostled forward through the scrum in front of the bar; Louis pulled out his wallet, and fished out a crisp ten pound note.

'I love it when you go to the hole in the wall and it delivers you a brand new notes,' he said. 'Seems such a shame to use it.'

'I know,' Kathryn laughed. 'Not that I'm usually that lucky. Got money out the other week, I swear the note came out almost in two halves!'

Louis nodded. He registered the way that the conversation was going, unfamiliar as he was at taking part in 'rounds'.

'What would you like?' he asked.

After a few minutes they eased themselves away from the bar, Kathryn with both pint glasses as Louis fumbled to put the change back in his wallet and stuff it into his trousers.

'Thanks for coming tonight,' he said, as he ushered Kathryn towards a quiet table in the corner.

'Aren't we going to re-join your friends?' Kathryn asked with surprise.

Louis was by now sat at the table, and now fidgeted uncomfortably. He frowned as he gazed up at Kathryn next to him.

'I guess...'

Louis eased himself regretfully out of his seat, and followed Kathryn back through to the main room to join his friends.

Beth, on vocals, led her own band in a cover of The Beatles' *Twist and Shout*. The lights swirled around the room, and the floor creaked with dancing. Louis sat at his table, watching the dancers and tapping his foot to the beat, his hand resting on the side of his pint glass.

The song died away, and Kathryn leant in towards him.

'You don't dance then?'

Louis looked sad.

'I can't.'

The tempo changed, and Beth started off with a song from *Grease*.

'Of course you can.'

Kathryn jumped to her feet, and tugged and cajoled at Louis.

'Come on. Let's dance.'

Louis stayed sitting resolutely, finding himself torn between staying put and going with Kathryn. The disco lights swept around the room, and on the floor Tom and Polly swayed and moved together. Towards the edge of the crowd, Kathryn danced, her dress sweeping around her, miming the words to *You're The One That I Want* and pointing emphatically at Louis when the moment dictated. She danced forwards, and reached out to Louis to entice him up; he winced coyly, and recoiled.

At the next verse Kathryn tried again, getting so far as to pull on his hand, but she couldn't persuade him to his feet. Louis sat, hand round his glass, watching Kathryn on the dance floor, and wanting so much to be up there with her. He saw Tom and

Polly, and Beth, through the masses, dancing and singing; what would they make of his clumsy rhythm and awkward moves?

No. He decided. He would do it. Putting down his glass, he readied himself to join Kathryn on the floor – just as the music faded and the set ended. He was left standing awkwardly at the table, applauding the band, and ready to hold Kathryn's chair as she returned to their table.

'You don't dance, then,' said Kathryn.

'Louis never dances, do you my boy?'

Tom was back at the table, loud and avuncular. He passed behind Louis to re-join Polly, giving him a slap on the back which made Louis feel even more awkward and displaced in front of Kathryn.

'I wanted to,' he said. 'I tried to; I was going to.'

Kathryn smiled.

'Next set; you, me, and the dance floor.'

She fixed him with a meaningful stare, that was only broken when a breathless and exhausted Beth eased herself into the empty chair next to her.

'So you must be Kathryn,' began Beth.

Louis opened his mouth to speak.

'Thanks so much for coming tonight. Louis can't stop talking about you.'

'Really?'

Kathryn blushed.

'No really,' continued Beth. 'Ever since he started the photography course at the end of term – you know we are both teachers—'

'I gathered.'

'—he's been saying how much of a photographer you are.'

'I don't know how he knows that!' Kathryn laughed.

'Did he tell you how worried he was about starting the course this summer?'

Beth talked to Kathryn as if Louis wasn't there, jabbering on like she'd known her for years.

'Why was he nervous?'

'Oh, you know. Apparently there were these two really old codgers last year, who just kind of latched onto Louis and bored him halfway to insanity.'

'Wasn't that long a journey,' chipped in Louis, with words that were scarcely noticed.

'Yeah, he's told me – well, warned me – about Colin...'

She flashed a smile in the direction of Louis, who just sat there, feeling increasingly like an observer as Beth and Kathryn talked. At times he found that snatches of Tom and Polly's conversation with the other work colleagues to the other side of him ebbed into his conversation, but not enough to entice him to switch fully. Neither was he part of Beth's conversation enough to drown out Tom's loud voice. And then he was left sitting alone on the edge of Tom's conversation, when Beth and Kathryn disappeared off together to the ladies' ahead of the band's next set.

Louis quipped a remark into Tom's conversation, which fell instantly into silence. Louis' confidence retreated inwards at the reaction, as he puzzled and agonised over what he had said.

'Oh, ma'am, good evening,' said Polly, over the top of Louis' shoulder.

Louis turned hastily, to find the tall figure of Miss Leroy standing behind him.

'Shouldn't you be – still...?' Polly queried.

'Hospitals are for the old and the infirm,' clipped Miss Leroy, casting a stern gaze over her 'children'. 'As I am neither, I have discharged myself.'

Polly returned Miss Leroy's gaze, with a mixture of surprise and expectation that she shared with those around her. Louis eased himself out of his chair, and moved to invite Miss Leroy to a seat.

'That is very kind of you,' clipped Miss Leroy. 'But I won't stay long. I just wished to give my regards to Beth. Where is the birthday girl?'

'Um – just gone to the, err...'

Louis realised that his explanation was going towards characteristic detail, and stopped himself.

'Ah, there she is,' Miss Leroy said, as she spotted Beth returning through the room, chatting all the time with Kathryn.

Sarah and Caz hid in the shadows of the car park, plotting how to get into the club house. They shared a bottle of cider between them, swigging alternate mouthfuls. They watched as Miss Leroy strode purposefully out of the club house towards a waiting cab.

'Come on, let's try round the back,' said Caz. 'At my uncle's birthday they were all spilling out onto the pitch by this time, and too drunk to notice who was who.'

'Sarah?' asked Caz, when her friend didn't respond straight away.

Sarah watched the cab all the way out of the car park and beyond it, disappearing right along the road.

'Huh?'

'Round the back. Come on.'

Sarah shrugged, and followed her friend to where, sure enough, the party was spilling out of the pavilion. The smokers stood around clouds of bitter-smelling fumes. A couple snogged passionately against the porch. Caz led Sarah brazenly up to the doors and into the bar, and Caz was quick to scour the tables and windowsills for bottles of booze, which she swiped unnoticed to bring back to Sarah.

'Not a bad party for a bunch of teachers,' said Caz, her head nodding to the beat. Beth's voice could be heard over the top.

'And Miss Vernal, she can sing!'

Again, when Caz looked for comment, she found Sarah's mind preoccupied. This time Sarah crept forward, the lip of her bottle almost to her mouth, mesmerised by the dance floor. Lewis danced in front of Kathryn, moving to the music with her.

The music ended, and Beth introduced the next and last of that set. After a mellow and moving introduction, the lights dipped to gentle swirls across the hall with the scattered light of a glitter ball, and Beth opened out into a romantic number. Lewis and Kathryn danced together on the floor, arm in arm, so close that breaths interspersed.

Sarah's surprise escaped her.

'Dad!'

PART TWO

Autumnal Leaves

agitato con fuoco

1

Louis was snuggled on the sofa with Kathryn, watching a DVD on her laptop. Much as he tried to fight the thoughts, the truth that tonight was the last night before the first morning of the new term was a hard thing to bury. These last few weeks of late August – ever since Beth's party – had been the best weeks of his life. It had been a rollercoaster, from his first, awkward kiss with Kathryn – if you didn't count the dream-induced craziness on White Horse Hill – to the daily meet-ups, to going for lunch at the University Press, and waiting for her when she finished work. Not to mention this last week, when, following Kathryn's announcement that she had some holiday to take, she had moved in for the duration, or as good as.

He remembered fondly the fun they had making jam, after one of Kathryn's colleagues presented them with the biggest bag of damsons ... and the hilarious chaos that had resulted. He remembered the long walks down by the Wrenshire canal, and foraging for sloes amongst the blackthorn bushes.

On the coffee table stood the remnants of the last bottle of wine of these summer holidays, the wine glasses standing tall with that slight smear of red in the base of the cup. He gave

Kathryn a gentle squeeze between his arms, and she glanced up at him with a smile.

The credits began to roll against the somewhat schmaltzy theme music.

'That was brilliant,' said Kathryn.

Louis didn't answer, just kissed the top of her head.

'Do we have to go back to work tomorrow?'

Kathryn pulled herself up and turned to face him. She shrugged.

'Sadly, yes.'

'This last week – this summer – it's been amazing.'

Louis held her tightly.

'Thank you.'

'Hey, stop it, you make it sound like we're never going to see each other again. It's only 8.5 hours of the day that we work.'

'You're right. We can still have fifteen and a half hours when we don't have to miss out.'

Kathryn nodded.

'And we have photography class,' she added. 'I still have to make sure I get a better mark than you!'

'Really?'

Kathryn nodded impetuously.

'You're good. But some of your composition, you just need...'

She laughed, and they kissed.

They kissed again in the hall, after Kathryn had shouldered her small rucksack, and gathered up her handbag and camera. Louis let his hands trail across Kathryn's waist, and slipped them beneath the fabric of her blouse for the touch of her skin.

'Louis—' Kathryn said, as she kissed him again. 'I have to go.'

'So go, I'm not stopping you.'

He followed his words with another kiss, and a continuance of their embrace.

Kathryn crossed the garden, glancing back over her shoulder again at Louis in the doorway to his home. When she was halfway through the door in the garden wall, Louis suddenly sprinted forwards to join her, and they tumbled out of the garden onto the pavement, where they kissed again.

A tram rumbled towards them along the street.

'I should go,' said Kathryn.

'You don't have to,' answered Louis. 'Stay. Like you did last night.'

Kathryn glanced from the approaching tram to Louis in front of her. She chewed on her bottom lip, and felt herself sway on her feet. She looked longingly at Louis, but found herself hoisting her bag onto her shoulders. She shook her head slowly.

'I can't. Not tonight.'

The tram rattled to a stop beside them, and suddenly they were flooded with the patchwork, criss-cross of light from the carriages. They kissed again, before Kathryn broke free and boarded the tram. With a hiss and a squeal, the wheels began to turn again, and the tram eased off and on its way. Louis continued to stand on the edge of the street and watched, waving, until it was out of sight. He turned and stepped back into the garden, and pulled the door closed behind him, until the lock clicked shut with a reassuring thunk.

2

Day came, and with it a soft breeze that blew through the leaves that were just on the turn towards autumn. It blew through the curtains into the room a little, floating waves of sunlight across the floorboards and the bed; Louis lay awake, listening to the headlines on BBC Radio 4.

He sat up on the edge of his bed and allowed the world to straighten itself, before he got up and crossed the room to the window in his pyjamas. Looking out through the open window, he could feel a touch of coldness in the air – a refreshing beginning to what he could tell was going to be another relentless, blazing day.

Glancing across the room, he saw his work clothes where he had laid them out ready last night. Once more to school, he considered; once more unto the breach. After showering and shaving he quickly dressed, tucking his checked cotton shirt into his brown corduroys, and he tied his tie in front of the mirror.

Leaving the bedroom, he went about his normal daily routine of making himself a breakfast of orange juice, muesli, and a large mug of coffee. Pausing before his toast, he reached across the counter to push open the window and put out a handful of bird seed and mealy worms onto the little stone ledge. As he stood in the kitchen, spreading a thick layer of butter and honey onto his toast, a wren was soon on the scene to fill his tummy too.

Half an hour later, and he was wheeling his bicycle out onto the street, with his trousers tucked into his socks and his satchel clipped to the rack. With a bit of a wobble to start off, he cycled off and turned left almost immediately into the side streets.

Arriving at school, he greeted everyone he met with a cheerful hello and a happy smile. Walking the corridors of the H-block, he did still remember those first tentative steps when he first walked the corridors as an adult and newly qualified teacher, but gone was that tentativeness now. Now he had a purpose, and an established class. He felt ready too, and maybe for the first time, properly ready. Which, he considered, was weird when he added up how little preparation time he had devoted to lesson plans this summer, compared to previous years. As he unlocked the door to his classroom, he remembered those few snatched hours in the garden, sorting out school work while Kathryn read. He smiled and closed the door behind him.

Across the other side of town, Kathryn woke late in her crowded bedroom in the two-up, two-down terraced house she shared on Juxon Street. At first she moved with slow and delirious movements as she raised her head from the pillow, and her eyes focussed on the blinking display of the clock radio. She soon dived out of bed in a hurry, muttering swear words as she ran for the bathroom.

She was still moving at double speed as she crashed around the kitchen, slurping down scalding coffee as she moved to make breakfast, quickly discovering that the milk was off, and she was out of bread. A bowl of dry cornflakes and a hurried cereal bar made her realise the need to make use of the staff canteen later.

She grabbed her shoulder bag and left, pulling the door closed behind her. From her front gate she ran up the road to Walton Street, where she skipped to avoid the tram rails where they cut through the cobbles and broken tarmac. Past the traditional, art-house cinema, and the upmarket deli, she ran past the grand frontage of the University Press, only slowing as she neared the entrance.

She greeted the friendly porter with a cheerful hello and flashed her ID, before swiping it through the slot and pushing past the clanking turnstiles. She belted across the lawn, with its ornamental duck pond and ancient copper bench, only slowing her pace as she reached the far side of the main quad. She was about to enter through the revolving doors, when Charlotte called her to a halt as she ran to catch up.

Soon they were catching up on gossip, with Charlotte asking about and Kathryn reporting on her week off, and more importantly the status of the relationship with Louis. Kathryn found it all very easy to tell, with stories gushing out, one after the other. She blushed more upon being told by Charlotte how the state of things was so evident in her face.

'Excuse me?'

Kathryn and Charlotte both looked round for the source of the voice; spoken in a serious tone. They both took a step aside to let a tall, auburn-haired woman in smart business dress – a sharp contrast to Kathryn and Charlotte's more casual attire – pass through into the building, even though there was plenty of room to go around.

'Who's she?'

'New commissioning editor in Classics, sadly,' said Charlotte. 'Started last week.'

'Brilliant,' said Kathryn. 'Is she on any of my lists?'

Charlotte nodded.

'And mine.' She frowned. 'Dr Amanda Jones. She's come to us from some post at The University. Friend of the Secretary – one in with the delegates.'

'One of those...' Kathryn sighed.

They pushed through the revolving door into the bright and airy, modern atrium, flashing their passes to security as they headed to the stairs.

'Mr Tumnal.'

Lewis swung round on his feet to find Miss Leroy standing by the doorway.

'You had a good summer break, I trust?'

'It was brilliant, yes,' he said, before adding, 'thank you.'

Lewis approached the headmistress, watching carefully for the signs of the stroke or other debilitation, but she seemed as sharp as always.

'You are quite recovered?' Louis asked tentatively.

'I am,' Miss Leroy said. 'It was an inconvenience, what happened to me. A setback Lewis, which I battled and won.'

For some reason Lewis felt she was not just talking about a stroke and a stay in hospital.

'You should know, of all my staff, that I do not lose battles lightly. And I do not take kindly to those that force them.'

She was not, Lewis reasoned, only referring to the stroke as a person. Avoiding Miss Leroy's omnipresent gaze, Lewis looked away to count his schoolbooks.

'Everything is alright with you, isn't it, Lewis?' continued Miss Leroy firmly. 'With all that has happened, we have missed our usual sessions to monitor progress.'

'Everything's fine,' Lewis nodded. 'Better than fine.'

'Good.'

Louis stood still for a moment, and listened to the clip of stilettos on the corridor floor. *Amanda?* He had forgotten that Miss Leroy knew all about Amanda.

Later that afternoon, during a moment when Louis found he had a respite from directing teaching, he looked out across the rows of bowed heads. He knew of course he should have been working on his prep for the next lesson, but instead he fell to dreaming.

Out there, somewhere amongst the heads, was a boy just like he used to be: friendless and lonely, ignored for the most part by his parents, and desperately reaching for something, anything. The boy would be waiting for somebody to notice him, just as Miss Leroy had noticed Louis. It had taken a three-boy attack at the back of school and a broken flute, but Miss Leroy had noticed him that day. She'd believed in him, given him the music lessons, and approved of the match when he had met Amanda Jones.

Amanda Jones. Was Miss Leroy the only other person to have known Amanda Jones?

'Sir—'

Louis woke up, suddenly aware of the first-year girl stood next to his desk, and the rows of expectant, amused and bemused faces watching him from the class.

'Sir,' the girl repeated.

'Yes?'

'It's Miss Leroy, sir. She asked me to come and get Sarah from your class.'

Even before Louis could answer he saw the girl with the fair hair tucked back in a ponytail, in the third row from the front, begin to gather her things. It was the girl from the flat above his own. He nodded to her to go.

He watched Sarah and the first-year girl leave, before setting the class back to their project. Sitting back in his chair now, all he could think about was the time when, as a boy, Miss Leroy had called him out of class to her office. What could she want with Sarah?

Charlotte sat with Eleanor at their pod, feigning a work conversation while watching Kathryn in the glass-fronted office opposite, as she was given instruction by her boss, and the animated and enthusiastic Dr Amanda Jones.

Eventually the meeting came to a close, and a wearisome Kathryn left the office to take the few short steps back to her desk and collapse into her seat. Charlotte and Eleanor both waited and watched for Amanda to stride off down the corridor, carrying her own self-importance with her. Once they were sure she'd definitely left, and their manager had slid the office door closed on another meeting, they sat forward.

'She's a nightmare, don't you think?' they both said, almost in chorus.

'Completely and utterly,' said Kathryn. She logged back into her computer, but quickly slung the mouse away and leaned towards the desk divide.

'She should just trust us to get on with the work. A week here, how can she presume to know our jobs better than us?'

'I know.' Charlotte said. 'And it's come from nowhere. The speed they make pointless decisions in this place. It's unbelievable.'

'And yet it takes them goodness knows forever to appoint a new PA,' added Eleanor.

'Who is she anyway?' growled Kathryn. 'Just because she's got letters after her name. What does she know about publishing?'

'Her father's the Dean of Emerson too, who's like that with the Leroy family.'

'Might have known. The Leroy's get everywhere in this town!' Kathryn raged, holding her head in her hands.

'She pulled one of mine out of class this morning, too,' Beth said.

'I wonder what she's planning?' mused Louis. 'And Sarah's a good student too – can't have been a disciplinary.'

Louis sat with Beth in the staff room with their Tupperware on their laps, eating their sandwiches.

'You had a good birthday then?' asked Louis, after a pause in conversation.

'Yeah, it was ace,' Beth said, beaming. 'And we got a new gig out of it. It's all good.'

Louis nodded.

'And you? You had a good time?'

Louis looked up and caught Beth's gaze. He could tell that she was angling for more than just an affirmation as to the quality of the party.

'I think you had the best time of anyone there,' Beth added, in an attempt to lead the conversation somewhere further.

Louis blushed.

'Sorry. We were a bit anti-social.'

'Don't apologise. It's great Louis, I'm so pleased for you—'

Polly rushed into the staff room and landed with a sigh in the chair opposite Louis and Beth, growling under her breath.

'Problem?' asked Beth.

Polly scowled furiously. 'Agh! That woman, she's impossible.'

'You're talking Miss Leroy. Not a parent?'

'The bitch!'

Polly pulled the cellophane from her sandwich carton and threw it aside.

'Not only does she interrupt my class to take out one of my best students, but now she stops me as I'm trying to go to lunch to ask me all these questions.'

'What questions?' asked Louis curiously.

Polly was about to answer, but hesitated long enough to stop herself.

'Doesn't matter. If she hasn't talked to you yet, it's probably best if I don't say.'

'She told me she was going to reorganise our year groups,' said Beth, 'Something's not working, apparently.'

3

Louis pulled a lively discussion about characterisation in modern, nineteenth-century, and Shakespearean literature to a close, in a way as to set the class' first homework assignment. As the clock ticked closer to three-thirty, he let them pack up their bags and leave as soon as the bell rang for the end of school.

He sat back in his chair and relaxed for a few moments, before tackling the pile of marking that had already built up. Eventually he sat forward, picked up his pen, and dragged the first book off the pile onto the desk in front of him. And there it sat while he tried to work up the enthusiasm to attack the task. He lifted his head and looked out the window at the beautiful evening sun. He glanced at his watch. The minute hand was fast approaching four o'clock. Kathryn finished work at four-thirty, he mused. If he left now, then he still had time to get down the hill and get across town and meet her.

His gaze refocused on the pile of marking. It would be even bigger this time tomorrow.

Beth sped down the stairs and around the corner, into the long corridor that ran down the whole of the west side of

H-block. She stopped outside Louis' classroom and knocked. No answer. She knocked again and tried the handle. Locked. She pressed her face close to the wired glass and peered through, to see Louis' desk chair left standing free on the floor, instead of pushed neatly back under the desk, and a pile of marking, still on the left side of the desk. Both his jacket and satchel – *and Louis too* – were gone already.

She stepped back and frowned, puzzled.

Louis jumped, almost carefree, from the tram at its stop on Walton Street. He walked briskly to cross the road, and waited outside the entrance of the University Press. As the minutes passed, so the occasional person who passed through the gate increased to a slow trickle of people, spilling this way and that onto Walton Street, some to gather on the pavement before boarding a tram, and some to saddle up onto their bicycles.

Louis fidgeted and sidled from foot to foot as he waited, straining sometimes to peer through the railings to see if Kathryn was on her way. As he waited, thoughts came and went through his mind. The pile of ironing waiting for him back home, the washing up from last night, and the pile of marking still looming over his desk at school all weighed heavy on his conscience.

Voices crept into his consciousness, and Louis looked up. The turnstiles creaked and clanked, and Amanda emerged from the archway into the light.

'Amanda?'

Louis stepped forward.

'What are you doing here?'

Amanda stopped, her conversation momentarily interrupted, to look Louis up and down.

'I'm sorry,' she said, 'Am I supposed to know you?'

Louis stepped back, pressing himself against the hard, parallel bars of the railing. It had been bad enough that he had seen Amanda here, now, in public when he was waiting for Kathryn; but for her not to recognise him? How could she not have recognised him? Why had she not? When Kathryn did eventually exit the turnstiles, her face beamed as she saw Louis waiting for her. He was at first awkward and uncertain. After a brief commentary over how their respective days were, they headed off together down the street towards town.

They turned off the street, down a stone stairway beneath an antique shop and a wine bar, into a vaulted cloister-like room. A cellar beneath several properties, there was a kitchen at the back and tables spread around a series of rooms, and nestled into alcoves. In a cleared area to the middle of one side, a handful of musicians were setting up their instruments and amps.

The waitress showed Kathryn and Louis to their table, one of those in the furthest corner and secluded in an alcove. As he passed by other tables, he noticed Amanda at a long table surrounded by a group of her friends and co-workers, none of whom he recognised. They reached their own table and eased themselves into their seats. The waitress handed them both menus and left them. It was only then that Kathryn leant forward towards Louis to speak.

'Are you okay?' she asked.

Louis looked up and nodded, then smiled. For some reason he felt that he had to tell Kathryn about Amanda; but how? It still seemed impossible that she was here.

'Louis?'

He shook his head.

'Just thought I recognised someone.'

Kathryn frowned, and returned to studying the menu.

Later that evening, the shared platter of bread, pâté, houmous and olives was going down well, as was the bottle of wine, as the jazz singer lifted the atmosphere in the room. A song ended as Louis moved to refill their glasses.

'I never know if you are supposed to talk through the songs at occasions like this,' he whispered.

'I know what you mean,' Kathryn laughed. 'That table over there, though.'

She pointed to the long one, where Amanda and her friends were enjoying an enthusiastic, raucous night.

'It doesn't help that I do recognise someone on that table,' Kathryn said bitterly.

Louis looked up, interested.

'It's her, third in from the right,' said Kathryn. 'Dr Amanda Jones. Or the bitch editor from hell.'

Louis raised his eyebrows with curiosity.

'I didn't tell you,' said Kathryn. 'Even before I got back to my desk this morning, I discovered that she was all but my new boss.'

'You never said—'

'Well not my actual boss. She's the new commissioning editor for a package of my journals. I spent most of the morning being lectured by her about how to do my job.'

Louis' mind buzzed with questions. He was about to speak when the singer began again, an upbeat number. He smiled across the table as Kathryn settled back in her chair. He speared an olive with a cocktail stick.

Across the room, he watched Amanda drink more wine and exchange conversation with her girlfriends. *Why had she not recognised him? Who was she if not the Amanda he knew?* Louis almost missed the applause for the last song.

Louis smiled uncomfortably and tried to cover up his awkwardness by laying another slice of pâté onto the soft, warm French bread, refilling their wine glasses as the singer began again.

The first set finished and the waitresses began swarming round the room, bringing out platefuls of sausages and mash. Louis glanced up and again across the room. Kathryn sat forward, her chin resting on her hands with her gaze fixed upon him.

'What's with you tonight, Louis?'

Louis looked up again. He shrugged.

'Huh? Nothing.'

Kathryn frowned.

'Yes there is. Something's up – you're not acting like yourself.'

Louis didn't answer for a while. He didn't know what to say. He just sat still, returning Kathryn's gaze, and wondering how he could explain.

'Just been a long day. First day back and all. I'm a bit tired.'

Kathryn's probing gaze was relented as she offered him a friendly smile and raised her glass to him. They exchanged salutations and tucked into their sausages and mash. It was absolutely delicious, the mash creamy and dripping with caramelised onion gravy. The sausages were firm and meaty, and full of rich flavour. Even so, Louis found the taste marred by his preoccupations. How had Kathryn accepted his lame explanation so readily? Or had she seen through the paper thin and transparent walls of his exterior?

Amanda's laugh cut into his thoughts as it strayed across the room. Louis looked up, as did Kathryn.

Kathryn shook her head and frowned.

'It's no good,' said Kathryn. 'I just can't relax with her here.'

The next set changed all that, with some truly, hauntingly beautiful songs. Louis pushed back the table mid-way through, so that they could adjust their seating and snuggle in together.

One song involved a solo by the man on double bass, improvising through a fiendish rhythm that had him bent double, strumming and slapping and bashing the strings. His face and fingers were stretched and contorted through the music. As the keyboard and vocals picked up the tune, Louis cast an aside towards Kathryn.

'That can't be comfortable,' he grinned.

'Brilliant, though. Bloody brilliant,' whispered Kathryn.

Louis and Kathryn giggled their way out of the jazz cellar, up the stairs and out into the open air, and made their way up Walton Street. They stopped outside the Phoenix to look at posters for art house films. Louis nodded towards one of them.

'I've read something about that. *Stolen Lives*, I think it's based on some old English ballads – *Thomas The Rhymer*? I forget. Good reviews, though.'

'And Julie Delpy, she's always good,' commented Kathryn.

They walked on, making plans to go and see it when it came to town. Turning off the main road they headed down Juxon Street, past the tiny front gardens; some tangled and overgrown, some well-kept and blooming, and some open to the pavement and stacked with bicycles, until Kathryn brought them to a halt outside a slightly tatty mid-terraced Victorian house. Once the working-class homes to the printers at The Press they were now sought after city centre properties for young and single professionals.

Louis followed Kathryn up the path to her door. Kathryn paused with the key in the latch, and turned to face him.

'Thank you.'

She smiled. Their arms reached out at the same time to pull the other into an embrace.

'Tonight,' she began, 'despite, you know … it's been wonderful.'

She leaned forward and raised herself up to kiss him. He kissed back. Under the shadowy light of the streetlamps, they kissed again. Eventually Kathryn slipped back and twisted the key in the lock, pushed open the door, and flooded the front garden with light from the hall.

She turned again.

'Are you coming?'

Louis shuffled on his feet.

'Best not. School tomorrow, you know.'

Back home, Lewis eased the door shut, controlling the release of the lock to minimise any sound. He turned and leaned gently back on the door and sighed quietly, a smile on his face as he remembered the beautiful evening. He held the image of Kathryn from that night in his mind. He replayed in his mind how they had fallen into each other's embrace in the jazz cellar, and the way they had made their way out onto the street up those steps, all but as one. He remembered again for fear of forgetting it.

'Where have you been!'

Lewis was startled out of his dreaming. Half way up the stairs opposite him stood Sarah in her dressing gown. She approached him slowly, rounding him.

'You were supposed to be here tonight because Mum was out!'

Lewis stuttered and stumbled over his words, and completely failed to say anything.

'You forgot, didn't you!' yelled Sarah.

4

Lewis spent a troubled night in a place between wakefulness and sleep, Sarah's words reverberating through his thoughts again and again. When eventually Amanda did come home from her night out with the girls, Lewis pretended to be asleep, and when in the morning over breakfast Sarah didn't mention it, he decided that he needn't worry mentioning his forgetfulness the night before, even though his heart burned with the deception.

'So, do you have another busy day ahead?' asked Lewis.

Amanda looked up and considered the question.

'Every day's a busy day in publishing.'

A few moments later she frowned.

'Actually, I think I may have some bridges to build. We've just taken over quite a big package of journals; you know, the kind that come with a large society and a radiation sticker attached.'

Amanda paused again.

'I think I may have been a bit heavy-handed with one of my production editors.'

Lewis nodded. He remembered something in his dream. Maybe the conversation with Amanda hadn't been a dream after all?

'She's a nice enough girl. She has a good brain on her shoulders, Cathy – or Katy–'

'Kathryn,' interrupted Lewis.

Amanda looked slightly blank and bewildered.

'You told me about her before, remember?'

Amanda shook her head.

'Did I? I don't remember.'

The conversation stumbled into silence. Lewis pottered slowly, clearing the table and washing up the breakfast things. At some point Caz arrived for Sarah, and they both headed out to school. Amanda read through some emails on her Blackberry, lingering over a piece of toast and marmite and the remainder of her mug of coffee.

'I didn't know you liked Marmite.'

Lewis had stopped to clear away Amanda's plate.

'Come to think of it, I didn't know we had Marmite.'

Amanda's reaction was blank and quizzical. She shook her head and went on with her reading. Lewis continued pottering about, wiping down the surfaces and sorting out the contents of his satchel.

'I guess I should be going then,' he said eventually.

Amanda looked up and smiled, and got up from the table to give him a hug and a kiss and wish him a good day.

It was already too hot, even at eight o'clock on a September morning, and so Lewis bundled his tweed jacket onto the rack of his bicycle with his satchel, and cycled across town with his shirt sleeves rolled up. All across town his thoughts were all about his crazy, mixed-up memories. The Marmite issue pressed on his thoughts. He hated the stuff – detested it – and so did Amanda. He could remember times in the past, when she had stayed over as a child or in the shared house during the second year of university. So how did the jar of Marmite come to be there this morning? Why was she eating it?

And how did he know Amanda's colleague was called Kathryn? She hadn't mentioned her. There were just too many gaps and inconsistencies opening up in his memories for his liking. He stopped at a set of lights and heard, through the open window of the car next to him, the tune

– his tune – *if only a rock cover of it.* Why couldn't he remember what that tune was? As the lights changed and he wobbled to a start again, he resolved to find out.

When Lewis arrived at school, he deviated from his normal route to his classroom to stop by Miss Leroy's office. He knocked, and waited for the clear, commanding voice. He opened the door, and stepped past the headmistress' name plate into Miss Leroy's suite of offices. He found her writing a letter, sat as usual at her antique desk with the burgundy leather top. She paused briefly to signal, with a slight wave of the hand, for him to sit, but did not look up until she had finished and carefully roll-blotted the signature.

Putting the letter carefully and precisely to one side, she folded her hands together and sat forward over the desk.

'Now, Lewis. What is it I can do for you today?'

Lewis felt himself shrink before Miss Leroy's quietly imposing manner. He might have entered this room as a member of staff in his early thirties, but now, sitting before her again in her office, he felt every inch the frightened little eleven-year old that he had been that first day.

'Lewis?' Miss Leroy prompted, not unkindly.

'I know you said it was unimportant,' began Lewis. 'But I really have to know.'

Miss Leroy smiled thinly.

'Nothing is wholly unimportant, Lewis. What is it that you feel you must know?'

'The tune, the one you taught me – my tune,' said Lewis. 'This tune–'

He began to sing the haunting melody. To hear the song again, sung in this way, seemed to cause pain to Miss Leroy. Eventually, when she could take it no longer, she got up from her desk and walked to the window, turning her back on Lewis. Lewis' singing faltered and he stopped. He began to get up.

Miss Leroy swung round and screamed–

'Stay where you are!'

Lewis slid back into his seat, feeling very much like the naughty school child.

'It's just a tune Lewis. And yes, you call it your tune because it's very much Your tune. It's the first piece that I could get you to play successfully, but in truth it's just a random collection of notes.'

'No.'

This time Lewis did get up.

'It's more than that. This very morning I heard it in someone's car; a rock cover of it, but the same tune.'

'You're mistaken, Lewis,' said Miss Leroy calmly. 'Of course you thought you heard it. We are all, always, mistaking part of one song for the totality of another.'

Lewis shook his head dismissively.

'You of all people Lewis, must realise that there are only seven basic plots in the world. Just as this is the case for novels, so it is true for musical notation.'

Lewis shook his head.

'Why won't you tell me?'

'Lewis, Lewis…'

Miss Leroy attempted to placate her English and Creative Studies teacher with calming words.

'Why the anger, Lewis? It's not like you.'

Lewis glared at the Headmistress.

'I have to know.'

'I can see that,' said Miss Leroy, placing her words carefully. 'But I ask you, why does it matter so much? It really doesn't matter.'

'Don't keep saying that. It matters. It matters very much to me. It's me that is losing track of what are my dreams, and what are my memories!'

As soon as Lewis had uttered the words, and heard them in a voice of anger and upset, he regretted them. He fell silent, hoping beyond hope that by some miracle Miss Leroy had not been listening.

'Dreams? Memories?'

She had heard. Instinct took hold of Lewis, and he knew he had said too much.

'What, could you possibly mean, Lewis?'

Miss Leroy smiled, a smile which betrayed some further knowledge. Lewis pressed himself into his chair, suddenly fearful of the interest, almost menacingly so, that Miss Leroy held in his foolish and unintentional disclosure. Even so, he found himself compelled to answer, an urge to fight Miss Leroy's controlled and conniving probing.

'There are just bits of my life. They don't make sense anymore, and I have these odd memories.'

Miss Leroy smiled.

'Lewis, your life is as it always was, and what you always wanted it to be.'

Lewis shook his head, and in flinging himself out of his seat he turned to the door.

'Lewis, no!' Miss Leroy called after him. 'I can help you.'

Lewis turned.

'Then tell me,' he said. 'What is the song that has been with me all my life, but that I can't remember?'

Miss Leroy stepped towards Lewis.

'Lewis, you don't need to worry yourself about this. You've just lost some of your direction. I can help you refocus.'

Lewis took one step, and one step only, towards her.

'Keep away from me.'

He turned and left the room, leaving Miss Leroy's plaintive cries and calling of his name behind.

5

During the five minutes between classes, Louis went to check his pigeon hole in the small anti-chamber between the corridor and the staff room. Lying between a set of union newsletters and some sales fliers was a single sheet of A4, folded once: a memo from the Headmistress.

'Oh, you've got one as well,' Beth commented.

Louis swung round to find his friend standing just behind him, clutching a stack of books and files to her breast.

'You too?' said Louis. 'I wonder what it's about?'

Beth shrugged.

'Dunno. Polly's had one too.'

Louis stuffed the memo into the front pocket of his satchel and frowned.

'Guess we'll find out on Wednesday,' Beth said. 'Do you feel like going for a drink after?'

Louis nodded, but she could tell by his somewhat vacant air that he hadn't really heard, and was already off in his mind considering some other thought.

'Louis.'

He turned.

'Wednesday. The pub, after Leroy's thing?'

'Yes,' replied Louis. 'Sorry, Beth, got to go.'

Beth was left standing at the pigeon holes alone. An elderly science teacher, whom Beth fondly referred to as The Professor, stepped into the lobby, snatched his post out of the tray, doffed his head towards Beth, and went on his way. She frowned again, stuffed her own post into her shoulder bag, and was about to leave when Polly burst in, gushing brightly and relieved to find her friend.

'Beth, I thought I could find you here,' she said; then winced. 'No Louis though, where...?'

'Poll,' Beth laughed. 'What is wrong with you?'

She then noticed the flash of silver, and the star of reflected light on Polly's finger. Polly saw straight away that Beth had noticed, and she beamed.

'Tom – it was a complete surprise – he just came out with it, last night. When he brought out the box I had no idea.'

She spread the fingers of her left hand to show off the ring.

'It's fantastic news Polly,' exclaimed Beth. 'Have you told Louis yet?'

Louis stood at the back of his classroom, with a poster of English grammar and a ball of Blu-Tak in his hands. He watched Polly leave. He was excited for her – he really was – but something about the speed of the announcement made him feel somewhat uneasy.

Polly getting married meant only one thing to Louis. It meant the prospect of enduring yet another social situation; of going to something where he knew only a few people, and having to make small talk. He never knew how to begin conversations with strangers, and he was too self-conscious to lose himself on the dance floor. He reached up to his neck and felt the gold wedding ring where it hung next to his skin. Why was everything so complicated?

Standing outside The Press later that afternoon, Louis was again fiddling nervously with the wedding ring on its chain. He was sure Kathryn would go with him, but did the invite include a plus-one? He stopped suddenly, as he saw Kathryn leave the gate. He beamed a broad, happy smile, which slackened as he saw her followed out by Amanda. He screwed up his face, and puzzled over seeing them chatting quite happily with each other.

Kathryn said goodbye to Amanda before walking up to Louis. Kathryn looked directly into his eyes.

'Lewis,' she said, nodding her head slowly towards him as she passed.

Louis frowned and turned to Kathryn, giving her a quick kiss.

'You ready, then?'

Kathryn nodded, beaming brightly. They turned and began the walk into town. For a moment they discussed their respective days, then, as they passed the end of Little Clarendon Street and started along the terrace of Victorian and Edwardian houses, their conversation faltered.

'Kathryn, I'm confused.'

Kathryn glanced across at Louis.

'How so?'

'That woman, Amanda. I thought you hated her?'

Kathryn laughed.

'Yeah, I thought so too. We've come to a sort of understanding though - she's actually not that bad.'

'Not a control freak then?'

Kathryn shook her head.

'Not at all, I don't think she's that much of a control freak really - she just likes to get things right. Now she knows that's what I'm about too, it's all good.'

Louis smiled, somewhat uneasy about this new alliance between Kathryn and Amanda, though unsure as to why.

'And I think I've got some part-time work out of it!' Kathryn grinned.

Louis' interest was piqued.

'Yeah, one of her friends needs a babysitter on Friday night. That's okay isn't it? She said it would be okay if I brought a friend with me.'

Louis remained quiet.

'Just I could really do with the money this month,' continued Kathryn.

She looked up, watching Louis' subdued response.

'Louis?' she queried.

Louis started, awoken abruptly from a daydream.

'No, it's fine.'

Ask her, he pushed himself silently. Tell her about Polly's invite, and the wedding.

Kathryn smiled wryly during the lapse in conversation.

'Are you nervous about this?' she asked, laughing. 'I'm terrified. Don't think I've done any studio work.'

Louis stood in the college studio, in reality nothing more than an old classroom with boarded over windows and rigged with lights, reflectors, and a miscellany of left-over props from previous shoots and old drama productions. 'I don't really know what I'm doing, you know,' he admitted, wheeling a tungsten lamp into position.

Kathryn laughed.

'I think there's probably even more pretension surrounding studio photography than any other kind.'

She wheeled a reflector over to a position opposite where Louis was standing.

'I'm just setting this up like you imagine a studio to look really. I'm with you – I haven't a clue,' she explained. 'Surely, given the perfect lighting positions, beautiful models, and no surprise gusts of wind, any fool can come up with half decent photographs.'

Louis shrugged.

'And yet you read all this stuff, look at the reviews, and it's all held in so much higher regard than good natural photography and landscapes. But we're all still working with the same properties, it's just that in the field we can't control the lighting. Not absolutely.'

'I guess it's the difference between the photo artist who goes out time and time again to take the one perfect shot in the conditions that will tell their story, and Joe Bloggs who takes the odd snap on his day out because he's there.'

Louis began to unpack his camera and set it up on the tripod. Kathryn moved her bag closer and joined him in setting up.

'And that makes it more real? Because the 'artist' has to come back and take the shot that fits their 'story'?'

Kathryn tossed her head back and laughed dismissively at the suggestion.

'What if the story, as you put it, is the journey? Isn't it artificial to then go back to re-shoot something? Better to be good at having the skills to capture the moment.'

'I guess...'

The flash fired, the motor whirred, and the picture was taken; Louis' face of thoughtful composure was captured in the lens of Kathryn's camera. She bundled him across the studio, to the stool with the varnish flaking off in front of the white screen. She took his camera from his hands and retreated back across the room.

'I've decided. I'm going first.'

Kathryn directed Louis into a series of poses, once suggesting a catalogue pose to great hilarity before they fell into a natural rhythm of photographer and subject. She was fast and nimble, between focus and exposure dials and the click of the shutter. She paused.

'Like those goddamn awful travel documentaries on television.'

Louis looked perplexed as to the conversation.

'Artificiality,' answered Kathryn by way of explanation. 'They always claim it's some random celebrity on a journey, possibly with a time constraint, or limited to travel by land or sea, but as soon as the ubiquitous helicopter shot hoves into view, you know that it's random celebrity *plus* a posse of sound, lighting, film crew, director and producer along for the ride, and they are flying in and out to film segments according to weather conditions, and worse, the needs of other projects.'

She fires off more photographs.

'It's just all so *fake*.'

Louis nodded, and Kathryn captured the agreement. The shoot continued, with Kathryn getting ever more creative with camera angles. She clambered up on stools, so that just like when they were on the White Horse Hill she shot high and crouched low to throw the perspective, twisting the camera. She represented Louis with his camera, and so began a session of taking-photographs-of-you-taking-photographs-of-me until—

'My turn, I think,' Louis said.

Kathryn laughed, and snapped a picture of Louis' petulant face. Slowly she lowered the camera from her eye, and noticed Louis' outstretched palm. She smiled almost apologetically, and handed over her camera. Placing Kathryn's camera carefully back into her bag, Louis fixed his into position onto the tripod before fixing the shutter release to it.

In contrast to Louis' hesitancy as a model and Kathryn's flirty way with the camera, it was Kathryn to be a model who teased and taunted an uncertain Louis. He composed the shots carefully, taking careful account of metre readings and adjusting the settings between each take. He had to keep on asking Kathryn to return to a previous expression and pose, which just made her more bored and restless. She unfastened a button to her shirt, and slipped the neckline off one shoulder. Louis photographed the pose, but his over-staging killed the flow.

'Louis,' said Kathryn.

Louis had his face buried in the eye-piece, and was twiddling with the exposure.

'Louis,' Kathryn repeated, as she scrambled to her feet and moved to interrupt him. She grabbed the camera from him and flicked the quick-release to the tripod. As he protested about missed shots, she presented the camera into his hands and looped the strap over his head.

'Now, Louis,' she told him. 'Photograph me. Properly. Just use your instincts.'

She followed up the words with a stare that reflected the seriousness with which she spoke.

Louis was left holding the camera as Kathryn walked back across the studio in bare feet, having kicked off her sandals. She stopped halfway, and from within her shirt released her bra. She turned her head and looked back over her bare shoulder, her shirt stretched across the other and her arm.

'Well, are you ready?'

She grinned.

'Shoot.'

Louis slowly lifted the camera to his eye, zoomed, focused, and—

—captured the image.

Later that evening, Lewis cycled up to, and dismounted in front of, the door in the wall, as a mottled moonlight filtered down past the skeletal framework of autumn trees. He unlocked the door and lifted his bike through. A little later, he walked round the outside of the large Edwardian building to the front door.

A chill wind blew through the garden and whipped up the fallen leaves in small eddies of movement. Lewis shivered as he fetched out his keys. He looked up to where the almost full moon was clearly visible alongside the array of stars. He picked out the plough, and the North Star, and Orion's belt. Again the wind blew, and again Lewis shivered. He fiddled with the ring on the chain around his neck. Unhooking it in an often-practiced movement, he replaced it onto his left ring-finger. He turned and let himself through the front door.

Lewis poured boiling milk into his mug, and watched as the flow of white spiralled into the chocolate. Taking the mug in his hands, he carried it through to the lounge and to the sounds of forced Australian dialogue of the latest soap-pretending-to-be-drama. As he rounded the doorway, Amanda looked up from the settee.

Lewis smiled and took a seat next to his wife.

'You had a good evening, then?' she asked, turning her head towards her husband in such a way as to toss back her rich, auburn hair.

Lewis nodded. 'It was good, yeah. I think we're making good progress. With the project, it's very good.'

'Are you going to be ready for the exhibition?'

'—mind you, the new girl I told you about, who I'm working with,' continued Lewis. 'Well I say girl. She's not much younger than us. Kathryn – brilliant photographer.'

He laughed.

'I'm going to have to watch my game!'

Amanda smiled thinly, and eventually Lewis eased off with his self-congratulatory chortles.

'How's Sarah?' Lewis asked. 'Did she have a good day at school?'

'She missed seeing her father before going to bed. If it's not photography class or staff meetings, she hardly ever gets to see you, Louis.'

Louis? Lewis stared at his wife. Again she called him Louis?

'I'm sorry. Just, it's been a hectic few weeks.'

'She needs you, Lewis,' Amanda told him. 'And I don't just mean for homework.'

Lewis lowered his head.

'I need you too,' said Amanda.

'I'm sorry, love.'

Lewis reached forward to hold her, to take her hands and caress her soft skin.

'I really am so sorry. I'm stupid. I should have thought.'

'Yes. Yes, you should.'

'I'm here now,' Lewis said, with a smile. He looked deeply into Amanda's blue eyes. He leaned closer, gently touching her neck and angling himself up to her; to kiss her.

'No, Lewis.'

She pulled away.

'I'm really not in the mood.'

'But Amanda,' Lewis said, twisting his mouth with disappointment. He reached for her hand, holding it. She pulled away again.

'Really, Lewis. No. I'm going to bed.'

Lewis sunk back into the settee as Amanda left the room, and fell to silent brooding. Questioning thoughts entered his mind. Amanda returned to the room, if briefly, to stand in the doorway.

'Don't forget that we are out to dinner on Friday night,' said Amanda. 'We'll be back late, so I've arranged for Sarah to stay at a friend's.'

Louis sat alone in the centre of the settee in the dim light of a single table lamp. In his lap he held a bear, a little threadbare round the arms and the head, and with eyes that did not match.

'Oh Ardizzone, what have I done?'

He pulled the bear closer to him, hugging him tightly. He extracted reassurance from its familiar touch.

He couldn't help but feel the loneliness and the isolation. Tears began to form in the corner of his eyes. He wiped them away defiantly, and they came again quicker. He squeezed Ardizzone tighter, hugged him closer, and stared through the clouded vision of his damp eyes at the door across the other side of the room. The door loomed closer in his vision. He slammed shut his eyes and squeezed them tight.

Lewis jolted forward. Suddenly awake, his head was still groggy. He glanced across at the clock on the front of the video recorder. 00:15. Shit. Bedtime. He leapt up from the settee, but was careful to replace Ardizzone in his place in front of the cushions.

Lewis brushed his teeth in front of the bathroom mirror, and deposited the toothbrush into the glass with a reassuring clunk. He wiped his mouth dry and left the room, pulling the light off as he went. As he crossed the landing, he stopped outside a door. Moving his head closer, he spoke softly.

'Goodnight, Sarah.'

He crossed the landing again and entered the bedroom. One wall was lined with books and papers, the others filled with photographs. He stood at the foot of the bed for a few moments and stared at the duvet, before he pulled off his clothes and climbed in, propping himself up in the centre of the bed with a book in his hands, ready to read.

Louis lay still and looked about the room, considering the evening which had just passed. He remembered the brightness in Kathryn's eyes and the ease of her conversation towards – with – him. Back further, images returned to him of the class when they had both worked together. He cursed himself for not having asked her when he had the chance to go with him to Tom and Polly's wedding. His eyes felt tired and heavy. He pushed back the pillows, put his book on the side, and flicked off the light.

Behind him, the covers moved, and a hand slipped round his shoulders and caressed his shoulders. Lewis smiled as he felt Amanda laying behind him, curved into his position. Lewis turned over, reached across, and embraced his wife. Amanda muttered his name in her sleep. He continued to lie on his side and gaze at her. He was so lucky.

6

Sarah crossed the playground with Caz, clutching her school books to her front, and chatting. Behind her she could hear the unmistakable click of heels approaching, and Miss Leroy's stern voice.

'Sarah!'

Both Sarah and Caz stopped and turned, waiting patiently for Miss Leroy to reach them.

'It's alright Miss Cooper,' Miss Leroy directed her words to Caz. 'You can go.'

Sarah threw her gaze aloft and shook her head. She bid Caz to go.

'Yes, Miss?' Sarah asked, with weary resignation.

'I need to talk to you, Sarah,' said Miss Leroy directly. 'About your parents. Your father.'

'Lewis!'

Louis stopped short, mid-stride, halfway down the school corridor, and turned upon hearing his name. Beth was standing resolutely firm outside of the staff room door. She beckoned slowly, and silently. Feeling instinctively like a small boy again, he returned to his friend.

'You, Lewis Tumnal—'

Louis couldn't remember the last time that Beth had called him Lewis.

'You stood me up last night,' said Beth.

'I – I did?'

'Yes. We were meeting up in *The Downloader* for a drink after work.'

'Sorry, Beth. I guess I forgot.'

'Yeah,' sighed Beth. 'I wished I'd forgotten when this sleazy banker type started to chat me up.'

Louis frowned and looked back at her meekly.

'So where were you?' asked Beth. 'No, don't tell me. You were meeting your new wife-lady. Going well, is it?'

Louis smiled and tried to answer, before ending up just nodding. Beth cocked her head to one side and looked sorrowfully at Louis. She slipped an arm round his shoulders, and hugged him tight.

'Still, I don't blame you for skiving off Leroy's meeting—'

Louis gaped.

'Ah, that too. I completely forgot.'

'Yeah. And I don't think she's happy.'

Louis pulled free and turned to face his friend.

'So what was it about?'

Beth frowned.

'Reorg. All our classes are going to change come January. There's a new teacher starting, and she'll be taking six month's sabbatical.'

Louis nodded.

'Every eleven years apparently, Miss Leroy was telling me – she takes time off, coincides with her birthday and she gets a new teacher in.'

'Eleven years,' said Louis. 'In January we'll have been working here for eleven years.'

Beth laughed.

'How did that happen?'

Louis laughed too, if with a certain amount of uneasiness.

'Maybe it's time to look for a new job,' Beth quipped.

Louis shrugged. *Eleven years?* Was it really eleven years now since he finished university? And since Miss Leroy told him he had the job here?

'Post,' announced Charlotte as she arrived back at her pod with a stack of mail and one parcel. She tossed a couple of slim envelopes at her own desk, and handed a couple of jiffy bags to Eleanor before turning to Kathryn.

'What've you sent for, Kathy?' Charlotte asked brightly.

Kathryn looked up and saw the parcel; recognising it immediately, she took it quickly.

'Kathryn?

Kathryn sucked on her lip.

'Well, if it's what I think it is, then it's a present.'

She dug her fingers through the thick plastic and ripped open the courier bag. She brought out the immaculately presented, matt-laminate Apple box. She reached for her paper knife to slit through the seals and opened it. She carefully took out the iPod, and smiled.

'Who's the iPod for?' asked Charlotte. 'That is some present.'

Kathryn didn't answer, but bit again at her lip and smiled as she turned over to check the engraving:

Louis, for your music collection and mine. K xx

Kathryn beamed as she stared at it.

'No, Kathryn. No,' continued Charlotte. 'You've only just

met the man. It's too soon. You don't know him.'

Eleanor nodded in agreement.

'Charlotte's right. My brother gave his girlfriend an iRiver actually, but when you knew what they'd gone through...'

'Are you sure about this? Really sure?' Charlotte asked, pulling up a spare chair next to Kathryn.

Kathryn sat at her desk, holding the iPod in both hands, turning it over and over and reading the inscription again. Her smile changed into a great beaming grin.

Kathryn looked up, and glancing between Eleanor and Charlotte, she gushed excitedly:

'I hope he will like it. Can you believe that Louis still has a Sony Walkman circa. 1990?!'

Eleanor laughed.

'I think I do too, somewhere.'

'And still uses it!' Kathryn embellished. She began to put the iPod away, carefully sliding it back into the sleeve and boxes. Charlotte returned to her desk, and Eleanor began to slit open the wholly more uninteresting post of new manuscripts.

Eleanor looked up, twisting her face at the same time as ruminating her thoughts.

'That's still a pretty major present for a boyfriend of a month,' she said.

'We met in July, 'corrected Kathryn.

Caz flicked off her mobile phone and returned her attention to Sarah.

'That's fine. Friday night, you can stay over too.'

'Cool,' Sarah replied.

'Mum's got some babysitter,' Caz said, sneering as she said the word. 'But we can deal with her. I've got a DVD player in my room- we don't have to see her.'

Sarah grinned. Friday night. It was going to be good. She loved her mum and dad loads, but just recently it was simply awful.

'How's your dad been lately?' asked Caz.

'Fine,' said Sarah. 'When I see him. He's always shut away in his study writing his book, or out at his photography night school. It's mum that's been the pain; ever since she started her new job. They hardly ever seem to be in the house together these days. Leaves me—'

'A latchkey kid,' said Caz.

'I used to envy your life, your freedom.'

'Ha! Grass greener?' Caz laughed. 'I was the one who envied your life. Your family always seemed so sorted, and perfect.'

Sarah frowned. She looked down, saddened.

'I – I think – dad's seeing someone else.'

'The girl from the party?'

Sarah nodded, and hung her head.

Louis stood near to the school gates astride his bicycle, talking on his mobile phone. He nodded emphatically.

'Yeah,' he responded. 'Yes, that sounds good.' Then a little later: 'Yeah, see you later, love you too – and you...'

He giggled and hung up. Slipping his mobile phone back into his satchel, he sat back on his saddle and set off, wobbling slightly as he swung left onto the main road for the ride home.

Letting himself into the house a short while later, he set down his satchel in the hall and hung his jacket on the peg in the hallway, before moving on into the kitchen. He fetched himself a long glass of orange squash and headed back towards the lounge, thinking about Friday, and of seeing Kathryn again.

'Hi love,' Amanda said as she passed him in the hallway. 'Good day at work?'

Lewis nodded and replied with a Yes, almost under his breath.

'Oh, Lewis?'

Amanda stopped and turned.

'One thing. You've not forgotten about Friday, have you?'

'Friday?'

Lewis stared blankly back at Amanda.

'Yes, Friday,' she reiterated 'Dinner party at the college. My father's presentation.'

Lewis stared back, perplexed. He nodded and agreed. Friday. College dinner. Damn. He turned and sighed. He would have to go, he guessed. He was sure Kathryn would understand.

7

Louis reached for the phone – an old BT standard issue corded one – and was about to dial Kathryn's number. He stopped himself and looked again at the email response, all the while fiddling with the receiver in his hands. She had accepted his apology and his reasons readily enough, but it still didn't seem right to him.

He had wanted to speak to her about it and explain properly. He had just wanted to hear her voice again, but he also knew that if he spoke to her he wouldn't be able to continue with the carefully worded excuse, which was of course the very reason for sending an email in the first place.

Friday. Why had he agreed so readily anyway? Babysitting of all things, and for someone he taught English to? It really hadn't been a good idea, especially as he would have seen Kathryn again. His brain ached with the differences in opinion, the whys and the wherefores. He replaced the receiver in its cradle, and it chimed out the reassuring ding.

He sat forward and scrolled up the screen, staring at what he had written. Reading it back now it was the most pathetic excuse that he had ever seen. And yet Kathryn had accepted it with so much grace. She really was lovely – kind and compassionate and caring. She was loving.

Friday finally came, and Louis found it tediously long. With no free periods, and all the children he taught seemingly already in weekend mode, classes were hard work. The afternoon dragged on, until finally the bell rang for the end of school. Louis didn't even bother trying to set homework; he just let them all leave, packed up his own things into his satchel, gathered up his jacket, and left.

He walked slowly back towards the staffroom, fearing the inevitable questions about weekend plans which he had so far managed to avoid by not going to the staffroom at lunchtime. Ever since he had pulled out of babysitting with Kathryn on Friday night, he didn't have any plans. Kathryn's mum and dad were visiting on Saturday, and they hadn't said anything about Sunday.

Louis heard Beth and Polly's voices, and panicked. He couldn't face the thought of the questions, and turned quickly into an empty English lab and out into the courtyard in the middle of H-block, scurrying on further to slip out a side entrance of the school a few minutes later to collect his bike.

Later that evening Louis sat in front of his computer, the flare from the monitor and a pool of light from the door lamp the only light in an otherwise darkened room. He flicked backwards and forwards through the folder of images, and the results from the studio session of a few days ago. This was his first opportunity to look at them. From the score of shots he had to pick just a handful to work on, and produce a photo story for his next project. He had the idea in his mind of how he wanted the project to look, he could see it clearly in his mind. Looking at the images before him now made him realise just how much he missed Kathryn.

Louis glanced at his watch. It was just coming up to 7:30 – somewhere across town, Kathryn would be arriving at the house where she was going to be babysitting.

*

Kathryn pressed the bell and stepped back. When the door was opened by a woman in her late thirties, nervousness gave way to giddy chatter. She and her older husband were friendly to the point of jovial. They showed Kathryn around their house, told her to help herself to anything she liked in the kitchen, and then introduced their daughter Caz.

Caz was a slim girl with short, bleached blonde hair, with the beginnings of darker roots showing which may or may not have been a deliberate style. She was quiet when introduced to Kathryn, but seemed nice enough. She had a friend staying with her, Mr Cooper explained; Sarah, who seemed all the more sprightly.

Kathryn was told by Mrs Cooper that they would be back around eleven, and then they were leaving. Kathryn stood at the front door, and watched as the Coopers walked for their tram before closing the door. She turned, to find herself confronted with Caz and Sarah, two girls on the verge of their teenage years.

'We don't need a babysitter,' said Caz firmly. 'You do know that?'

Kathryn looked back at the girls and shrugged.

'I know,' she said. 'But your folks are paying me, so we might as well get along.'

'Whatever,' Caz shrugged. 'We're going to watch DVDs.'

Kathryn smiled, and followed her two charges into the lounge. Caz threw herself into one of the armchairs, and Sarah took one end of the sofa. Kathryn settled at the other end, putting down her shoulder bag on the floor next to her. For a few minutes they sat in silence.

'So what are we watching?' asked Kathryn, breaking the silence.

Caz darted across the room and pulled out a selection of DVDs, which she presented to Sarah. Kathryn watched with amusement from across the room as they discussed the options, and thrilled and squealed over the stories and the actors.

Kathryn's phone tingled out that she had a new message, and she reached to retrieve it from her bag. It was a message from Louis. She smiled as she read the message that was carefully keyed with all the correct spelling and punctuation of a letter. It was an invitation to a concert – Stravinsky's *Firebird* and some other things, with one of Louis' colleagues playing in the orchestra. She smiled and eagerly replied, before putting her phone back down on the arm of the chair.

The film, Kathryn quickly discovered, was utter bilge, but the two girls seemed to be enjoying it; an American high school romp, with an admittedly dreamily gorgeous male lead.

'It is ridiculous, this film – we do know that,' announced Sarah, after one particularly saccharine-coated scene between the male lead and the object of his affections, the school cheerleader.

'Fun though,' said Kathryn.

Kathryn smiled, and noticed that Sarah's attention had been taken by something else. Following Sarah's gaze led back to her own shoulder bag, the contents of which had, when Kathryn had retrieved her mobile phone, been disturbed so that now, sticking out the top, was the booklet of A4 paper containing a slightly dog-eared draft of Louis' novel.

'Where did you get that?'

Kathryn pulled the novel from her bag and looked at it, then at Sarah.

'It's my boyfriend's. He gave it to me to read.'

'That's my dad's!'

Kathryn shrugged.

'Maybe he loaned it to your dad as well?'

'No. It's *my* dad's novel. He wrote it,' said Sarah ferociously. 'How do you know my dad? And what do you mean, boyfriend?'

Kathryn gaped.

'Louis doesn't have a child – or a wife.'

'His name's Lewis,' countered Sarah.

Kathryn was about to reply, but stopped herself. She looked down at Lewis' novel in her hand, a story of double lives and mistaken memories. What she had read of it so far had been brilliant, and now she wondered if that was because it was his own life he was telling.

'Have you read this?'

Sarah shook her head.

'Dad's very protective over his work. I don't think even mum has read it.'

Kathryn gazed at Sarah, as she attempted to take all of it in. She glanced down at the manuscript in her hands, and at Louis' name on the cover: L. Tumnal. Her whole world was suddenly, in one moment collapsing in freefall around her.

'I read the first few pages once,' admitted Sarah. 'Dad was with mum in the kitchen, and it was there on the desk. Didn't really get far enough into it though to know much about it.'

Kathryn looked up again, picking her words carefully.

'I still don't – I don't remember—'

She stopped and started again.

'If you don't mind me asking, where do you live? North Wren Hoe…?'

'On the corner of the Woodstock and Bevington roads,' continued Sarah.

'It's a huge house. Massive,' added Caz.

'I know it,' said Kathryn. 'An Edwardian building. The ground floor flat.'

Caz shook her head.

'Not a flat,' Sarah said. 'The whole building. It was grandfather's.'

Kathryn stared blankly at Sarah.

'We can't be talking about the same place.'

Kathryn shook her head. Louis' flat had always seemed like, and felt like, a self-contained home. She remembered the blocked-in stairwell with the newel post jutting out of the wall. There had been other doors in the flat that had been locked – but the stairs, she remembered the missing stairs. It had to be a flat, and so in which case it must be a different house.

'It's right on the corner isn't it? Behind a high stone wall. You get to it through a blue door in the wall which has a Yale lock.'

Sarah nodded, as did Caz.

'That's my house.'

Kathryn fell silent. Her brain was somersaulting with questions and uncertainness. Eventually she looked up and back to Sarah, who had gone back to watching the film. Sarah glanced back, and in her stare Kathryn could see that this was not finished.

'I didn't know,' said Kathryn. 'I swear I didn't know he was married.'

Sarah frowned.

'So what are you going to do now you do?'

Kathryn shook her head, shrinking back under the intensity of Sarah's stare. Her hand went to her neck, her fingers feeling at her necklace. She saw Louis in her mind, fiddling with the chain around his neck; the chain with the ring hooked through it. The ring – the wedding ring – Kathryn remembered Louis telling her that it was his father's wedding ring. What if it was not his father's, but his own? But the flat, the house, the stairs; it would have been so easy to move a ring from a finger to a chain around his neck, but how could he restructure a house and arrange for it to be remodelled? And where were Sarah and her mum when she stayed there?

It had to be okay.

'So what are you going to do?' asked Sarah forcefully.

Kathryn glanced up. She looked back at Sarah, and frowned uncomfortably.

8

Louis stood on the pavement at the end of Broad Street where it curved around the gothic front of the Wrensong Theatre. It was a chill autumnal evening, and crisp, dry leaves danced and scuttled across the paving. Beth hurried towards him down the street, keeping her scarf in place with her hand. Louis smiled as he greeted her.

'Sorry I'm late,' said Beth. 'Parking, you know. Are we all here?'

Louis saw Beth glance around, and scanned the other people gathering around the theatre.

'Where's Kathryn?'

'Still got five minutes,' said Louis, by way of a reply. He glanced at his watch to confirm the time.

'She'll be here. Don't worry.'

Beth smiled, and pulled her coat tighter.

'It's a bit of raw one this evening.'

Louis nodded. There was indeed a chill wind blowing down Parks Road towards them. Glancing up, Beth already looked frozen. He dug his hand into the inside breast pocket of his corduroy jacket and pulled out the strip of tickets. He tore one off and handed it to Beth.

'Go on, take it,' said Louis. 'You go on. We'll meet you inside.'

Beth frowned as she received the ticket, but thanked him before bounding up the steps under an arch flanked by gargoyles, and headed across the quad.

Louis watched his friend go, turning only after Beth had disappeared inside the Wrensong. He wandered up and down the pavement at the front of the theatre, scanning the faces of the pedestrians. Coming from Jericho, he guessed that she might be coming down Broad Street; then he switched his attention to the surge of people who came up the steps from the metro station after the rumbling arrival under his feet of each train. Where was she?

Louis checked his watch again. Kathryn's reply to his text message had been so enthusiastic. He checked through his sent messages to see if he had told her the right time. He had. He scanned the people in the street again. *Where was she?*

Turning to look at the theatre again, Louis could see the last of the audience gathering around the doors and going in. What had been a steady stream was now just a trickle of late-comers. He jigged up and down impatiently, needing to go on inside but wanting to see Kathryn arrive first.

Louis saw the ushers starting to go from entrance to entrance, closing the doors. He had to go now, and began to make his way up the steps and across the courtyard. Producing his ticket to the lady on the door, he took one last glance round in case Kathryn had arrived at the last minute, and then stepped in.

A few minutes earlier, Kathryn had been standing at the bar of The White Horse; a very narrow pub, the floor of which was several steps down from street level. Her hand closed around a half-finished gin and tonic. From where she stood she could see across the street to the Wrensong Theatre opposite. She could see Louis standing outside, waiting and watching as he was joined by another woman of about his age – she supposed this must be his colleague Beth that he talked about – and then a little later watched again as she left him to go into the theatre.

Kathryn took another drink from her glass and puzzled again over her predicament. She had wanted to come tonight, that much she had proved; but in that case why was she hiding out in the world's smallest pub, nursing a drink on her own?

Last night continued to bother her. There were so many questions left unanswered that Kathryn felt unable to judge how she really felt. She loved Louis, or at least she loved the Louis she thought she knew. At the same time, if it turned out that he really was Sarah's father, and he had a wife behind one of those locked doors in the flat, then did she really want to go to a concert with him now? Tonight? She took another drink and looked out the window.

Glancing at her watch, Kathryn could see that it was time. Across the street, the ushers were closing up the theatre for the performance. Louis was about to make a move now, she could see that. Quickly, Kathryn downed the rest of her drink and slapped the glass back on the bar, before hurrying to the door and up the steps to the pavement.

She stopped. Across the street she could see Louis stepping into the theatre, the last of the patrons. And behind him the doors were closed. She sighed and looked downbeat. She was too late. Kathryn returned to the bar and ordered herself another drink.

Louis sat in his seat at the back of the circle, fidgeting with his fingers as the orchestra played through a modern piece that at every turn failed to engage and thrill him. His gaze went from Tom, as he bowed his cello with great forceful sweeps, to Polly where she sat near the back, tucked around her French Horn.

His gaze and his attention drifted frequently to the carved panel work around the hall, and to the brass lamps hanging from the decoratively painted ceiling. He found himself plotting ideas for his novel, until suddenly, almost without warning, it was over and the audience were applauding.

Louis dropped the programme to his lap and clapped with a lacklustre sense of duty. Down in the stalls he could see maybe a dozen or more people standing in rapturous ovation to the piece. He leant in towards Beth.

'Didn't really get that, at all.'

'Me neither.' Beth shook her head.

The applause subsided, and down on the stage the orchestra began rearranging itself for the next piece. Stagehands brought more chairs back on, swelling the ranks of the string section, and the percussionists set about arranging their toolkit of instruments.

Next to Louis, someone eased themselves into a seat. He turned, ready to ward them off as being taken, and stopped, face to face with Kathryn. He smiled, if weakly.

'Sorry I'm late, work you know,' excused Kathryn. 'Thanks for leaving my ticket—'

She waved her hand back down in the direction of the box office. Louis was about to answer, when he found himself out of time as the orchestra filed back into their places and began tuning up for the next piece. The auditorium descended into a hushed silence.

Louis managed to snatch a few words.

'I'm glad you made it.'

Another modern work followed, this one much improved over the last, with, Louis felt, an air of genuine musicality about it. He quickly found himself lost in the long, ebbing chords, and the lone horn player - Polly - carrying an enduring tune.

Louis glanced at Kathryn. She seemed to be enjoying it. He looked back at the stage as the bowing undercurrent of chords was reaching an enthusiastic crescendo. Tom was in the front row of the cellos, almost bent double over his instrument and forcing the strings under the full length of the bow.

And quiet. The solitary horn played on, and picked up a miscellany of other instruments on its way, before bringing the whole orchestra into a poignant finale.

The audience exploded in applause, and the conductor was quick to pick Polly out for solo thanks. Louis clapped enthusiastically, and when he turned to see Kathryn's reaction she too was beaming broadly.

'Is that your friend?' Kathryn asked, after leaning in towards Louis to make herself heard.

Louis nodded.

'She's brilliant,' he said. 'I knew that she was good, but that was just blooming amazing.'

'Did you see the leader of the cellos, too?' said Kathryn. 'The way he pushed his bow over the instrument.'

'That was Tom. Polly's fiancé.'

He saw Kathryn nod with recognition at this, and felt it the ideal time to mention the wedding and the invitation. He was about to speak when Beth interrupted him about going down to the bar.

A little later, Louis fought his way through the throng of concert-goers to emerge with three clinking glasses into the open air and the autumn dusk over the quad between the Wrensong Theatre and the Bodleian Library. He rejoined Kathryn and Beth, who had in turn been joined by Tom and Polly.

Louis handed Beth her drink, then Kathryn, pausing to smile at her and ask her if she had been introduced.

'Yeah, just have,' answered Kathryn. 'We were just all saying how good that last piece was.'

Louis could see Polly blush brightly, her face going the colour of Beth's cranberry juice. Kathryn took Louis to one side briefly.

'I'm sorry I wasn't here from the beginning.'

'It's okay,' Louis reassured. 'You're here now.'

Kathryn nodded slightly, and smiled. She found that she couldn't stop staring at the wedding ring where it hung, just behind the open collar of Louis' shirt.

'So Kathryn,' began Polly. 'Have you heard *The Firebird* before?'

Kathryn nodded enthusiastically.

'Love it!' she said, grinning. 'It's proof modern music doesn't have to be plink-plunk—'

'Like our first piece tonight?' said Polly, 'Yeah, I apologise for that.'

'Can you still call Stravinsky modern?' Louis mused out loud.

Kathryn rolled her eyes despairingly.

'Twentieth century. You know what I mean, Louis,' she added, before turning again to Polly. 'You were *very* good, I mean *really* good. I guess you've been playing since you were so high?'

She gestured the height of a small child, and Polly laughed.

'Something like that!'

'I wish I had continued,' sighed Kathryn. After Polly had responded enthusiastically to this, she added, 'Oboe. Did my grade eight but I wasn't very good. Then, since the frenzy of A-Level revision and going off to uni, I haven't really touched it.

'You should get it out again,' encouraged Polly. 'And get Louis to dust of his flute. Duets.'

She grinned. Tom was hovering impatiently next to his fiancé.

'Best get back then, and tune up,' said Polly. 'Nice meeting you.'

Kathryn, Beth and Louis all wished them good luck, and closed in to a tighter group as Tom and Polly weaved their way back through the throng of dinner jackets for the second half.

Louis followed the two girls back into the theatre, a little separate from their laughing and joking conversation. As they took their seats again he felt on the outside of things. He felt his emotions were torn between pleasure that Kathryn was liked by his colleagues, and jealousy that they were able to talk to her so easily. For the rest of the interval he sat in silence next to Kathryn, listening to her conversation with Beth while remaining unable to recall what it was they were talking about, and brooding over this.

It was with relief then, for Louis, when the stage, now reset once more for the larger orchestra, began to fill again with musicians, and the tuning up began. Kathryn and Beth's conversation ebbed away, and Louis felt at ease once more with the three of them facing the front again.

The leader of the first violins returned to the stage to enthusiastic applause, and the whole orchestra turned once more. Then the conductor took to the stage, and more applause. Kathryn leaned in closer to Louis.

'*The Firebird* is one of my most favourite pieces,' she told him. 'Thanks for inviting me.'

Louis nodded and smiled.

As Kathryn finished applauding, she slipped her hand down and found Louis', entwining their fingers together.

A lone flute sung out across the hall, joined progressively by other instruments as the piece built towards its finale. Louis glanced across at Kathryn, who was every bit as captivated. They watched the orchestra to the end, and the auditorium exploded in applause.

'That was brilliant,' exclaimed Kathryn, clapping furiously.

Louis nodded enthusiastically.

'I just love it. The end section – always thought it should be used in a movie.'

Kathryn narrowed her gaze as she considered this.

'Yeah, I know what you mean.'

The conductor was now picking out various soloists, and the applause deepened with each one. Around the hall there were even some standing ovations, including, Louis could see, from the stately presence of Miss Leroy in her private box. His gaze lingered on the head teacher for a moment – long enough for her to turn and pick him out from the crowd. He felt the intensity of her gaze burn into him.

Next to him, Kathryn was gathering up her coat and programme.

'Are we off?'

Louis started. Kathryn's words had broken Miss Leroy's hold on him. He looked around, wincing uncomfortably.

'Sure. Yes.'

As they filed out to the end of the row, Kathryn hooked her arm through Louis' and pressed herself closer.

'Louis, are you alright?'

Louis let out a gasp, then nodded.

'Yes. Just saw someone – I thought I knew...'

Outside the Wrensong Theatre again, under the light from the wrought-iron street lamps of Broad Street, Louis and Kathryn regrouped with Beth. Louis felt comfortable with Kathryn's hand in his. They descended the steps from the quad to street level, where Louis began to lead them across the street towards the White Horse.

'Tom and Polly said they'd meet us across the road,' he said. 'Shall we?'

Kathryn looked hesitant. Beth shook her head.

'Sorry. I need to get back – busy day tomorrow.'

Kathryn looked from one to the other.

'And Beth said she'd give me a lift back. You don't mind, do you?'

Kathryn felt Louis give her hand a gentle squeeze before releasing it. He seemed quietly crestfallen.

'No. No it's fine,' he said quietly.

9

Kathryn headed back across town with Beth, weaving their way through the warren of streets to the multi-storey car park on the far side of the town centre. Their conversation ebbed and flowed as they dodged the throngs of students out for the night.

Arriving at last at Beth's car, alone on the upper level of the dimly lit concrete shell of a utilitarian car park, Kathryn realised that she probably could have been home by now if she'd walked. But she needed the time with Beth, to talk to her, to ask her.

Kathryn settled into the passenger seat and fastened the belt, as Beth fired up the ignition and silenced the annoying local commercial radio station.

'Can I talk to you?' began Kathryn. 'About Louis, I mean,' she added, after receiving an oddly quizzical expression from Beth. 'It's just I was doing some babysitting last night, and I found out something – well, I don't know if it's true – if it is then it doesn't make sense.'

Kathryn was all too aware that she was making little to no sense as she tried to rearrange her thoughts into intelligible speech.

'Amongst everything else he does Louis is writing a novel, isn't he?'

Beth nodded.

'Very secretive about it, though. I so want to read it,' she answered. 'Why? Has he let you?'

Kathryn slowly nodded, and chewed on her lip hesitantly.

'He has, yes. It's good - very good.'

'I sense a but coming on.'

Beth pulled the car up at a set of lights, and waited as a tram trundled across in front.

'One of the girls I was babysitting for, she was a friend of this family - but she recognised the novel in my bag. She said—'

Kathryn thought over her words, picking them carefully, as if lining them up in her mouth.

'She said that it was written - by her Dad - Louis, that is; that he was her father.'

'Louis doesn't have children.'

Beth shook her head quickly and vociferously.

'That's what I thought,' said Kathryn. 'She knew everything, though. Her house was Louis' home...'

Kathryn winced.

'Well, she said it was a house, the whole building. His place is a flat though, in a larger building.'

'Sounds like one of his students making trouble,' said Beth. 'We get this quite a lot. They find out where you live, then they tell all kinds of lies.'

'What about the wedding ring that he wears around his neck?' asked Kathryn.

Beth overtook a tram as she turned off the end of Beaumont Street into the Jericho area of town.

'I think it's his father's,' said Beth. 'He's worn that like forever.'

Kathryn kept her gaze fixed straight ahead. Far from straightening out the answers to her questions, she was more hopelessly confused than ever. As Beth approached the old Phoenix cinema Kathryn spoke again, this time just to say that she could drop her off outside; that her house was just around the corner.

Minutes later, Kathryn stood on the pavement, bent to the open car door and thanked Beth for the lift. She pushed the door closed, and watched as Beth drove off up the road. She then she turned and headed round the corner, down the road of small Victorian terraced houses. She let herself in through her own front door, finding her housemate Nina draped around another young man Kathryn did not recognise as the current boyfriend. She waved goodnight as she passed, and continued up the stairs.

Upstairs in her room, she deposited her work bag on the floor by her sprawling desk and began pulling off her clothes, and slipping into her nightie.

Her face twitched with thought. She crossed to her desk and pushed up the lid to her laptop, pressing down on the power key to bring it out of hibernation while she pulled her robe across her, and ducked out to the bathroom to brush her teeth.

Back in the room a few minutes later, Kathryn freed her laptop from its power cable and withdrew with it to her bed. Sitting with it, she began, drawing on the tips she had learnt and used when helping her uncle with his family research, to search for Louis Tumnal.

An hour or more later, and her searching had generated pages of hastily scribbled notes on countless scraps of paper that now littered the surface of her duvet to either side of her. She picked up one piece of paper and stared at it. Louis Tumnal was born in the house he lived in now, and she had the electoral role for the last three elections to show that his name and the age tallied up, and that he was single, but...

Kathryn picked up another piece of paper. A birth record for Sarah Tumnal eleven years ago, to a Lewis Tumnal and Amanda Jones of the same address. But here was another thing, there was no birth or marriage details for Lewis. Her brain ached as she tried to make sense of it. Louis existed and Sarah existed, but Sarah had no father and Louis had no child. She stared at the address on each scrap of paper, the same address. She was no further on with her investigations. If anything, she was more hopelessly confused than ever. Kathryn gathered up the sheets of paper and deposited them on top of the keyboard, sandwiching them in the computer as she closed the lid on them.

Minutes later, she switched the bedside lamp back on, and reached down to retrieve the papers from under the lid of her laptop. She stared at the marriage records until the names were etched to the back of her eyes. *Amanda Jones?* The more she stared at the name, the more she couldn't shed the image of Louis stood at the alter of some college chapel with her boss. She dropped the paper to the floor, flung off the light, and tried to push those thoughts from her mind.

Kathryn finally woke mid-morning, with the late September sun streaming in through the curtains. She felt rough, not through drink but through a sleep that had been much disturbed by restless, over-active thoughts. They had *finally* bedded themselves for the night, but only after many hours, hence the late Sunday rising.

She showered and dressed herself in warm, comfortable clothes, had a quick breakfast of toast and cereal while she checked her email and had a quick glance over her Facebook, before heading out to enjoy the day. Walking down through Jericho, she crossed the canal and headed out onto Port Meadow, where she intended to lose herself with her camera. An hour, and a very long, bracing walk later, she found herself at the far end of Port Meadow, and outside the Trout in Wolvercote.

Kathryn went to the bar and bought a half of cider and some crisps to take back outside into the autumn sunshine; she sat on the riverbank, watching the river pass by beneath her, and munched her way through her packet of crisps. Looking up, she could see the table where, a month earlier, she had sat with Louis and laughed and joked.

Louis. He didn't seem like the cheating kind. And Beth, she knew him. But Sarah had known him, and last night she had found her birth certificate and it had been the right address. And Amanda Jones? It had to be the same person, and she did have a husband and child, she knew that. Kathryn didn't understand. She frowned, before downing the last of her drink. She had to talk to him, and now was a better time than any.

The tram rattled down the side of Woodstock Road past Squitchey Lane, and Kathryn reached to yank the alarm. At the next stop it drew to a halt, and she disembarked on the opposite corner from the high stone wall behind which Louis' house stood.

The tall trees within the garden were just losing the last of their leaves, and the tall three-storey Edwardian house with the steeply pitched and gabled roofs was more visible than usual through the skeleton of branches.

Kathryn crossed the side street, and, instead of going to the door in the wall that she used when she was with Louis, she ducked down Bevington Road and squeezed through a gap in the wall and next door's fence, before crossing the gravel at the front of the house to Louis' front door.

She marched up to the front door, noting the buzzers to the other flats, as she pressed the doorbell for Louis. After a few minutes the door opened inward to reveal a surprised Louis.

'Kathryn, I didn't know. Did we arrange...?'

Kathryn smiled.

'I was in the area. I was walking – walked further than I thought. Thought I'd drop in.'

'Are you okay?'

Louis ushered her into the hallway, and she found herself immediately staring at the protuberance of the old stairs where they were still showing after being walled in. She reached out and stroked the wooden detailing in the end of the newel post.

'Kathryn?'

She blinked herself awake from the absentmindedness she was lost in.

'Where are the front doors to the other flats?' she asked eventually.

Louis stopped and looked at her, surprised by the apparent randomness of the question.

'There's a lobby round the back. It's a modern extension where the coal shed used to be.'

'So what's behind here now?' Kathryn asked, pressing her hand to the new wall.

Louis laughed.

'Cupboard under the stairs – as there would always have been.'

He flung open the half-height door to reveal a home for vacuum cleaners, cleaning products and old newspapers.

'And—'

Louis closed the door and dashed round the corner to where the foot of stairs should have been, but instead was another smaller-than-average door.

'A cupboard *over* the stairs.'

He opened this one too, grinning broadly. Kathryn peered in through the door at where the stairs continued up, ending in a ceiling. Each step was stacked with books and files.

'Apparently the architect wanted to preserve as much of the house as they could after it was divided up.'

Kathryn nodded. It was kind of cool.

'Wouldn't it be great to buy the whole building and put it back to how it had been?'

Louis swallowed and gulped awkwardly, but remained otherwise quiet.

A little while later, he led Kathryn back through to the lounge. Depositing his mug down on a shelf, he directed Kathryn, holding her own mug of tea in both hands, to one of the other doors in the room.

'Another oddity of this flat,' he said, fetching a bunch of keys from his desk drawer. 'They left these doors here; locked of course, but pointlessly so.'

He turned the key in the lock and opened the door for Kathryn to see – the solid wall immediately behind.

'Weird!' Kathryn laughed.

Louis closed the door again and relocked it, before returning the keys to the desk. He stood for a moment, absentmindedly looking down at his desk, gazing at a couple of his pictures and some pages of notes.

'How's your project going?' he asked as he looked up again and gestured to Kathryn to sit. She remained standing, replying with an insubstantial and noncommittal update.

'It was good last night, wasn't it?' Louis began again.

'It *was* actually,' agreed Kathryn, 'Thank you so much for the invite.'

Louis grinned.

'Well, who else would I have invited?'

Kathryn looked up, directly into Louis' eyes.

'I'm so used to going to these things alone.

Kathryn stood in front of him, wondering at Louis' peculiar choice of words.

'You've never had friends – *a friend* – to go to things with?'

Louis shrugged.

'Well, I'd go with Beth, or with her girlfriend sometimes when they were together.'

'Never a girlfriend yourself, or...'

Kathryn picked through her words carefully, hinting for a response.

'You know the answer to that!' Louis said defensively.

'Or a wife? Amanda maybe?' Kathryn asked, not quite believing that she had said it.

'Kathryn, I don't have a wife!'

'Uh-huh. Next you'll be telling me that Sarah's not your daughter.'

Louis' protestations ceased immediately. How did she know? Sarah – what could he say?

'How do you know about Sarah?'

Louis regretted the question as soon as it was out of his mouth.

'I met her, Louis,' Kathryn told him, observing his incredulous gaze back at her. 'The night I was babysitting. One of the girls, she was your daughter!'

'I don't have a daughter,' protested Louis again.

'She knew about your novel,' continued Kathryn. 'She recognised it in my bag.'

'You've got it all wrong.'

'She was born in this house, Louis! She has your name.'

Louis shook his head.

'Are you denying that you have a daughter? Louis, you lied to me.'

'Yes. No – I mean—' Louis' words were twisted on his tongue. 'Do you see any sign of a daughter here? Have you ever?'

'I don't know how you do it Louis? I simply don't know how you can have your friends lie for you—'

'You've been talking to Beth about this? Last night? Of course...'

'I don't know how you do it,' Kathryn continued unabated. 'Where you put your wife and child when you're with me, I don't know. But it ends here!'

Louis stuttered as he tried to explain, to tell her about Amanda and Sarah, and why it wasn't as she was guessing.

'Don't even try, Louis. You can't explain this. You can't make me understand why you would do this to your wife – your child – to me.'

'I want to,' pleaded Louis pitifully.

'Don't,' Kathryn told him. 'Don't even try.'

Louis felt tears well up in his eyes. Slowly he sunk down onto the edge of the sofa, devastated by his confrontation with Kathryn.

'Goodbye Louis.'

Kathryn turned and walked quickly but composedly from the room, snatching up her bag in the hall before leaving the building, only letting out her tears and anguished screams once outside. She ran from the garden and across the street, leapt aboard a fortuitously waiting tram, and sunk onto a bench behind the driver. She put her head into her hands and sobbed. Her face was red and streaming with tears.

Louis just stood at the front door of his house long after Kathryn had run. Eventually he crossed the garden and shut the door in the wall, pushing the latch closed until it clunked shut. He turned and looked back across the garden, through the overgrown trees and straggly shrubs at the now slightly forlorn looking house.

And then he heard it. The tune from his childhood, with its haunting melody. For a moment he thought he saw himself as a small boy in the window playing his flute.

'Lewis,' he said.

Suddenly, the tune that had been ever-present in his life made sense. It was the soundtrack to his time with Amanda, the childhood friend whom had made his schooldays bearable. When his classmates had been pairing off at the disco, seeing movies, and going to parties, it was okay because he had had Amanda. His secret. His invention.

But how had Kathryn found out? No one had known - *knew even* - of Amanda. Kathryn had behaved as if Amanda was real. It wasn't possible.

Louis returned to the house, stomping angrily across the garden. He should have told her the truth, he decided. Better to admit to living an imaginary life, than to lose his one real love.

10

Lewis sat in the lounge, dimly lit by the light from a solitary lamp. Somewhere outside he could hear the sounds of a gate opening and closing, and footsteps on the gravel, with voices in the dusk. Thoughts pummelled at his brain without taking in what they were about; they beat the sense out of him, so that he felt woozy and exhausted. The front door opened, and then more voices, both inside and out; footsteps on the gravel, and the gate again.

'Hi, Dad!'

Lewis looked up, as Sarah slung her school bag onto the stairs.

'Dad? What's wrong?' asked Sarah suddenly, rushing to him.

Lewis looked up, unable to answer. He felt the wetness round his eyes, and the heavy-set lids.

'It's Mum, isn't it?' said Sarah. 'She's left us, hasn't she?'

Lewis nodded.

'I didn't know what to do,' he said. 'I tried to explain. I tried to tell her, but she wouldn't listen.'

Sarah sat down next to her father and put her arm around him. She gave him a gentle, comforting squeeze. Then, turning her head towards him, she narrowed her gaze on him.

'Mum found out, didn't she?'

Lewis shook his head involuntarily, questioning Sarah's thinking.

172

'I saw you, Dad,' said Sarah. 'Who is she?'

'Who?'

'The girl you're cheating on us with.'

Lewis shook his head again.

'I saw you, Dad. At Beth's birthday party. You were with that girl. Who was she?'

Lewis sunk into a kind of daze as he remembered.

'Kathryn,' he said. 'She's a friend of Beth's. I teach her in photography class.'

'I saw you kiss her!' Sarah said, rounding on her father, 'How long has Mum known?'

Lewis shrugged.

'I didn't know that she did, until today. She just ambushed me with it this afternoon – I tried to explain, but I think she had already decided.'

Sarah stared at her father with disbelief, at the way he was now moping about something that he could have done something about.

'Why did you do it?' she questioned him.

Lewis sighed deeply.

'Your mum and I, our love,' he said hesitantly. 'It was never real.'

Later that night, Lewis crossed the floor of the hallway from the kitchen to the stairs. He gathered up his books from the hall stand, and made his slow, preoccupied way up the stairs. On the top landing he paused for a moment outside Sarah's bedroom door. Through the gap in it where it stood ajar, he could see her sat cross-legged on her bed, looking at her laptop. After a while Sarah looked up, suddenly aware of someone watching her. Her stare met Lewis', and he turned without a further word and continued on to his own bedroom.

Lewis went through his nightly routine on autopilot. He could not have said how he got to sitting up in his bed in his pyjamas with his book open in front of him. And even when he was, his eyes could not

He looked to his book and found his place again. Reading the next page, Louis realised he had read this same page at least three times previously. He battled on reading the words, while remaining oblivious to the story. An hour or so later he woke with a start, slumped on his pillow with his glasses crooked on his nose, and the book somewhere next to him on the floor. He returned the book to the bedside cabinet, took off his glasses, and switched off the light before snuggling down into his pillow and waiting for sleep.

The following morning Louis woke with a start. Even before he had fumbled for his watch and checked the time, he knew he was late. Monday morning, and somewhere across town, someone else would be taking registration for him. He cursed out loud and jumped out of bed, only to have to sit again, quietly for a few minutes while his head stopped spinning. He uttered more swear words, and continued to punctuate the hasty act of washing and dressing with them. Somehow he got from the bedroom to the kitchen, and got a mug of strong, black coffee and a slice of toast down him. Without checking his satchel, he slung it over his tweed jacket and left the house.

At school he diverted away from the main entrance and sneaked in through the side entrance to the staff room, feeling incredibly like both a naughty school child and a criminal.

Fortuitously, Monday mornings were a free period for Beth, and on this morning she had chosen to work through some lesson plans in the comfort of the staffroom. She looked up as Louis entered, expressing body language that exuded guilt.

'We thought you must've been ill?'

Louis shook his head.

'Just overslept. I *never* oversleep—' he said, swallowing another curse. 'Has the Head noticed?'

Beth shrugged.

'I don't think so,' she said. 'Polly's got a free too, so she covered your class. We could get you back in at break.'

The rest of the morning passed without incident. Louis helped Beth with some class prep work until just before break, when they headed down to the English labs and spent the time until next lesson chatting with Polly. At lunch, Louis left the school to buy a sandwich from the petrol station across the road, before returning to brave the staff room to eat it. The only thing in his pigeon hole was a union newsletter. He had gone to check for post nervously, sure that he would find a memo summoning him to see the Head, and every time he heard the staff room door he felt sure it was going to be Miss Leroy, or a pupil sent to fetch him to her. Slowly Louis began to relax, to think that he had got away with his earlier absence.

The afternoon passed even better than the morning; a double period of English Lit, followed by Creative Writing with his 'good group'. There was nothing that Louis like better than an intelligent and animated discussion about the innocence of childhood, sexual awakening, and maturity in relation to Laurie Lee's *Cider With Rosie*, that ended only, and abruptly, when the school bell rang for the end of school.

The class piled out, and Louis smiled as he overheard some of them still talking over the themes as they left. He went around the classroom, tidying up and making it right for the morning, before he himself gathered up his belongings, slipped back into his tweed jacket, shouldered the scuffed and worn satchel, and left.

Louis left H-block and began to cross the playground diagonally towards the two-storey 1960s Humanities wing. He had just began to pick out a tune through pursed lips – the tune from his childhood and his flute lessons – when it was punctuated by the unmistakeable rhythmic percussion of Miss Leroy's heels behind him.

'Lewis Tumnal,' Miss Leroy said, her voice clear and clipped, and with perfect precision.

Lewis stopped and turned. He nodded to the headmistress and she drew level.

'Do please continue,' she said. 'We can walk together.'

They walked on, together across the playground.

'You were late then, this morning, Lewis.'

'I – err…'

Lewis didn't know what to say. He glanced up to see Miss Leroy looking at him across her half-moon spectacles, expectant of some kind of explanation.

'Overslept,' he said. 'Yesterday was stressful. It won't happen again.'

'Quite right,' Miss Leroy agreed. 'I have every confidence in you to be strong, Lewis.'

Lewis stopped, and turned to gaze bewilderingly at her.

'I'm not sure if I understand you.'

Miss Leroy took a step towards her English teacher and smiled warmly. She reached out and took hold of his hand, patting it affectionately.

'It is imperative, Lewis, that you resolve your differences with Amanda.'

'Amanda?' How did she know about Amanda?

'Yes, Lewis,' she told him. 'Absolutely imperative. You need to be strong. I need you to be strong.'

'She's left me, though. She said she didn't know who I was anymore.' Lewis said, a sense of panic in his voice.

'Hush now, Lewis,' Miss Leroy added warmly. 'You are Lewis Tumnal; a teacher, and a successful one at that. You write, and play music, and you have the most gorgeous wife.'

'I – I guess...'

'And where did you meet Amanda? In orchestra, at this very school. And you've been together ever since. It's beautiful.'

As they neared the Humanities block, Lewis could see Beth and Polly waiting for them.

'There, see, and you have friends,' said Miss Leroy. 'Go, talk to them, and find your strength, Lewis. Be strong, for me.'

Louis carried his pint of mild bitter back from the bar to where his friends were already sitting on the low sprawling sofas, in the snug area of the pub.

'We've not seen much of you of late here in the old *Downloader*,' Tom said, once Louis had arranged himself on the leather sofa opposite.

'Louis has been busy seeing his girlfriend, haven't you,' Polly said, grinning at him.

'Oh yes,' said Tom,. 'Katy - Caroline—'

'Kathryn,' corrected Beth.

'Late night with Kathryn was it, last night?' asked Tom. 'It's alright, Polly filled me in on your late arrival at the asylum this morning.'

Louis remained silent. There was sometimes very little that he could say about Tom's ever-present sense of humour.

'Louis?'

Beth turned to look at her friend next to her on the sofa.

'Is everything okay?'

Louis shook his head slowly, and puzzled privately over his choice of words.

'Is it Kathryn?' Beth gulped the question.

'Last night, we had a row. She walked out.'

Polly leaned forward, reaching out to offer support.

'Everyone has rows – look at Tom and I – she'll come back.'

Louis shook his head again.

'I don't think so, not from what she said. It's all over.'

'But why?' asked Beth. 'What did she say.'

'It's not what she said. It's what I couldn't tell her.'

Beth, Polly, and Tom gaped. Louis shook his head a third time.

'I can't talk about it.'

The conversation fell silent. One by one, the three friends sat back again in their seats, Beth the last to do so, intent as she was to demonstrate support and compassion.

Louis laughed, a brief, punctuating chuckle that broke the silence.

'So, how was everyone else's day?'

There followed nods, and muttered subdued agreement. Louis took a drink from his glass, sat forward, and placed it down on the table in front of them.

'So, are we all set to go to the fair next week?' Louis asked with false brightness.

Lewis' bicycle stood chained to the railings outside the riverside branch of Pizza Express, the lights from which spilled out onto the pavement. At the small table inside by the window, he sat opposite Sarah. As he worked steadily through the pizza with a knife and fork, his daughter ate each triangular slice by hand, balancing the thin crust stretched with strings of mozzarella across her fingers.

Lewis would occasionally take pauses to open his notebook and jot down ideas. Sarah reflected on this activity with a doleful look and big, wide eyes.

'Your novel again? Or lesson plans for tonight's class?' Sarah asked, smiling at her father.

'In this instance?' Lewis answered. 'I guess you could say both.'

Sarah raised an eyebrow of interest.

'It's actually notes for the lesson tonight, but as one of my characters is doing a course in photography, the one informs the other.'

Sarah grinned.

'You love teaching, don't you?'

Lewis looked up, mid-mouthful. He nodded again.

'I just like sharing my knowledge.'

'So who do you find easier. The adults or us lot?'

Lewis paused. He chewed on the pizza and considered the question.

'Has to be children,' he answered eventually. 'With the adults, if they think they know better than you, they just continue on and on at you...'

'Is that Colin?' Sarah grinned.

'He's so tiresome.'

They finished up the meal and Lewis checked his watch. He hastily packed his notebook into his satchel and slipped on his jacket.

'Come on, we'd better pay. It's almost half seven.'

A few minutes later and they were crossing the street outside the restaurant, dodging a passing tram as it rattled its way to a stop, and heading for the college building. Sarah walked with her dad up to the entrance, where Lewis fished twenty quid out of his wallet and handed it over.

'Have fun at the cinema. Is Caz joining you?'

Sarah nodded enthusiastically.

'Yeah, I'd better dash – but I should be back here about nine.'

Lewis agreed. For a moment an awkward silence endured, while they hesitated over goodbyes. Lewis turned and disappeared into reception.

Louis turned right out of the stairwell into the subterranean corridor and walked its length. His mind kept running over what he would say to Kathryn when he saw her. He would explain everything – about Amanda and Sarah – of how they weren't real. He kept piecing together the words, replaying the opening line, and realising that it wouldn't work, all the way along the corridor, until he reached the door to the photography lab.

He stopped and composed himself. Kathryn would be sat in their usual spot on the far side of the room. He could picture the look on her face when he entered so clearly he began to beam at the thought. Louis pushed open the door, and stopped almost immediately. Kathryn was not there, and Louis could not hide the unrepressed disappointment on his face as he scanned the room, desperate to see her. Brian and Colin looked up, from where Colin was evidently in the midst of some long and detailed explanation, and greeted Louis, before returning their attention to what they were looking through on the light box. Louis glanced at his watch; there was still five minutes for her to arrive.

The minutes ticked by, and at eight o'clock as Brian began the class, Kathryn was still nowhere to be seen. Louis was so wrapped up in his thoughts he missed the whole of Brian's introduction into tonight's exercise, and was consequently surprised when Colin was suddenly at his side, sliding his chair in next to him.

'Colin, what are you doing?'

'Working with you, like Brian told us,' said Colin. 'I know how you normally work with that Katy lass, but as she's not turned up...'

Louis stuttered with uncertainty.

'Of course. Now, what were we doing again?'

Louis shifted his chair across and let Colin take the driving seat, as they discussed the different ways of working with wide apertures and long exposures. Louis glazed over at some of Colin's explanations, and couldn't bring himself to argue against some of his more preposterous suggestions. The lesson dragged like no other, and at break time he lingered in the corridor after a toilet break, so as to be sure Colin was fully-engrossed in another tedious conversation with another classmate. Louis sidled into the room and joined the conversation of a younger group of students, but their talk just made him miss Kathryn all the more, and he soon slipped away and back to his desk.

It was somewhat with relief, then, that the clock ticked round to ten o'clock, and Louis was able to escape down the corridor while Colin was still going over the details of his project work for about the fifth time to some hapless student. Louis dashed up the stairs into reception and out onto the street.

Lewis ambled around the small square at the front of the college, looking at advertising hoardings and reading planning notices strapped to lamp posts. He glanced up occasionally, looking this way and that for a sign of Sarah waiting for him. He saw Colin heading through college reception, and hastily moved off further down the street away from the tram stops. Finding himself opposite Pizza Express, he looked up through the window next to where he and Sarah had eaten earlier. A girl with blonde hair tucked back in a ponytail sat opposite a man with short, slightly greying hair and glasses. It couldn't be? Could it...?

Lewis sprang forward into a run, stopping almost as quickly as a cyclist swerved and a car blasted on its horn. He looked down the road again, and crossed at the earliest gap, all the time keeping an eye on the window, but as he neared he could see it wasn't Kathryn. He shook his head sadly, and crossed the road to where Sarah was, by now, waiting for him.

'It's going to be okay, you know,' Sarah said curtly as he approached. 'You don't have to go and get yourself run over, just because mum left you.

Lewis shrugged.

'Was it a good film?'

'It was brill.'

And Sarah proceeded to tell Lewis all about it as they headed off down the road on their way home.

11

The production office was a long room open to the Old Quad down one side that slowly emptied as people shut down their computers, collected their coats, and headed off home, leaving just a core of people working as the light dimmed outside. At Kathryn's pod, she, Charlotte, and Eleanor continued to work. One of their friends from another department stopped by as they passed through the office on their way out.

'We're going to the fair later. Eleanor and I that is – Kathryn's off with her man,' Eleanor said.

'Well, that and I've got this issue to get to press,' added Charlotte. 'Actually, I'm a bit up against the clock at the moment.'

She frowned, and focussed again on her pile of revisions. The friend nodded, and, after wishing them a good time, headed off to join up with another friend as they left the office chatting.

Kathryn broke from her corrections work for a moment to watch them go. She turned again towards Eleanor and Charlotte.

'Can I ask something?'

Both Eleanor and Charlotte looked up.

'Sure,' Charlotte said, confused that Kathryn was even asking.

'I was wondering—'

'Kathryn!'

Kathryn stopped at the sound of her name. She turned and saw Amanda leaning out of her office door.

'Can I have a word please?' continued Amanda.

Kathryn sighed quietly under her breath, before mouthing something to her friends. She got up, grabbed her notepad and pen, and smiled brightly at Amanda.

'Of course,' Kathryn replied politely.

Amanda ushered Kathryn into her office and slid shut the glass door. Kathryn sat at the meeting table, but Amanda remained standing to tower over her employee. From the main office, Charlotte and Eleanor watched. At first they tried to go back to their own work, but the voices that gradually raised in volume soon distracted them.

Kathryn looked to be trying to explain something, but Amanda was pounding variations of the same few words at her. At one point she returned to her computer, and she was pulling up schedule screens with lines of pink across them – and Kathryn was then on her feet and leaning over Amanda, pointing, and obviously trying to explain.

Charlotte and Eleanor turned and looked nervously from one to another. Suddenly everything was quiet again. Kathryn flung the office door back with such force that it shook on its hinges, and she stormed back to her desk and slumped into her chair. She scowled with intense fury.

'Please tell me you didn't just throw the ash tray,' Eleanor said quietly.

Kathryn glared at her friend. After a few moments she glanced over her shoulder as Amanda slid the office door shut, sending a pointedly fixed stare across the room at Kathryn before returning to her desk.

'Evil witch,' Kathryn said, through gritted teeth.

Charlotte leaned forward.

'What was that all about?'

'Absolutely nothing,' replied Kathryn. 'A complete non-problem.'

Both Charlotte and Eleanor exchanged concerned glances, and leaned closer in an attempt to encourage more explanation out of Kathryn.

'I've fallen behind schedule by one day. There's five days' slack for pity's sake, and it's not even as if there wasn't a good reason for it.'

Kathryn's words tumbled out with adrenaline.

'I tried to explain how I was waiting for an author to clarify a crucial scientific point, and how he had promised to do this by today, which incidentally he has now done; but no, apparently that's not good enough. I mean honestly, the bloody thing is still probably going to go to press ahead of time.'

Charlotte frowned.

'She's having a bad day, I guess.'

'Bad day? Bad week, more like,' retorted Kathryn. 'She's been constantly on my case.'

'I heard Gillian and Edward talking in the kitchen the other day – apparently she's left her husband or something.'

Kathryn rolled her eyes.

'Really not my problem. Louis and I split this weekend, and I'm not acting like the bitch reborn.'

She stopped, aware suddenly that Charlotte and Eleanor were staring at her.

'I didn't tell you that, did I?'

'We—' Charlotte began, glancing at Eleanor. 'We suspected something wasn't right.'

'What happened?' asked Eleanor.

'Only that he's got a wife and child,' Kathryn told them.

Charlotte gaped, wide-eyed.

'How?' she asked with bewilderment. 'You've been to his house?'

'I have literally no idea,' Kathryn said, sorrowfully. 'You know when I did that babysitting the other week? The girl's friend was his daughter. And he couldn't deny it.'

'That's terrible,' said Charlotte. 'Why do men do that?'

Kathryn shrugged. She looked down at the work on her desk and sighed.

'Guess I better get this issue off then,' she said. 'What time were you guys going to the fair?'

Charlotte glanced at Eleanor, expressing uncertainty.

'When we're ready, I guess; no plans. Did you—'

'Because – do you mind if I come along with you?' asked Kathryn.

'Sure,' answered Charlotte. 'We only didn't ask you before because we assumed that you would be meeting up with Louis.'

Kathryn was silent.

'Of course you can. You don't have to ask,' added Charlotte.

The spiralling, circling Scorpion ride flung the fair-goers down into the crowd, before casting them up towards the high fifteenth-century turreted walls of the colleges. Lights flashed and swirled, and music boomed out of speakers from every ride. Kathryn dodged people and weaved her way through the throng with Charlotte and Eleanor, munching on some candyfloss, allowing it to melt on her tongue.

They stopped outside a stall while Charlotte tried in vain to win a goldfish, then turned around to find Eleanor at the next stall, firing coconuts at targets. A round-faced man with a large belly hanging over his jeans laughed endlessly as he presented Eleanor, blushing red, with a large squidgy bear.

Across the other side of the fair, Louis stood looking up at the old fashioned helter-skelter as first Beth, then Tom, and lastly Polly slid round and round on seagrass mats. They worked their way onwards down the street, seduced by the smell of roasting chestnuts. Through the crowd, for a moment, Louis thought he saw Kathryn, but after looking again a moment later she was gone, either subsumed into the swelling crowd or never there.

Beth grabbed Louis' hand and tugged him forward, pushing him to a turnstile at the front of the queue. She pushed a fiver into the hands of the man at the gate.

'Two please.'

The man handed Beth a couple of stubby tickets in return.

'Beth?'

'You can't object to the big wheel,' said Beth. 'No arguments. You're coming with me.'

Louis glared at his friend, whilst feeling a secret, internal pleasure that she was forcing him onto a ride. Moments later and he was jostled into a cradle, and jolted forwards by degrees, further into the sky. At its highest point he and Beth were sitting level with the rooftops and looking down, not just across the tops of the plain trees, but the whole fairground that sprawled across the wide St. Giles Street, and down into neighbouring streets.

Beth snapped photographs, and Louis saw shots form in his mind from the vista set out beneath him, beside him, above him, that made him wish that he had brought his own camera with him. For a moment, as he looked down, he thought his gaze met with that of Kathryn, looking up. But he blinked and she was gone, vanished again into the milling crowd.

They jolted forwards again, and down by degrees until the cradle in front of them was filled by a father and daughter, and with a slow grinding of gears the wheel shifted and turned into action. Up, up, up, and the people below were tiny and the sound system was a distant hum, drowned out by the quiet of the night and the wind that whistled across the roofline. Down, down, down, and they were plunged back into noise and flashing lights and the relentless fair. No sooner than they were down again but they were lifted back out into another circle. Louis and Beth waved to Tom and Polly, and they waved back.

Back up at the roofline, Louis glanced to his right and his gaze met with that of Miss Leroy. She stood in one of the attic rooms of the college with a younger, tall, and dark-haired man at her side. The wheel continued on its way and took Louis and Beth back down, away from Miss Leroy's prying gaze.

Kathryn walked through the fair, laughing and joking and sharing gossip with her friends. At the top end of the street, just beyond *The Eagle & Child* and separated from the rest of the fair by the tram lines, was the house of mirrors.

'Hey! Shall we?' suggested Charlotte.

The others agreed, and they joined the queue. They shuffled forward with the rest of the fair-goers, and as they reached the gate Kathryn looked up in time to see Louis and his friends ahead of them. A pang of uncertainness wrenched through her, but Eleanor had already handed over the entry money, and the jostling of the crowd pushed her through the gate. Her breath quickened to match her feelings. Separated by another group of friends, Kathryn could see the back of Louis' head as he disappeared into the interior.

Kathryn stepped forward and up through the entrance, immediately confronted with a reflection, a distorted rear view. She glanced round, and saw the warped floor-to-ceiling mirror behind her that twisted and contorted her view.

Shrieks and giggles from the crowd inside echoed around the walls of the ride, over the top of the rhythmic hum of the generator and the clanking of the machinery, as the mirror walls shifted positions to close off pathways and open up new ones as they walked through the mirrored maze.

'It's like being inside a mirror,' said Kathryn.

'Disorientation city!' agreed Charlotte.

The walls clanked again, and the scene was instantly different. Kathryn swung round, searching the people around her and the reflections in the mirrors.

'Where's Eleanor?' she panicked.

Charlotte swung round too, staring through the distortion. 'She was right beside me – just now—'

'Not anymore,' said Kathryn.

The machine grinded into motion again, the mirrored walls in front of them parted to reveal a new chamber, and they shuffled forward. Behind them the walls clanked and moved and snapped shut.

'Charlotte!' Kathryn shouted out. The walls had separated them.

Kathryn moved forward again. Where once she had enjoyed the childlike delight of the twisted reflections, now the claustrophobia and the disorientation scared her. The walls turned and flipped, and the corridor opened out to another chamber and a different set of people, but there was still no sign of her friends. She moved on as the walls grinded across the floor, flipping their reflections here and there, pushing between the people and sorting them into different directions. Kathryn tried to remember how big the trailer had been, then tried to keep a focus on where she was in relation to the outside world, but it was hopeless. Her head ached, her mind confused by the convex and the concave reflections of other equally twisted images. As the panels parted once more, she stepped forward to where, in front of her, a solitary man stood, staring at his reflection. The walls moved and pushed her on, and she stepped up alongside him. Glancing to her side, she confirmed what she knew already.

'Louis,' Kathryn said dispassionately.

He didn't answer. She looked at him, at the way he stared straight ahead, his gaze fixed on something in the reflection. Around them the ride groaned, sending vibrations through the floor.

Lewis stood in front of the mirror, staring at the warped and refracted reflections. At his side, he could see Amanda standing with him. And across his shoulder, in the reflection of a reflection from another mirror, there was Miss Leroy, looking back at him.

'Lewis,' said Miss Leroy. 'Amanda. It's so nice to see you both together.'

Lewis didn't answer. He looked to his side, to Amanda. His hand slipped easily into hers, and he smiled.

'Keep hold of her Lewis—'

Lewis straightened up, still smiling, and looked again to Miss Leroy.

'She makes you Lewis,' Miss Leroy continued.

'Louis, what are you doing?' Kathryn pulled her hand from his. 'What are you looking at!'

Louis turned to face Kathryn.

'I'm sorry. It was never meant to end up like this,' he said, sorrowfully.

'No? Well...!'

Kathryn stopped, noticing a lack of comprehension on Louis' face. She returned a stern gaze at him.

'If you never had used me to cheat on your wife—'

'It's not like that,' said Louis. 'Amanda, she's not—'

'Amanda? I was right then?'

Louis nodded.

'I need to explain.'

Kathryn jumped back as the realisation hit her.

'And – she doesn't work for The Press too, does she?'

Louis nodded.

'Not that it matters.'

'The hell it matters, Louis. Your *wife* is my boss! And because of our affair, she's been giving me absolute hell.'

Louis stared back at her blankly.

'It matters very much.'

The grinding of the machinery was suddenly louder. The next mirrored panels began to move, jolting forwards and back, and jammed. The grinding and the groaning intensified, as metal strained over dry metal. Shrieks of alarm penetrated the increasing din from elsewhere in the ride.

With an alarming pop of electricity and a flare of blue flame, the ride went dark, screams echoing around the house of mirrors. The gears grinded noisily, and a mirrored panel flipped open with such force that the glass shattered and caused Kathryn to jump back. She crashed into another panel, and felt the glass give behind her.

'Kathryn!' Louis called out. His voice sounded further away than it should be. The emergency lighting flicked and flashed back into life. Kathryn found herself on the reverse side of the mirrors between the grinding levers and the sides of the truck. Through a gap in the panels she could see Louis, standing hapless in front of the mirrors.

'Louis!' Kathryn shouted.

She dove towards the gap and tried to squeeze through. Something tore, and her arm stung with pain. She pulled back. Louis was at the panel now, pulling against the direction that it was closing, now kicking at it. He was saying something under his breath, but under the now thunderous roar of machinery, Kathryn couldn't hear what he said.

'Take my hand!' Louis shouted eventually, as he reached out for her.

Kathryn grabbed it without thinking. There was no way she could get through, nor he to her. She released his grip and pushed his hand away, moments before the panels snapped closed.

Kathryn screamed out, at the same moment that Louis shouted out her name. She hit the panel with her fists. It rattled but remained in place. It was then that she noticed the smear of blood near to where Louis' hand had been. Her breathing became fast and breathless, as she realised she was trapped in this space, that with every panel movement was becoming smaller and smaller.

She looked up, wondering if she could climb over the glass panels, but above head height was where the gears and levers were working this way and that. Kathryn looked round again, noticing at last a narrow crack in the side of the truck through which she could see the light from the floodlights outside. Upon closer inspection, Kathryn saw that the side panel of the truck was just bolted to an upright, and that the bolt was loose. She fiddled, with fumbling, aching fingers, and sprang it loose. The next was more of a reach to get to, but after several easy turns she found the threads to be rusted solid. She sighed with heavy frustration, elbowing the side of the truck. It moved a little, but her shoulder ached with pain. She aimed a kick at it, and almost toppled over herself. Then, bracing herself against every available support, she kicked again, and again.

Finally another of the bolts sprang clear, hitting her sharply in the leg. She was able to push the corner of the side panel out enough to squeeze through and drop down onto the road at the back of the ride, amongst the vans and cables, and the petrol-guzzling, throbbing generator.

Kathryn straightened up and looked around. Somewhere up above, the Scorpion ride whizzed around above the tree top.

She stepped over the cables and around cases to get out from behind the ride, and as she rounded the end of the trailer, she saw the packed and silent crowd gathered in front of the House of Mirrors, with a couple of ambulances pulled up outside with their blue lights flashing. She scanned the people being led out of the ride, but could see no sign of Louis. She did catch sight of Charlotte and Eleanor talking to a policeman; at least they were safe. Then she noticed something out of the corner of her eye. She turned to look closer, at the smear of blood on the shop window of the nice deli on the corner of Little Clarendon Street. *Louis?* She wondered.

She followed the trail of blood around the corner and stopped. She could see him down the far end of the street, just beyond a pool of light from a streetlamp. In the gloom of the night, Kathryn could see the silhouette of a tall woman, stepping out of the shadows towards Louis.

Kathryn held back at the end of the street, watching, and wondering. Eventually, slowly, she moved forward, keeping close to the side of the street and in the shadow of the buildings. Halfway down she stopped again. There was something familiar about the woman talking to Louis. She was old, stern, and by the looks of it, possessed with an air of old-fashioned properness. And then the woman looked up, down the street, directly at Kathryn.

Kathryn froze, and shrank back against the wall. The lady kept her gaze on her, eyes fixed, burning her with their force. Louis remained with his back to Kathryn, stooped low and humbled. A stillness descended over the street, the sounds of the fair now far off in the distance.

Momentarily the gaze-hold was broken as a young couple walked down the street, passing between Kathryn and Miss Leroy before turning off towards Wellington Square. A light wind whipped up and stirred the leaves in the gutter. The dry brown, curled leaves rustled and whispered before scuttering across the road, and then as the wind turned, back again. Kathryn glanced up again. It looked like Louis was now arguing with the woman, but only the faintest of murmurs drifted across to her on the wind.

The leaves continued to swirl and stop in the gutter. The wind was picking up now, brushing more off the swaying branches of the trees that lined the street. Kathryn drew her coat around her, and her arm stung again. She touched her hand to the pain, and felt the stickiness that was blood. She winced and shivered. The moment that the mirror had crashed back on her flashed through her mind. The pain seared through her once more.

A blast of cold, dry wind howled mournfully down the street. It swirled round, up through the rustling leaves with the litter from the gutter; paper cups and food cones dropped by people leaving the fair.

Kathryn jumped back, startled, and looked again where Louis and Miss Leroy were arguing. Another gust of wind from one end of the street, and from the other a waste bin fell over, clattering loudly as it rolled into the road. The wind picked out the rubbish, casting it into the air, then playing with it in the gutter.

'Leave her out of it!' pleaded Lewis, pointing back across at Kathryn.
'I can't,' Miss Leroy said coldly. 'She's become too involved.'
Lewis shook his head.
'Where's Amanda, Lewis?' asked Miss Leroy. 'She was everything you wanted once.'
'She doesn't exist.'
'She is your wife.'
'In our stories, once,' countered Lewis.
'She was your one companion.'
'She was make believe!'

Lewis lunged for Miss Leroy, his eyes suddenly alive with fire. Miss Leroy staggered back awkwardly, supported by her stick, which she now raised toward Lewis. She fixed him with her gaze and raised another, outstretched, hand toward Kathryn.

The wind whipped around Kathryn, blowing her long hair around her face. She had to help him, but her feet felt like lead weights holding her to the ground.

The wind whirled round, roaring down the narrow street. A shadow fell across her, and she turned to look. Leaves and litter were blowing about above her head; she gaped. There were arms and legs; a figure that loomed over her, lashing out at her with leafy arms. The wind roared; or was it the monster?

'Louis!' she screamed.

'Let her go!' Lewis shouted at Miss Leroy. He, too, could see the monster of leaves and litter bearing down the street towards Kathryn.

Miss Leroy's eyes burned brightly.

'First, swear to give the girl up,' she said coldly. 'Return to your wife, and do the one thing that I need of you.'

'And you'll call that thing off?'

Miss Leroy returned one slow, careful nod to Lewis. Lewis glanced back at where Kathryn was flapping and flinging her arms about, as the monster pushed her to the wall, scratched at her face, and clawed at her coat.

'Alright,' he turned to Miss Leroy. 'I'll do it.'

Kathryn stumbled backwards, and fell to the ground. As the monster bore down on her, the arms of leaves slashing at her face, she screamed, and squeezed her eyes tight shut. And suddenly everything was quiet. Slowly she peeked open each eye and looked about her. A calm had descended over the street; the leaves lay in the gutter, and the odd plastic cup rolled across the street. Opposite, a man knelt, crumpled to the floor – Louis.

Kathryn picked herself up and ran to him, throwing herself at his side. She pulled his head out of his hands, clutched the sides of his face, and stared into his eyes.

'Louis, what was that? Who was that woman?' she blurted out, all too fast.

Louis looked up, into Kathryn's eyes, feeling the tears that ran down his face. He shook his head. He looked away.

'Louis?' asked Kathryn. 'What's wrong?'

'It's over,' he mumbled, face buried in Kathryn's front.

Kathryn knelt with Louis at first, helping him, little by little, to his feet. They were standing at the furthest end of the street from the noise of the fair, facing each other.

'I'm sorry I doubted you,' said Kathryn.

'Don't be sorry,' Louis said, holding her tightly. 'You were right, my life's too complicated.'

'Let's not talk about that now,' Kathryn said, breathing the words softly. Then, with a smile, she asked: 'Walk me home?'

Louis nodded, and they set off, turning the corner into Walton Street. Up ahead, the lights of a tram approached through the night.

Kathryn reached out for Louis' hand. She stopped. He stopped too, as she lifted his hand to look at where the skin was severed and scraped.

'Your hand! I completely forgot,' she said. 'That must sting.'

She touched it gently, and he withdrew, wincing.

'It's fine! Come on let's get you home.'

Outside Kathryn's front gate, they stopped again. She took his hands, one in each of hers.

'You can come in if you like,' she told him. 'For a coffee, and – I can clean up your hand.'

Louis shook his head.

'I can't,' he answered with regret. 'Goodbye, Kathryn.'

Kathryn shook her head vehemently, and flung her arms upwards to pull Louis into an embrace. She kissed him. For a moment he allowed himself to reciprocate, but eventually pulled back quickly.

'This is goodbye,' he said. 'It has to be.'

He took a couple of steps back and turned away, forcing himself to make the steps.

'Why does it?' Kathryn called after him.

Louis lingered, considering turning back, but forced himself to walk on, leaving Kathryn standing on the pavement outside her house, watching him.

PART THREE

Cold Winter

adagietto misterioso

1

Kathryn had endured several very long weeks through the latter end of autumn – weeks in which she had done little except work and sleep. Following the fair she had gone back to photography class, expecting – hoping – to see Louis; but he had stopped going, and she quickly lost the enthusiasm she once had.

Christmas arrived at last, and with it the first snowfall of winter. Kathryn packed up her bags, shut up her little house in Wren Hoe, and fought her way home on overcrowded trains to her parent's house outside Bristol. She unpacked her bags in her old bedroom, in the little stone cottage on the outskirts of town, and settled into a new routine that consisted of little more than walking the family dog, giving requisite amounts of love and affection to Humphrey, the elderly tabby cat, and reading in front of the fire.

The evening she arrived home they decorated the tree, and the following morning Grannie arrived by taxi. Kathryn was sat in the lounge, feet tucked back under her, enjoying the latest in a series of fantasy books for young adults, when she heard her mother call her from the kitchen. Kathryn frowned, annoyed to be disturbed from her reading, and slipped an old train ticket in between the pages to mark her place. She got up and headed through to the kitchen, bashing her shoulder on a protruding coat hook on the way through the hall and wincing at the pain. The injury she had sustained at the fair, worse than she first thought, still bothered her.

Walking between the lounge and the kitchen, Kathryn left a room that was toasty warm from the wood burner, through a comparatively cold hall to arrive in a kitchen that steamed with warmth, and where condensation fogged the windows. Her mother was busying herself over the stove.

'Ah, there you are,' Kathryn's mother pronounced.

'What can I do, Mum?' Kathryn asked brightly. Her mum gestured to the fridge.

'Your grandmother and I are trying to get as much as we can done before tomorrow. But we've got tonight's dinner to arrange, and–'

She stopped still, staring vacantly at the fridge as if trying to remember something.

'There's sausage meat and bacon, if you'd like to do your usual with them.'

'Sure, okay,' Kathryn said, moving to the sink to wash her hands.

'And then maybe make up the stuffing balls after?'

Kathryn nodded again, as she began getting food out of the fridge and a large earthenware dish out of a cupboard. As she settled into the routine of breaking off lumps of sausage meat and rolling it in between her hands, before wrapping a rasher of streaky bacon around it, she listened quietly to her Mum and Grannie's conversation; Grannie fussed over the preparation of vegetables, relating a tale of woe of trying to find something at the supermarket. Kathryn's mother got Grannie talking about how she was getting on with her school visits; Kathryn didn't know this until now, but Grannie had started volunteering at the local primary school, taking some of the children through their reading.

Kathryn began to recall her own cherished memories of sitting on Grannie's lap, in the big wicker chair that stood overlooking the garden in the house in Middleton. Grannie would take her to the library, where she would be seduced by all the wonderful books, and they would go home, loaded down with as many books as was allowed, and then they would read them together.

'They are dreadful, Louisa,' said Grannie forthrightly. 'I've noticed such a change over the years. They just don't have the attention span to read. It's a real effort.'

Kathryn watched her mother chopping some carrots, bemoaning child literacy with Grannie.

'Of course I blame these computers and telephones that they all have,' continued Grannie. 'I remember when the focal point of the classroom was the library shelf. And even the dictionary you had to understand—'

Kathryn rolled her eyes. She loved her Grannie, dearly, but she did have this awful tendency to pronounce as evil anything which was new.

'Did you know, Louisa, that to find out how to spell something now, they just have to type what they think it might be and the computer tells them what it should be?'

'There's nothing wrong with spellchecker, Grannie,' piped up Kathryn.

Grannie looked up from across the room, affronted by Kathryn's interjection.

'These children don't even check to see if it's the right word they are correcting though,' explained Grannie. 'They just see the suggestion and accept it.'

Kathryn frowned and continued to roll her sausage meat.

'They spend too much time on these computers if you ask me,' continued Grannie.

Kathryn sighed. *Here we go again...* She glanced up every so often to keep an eye on her Grannie.

'I blame all this Facebook and Twitter nonsense if you ask me. It's not healthy,' agreed Louisa. 'Makes them unstable in my opinion.'

Kathryn's head spun towards her mother.

'There was that case recently wasn't there, of a boy who spent every waking moment on his computer, and then flipped out and killed his sister – slashed at his mother's face with a carving knife too.'

Louisa shook her head.

'Dreadful behaviour,' Grannie said.

'He had one of those learning difficulties I think,' added Louisa. 'Autism or Asperger's it was. If he had spent a little less time glued to the computer screen in those second life programs, he would have been better able to cope with real life.'

'Oh, I agree,' said Grannie. 'I asked one of the boys about his Facebook thing, and who all these friends were. He's nine years old – how does he know three hundred people? They get these 'friend' requests, and they just say yes.'

'You have to be thirteen to go on Facebook,' interrupted Kathryn.

Louisa stared back at her daughter with a look of trying to work out the relevance of the statement.

'And anyway, it's actually quite interesting,' continued Kathryn with self-assurance. 'They've done quite a lot of research, and its shown that social networking is a brilliant way of enabling people with Asperger's Syndrome to socialise and network.'

'Was this in one of your journals?' Louisa frowned.

Kathryn ignored the remark. 'Where a kid with Asperger's would perhaps never be able to speak up in a crowded room, they've seen it happen that online they can speak up, answer, provide support, and land jobs that lead them to have a successful *real* life – as you call it.'

Kathryn punctuated the last words of her argument with a forceful passion that, for a moment, silenced her Mum and Grannie.

'That's very interesting, Kathryn,' Louisa replied, before turning back to Grannie with a barely disguised frown.

Kathryn rolled her eyes towards the ceiling, and slapped together some more sausage meat and bacon. She moved on to the stuffing mixture, mixing up sticky balls of flavour, and trying to ignore her mother and grandmother's conversation as it returned in time to the news reports and the faults of social networking. She quietly returned the dish of sausage meat and stuffing to the fridge, did some basic clearing up, and slipped away from the conversation. She returned to the lounge and slipped easily back into her spot at the end of the sofa. Retrieving her book, she opened it to where she had got to, but found herself unable to read. Scowling at the page in front of her, she was fuming inside over her mother's prejudice and lack of understanding. And the more she got angry over people's lack of understanding, the more she thought of Louis.

For a moment, Kathryn pictured Louis next to her. She remembered the invitation coming to her from her parents, and Louis' glad acceptance of Christmas in this house.

She felt Louis' arm slip around her shoulders, and his breath close to her. They looked through the holiday brochure on her lap, leafing through the pages and exclaiming occasionally over something that one of them had seen. It felt nice – proper – to be sat here in her parent's living room, with wood burner blazing and her boyfriend sitting next to her.

'Aperitif?'

Kathryn jumped in her seat and looked up. Her dad was stood in front of her, with a glass of port in one hand and a bottle in the other.

'Err, yeah – thanks.'

'So what would you like? Port, sherry, glass of wine? I think we might have some of last year's sloe gin left.'

Wine was almost across her lips before she hesitated, overwhelmed by the choice.

'Oh, sloe gin, please.'

She glanced round, about to ask Louis what he wanted before she remembered that he wasn't there. As her father bustled out of the room she looked back down into her lap, where the holiday brochure was now once again her book.

Finding her place once more, she delved back into the story, reading the rest of the current chapter and one more after that, before the rest of the family joined her in the lounge for their pre-dinner drinks. Kathryn joined in with the meandering conversation that followed, while staring into the sparkling, magical Christmas tree across the room. Through squinting and half-closed eyes, Kathryn made the fairy lights do funny effects in front of her, and she lost herself in her imagination and the potential photographic shots that formed themselves in her mind.

2

Christmas morning came, and for maybe the first ever time, Kathryn slept through to a leisurely, festive lie-in. Her phone winked new messages at her from the bedside table. She sat herself up in bed and pulled the phone to her. There were two messages, one each from Charlotte and Eleanor, both wishing her Happy Christmas. She smiled, and sent her good wishes in return.

Downstairs she could begin to hear the crashing and clattering of breakfast being made, and a turkey being put into the oven. Kathryn swung her legs out of bed, grabbed her dressing gown, and headed to the bathroom.

A little while later, she headed downstairs with a small handful of presents to add to those at the base of the tree, before going to join her family. The normal breakfast table of cereal and toast was augmented with servings of scrambled eggs - a deep rich yellow from their neighbours' chickens - and smoked salmon.

Kathryn wished everyone a happy Christmas and slipped into her usual place. Her mother and Grannie were already in their best Christmas clothes, and so Kathryn - after glancing down at her own outfit of old jeans and lumberjack shirt - shared a relaxed grin with her father, who was similarly casually dressed in soft corduroys and comfortable sweater.

With breakfast cleared away, Kathryn's mother and grandmother set to preparing the lunch, while Kathryn set out with her dad, in their boots, into the woods to walk the dog. Scruff bounded back through the woods with a soggy stick between his teeth, a festive ribbon hanging from his collar, and mud splattered up his hocks. If dogs could smile, then Scruff was definitely smiling. He looped round behind Kathryn's legs and bounded back off up the path. Kathryn laughed as they stomped through the woods. They laughed and joked, taking the mickey mercilessly out of Grannie.

'Aagghh, Dad!' Kathryn vented. 'They annoyed me so much yesterday.'

Her father's response was everything that Kathryn could have wished for, understanding, compassionate, and moreover intelligent. He didn't pretend to know much about autism, and much less about Asperger's, but believed what Kathryn said about it, and seemed to find the whole social networking as a tool toward social understanding as something that was completely understandable.

Kathryn loved her dad. He had retired earlier this year from his nine to five office job, and was loving the new found opportunities to work with his hands in the outdoors. He had started going to a green gym that worked out in the woods, and he started to point out things in the woodland that he had been involved with setting up and clearing.

They turned down another path, pausing for a moment while they called Scruff, and watched as he stopped, listened, bounded around in circles in a hopeless attempt to chase squirrels, and ran to join them. They moved on again, taking a narrower path down the side of the hill that led them eventually into a lane between two gardens, and to the road right next to the village pub.

Dad headed indoors, leaving Kathryn waiting at a table holding onto Scruff by his lead. It was only a minute or so later that her dad came back out, carrying a couple of pints of the local ale, and took a seat opposite Kathryn. Scruff moved suddenly, as Rupert took his seat, and wrenched her arm sharply. She winced as a shot of pain stung the fairground wound on her arm.

'Still bothering you,' her dad said, taking a first sip of beer. 'How did you get on with trying to get compensation?'

Kathryn shook her head slowly.

'No luck,' she answered. 'The council put me in touch with the ride operators, but they don't exist. The address was a field outside of Charlbury.'

Her dad frowned.

'That kind of irresponsibility makes me so angry.'

Kathryn nodded and frowned sadly. She drank from her beer.

'Your mum and I, we were sorry to hear about – Lewis, wasn't it?'

'Louis,' Kathryn corrected.

Her father nodded.

'It was stupid of me, really,' she said with regret in her mouth. 'One big, stupid misunderstanding on my part. I thought one thing, and acted too rashly.'

Her dad reached across the table to take his daughter's hand in his.

'I'm sure it wasn't like that. These things always have reasons, and you can only act on your best knowledge at the time.'

Kathryn smiled weakly.

Bang! A cheap plastic toy leapt from the end of the cracker along with a tissue paper hat. Kathryn sat around the dining table with her closest of family, with plates of golden meat and serving dishes of steaming vegetables. Her dad told a bad joke very well, and everyone groaned over poorly disguised laughter. As Kathryn tucked into the delicious dinner, she glanced up at the space at the end of the table where Louis could have been sitting. As she looked away, she saw her dad catch her eye. She knew that he knew what she was thinking.

After dinner they all moved to the lounge where presents were waiting, and Kathryn set about passing them out from under the tree. As she picked out her own presents, she noted the size and shape of them, mostly guessing from the book or CD shape what they were; all except for one from her parents, that was a larger, rectangular box. When it came to retreating to her end of the sofa with her stash of presents, she vowed to leave that one until last.

Kathryn peeled back the Sellotape securing her present from Grannie. She could tell it was a book from the outset, and a sizeable one at that. She gasped, hardly believing what it might be, and tore back the paper to reveal a large, lavishly bound single volume of stories.

'What's that you've got there?' asked Louisa.

Kathryn held up the book for her mother to see.

'A new edition of *The Albion Book of Ballads*,' Kathryn beamed. 'Thanks Grannie, this is brilliant.'

'I hope it's the right one,' said Grannie. 'Of course, if I'd known, I'd have asked you to make use of your discount and given you a cheque. It's one of your lot's publications.'

Kathryn turned the book over and saw, as Grannie had said, the stylised image of the wren on the book of learning that signified a University Press book. She flicked through the book, opening the pages at random to soak up the words.

Towards the end of the present session, the large, rectangular present from 'Mum and Dad' was still left to be opened. Amongst the presents neatly stashed on the cushion next to her, there were already individual presents from both 'Mum' and 'Dad', a novel from the current bestsellers list, and from her father a CD of classical string music by *The Dumas Quartet*. Kathryn lifted the last remaining present up and considered it. She gave it a gentle shake, but it didn't rattle.

'It was your father's idea,' said Louisa. 'As usual he's spent far too much on you.'

'We thought you deserved something special,' he said. 'After what you've been through.'

Kathryn started fiddling with the Sellotape; peeling it back, her heart raced with childish excitement as to what it could be. She hung back from tearing the paper away through, not wanting the surprise or the anticipation to be over.

'Are you not going to open it?' Grannie asked brashly.

Kathryn grinned. She peeled away the tape from the ends, and smoothed out the paper. Gently she folded it back, and gasped. She looked up at her dad, and across to her mum, before returning her gaze to her dad.

'You haven't?'

She had only seen a few letters and half a picture, but she couldn't believe what was in her lap. Kathryn pulled back the last fold of paper, and there in front of her, on her lap, was a box containing a Tamron 70–300 lens.

'You shouldn't have. This is too much.'

'I hope it's the right one. The Canon one was about four times the price, but the man in the shop recommended it–'

'It's perfect, Dad.'

With the box still in her hands, she got to her feet to go and thank her parents properly, pressing a kiss to her Dad's cheek.

'We thought, since your course seemed to be going well – that you would find it useful,' continued Rupert.

Kathryn couldn't shift the broadest grin from her face. She kissed her mum too, and stood for some moments longer in the middle of the lounge just staring at the box. Eventually she returned to the sofa and unpacked it from its polystyrene and plastic wrapping. She stared at the lens in awe, hardly believing in its existence. She tried twisting the zoom.

'I've got to try it.'

Kathryn placed it carefully back in the box and dashed out of the room, to scamper up the stairs. Her footsteps padded across the ceiling of the lounge and back. Moments later and she burst back into the room, where she promptly set about switching lenses on her camera, and began playing with it.

She lifted the viewfinder to her eye and moved it around the room, zooming in, and in, on her Dad's eye.

'Wow!'

She pressed down on the shutter. Reviewing the picture on the tiny three-inch screen, she could see the razor sharp definition of her Dad's eye and lashes, set against the soft depth of field of the surrounding face.

Over the next few days, between sleeping and eating nice food and all those festive extras, Kathryn divided her time between playing with her newly revitalised camera and delving into the thickly rich book of ballads.

Walks with Scruff became longer in time, if shorter in distance. She would head up through the woods behind the house and walk out across the fields above the village. On each new walk she would go out having learnt something new, from a combination of her books, the internet, and the manual, and would shoot shot after shot of the wildest outcrop of rock or rotting post, each with subtly different effects. During all of this Scruff would head off on his own chasing smells, only to bounce back to Kathryn and bark at her heels.

The book was an altogether different pleasure, one to be had in front of the fire. She would curl up on the end of the sofa, or in an armchair with her feet tucked back under her, and lose herself in the words. With her would be a mug of tea and some Christmas chocolates, or a glass of port or sloe gin and a bowl of mixed nuts and raisins.

She found some of the stories vaguely familiar, like she had read them before; others she was discovering completely anew. At every turn of the page she discovered something new; an echo here, a memory there, of stories she already knew. She felt that this book was going to be the beginning of so many journeys. She tried dipping into the stories, but found it impossible not to just keep on turning the pages, reading it from front to back cover. The folklore and legend of England and its neighbouring isles came thickly through the words. Kathryn loved it; how there were good elves and bad elves; tree nymphs and pixies; witches and wizards.

When she went out with her camera now and focused tightly on the intricacies of nature, she saw these places as houses in miniature for another world. Alone in the woods it was another world, one where she stood still and the silence would be broken by the snapping of a twig, or a scuffle of leaves from an unseen stranger. It was evidence that the other people of the world were also in the woods. Oddly, when Kathryn was on her own amongst the trees, she did not feel alone.

She did not feel alone either when she was lost in the book with characters who were so alive. As she read through the poetry, she could see literary epicentres for so many of the books she loved and adored. And she could see why it was that writers kept on coming back to this one book verse for the imaginative spur for their tales.

3

Grannie left two days after Boxing Day. Kathryn's father took her to get the bus, and Kathryn went along with him in the car. The hour and a half round trip was maybe the longest that Kathryn had been parted from both her camera and *The Albion Book of Ballads*. On the way home with her dad, she tried to explain to him how much that book meant to her.

'I don't think Grannie really knew what she was getting me, you know.'

Kathryn laughed, talking enthusiastically about her book as Rupert turned the car back onto the main road to Miles Cross.

'Your Grannie has very – conservative tastes. You shouldn't be mean about her.'

'Oh I'm not. It's a brilliant present,' said Kathryn. 'I just wish that Grannie could have known how fabulous it was, for herself.'

'We can't all have your refined intellect for literature,' Rupert chortled.

Kathryn grinned.

'Thanks for a great Christmas, Dad. I feel so spoilt – so many nice presents, and—'

She stopped on receiving a sideways glance from Rupert, that told her in no uncertain terms that she was being ridiculous.

'I know I said this before, Kathy,' he said. 'But you've been through it these past few months. You deserved a break.'

Kathryn smiled, looking down as she felt the warmth of her face blushing. Someone else who deserved a break, Kathryn considered later that afternoon when ensconced once more in her book, was Tam Lin. Between Janet and the Faery Queen, he was having a rough time of it. Not content with having him wrong his true love, the Faery Queen had entrapped him so that every seven years he relived the same life, having to wrong his true love again and again. The writer, the storyteller of this tale, certainly had it in for Tam. She supposed that she was feeling for Janet, but how could she? She decided, decisively that, if anyone was in need of a break, it was her Tam.

Kathryn felt the passion of this story more than any other. She felt in her heart the pain of Tam's life, and through it a connection to his story. Immediately upon finishing it she read it over again, and returned to it later that night in bed before she turned off the light.

In her dreams she lived the story again, where she was both storyteller and Janet. She travelled away from home through the forbidden woods. *Why did these stories always involve dark and foreboding woods?* She met with Tam Lin, but a Tam with the face and voice of Louis. Back home, the old knight – a wistful, smiling version of her own dad – advised her of a herbal remedy for her injury.

She woke, with a start, a cold sweat on her brow and a stinging pain down her left arm. She sat bolt upright in her bed and reached to turn on the light, before guzzling down half a glass of water. She collapsed back into her pillow.

Looking at her phone she saw the time was only 3:30am, and it was pitch black and deathly quiet outside. As she sat still, with the covers pulled to her, she could hear the slow ticking clock from downstairs, and the mournful whine and whistle of the pipes.

She frowned, and reaching for her laptop where it lay on the floorboards, she pushed up the lid to an illuminated, virtual world. Hitting refresh on her Facebook, she read a couple of comments to a status update which made her smile before turning to her messages. There was one from Eleanor about tomorrow...

Kathryn tapped out her reply, realising at the end of three long paragraphs that it was no longer the quick response that it had been intended to be. She clicked send, checked her news feed, browsed the latest items on her Twitter page, and checked her email, before closing the lid and snuggling back down in her bed.

Lying there in her bed, she listened to the sounds of the night – at a fox out there in the woods, and the whining and the murmuring of the pipes. Her mind emptied, and suddenly she was asleep.

Day broke, and the early morning sun slanted in through the windows. Kathryn woke, lying still for a moment before propping herself up on her pillows and reading for a bit, until she heard her mum and dad surfacing. She got up, washed and dressed warmly, and headed downstairs. Scruff greeted her enthusiastically in the hall, and she offered to take him for his first early-morning walk.

Kathryn fastened up her duffle coat and slid her hands down into her gloves, toasty warm from being left in the cupboard over the boiler. She tramped out into the frosty late December day, with Scruff charging excitedly off across and around the garden. She called him back to her as they slipped through the gate at the back of the garden, and into the woods.

'I'm going to miss our walks together,' she said out loud to the dog, who pricked up his ears in response, wagged his tail, and bounded off after another squirrel.

After breakfast Kathryn retreated to her bedroom to repack her bags, a task that involved her retrieving her belongings from locations around the house. She left *The Albion Book of Ballads* out for as long as possible, always hoping that she would find herself with only just enough time to sort herself out a turkey sandwich and some festive nibbles in a Tupperware box, before her dad gave her a lift to Bristol to catch her train.

The book of ballads remained close to the top of her shoulder bag on the train, but her journey was instead spent browsing a photography book, eating her lunch and texting her friends. The train rattled its way slowly through the English countryside, along the branch line to the quiet Cotswold town of Little Gidding. As the sun was just beginning to set the train slid into the platform, and Kathryn alighted to be met by Eleanor, with her brother Ben and his wife Kirsten.

Kathryn settled into her friend's family's house with ease. It was an old farm on the edge of the next village, although the family were as far from farmers as they could be. The whole family had an academic bent to them. Eleanor's father Guðni, an Anglophile Icelander, was a professor at the university, and Ben was rapidly making a name for himself in the world of climate science. His wife Kirsten was actually Eleanor's friend originally, having met on a conservation holiday abroad, and was now a locum veterinary nurse. The meal table discussions tended to border on intense theoretical debates across a range of subjects, whether it be news, politics, science, or any one of the arts.

Kathryn found it wonderful to be able to really discuss ideas, without the fear of it sparking one of her mother's or Grannie's prejudices. Even though Guðni and Ben did have good senses of humour, she did at times pine for her own father's sometimes off the wall goofiness.

Following Kathryn's first meal in Little Gidding – a sumptuously tender and rich venison casserole, followed by a large slice of Christmas pudding – the family all retired to the low-ceilinged lounge with an open log fire, and to another round of presents. As Kathryn added her few to the pile under the tree, it seemed to her that for a day closer to New Year, there was an alarmingly large number of them.

Kathryn sat with the warm glow of contentment – possibly also from the hearth of the fire – as her friends opened their presents from her; the bottle of single malt for Guðni, and hyacinth bulbs for Eleanor's mother. Ben seemed to like the popular science book, as did Kirsten seem to be happy with her novel. She watched, grinning, as Eleanor unwrapped her present; one of her own photographs framed – a black and white picture of The Press with selective tinting.

'Oh Kathryn, that's brilliant,' Eleanor gushed. She got up from her place on the hearth rug and hugged her thanks to her friend.

Kathryn remained mute, caught between pleasure at the reaction to her present and embarrassment for how well it had gone down. She glanced down at her own pile of presents, all still unopened.

She chose the first to open – from Ben and Kirsten – and carefully tore through the paper around the Sellotape, pulling from the wrapping a DVD boxset of *Battlestar Galactica*.

'You haven't got them, have you?' asked Ben, hesitantly.

Kathryn shook her head, excitedly.

'No, and I've not seen them either,' she said. 'Been meaning to – but you know – always too much month left at the end of the money.'

'We decided to get it for you back last Easter when we saw you,' Kirsten added. 'Remember? You had just read the *Four Quartets—*'

'For about the fifteenth time,' Kathryn said, beaming.

'We were all talking about it, and we decided then that you'd like this. If you watch it at the same time as reading the Quartets, you can see some amazing parallels,' continued Kirsten.

'Yeah?' Kathryn nodded vigorously. 'Cool.'

There was a present from Charlotte too, the new album from one of their favourite bands. Kathryn grinned with pleasure as she remembered sending Charlotte off for the Christmas holidays with exactly the same present.

Next up was a present from Eleanor. A preliminary feel around the edges told Kathryn it was a book, and a slim hardback at that. She peeled back the tape and unfolded the wrapping. The cover struck her immediately. It was a black and white photograph, with some selective tinting, of a field in autumn, with a dark silhouette of a hemlock stalk set against a misty, smoky background, and some faint blurs that could be people. *J. Rawson's Book of Essays & Stories* – the title and author were blended into one.

'She works in one of the university libraries in Wren Hoe, I think,' said Eleanor.

Kathryn nodded, unable to take her gaze away from the picture.

'I've read a couple of bits in it,' continued Eleanor. 'Thought of you – Rawson evidently shares your same passion for old myth and reworking stories, which she then talks about along with other books in her essays.'

Kathryn opened the beautifully bound and typeset book, leafing slowly through the pages to the contents list.

'There's a brilliant essay on Diana Wynne Jones, and then her own version of Tam Lin – you've got to read *The Hyacinth Girl* first.'

Kathryn looked up as Eleanor mentioned Tam Lin. She saw an image of Louis, standing bare-chested in the forest in his guise as the Anglo Saxon nobleman. She felt the explanation of her dream tumbling forward out of her mind towards her mouth, only stopping herself just in time. She felt her cheeks burn with embarrassment. She ducked her head down and leafed through the pages. There, at page forty-three, was the start of *The Hyacinth Girl.*

'Thanks, Ellie,' said Kathryn. 'This is brilliant.'

4

Charlotte arrived the following day, and together they all saw in the New Year. Guðni cooked a massive four-course roast dinner, with a cheese board to follow; later on they played board games, and some card games that Eleanor and Ben had learnt while travelling. The house rocked to the sound of laughter and merriment.

At midnight itself they switched on the television for Big Ben and the fireworks live from London, and Guðni charged their glasses with champagne. They sang *Alde Lang Syne*, and each greeted the other, in turn, into the New Year. For a while they stood outside in the garden and listened to the church bells of Little Gidding, and then Guðni stoked up the fire and brought out the whisky. They sank into their chairs and chatted, drinking their way through the bottle of single malt as the fire died in the grate.

One by one they each staggered off to bed, until Kathryn, Eleanor and Charlotte were left. Kathryn lifted her whisky glass to her eye and peered through the finger of amber liquid, watching as the scene through it became distorted. She frowned at her thoughts and sighed.

'You still thinking of Louis?' Eleanor asked.

Kathryn glanced up briefly before taking a sip of her drink.

'Have you tried texting him?' Charlotte joined in.

'I can't.'

'Of course you can, just text him. Wish him a happy New Year. Here,' Eleanor said, reaching for Kathryn's mobile.

'No really, I can't,' said Kathryn. 'I don't have his number.'

Eleanor and Charlotte both looked up, surprised.

Kathryn swigged down more whisky and sighed.

'After that night at the fair I was going to text him, but his number was gone. I must have deleted it – not that I remember. And every message.'

'That's weird...?' Eleanor said, glancing at Charlotte.

'I really don't remember doing it. But it's like it never existed.'

Eleanor shook her head slowly.

'Send him an email, then.'

'Suppose I could.' Kathryn said, then shrugged. 'I'll do it tomorrow.'

'It is tomorrow,' said Eleanor.

Kathryn rolled her eyes at the retort, and sank further into her armchair with her whisky.

'I'll get your computer if you like?' Charlotte offered brightly, half out of her seat already.

'It's on the shelf next to my bed,' Kathryn replied, lazily and reluctantly.

Charlotte nodded and left the room at a bound. She left Kathryn and Eleanor sitting opposite each other in a state of bleary-eyed tiredness. After a few minutes Charlotte returned to the room, already lifting up the lid and bringing it out of hibernation, so that by the time she handed it to Kathryn it was downloading emails. She crouched down next to Kathryn and leaned across the arm of the chair to watch.

Kathryn passed her glass to Charlotte to hold, and settled her fingers to the keyboard. Nimbly she brought up a new message and clicked to begin typing Louis' email address. She stopped.

'Damn it! I can't even remember the address.'

She dragged the mouse across the screen and brought up her address book. Scrolling through the list forwards and backwards, she resorted to searching.

'I'm sure it was here—' Kathryn cursed through her teeth and narrowed her gaze onto the laptop screen.

After a few seconds more, she looked up. She glanced from Charlotte to Eleanor with a worried frown across her face, and a panic-ridden voice.

'All my emails to and from Louis are gone.'

'Has your computer been hacked?' asked Eleanor.

Kathryn shook her head and shrugged. Charlotte took the laptop from her and performed her own searches, balancing it on the arm of the chair.

'I'd have said a virus had got you, but it would have been more indiscriminate.'

'I must have deleted them – *all* of them. You'd think I'd remember doing something like that. Something so deliberate.'

She shook her head slowly and closed the lid of her laptop. Her mind bothered her over the lost emails. She frowned deeply, unable to shake the thoughts from her mind. They were still circling in her head later, as she tucked herself down in her bed and tried to get some sleep. Across the room in the other bed, Charlotte was already asleep; and Kathryn lay, head snuggled down in the pillow, with the lamp on, just drifting.

She woke sometime long after dawn, not being able to remember when she had turned out the light, and though unable to remember her dream, knowing that she had slept well, and deeply. No one mentioned the lost emails or the lack of contact details again, and Kathryn was able to push the thoughts to the back of her mind, burying them beneath the excitement of taking her camera with its new lens out for a walk with her friends in the Wrenshire countryside; not to mention the delights of intelligent science fiction from the DVD boxset that Ben had given her. The following night, all that Kathryn could dream of were galactic fighter pilots, and the alternate realities and dreamscapes of Cylons inside one's head.

The following day, Kathryn packed her rucksack again and got the bus from Little Gidding back to Wren Hoe. Changing to a tram at Wolvercote to take her back down into the city centre, Kathryn found herself feeling the achy, empty pit in her stomach that she always felt after a sustained time with people, and the comfort of being with family and friends.

Then she passed the corner of Bevington Road, and the snatched glimpse of the house where Louis had his flat. Through the bare branches of trees in winter, Kathryn saw the boarding across the windows and the For Sale sign hanging over the wall. She swung her head round to see it for longer, to catch the name of the company. *Where did Louis live now? When did he move out?* Suddenly she had a need to track him down and ask him yet more questions; but how to do that when she had no contact details?

The tram rattled on into the centre of town and Kathryn got off at the top end of St Giles, walking with her bags down Little Clarendon Street into Jericho. Back home at the little house in Juxon Street, Kathryn unpacked her bags, keeping her stash of presents neatly stacked on her desk. Her feelings did a somersault inside of her, and she felt a little ill with the emptiness of life at home. She took her presents downstairs, along with her laptop, and settled in the lounge to read and surf the web, with the last of the Christmas television turned on in the corner for comfort.

The coloured lights twinkled on the half-size artificial tree, slightly sad-looking in front of the fireplace. Kathryn sat, legs curled up next to her on the sofa, reading her books. She had read J. Rawson's *Hyacinth Girl* twice by now, and her essay on Diana Wynne Jones' *Fire & Hemlock* which went some way to explaining the inspiration behind the story.

As the evening wore on, Kathryn felt her eyes begin to tire; her head nodded down into her lap, and more than once she woke herself up with a nod and a snore. It was the last night of the holidays, and so, with some reluctance, Kathryn gathered up her belongings, switched out the lights, and headed up to her room.

It wasn't until she was washed, in her pyjamas and brushing her teeth that she remembered the For Sale sign outside Bevington House. When she had drawn back the covers and retreated to her bed, she did so taking her laptop with her and was quickly accessing the property websites. It took several attempts at tweaking the search criteria, but eventually she found it; the façade of the Edwardian house looming over the stone wall, with the blue door along the side. She clicked through to the details, while still reeling at the price, expecting to see details for several well-appointed flats, she quickly discovered that the whole building was up for sale.

She browsed through the gallery of room images and floor plans, recognising bits of it from her time there with Louis, but confused to see it as a whole house.

'It must have been done up by developers at the end of last year,' reasoned Charlotte, when they talked about it the following day at work.

'I thought that,' said Kathryn. She stared at the details again on her work computer. 'But some of Louis' furniture is still there. If a developer had gone through it, it would be all glistening white and new looking.'

'And they're more likely to divide it *into* flats than vice-versa,' Charlotte agreed.

'I'm beginning to think that I dreamt the whole thing.'

Kathryn clicked away from the house details and returned to the production database. She pulled open her filing drawer and browsed through the tabs for her article file, which she pulled out onto the desk. Then she stopped, staring at something at the back of her drawer.

'Kathryn?'

Charlotte stood up and looked over the divider between the two desks.

'What is it? What's wrong?'

Kathryn sat and stared. Eventually she bent closer, pulling back the rack of files to pull the box out from where it lay mostly concealed at the back of the drawer. It was a box for an iPod, and Kathryn quickly opened it to pick out the music player. She turned it over in her hands and read the inscription on the reverse.

'Kath?' Charlotte repeated.

Kathryn sat staring at the words etched into the metal casing in front of her.

'So he does exist,' she said.

'Kathryn?' Charlotte repeated.

Kathryn got to her feet, and passed the iPod across to Charlotte.

'Read what it says, for me, please.'

Charlotte took the iPod and read the inscription.

'Louis, for your music collection and mine, love Kathryn.'

Charlotte looked up.

'Seems pretty conclusive.'

5

Later that evening, after Kathryn finished work, she got the tram up to the Woodstock Road and walked the rest of the way to Bevington House. With still little idea of what she was actually going to do, she climbed down off the tram and waited for what might have been an age as it rattled off up the line. In the dark of the January night, Bevington House looked a dark, foreboding, and unwelcoming place.

Eventually she made up her mind and crossed the road. Her gaze was drawn to the For Sale sign hanging over the wall. The gate was, as expected, locked, and so Kathryn followed the wall around the corner into Bevington Road, where she found the gap between the end of the wall and next door's fence. She squeezed and pushed her way through the shrubbery, to stand in the garden at the side of the house.

Kathryn stopped. A haunting flute melody sang out from somewhere nearby. She spun around on her feet, expecting to see someone but found nothing more than a deserted street. She caught her arm on a clawing yew branch, tripped, and fell. The music had stopped, but now there was laughter, the sound of giggling children's voices, and their feet in the grass as they ran off.

'Who's there?' Kathryn called out.

There was no answer.

Kathryn moved on slowly through the shadows, and listened for anything; beyond the wall came the sound of cars on the road, and the rattle of another tram. She trod the path to the front door. The porch was a darker shadow, beyond the long shadows that stretched across the moonlit garden. Looking down at the doorstep and the mat which proudly welcomed visitors, she found that it was muddy and threadbare, and stank somewhat of pee. Kathryn screwed up her nose, and remembered how a few months ago the garden might have needed work, but not like this. Then it had still looked lived in. How could it have changed so dramatically, to something so rundown and dilapidated so soon?

On the off-chance, Kathryn reached out and turned the handle. It moved, and the door gave a little. She pushed a little harder, and the swollen wood that was stuck in the frame gave a bit more. After a more determined shove with her shoulder it swung inward, and she staggered forwards into the hall, hardly able to believe what she was doing.

From the little light that filtered in from outside, she could make out that the hallway was completely deserted, and the stairs swept upwards into the darkening gloom. This was not the flat that Louis had shown her round, and yet there were echoes of the place in which she had spent so much of her time only a few months previously.

She stepped forward cautiously and pushed open the door at the far end of the hall. She found herself in a kitchen that was unmistakably Louis'. Instinctively she reached out to where the light switch should be and flicked it. Nothing. She flicked it again, and moved on. Her eyes began to become accustomed to the dark. Over on the counter, she could recognise Louis' kettle and toaster; and there – the mug tree. She reached out and picked off a mug. In the dark she could make out the illustrated mug that she had given him, for the anniversary of their first month together.

Her heart leapt as she picked out the visible signs of Louis' presence – his existence even. Glad thoughts, though, turned sour, as the thought hit her of where Louis was now. Kathryn shivered, feeling the goose bumps rise along her arms. Above her, the old house creaked and groaned. Kathryn froze as her heart thumped, listening to the rhythmic beat slow down again while the house fell silent.

Kathryn returned to the hall, about to leave the house when she stopped again, looking back over her shoulder. The stairs. She turned and returned to the newel post and stroked the oiled wood, feeling the dust beneath her fingers. Nervously and cautiously, Kathryn climbed the stairs, the treads creaking under her with every step. She turned at the half-flight and continued on to the first landing. A shaft of moonlight sliced in through the window, giving her light to see the old nursery at the end of the corridor. She moved on slowly across the floorboards, and pushed the door open further. Beyond the dark shadows she could see that the room was sparsely furnished; a child's playroom that had been left suddenly. On a tiny cane chair across the room sat a bear. Kathryn recognised it immediately, and rushing forward she grabbed it up and hugged it tightly.

'Ardizzoni!' she exclaimed. 'Oh Louis, where are you?'

She buried her face in the familiar smell of Louis' tattered and much-loved bear, breathing in the musty smell.

Her thoughts were broken by a scream that curdled her blood – a child's scream. She swung round and leapt back. The white face of an owl was at the window, wings flapping at the glass. Kathryn relaxed and composed herself as she realised what it was. She clutched the bear tightly, and ran quickly down the stairs and out through the hall. Squeezing through the gap in the garden wall, she continued to run to the further tram stop before boarding.

She stayed sat in her seat on the tram, clutching the teddy bear to her tightly. The tram rattled on down through St Giles to the last stop. Kathryn walked slowly, eyes fixed ahead of her, across the street in front of the Ashmolean. She walked on in a daze down, into Cornmarket where the lights reflected across her face. Groups of people ducked and weaved out of pubs and side streets, and Kathryn walked through them all, oblivious.

Around one corner a group of younger children came gabbling and excited, high-pitched voices that cut through the traffic noise. Kathryn turned her head as they passed and saw her – Sarah. She was with Caz and a gang of other mates, but it was unmistakably her. Sarah's head turned and looked back, as if suddenly aware that someone was watching. Kathryn's gaze met Sarah's; she looked away, and walked on down the street.

Later that night, Kathryn arrived home and slumped into the hall. She pushed the door closed behind her and continued upstairs to the room. Once inside, she sat the bear down at the head of her bed before dumping her bag by her desk, slipping off her winter coat. She returned to the bed again and sat in front of the bear, readjusting his seating position.

'You're a mess, Ardizzoni,' said Kathryn. 'So, so dusty.'

She retrieved a hair brush from a drawer, and set about brushing the dust and cobwebs from the bear's fur.

'Where's your daddy, then?' Kathryn asked the bear. She brushed the top of Ardizzoni's head, and caught herself in the bear's gaze. For a moment, it was like Louis himself was looking back at her.

Kathryn continued to brush the dirt from the fur, and felt tears form in the corners of her eyes and trickle down her cheeks.

'Oh Louis, where are you?'

Kathryn picked up the bear, held it in front of her and fixed her gaze on Ardizzoni, before hugging him tight and close. She lay down with the bear in her arms and drifted off into sleep; she woke again the following morning with the sun pouring in through the open window, and the sounds of people going to work.

Kathryn picked herself up slowly, sitting Ardizzoni back up on her pillow. She glanced across at the clock radio and the time hit her. She sat forward, bolt upright, and swore sharply.

Kathryn headed back out to the quad with Charlotte and Eleanor and their lunch, to settle themselves down on the wall that surrounded the duck pond.

'So—' Charlotte opened the conversation. 'What happened last night? Did you go to the house?'

Kathryn nodded. She held her sandwich in her hands, staring vacantly ahead; picking crumbs absentmindedly, which she flicked towards the ducks.

'It was really sad,' Kathryn began. 'The whole place is empty and boarded up, and you know, it looked like it's been like that for years.'

'How's that possible? You were always in and out of there last summer – and there were other families, you said.'

Charlotte looked up at her friend from where she had taken a seat, cross-legged on the lawn. Kathryn shook her head and shrugged.

'That's the other weird thing. When I saw the agent's details on the net – it *is* just one house...'

She stopped, as she caught the questioning expression from both Charlotte and Eleanor.

'The door was open. I probably shouldn't have but—'

'You didn't?' gasped Charlotte. 'No one saw you?'

Kathryn shook her head, and explained how the inside was both the same flat as she was used to, and also a different house. She told them about the child's voices, the footsteps she had heard in the garden, and of Louis' old bear that she had found in the nursery. She shivered at this last remembrance, thinking of where Ardizzoni was sitting now at the head of her own bed in the small house in Juxon Street.

'So he does exist then? Louis...' said Charlotte.

'Well he's not my imaginary friend, if that's what you're asking,' Kathryn laughed.

'Obviously.'

Eleanor forked up salad from her bowl.

'How do you suppose he did it?'

Kathryn glanced round, perplexed by Eleanor's question.

'Well, you knew him living in a clean and tidy flat; but there was a disused house behind it...'

Eleanor stopped. She could see that Kathryn's attention had drifted off elsewhere.

Kathryn sat on the floor next to her bed, with her laptop to one side and her books of ballads and poetry and legends spread out around her. She glanced back across her shoulder, to where Ardizzoni appeared to be watching her from his position on her pillow. She turned again and returned to her notebook, to write down all that she remembered about her Louis. She didn't know exactly why, but she felt it necessary to write down everything that she knew about him. Referring to her own diary and her blog, she filled in the gaps and remembered all the details of her relationship, smiling fondly at the memories.

The first thing she realised was those months with Louis were real, whatever the evidence of a deserted house, deleted emails and missing Facebook profiles. She had the memories and the diary entries, and – glancing back at Ardizzoni – she had his bear. She wasn't crazy, and she wasn't going mad; but at the same time she had begun to see the similarities between her own situation with Louis, and some of the stories in her books. She re-read J. Rawson's essay on *Fire & Hemlock* for the fourth time since Christmas, and that evening she dug out her old battered copy of the paperback.

She put down her journal and reached instead for the novel, and opening it to the first page she stared at the words. Two memories. Sitting in the bedroom of her little shared house in Wren Hoe, with her dearest possessions around her, Kathryn felt like Polly with her two sets of memories. She read on, reliving the story she had first read a decade ago and quickly, once again, found it impossible to stop turning the pages.

6

By the time the weekend came, Kathryn had read through the book to its thrilling if poignant conclusion, one that did not fail to delight her again just as it had done the first time that she read it. She was also becoming queasily aware of how similar she was herself to Polly. And if she were Polly, then surely that made Louis a version of Tom Lynn. Variations of these thoughts ebbed through her dreams, and the half-consciousness just before waking.

She woke eventually to the sound of a hammering on the door, and a telephone call from Charlotte on the front step. Kathryn flew out of bed and tumbled down the stairs to let Eleanor and Charlotte in, with garbled apologies as she set about making coffee and getting ready.

Half an hour or so later, the three of them headed out on their way to Bevington House. As it was a sunny if not cold January morning, they walked up through Jericho along the canal, past the boatyards and light industry that spilled out onto the tow path. When they arrived at the boarded-up Edwardian house, it felt straightaway different to how it had done in the dark.

'How did you get in?' asked Charlotte.

'Just round the corner, here,' said Kathryn, as she led them round the corner to the narrow gap between the wall and next door's fence.

'You squeezed through here?' Eleanor asked, pointing at the gap barely eight inches at its widest and overgrown with nettles.

'It didn't seem so narrow in the dark,' Kathryn said, as she squeezed herself through into the garden. Charlotte and Eleanor followed, keen to get off the public-facing road as quickly as possible. They scrambled through the bushes, unhooking themselves from thorny tendrils and clawing fingers of branches.

'This was where I heard those children laughing and playing.'

Eleanor glanced up at her friend, and then at Charlotte. They shrugged.

'And you didn't turn back then?'

Kathryn shook her head.

'I knew they were on the other side of the wall. It was just the way that the dark makes you think that sounds are elsewhere.'

She pushed on through the garden, leading her friends round the side of the house to the front door. Charlotte and Eleanor followed their friend through the ordered if unkempt garden.

'I thought you said it was overgrown?' asked Charlotte.

Kathryn stopped, looking about at the garden properly for the first time that afternoon; now that she did look at it, she could see that Charlotte was right. The flowerbeds were straggly, and the grass long, but nothing was completely wild and overgrown.

'Things do look differently in the dark,' Kathryn said, with a shrug.

She led them on around the side of the house, up to the porch with the ivy growing over it, and the front door.

'One house, you say?' said Eleanor.

Kathryn looked round at her friend to see her nod towards the front door. She turned and looked again. There, just to the side of the front door, was the grey metal box with doorbells for different flats. Kathryn peered closer. Wiping away cobwebs and thick layers of grime, she could make out one name clearly: TUMNAL.

'Flat one,' she said. 'That's the one!'

Kathryn pounced forward and turned the handle, half expecting it to be locked. The door handle turned in her hand and she felt the door give a little. She pushed it further, and it came free of the frame. She stepped through into the hall and, stopped. The hall was not like the other night, but the hall of the flat she knew so well, with the curious blocked-in stairwell. She shook her head vehemently, before standing and gaping in disbelief and confusion.

'I – I don't understand! The stairs? The other night they were here!'

Eleanor stepped forward and ran her finger down the scratched and worn paintwork, and the peeling flakes of woodchip paper where they curled up against the woodwork.

'Well it's not new, that's for sure,' said Eleanor.

'This,' Charlotte said, looking up at Kathryn. 'It's his flat though? The doorbell?'

Kathryn nodded.

'It's Louis' flat alright. The kitchen's just through there—'

She pointed further down the tiled hallway and led the way. It was still very much Louis' kitchen that she found on the other side of the door; stripped of much of the personal, but still very much his. She stopped and stared ahead of her. She remembered her first visit here, when Louis was at the stove cooking up the dinner, and she had found herself looking at his collection of postcards, council notices, and shopping lists, that formed some kind of oddly beautiful collage. Now, one particular postcard stood out like no other; the postcard of an illustration from a favourite children's book, that she had sent to Louis for no other reason than she had liked it. Kathryn stepped forward and unpinned the card from the board. She turned it over in her hands, and read the note in her own handwriting. Her vision blurred, and she felt the tears as they welled up and began to run down her face.

'Where is he?'

Charlotte struggled to reply, as Kathryn fled from the kitchen and tore through the rest of the flat. In the lounge she found the bookshelves and sofas just as Louis had left them, if devoid of all but a few lonely books. The only piece of missing furniture was his antique desk, now marked out on the floor by squares of dust.

'It's like he just upped and left, but still had time to take some his things,' she said, as Charlotte and Eleanor joined her in in the room.

Kathryn squeezed back through the gap in the fence after her friends, and out onto the pavement at the side of Bevington Street.

'I have to find him,' she said, fired by what she had seen in the house. 'I don't pretend to understand what's happening here, except now I'm sure of it – he's in trouble.'

She stopped, going silent with her own thoughts.

'Kath?' asked Charlotte.

Kathryn looked up, finding herself on the street corner after being lost in her thoughts.

'Monday morning,' Kathryn said, as her friend's looked back at her. 'I think I'm going to be late in.'

Charlotte looked back, unsurprised.

'Duvet day?'

'Something like that,' replied Kathryn. 'Something I need to do.'

Charlotte frowned, and nodded with unspoken understanding.

7

Kathryn stood on the street on the east side of Wren Hoe, outside the 1960s frontage of the County School. She still didn't have anything such as a plan of what she was about to do, but she was here now, and she just had to try.

Across the road, she heard the bell sound for morning lessons, and watched as the last of the children funnelled in through the entrance. Still hesitant about what she had to do, she felt the waves of uncertainty break at her again. Then she remembered Louis' flat, and his abandoned teddy bear, and she strode forward and crossed the street.

The walk up to the school entrance transported Kathryn straight back to when she was still a child, albeit at a different school, and the fact that after the hive of activity and the screams and shouts, it was now deathly quiet, made her feel like she was sneaking in late. The naughty schoolgirl feelings only grew stronger as she buzzed the door for entry, waiting to be allowed into the airlock between the outside and the school within.

Kathryn stood for ages at the reception desk, finding it necessary in the end to cough loudly to attract the attention of the tall, spindly, peroxide-blonde tanned-like-leather, and surly receptionist.

'You should have said—'

'I – I did actually,' answered Kathryn.

'Coughing is no way to attract my attention.'

Kathryn was about to reply, and to state that she had tried the normal approaches but had been completely ignored. She stopped herself just in time, and instead forced a smile.

'So what can I do for you? We don't take in forgotten lunch boxes anymore.'

'I've not got any lunch boxes,' Kathryn began.

'What's his name?'

'Excuse me?'

Kathryn was alarmed by the woman's cold abruptness.

'Your son? His name?' the woman repeated, stiffly.

Kathryn was taken aback by the suggestion, but decided to let it pass.

'It was actually one of the teachers I was interested in,' explained Kathryn, as she tried to maintain a calm approach; something which was becoming increasingly difficult when pitted against the obstructive lady behind the desk.

'They are all teaching now. This is a school.'

Kathryn suppressed a grimace and a growl at this latest comment. Instead she smiled and replied cheerfully: 'I realise that, but it's just—'

She chewed on her lip, tossing around her choice of words in her mind.

'You do have a Louis Tumnal work here?'

Kathryn might as well have threatened the woman's husband for the reception that it got her. She stared coldly back at Kathry,n and folded her arms.

'Louis, did you say? We don't have anyone called Louis in this school.'

'Lewis then?' asked Kathryn. 'Lewis Tumnal? He teaches English.'

Before the lady could reply, the inner door to the office opened and a tall, older lady clipped into the office to deliver some files to the surly woman. The lady looked up and saw Kathryn.

'Who's this?'

Kathryn recognised the lady immediately from numerous newspaper articles and local history books; Miss Leroy, the all-but patron of the city and long-serving headmistress of the county school. The sour-faced receptionist looked about to answer, but Kathryn took her opportunity and leapt in with a rush of explanation.

'I'm looking for Louis Tumnal. He works here, teaching English.'

'And who are you?' Miss Leroy replied curtly.

'I – I'm K— his, umm – a friend,' answered Kathryn. 'I've not heard from him for a few weeks, and I just wanted to... He's okay, isn't he?'

Miss Leroy stared back at Kathryn with a cold, impassionate gaze.

'Lewis doesn't work here anymore.'

'Oh...'

Kathryn felt her heart sink inside her.

'You're obviously not that much a friend, if you didn't know he had left us.'

'We lost touch a few months ago. You know how it is. You don't know where he's gone now?'

'I thought you said that it was only a couple of weeks that you hadn't heard from Lewis?'

Kathryn stuttered, flailing for a response.

'I think we need to speak, don't you?' Miss Leroy said. She turned her attention to the receptionist.

'Let her through.'

The receptionist seemed surprised by the request, but after receiving a nod from the Head, she glared at Kathryn and buzzed open the inner doors. Kathryn pulled them open, and stepped through into the cold, institutional corridor within.

The door clicked shut behind her, and Kathryn stood alone for a moment in the dimly lit, shadowy corridor, gripped with inexplicable fear for what was to come. She felt goose-bumps rise all the way up her arms beneath her thick duffle coat. The feeling did not go when Miss Leroy joined her in the corridor, with a singular, sharp, and icy stare. Without saying a word, she turned and led Kathryn along the corridor to her office.

Once in the office, Miss Leroy swept around the end of the desk and eased herself into her throne-like chair. She nodded to the small, upright chair opposite, and Kathryn took a seat in front of her; instantly, she felt like she was twelve or thirteen again.

Miss Leroy said nothing at first, but retrieved a fountain pen from the tray in front of her and uncapped the lid. She pulled a notebook towards her, turned to a fresh page, and did not seem to be about to speak anytime soon.

'You were going to tell me about Louis? Lewis, I mean—' began Kathryn.

Miss Leroy raised a hand to silence Kathryn. A few moments later and she sat forward and looked directly across the desk at her.

'I don't recall saying that I was going to tell you anything.'

'Then why –?'

'I thought that *you* might like to tell *me* how you know Mr Tumnal?'

Miss Leroy smiled thinly.

'So you admit he works here?'

Kathryn leapt on the slightest admission of Louis' existence eagerly. If she was hoping for any more, she was disappointed, for her words were returned with a cold, dispassionate glare.

'I told you,' she said eventually. 'He was a friend.'

'Only a friend?' Miss Leroy asked, her question a leading one.

For some reason that Kathryn could not put her finger on, she found that she could not admit her relationship with Louis to Miss Leroy.

'We go to the same photography class,' explained Kathryn, convincingly she thought. 'Or we did. We were working on a project together before Christmas, but he's stopped coming, you see.'

'Maybe he just had enough of your interfering?' suggested Miss Leroy. 'It is quite tedious.'

The suggestion angered Kathryn. How dare she say such a thing when she didn't know her? She scowled.

'Interfering in Louis' life? Tedious?' Kathryn said, her face burning. 'Who are you to say whether I should or should not be interfering – which for the record I've not been – in anybody's life!'

Miss Leroy smiled thinly, looking at Kathryn over the top of her half-moon spectacles.

'My dear girl, as Headmistress of this school, my duty of care is not just to the children. I also have pastoral responsibilities to my staff.'

'You admit that he works here, then?'

Kathryn took pleasure in silencing Miss Leroy, if for a short time. She sat back and folded her arms deliberately.

'I'd like to see him, please.'

Miss Leroy sat back in her throne too. She raised her head up and looked down on Kathryn.

'Mr. Lewis Tumnal doesn't work here anymore.' Miss Leroy said, smiling with pleasure at the expression of shock on Kathryn's face. 'He left us at the end of last term.'

'Do you know where he's moved to, or why he moved?'

She felt Louis slipping further and further away. She could see him standing in his jacket and corduroy trousers, calf-deep in a pool of still water; he had his arms flung out towards her, screaming her name as a wave broke across the surface of the pool, and swept him away across a large stately garden.

Kathryn shivered and startled herself awake, to find herself still in Miss Leroy's office, opposite the Headmistress.

'I think we are finished, are we not?'

Kathryn nodded slowly; it certainly seemed that way. School had been possibly the last chance that she had for finding Louis, and she had failed him. Her concentration drifted again, and she was startled back to the here and now by Miss Leroy's cold tinkle of a voice.

'Of course, if I do happen to see Mr Tumnal, or hear from him, I shall be sure to let him know that…?'

'Kathryn.'

'That Kathryn was looking for him.'

Miss Leroy smiled.

Kathryn knew instinctively that it had been a mistake to have said her name. She now felt just like in one of her story books, that when you tell a faery your true name it was to give it power over you. Kathryn hated herself for these thoughts, as her rational brain tried to reassure herself that after all, what could an old Headmistress do to her?

Kathryn now followed Miss Leroy back through the school, feeling every bit as though she were being escorted from the premises. At the bottom of the stairs, they passed Polly and Beth, who were chatting over some photocopying. Kathryn raised her hand to wave and offered them a smile, but they seemed to look right through her.

Miss Leroy was standing at the door to reception now, and Kathryn hastened to catch up. She mumbled a half-hearted thank you, and was glad she hadn't put more effort into it when it was received with an ignored silence. The door clicked shut behind her. Kathryn glanced through the hatchway, to where the misery who was the school receptionist glared back at her. Kathryn strode off, storming through the next set of doors and taking childish delight in letting them slam shut behind her. She marched onwards and out of the school grounds, fuming at what had gone on inside, and the obstructiveness of Miss Leroy.

Kathryn looked up again, coming face-to-face across the street with a young man about her age, who was standing on the pavement watching her. She shook her head, turned, and began to walk home. A few metres down the road, she glanced back; the man was still there, watching, or waiting, or both. At the end of the street, Kathryn turned and looked again. This time the man had been joined by another and they were talking, but as she was looking back they both glanced up and watched her.

She turned, quickening her pace until she was safely out of sight around the corner. A tram rattled its way to the next stop, and Kathryn ran to catch it. Thrusting coins into the tray next to the driver, she went and found a seat. Looking up again as the tram trundled off, she saw the man again standing on the street corner, watching her depart.

8

Rain pounded rhythmically on the roof of the production office. Even at two o'clock, the light coming in from outside was almost as dark as night. Lamps above each of the desks cast small circular pools of bright light under which the production editors worked. Amongst them, Kathryn sat at her desk, working her way through proof corrections.

The minutes passed into hours, manuscript after manuscript; transcribing authors' scrawl into something that the overseas typesetters would be able to understand. Sometimes the task was easy, and sometimes it was harder. She relished the opportunities to decipher the author's scrawl, only to delete it as not journal style, and sometimes she would share the more ludicrous of these requests with her nearest colleagues. A failure by the copy-editor to change one seemingly tiny matter of scientific detail throughout the *entire* paper had resulted in a half-page diatribe from the author concerning the state of British publishing; and Kathryn had needed to resort to line-by-line unpicking with the aid of a ruler to correct a gazillion corrections. It was a frustratingly complex task, and one that, upon completion, led her to let out the biggest, longest sigh of relief. Kathryn declared a break time, making her way through the office and down the corridor with Charlotte and Eleanor, in search of tea and biscuits.

It had been a week now since Kathryn's visit to the county school, and she had been almost successful at not brooding over it. She hadn't seen the strange man since boarding the tram either, and had blocked him from her mind. Ardizzoni had been confined to the bottom of her wardrobe to sit behind the hems of her few dresses, and she had been glad that photography class hadn't started back up yet after the long Christmas break.

The three friends arrived back at the pod just as the production intern was finishing the post round. Kathryn stood and stared at the pile of thick manila envelopes. She sighed and settled back at her desk, clutching her mug of tea out of a feeling of security.

'Brilliant.'

'Don't knock it. I'm chasing my authors for theirs, otherwise this is going to be the slimmest issue on record.'

Kathryn frowned, lifting the pile of papers up and depositing it in her in-tray. A smaller, thin envelope of embossed paper slipped out of the pile and onto the desk in front of her. She picked it up, suspicious of the Wren Hoe postmark and the elegant handwriting that was unusual for her work correspondence.

'What the...?'

'Kathryn?' Charlotte said, looking over the divide.

Kathryn sat and stared at the envelope. She shook her head suspiciously, and slit through the top of the envelope. Inside was a gilt-edged card – an invitation – to a wedding.

'Who...?' Kathryn said, even before reading the names. Polly? Tom? She detached a Post-it note from the reverse of the card.

> Sorry I couldn't say anything at school. Hope you can
> come. The four of us would love to see you again.

'Kath?'

Kathryn sat and stared from the note to the invitation. Four of them? That would be Polly and Tom, obviously, and Beth ... and Louis? It had to be. She grinned. She re-read the invite again, seeing that it was just a few weeks away at Laurel Place; a big house in the north of town.

'I've been invited to a wedding.'

Charlotte looked up, her interest piqued.

'Yeah,' said Kathryn. 'It's Tom and Polly. You know, I told you about them. Louis' friends.'

'Is it just for you, or both of you?'

'Just me,' replied Kathryn. 'But it mentions the four of them seeing me...'

She passed the card over the divide to show Charlotte.

'See? Four of them must be Tom, Polly, their friend Beth – and Louis.'

Charlotte shrugged.

'Weird,' she said, passing the invite back.

'Guess I have to find a dress to wear then,' said Kathryn. 'Which leaves me with an odd feeling. Am I going to this with Louis, or are we still split? Does he want me back, or is this just Polly match-making?'

She pulled out another file of corrections to check, still muttering.

'And February? It's got to be something warm. Who gets married in February, anyway?'

Kathryn pulled the card closer again to read the date, before tossing it aside.

'Fourteenth! Might've known. That will have been Tom – he's such an insidious romantic.'

Kathryn gathered up some paperwork and headed off to the photocopier, with Charlotte and Eleanor laughing as she left.

Between queues of people using the photocopiers and others displaying out of order notices, she had to walk the length of the old building, taking the stairs to the attic level on the far side of the quad to the little repro room under the eaves. Rain and wind continued to lash out violently at the sash window that Kathryn was sure was leaking, and it was dark out there still. The sun would be setting out there now, if it could be seen through the thick, broiling clouds. Already the streetlights were on, but they made little difference to the light on the street.

Kathryn set her papers into the auto-feed, tapped the controls, and stepped back as the machine cranked itself into life. Out of the corner of her eye she thought she saw something, and looked again. Peering out of the window, and down across the street, she saw it – him – hunched in a coat on a swing. It was him. The man from outside the school. He was looking down at the ground now, but she was sure that earlier he had been looking up at the window, at her.

When it came to home time the rain had, if anything, worsened. Kathryn pulled the hood of her waterproof tightly around her face. Under the Walton Street entrance, she stopped to catch a last few words with Charlotte, who, having retrieved her bicycle, was already resembling the figure of someone who had done battle on the deck of a tossing ship in a fearsome storm.

'Ready to make a run for it?' asked Eleanor, as her tram rattled into the stop opposite.

'I'm tempted to join you, even if it is just for one stop.'

Eleanor grinned before saying her goodbyes, and joking something about wishing Kathryn luck. Then she turned to make a run for it across the road, round the front of the tram and boarded it.

Charlotte turned to her other friend.

'You going to be okay?' she asked, as she mounted her bicycle.

Kathryn stared wide-eyed in return.

'I'll be fine. It's you who's going to be sopping.'

Charlotte frowned and pushed down on the pedals, setting off into the rain. Kathryn watched her friend cycle off into the driving rain, and began to muster her own courage to venture out. While she waited she saw him, the man from the swings and from outside the school, wandering out of a side street and across Walton Street. Kathryn watched, sure that he would be boarding the tram before it departed, but he was in no rush, and began reading the notices and advertisements plastered on the stone wall.

'He must be soaked, that man,' Kathryn said, speaking her thoughts out loud.

The porter at the gate looked up.

'What, him? That's Matthew.'

'You know him?'

'I know of him, if that's what you mean,' the porter replied in his thick gravelly local accent. 'Matthew Leroy-Song. He's the nephew of that Miss Leroy; head of the county school, ye know? Her and her family own most of this city – most of the county too, when all's said and done.'

'He was hanging around the playgrounds down the road. Could see him from the office.'

'Was he now? Now I wonder why that was?'

Kathryn shrugged.

'Anyway, best be off I guess. Thanks for—'

She pointed over the road again. The porter nodded and smiled; and with that, Kathryn ducked her head and stormed out into the cold, driving rain, running down the road through the shops of Jericho and to the end of her street, down to her own door. She fumbled with the key and hurried inside, not breathing until she slammed the door and shut out the rain.

She peeled her waterproofs off and hung them over the end of the stairs, kicked off her sodden shoes and squelched upstairs to her room, where she just stood and looked at her bedraggled self in the mirror. She sighed and began to unpack the damp contents of her shoulder bag. One such item was the invitation, now bent and curled around the edges where the rain had soaked into the gilt-edged card. She smoothed it out and stood it up on her dressing table.

Returning from the bathroom, clean and refreshed and drying the last of her hair, Kathryn dressed quickly, pulling on a comfy pair of jeans and her favourite soft-cotton cowboy shirt. She moved to the window and drew back the curtain to inspect the weather. The clouds were fracturing and the wind was possibly easing, but the rain still fell heavily. She looked again – across the street, under the orange glow of a street lamp and sucking on a cigarette, was the unmistakable figure of Matthew.

'Who are you?'

She dropped the curtain back into place, and went to make dinner.

'He's still there, you know,' Kathryn said into her mobile as she hooked back the lounge curtain and peered out across the street, to where Matthew was still kicking his heels on the street corner. 'Just hanging around.'

'You want me to come over?'

Kathryn dropped the curtain back into place, and slumped down onto the end of the sofa.

'I think I would. If you don't mind?'

She was so relieved that Charlotte had offered. She wanted to ask, but had felt silly about it. She settled back in the sofa to wait and tried to read her books, but it was not easy. The image of Matthew standing across the street kept coming back to her, looming larger on her mind with every reappearance. She pulled out her book of essays and short stories again, and delved into yet more dissections of old myths and modern retellings. She became, in fact, so lost in the words, that when Charlotte knocked at the door, Kathryn was startled so much she almost ended up on the floor.

'I brought my sleeping bag with me,' Charlotte rushed out breathlessly. 'You know, in case you need company tonight... Other than that, I came as quickly—'

Kathryn helped her friend in with her bags quickly, before rushing to close the door. She lingered for a moment, peering up and down the street.

'I think he's gone actually,' said Charlotte. 'I didn't see anyone acting suspicious.'

Kathryn pushed the door gently but securely closed, and flicked the catches to lock at it. Lastly, she slipped the door chain across. She sighed heavily and frowned.

'I'm sorry for getting you over like this, Charlotte, but Nina – she's away on business for a few days and – the guy was freaking me out. Really giving me the willies.'

'It's fine Kath, honestly.'

A little later and they both came back through to the lounge, clutching a mug of coffee and each with a huge bowl of popcorn. Settling down each to a two-seater sofa, Charlotte set down her coffee on the table and scooped up a large handful of buttery popcorn.

'I wonder who he was?'

Kathryn laughed.

'That was the weird thing. I said exactly the same thing outside work. Turns out the porter knows him. He's only some rich nephew of Miss Leroy.'

'Leroy?'

Kathryn gaped for a moment, surprised by the lack of instant understanding.

'Of course, you're fairly new – you don't know. The Leroy family own most of this town, well, any of the town that's not owned by the university. Miss Leroy is this massive matriarchal figure.'

Comprehension began to swell over Charlotte as Kathryn explained.

'Was she the woman who was ill...?'

'Last summer, yeah. Not long after I met Louis.'

Kathryn fell to thinking again of Louis, and of happier times; and then of the empty house that was all boarded up and lonely.

'And this stalker guy, he's a Leroy too?'

'A Leroy-something, yeah.' Kathryn nodded. 'Matthew.'

Charlotte grinned. 'Well at least you have one advantage over this Matthew character. *You* know *his* name.'

Kathryn smiled, if half-heartedly, and chewed on her lip as she remembered what she had felt as soon as she had told Miss Leroy her name. If Matthew was following her because of Miss Leroy, then surely she would have passed on the details of her name. But – her brain spiralled off in new directions – Matthew had shown up outside school right after Miss Leroy had shown her out. She had had no time to contact him. In which case, who was he?

'I'm going to have to confront him, aren't I?'

Charlotte nodded slowly and sadly.

'I think so, yes.'

9

The following morning, Kathryn woke after a good night's sleep, possibly aided by the knowledge that Charlotte was downstairs on the sofa. After the wild misery of yesterday's weather, bright winter sunshine poured into the bedroom of the little house on Juxon Street. When Kathryn and Charlotte left for work, there was no sign of Matthew anywhere outside the house, and neither was there at the end of Kathryn's road, nor anywhere on Walton Street as they walked down through a slowly waking Jericho. By the time they had got to work they had discussed the matter thoroughly, deciding that Matthew must have given up his stalking. That is, if the sightings of him *were* anything more than coincidental.

There was a birthday in the office that day, and so at twelve o'clock everyone paraded out of the office and down though the atrium, winding their way through the narrow backstreets, past the Wrenshire canal, to the Old Bookbinders. They queued around the bar for drinks and food, before heading through to the now-traditional backroom used on these outings. Charlotte pressed a ten-pound note into Kathryn's hand and passed on her order, before disappearing round the back in the direction of the toilets. Kathryn remained at the bar, patiently waiting her turn and

253

looking at the range of real cask ales and traditional ciders. Ever since the days when there had been an actual press at The Press, this had been the lunchtime retreat of printers and compositors, and thus this pub excelled in the finest beers and ciders.

Suddenly Kathryn woke from her daydream to discover the landlord, a round-faced and portly man who always seemed to serve them when the journal production crew descended, asking again for her order.

'Uh, sorry,' she said. 'Two pints of Birdsnest and – a couple of stilton burgers and chunky chips, please.'

The landlord nodded, having already rung up the order.

'Thirteen-sixty, lass.'

She handed over two notes and waited for her change, and then for the two pints to be pulled.

'Excellent choice.'

'Huh?'

Kathryn glanced round to find Matthew Leroy-Song stood at the bar, drinking his pint.

'You!' she gasped. 'How long have you…? I never saw – are you…?'

'Do you ever speak in whole sentences?'

He was well-, but not posh-spoken. Kathryn stared at him, taken in by his dark hair, dark searching eyes, and his chiselled face and chin with a fine coating of stubble. She shook her gaze from him, and cursed the feelings of desire that she had let stir within her. She forced her mind to refocus, and turned again to face him.

'It's Matthew, isn't it?'

Matthew didn't answer, but just continued to gaze searchingly from those dark eyes. His reaction only served to irritate her further.

'Why have you been following me?'

'What makes you say I have been following you?'

Kathryn stared, gaping at him with disbelief.

'Outside the school, you followed me all the way to the tram; and then yesterday at the park. You sat there for hours in the rain, and then again half the night, you were standing on the corner outside my house.'

'I think you are reading too much into this,' he laughed.

'I don't find it funny.'

This only made Matthew laugh more, though not cruelly. The landlord slid first one, then the second, pint of beer across the bar, and Kathryn thanked him. She picked up the glasses, and turned to stare at Matthew.

'Nice meeting you, but I've got friends.'

Matthew returned her gaze, seeming to look right inside of her with his dark, penetrating eyes.

'Lewis is alright, you know. He's happy.'

Kathryn stopped in mid-stride and stepped back.

'You know Louis?'

'He's a friend,' explained Matthew. 'Well, kind of cousins...'

Kathryn shook her head.

'Why are you telling me this?'

'So that you know he's okay, that you don't need to worry about him. He's happy. He doesn't need you anymore.'

Kathryn stared at Matthew, hardly believing she was hearing this. She shook her head vehemently, looking away decidedly as she stepped past Matthew to re-join her friends.

Her exchange with Matthew tainted the rest of lunchtime for Kathryn. She had already been quizzed over why she had been so long getting back from the bar; now she was quizzed again for being so silent while she bit into her stilton burger. She couldn't explain what she felt; she had difficulty enough working out what she was thinking. She spent the lunchtime on the outside of the conversations, listening and laughing to the jokes and the anecdotes, until burgers were eaten and beer was drunk, and it was time to return to the red pen and the manuscript papers.

Kathryn gathered up her bag, and followed Charlotte and Eleanor through the pub. Matthew was still leaning on the bar. As she headed out past the bar, he looked up and seemed to follow Kathryn with his gaze; as she passed behind him, he turned, reached out, and grabbed her arm – not roughly, but firmly enough. She turned and stared, and he fixed her with his gaze.

'Call me,' he said, and releasing her from his grip he pressed a crumpled piece of paper into her hands.

Kathryn gaped, incredulous as to his actions. She shook her head and stormed out of the pub to catch up with her friends.

'Can you believe that man?' she asked, as she ran to catch up, and fell in line, with Charlotte and Eleanor.

'What man?'

Kathryn narrowed her gaze.

'Matthew Leroy-Song,' she said, communicating each word with contempt. 'He just grabbed hold of me in there and told me – instructed me – to call him.'

She waved the screwed up piece of paper in front of her, before plunging it into the depths of her shoulder bag.

Charlotte shook her head.

'Kath, there wasn't anyone at the bar...?'

Kathryn stopped and stared.

'There were a couple of boatmen at the table to the right of the fire,' said Charlotte. 'There was no one at the bar.'

'But I spoke to him; that's why I was so long giving my order. Then he grabbed hold of me just now as we left, and said *Call me...*'

'I think we would have heard. We were right in front of you,' said Eleanor.

Kathryn shook her head dismissively.

'Are you saying I imagined it all?'

'We're saying that you're probably mistaken,' added Eleanor.

'You've been through a lot recently,' reasoned Charlotte. 'All this with Louis and the Leroy woman – it's been stressful. It doesn't make you a loony-bin to think–'

'I *didn't* make this up.'

Kathryn strode forwards, sidestepping some of the others, and stormed off. She heard her friends call after her, but continued on. She hadn't imagined it. Matthew had been there, and he had mentioned Louis. She had an invite to Polly's wedding back home, and Polly was Louis' friend. Why would Charlotte and Eleanor, of all her friends, lie about seeing Matthew?

Back at her desk she plugged herself into her iPod and swung the music up loud, not registering when her friends got back to their desks. At one moment she looked up just as Charlotte did too, and she just scowled. It was hard to stay mad at them though, and somewhere during the afternoon the musical barrier was silenced, and conversation and laughter returned. Neither Louis nor Matthew were mentioned.

When it came to that evening, it was also the night that photography class started. Kathryn just had time to pack up her camera with its new lens, download some of her favourite photographs from the Christmas break, and knock up a hasty pasta meal before she headed out to college. When she arrived, she had feared that she might have ended up working with Colin again, but there was a new girl that night, Sophie; she was very shy but incredibly nice, and once introduced she was easy to talk to. They got given their next essay question and the subject of this term's new project, then afterwards Sophie and Kathryn and a couple of the others went to the pub for a drink. Not once did Kathryn see strange men lurking on street corners watching her, and she didn't have time to think about either Matthew or Louis. At the end of the night she returned home and crashed onto her bed, falling asleep almost immediately.

It wasn't until the weekend that she next turned her attention to Matthew. Saturday morning came, with the realisation that she needed to sort out a dress for the wedding, and, in emptying out her bag she found the small, screwed up piece of paper with the phone number written on it in a not inelegant hand. She shook her head before screwing it up and lobbing it across the room, where it missed the rubbish bin and rolled under her desk.

After getting herself distracted again by a second mug of coffee and another chapter of her book, Kathryn headed out to walk the route past the front of work to town. She did linger under the colonnaded roads that ran down the side of Little Clarendon Street to look in the windows of the posh fashion boutiques, but baulked at an otherwise gorgeous dress when she saw the less than attractive price tag. Kathryn turned on her heels, and soon found herself browsing the racks of dresses in her favourite high street clothes shops.

She found the perfect dress remarkably easily as it turned out. She had to go back after browsing the other offerings, but she saw it the moment she walked into the shop. With the decision made she bought it, handing over plastic to pay for it, and headed out, determined to browse the shelves of her favourite bookstore. Turning out of the store on Queen Street, she all but knocked into Polly and Beth going in. Following an awkward exchange of apologies and greetings, Kathryn found herself following them back into the shop, where Polly led the way to the jewellery display.

'For the bridesmaids,' explained Polly. 'I had ordered these really nice, perfect necklaces and earrings online, but I only just had an email this morning. Out of stock and can't deliver—'

'Nightmare,' said Kathryn.

'So how are you, Katy?'

Kathryn grimaced at the unacceptable shortening of her name.

'I'm so glad you can come. Everyone was so pleased when we got your letter. Is that your dress?'

Kathryn nodded, and opened the bag a little to show.

'Perfect. You are going to look beautiful.'

Polly cast her gaze along another rack of jewellery, and zoned in on some delicate flower-like spirals of silver necklaces.

'Oh they are nice, and look – earrings to match. Brilliant.'

Polly pulled three sets of them off the shelf. Then, looking up again at Kathryn, she lifted one of the necklaces up to her neck.

'You wouldn't like a set yourself, would you?' asked Polly, but in in a way that was somehow not much of a question. Kathryn shrugged, and tried to answer.

'That's settled then.'

Polly grabbed another set of each and hastened to the cash desk. Kathryn remained a short distance away with Beth.

'Has she been like this a lot?' Kathryn asked quietly.

'It's been mental.'

As they left the shop, and Kathryn began to wonder when she could slope off to the bookstore, Polly announced another idea.

'You want to see where we are getting married, Katy?'

Kathryn shrugged, and was about to excuse herself.

'Beth and I were going up there now to drop some things off. You could come, if you wanted?'

This time Kathryn didn't even attempt to argue against the rhetorical nature of the question, and they rounded another corner out of Cornmarket to the Broad Street metro station, down the steps to where the train was waiting. Kathryn sat between Polly and Beth, feeling awkward, listening to yet more wedding plans and details about people she didn't know. Finally, the engine chugged into throbbing life along the length of the carriage beneath her feet.

A shriek of children echoed across the platform, and a couple of girls ran down the steps and boarded the train just as the doors slid shut behind them. It took a moment for her to realise that they were Sarah and Caz. Kathryn's gaze met Sarah, and for a moment she thought there was recognition there. Then she had to turn and listen to more of Polly's wedding talk.

Four stops down the line and they reached Park Town, the leafy suburban area in North Wren Hoe. Leaving the station with Polly and Beth, Kathryn couldn't fail to notice that Sarah and Caz were trailing them, or at least heading in the same direction. They crossed the park area in the centre of the circus, dipping in and out of the shadows of the tall trees and the pools of light from the streetlamps.

A long black car turned in and crunched up the gravel driveway, its headlights sweeping across the lawns and the great expanse of the stately home. Even from far away, Kathryn could make out the shape of the man standing waiting for the car to arrive – Matthew Leroy-Song. She flinched away and stopped.

'Kathryn?' asked Beth. 'You okay?'

'Actually, I've just remembered – I'm sorry, but I need to get going...'

Polly tried to convince her it wouldn't take long, and Beth offered her calming words and support, but Kathryn had decided. She thanked them for a lovely afternoon, and Polly for the jewellery, told them that she would see them soon, then turned and left. As she skirted back around the edge of the park, she glanced back over her shoulder at where Polly and Beth were walking up the drive, to where Matthew was now talking to Sarah and Caz at the gate. She turned again and walked on, briskly crossing the road to cut through to the Woodstock Road.

Back home, Kathryn retrieved the screwed-up ball of paper from under her deck and flattened it out. She stood and stared at it, trying to work out if she should call or not. She got as far as entering the number into the phone, but her thumb held back from pressing Call. She cancelled the number, and slammed the phone back onto the desk.

10

The day of the wedding eventually came, and after a week of early-February gloom and mizzle, Saturday's weather was bright and sunny. Kathryn woke with the sun pouring in through the windows, and one of the first things she saw was the dress, turquoise blue with navy and white swirls, where it hung on the end of her wardrobe.

Since the day of the shopping trip to buy the dress, Kathryn had been worrying more and more about the wedding. Not once had she considered not going. She felt it was somehow important – that there was something else riding on it – and not just because some girl she only vaguely knew through a friend wanted her to go. Several times in the intervening weeks, Kathryn had considered the scrap of paper with Matthew's phone number. Once even, she had gone to the phone box at the end of the road and dialled the number. She didn't know what she would have said to him, and when he had guessed it was her, it was all she could do to hang up and flee from the red telephone box. The following day she had seen him again on the playground opposite work. She hadn't telephoned Matthew's number again.

Kathryn got up, pulled her dressing gown around her, and traipsed bleary-eyed downstairs to make breakfast. An hour or so later, she pulled herself away from her books and the internet to shower and get herself ready for the wedding. Odd feelings ebbed through her mind, reminiscent of the time when she was getting ready for her first 'date' with Louis.

She imagined him there, standing on the edge of the dance floor, and going up to him. Then she was sitting in the ceremony waiting for things to start, when suddenly there was a cold draught behind her, and someone was behind her, and someone was taking a seat next to her, and it was Louis. She looked down at her hand, and saw Louis' reach out and take it.

Kathryn shuddered, woken from her daydreaming where she sat at her dressing table. Between herself and her reflection, she saw the invitation propped against the mirror. She saw the time of the service, and realised she needed to get a move on.

Finally she got to the point of putting on the necklace and earrings that Polly had given her, and in doing so they made her feel like she was carrying charms for her protection. She applied a small amount of naturalistic make-up, and lastly fixed the small posy of red flower petals in her hair. A last check over, and a final sort of her handbag, and she declared herself ready.

When Kathryn left the house she was reminded at how unused she was to walking the uneven flags of Juxon Street in heels, having to walk at a slower than normal pace to the tram stop at the end of the road. Riding the tram north, her thick duffle coat pulled tightly around her dress, Kathryn felt overdressed amongst the other passengers in their thick winter clothes, and while she felt good dressed up, she also longed for the comfort of jeans and a cosy sweater.

At Jericho Green she alighted to cut through a cross-street between the Woodstock and Banbury roads, before descending into the metro station to travel back into the city centre and to Park Town. She travelled on the city trams all the time; she loved the sun-bleached yellow of them, the wood-slatted seats and the ticket punching machines. But she loved the cities only Metro line even more. Running immediately beneath the road for most of its route from Kidlington to the terminus in the one deep section under The Broad, it was small and enchantingly cute. The stations were tiled with mosaics that resembled the places above ground they were named after, and the one kiosk on each platform was detailed with ornate woodwork. Summertown was always the busiest of stops, whatever time of day you travelled, and Kathryn sat and watched the changeover of passengers, amongst them an influx of people dressed for a wedding, and well-spoken to the point of the surreal. They made Kathryn feel like she had to tuck herself in closer.

Another couple of stops and it was Park Town, with its black and white tiling of the grand houses that surrounded the circus, and of the Leroy family crest. The train slid in alongside the platform and Kathryn discovered, as predicted, that this was also the stop for half the passengers in her carriage. She followed all the well-dressed and well-spoken people out of the station and across the platform. She hung back for a moment, under the pretence of reading the headlines of the local paper where they were stacked in front of the kiosk. Her nerves at going to Laurel Place had multiplied. She was passed by others, running down the last of the steps to catch their train.

Finally, and just after the train rumbled off out of the station, she turned again towards the entrance and the sweep of polished limestone steps that led to the street above. She passed the wrought-iron gates and the Victorian lanterns that marked the entrance. The park, which a few weeks ago had seemed so cold and unwelcoming, was now welcoming in the bright winter sunshine and the carpet of snowdrops and crocuses. She walked across the park, delighting in all the spring flowers, and wished that she had her camera with her. Then she stopped and fished a small compact digital out, and crouched down, balancing, if a little awkwardly, on her heels to take macro, and up the bell, shots of snowdrops. Flicking through the results quickly, she smiled and continued on her way. Waiting to cross the road, she was passed by a procession of plush cars that turned into the long gravel driveway of Laurel Place. She crossed the road, flashed her invite at the faceless porter on the gate, and began the long, awkward walk up to the house.

Kathryn looked ahead of her, scanning the faces of the guests getting out of cars for anyone she recognised. Her heart beat faster and faster, and she wondered whether it was too late to turn on her heels and leave.

'Kathryn, hi!'

Matthew's voice was clear and unmistakable. She swung round to find him standing all but on top of her, dressed in a sharp suit. Kathryn gasped, and jumping back in surprise she stumbled, tripping over her own feet. Matthew threw out a strong hand and caught her as she fell. Kathryn shrieked uncontrollably and felt the posy slip from her hair, scattering red petals around her like beads of blood. For a moment Kathryn remained there, held in Matthew's arms, sure that everyone must be staring at her. He brought her back to her feet, and stepped back immediately.

'What the hell do you think you are doing?' she snapped.

'You would have preferred it if I let you fall?' asked Matthew. 'And let you ruin that lovely dress of yours?'

'If you hadn't surprised me then I wouldn't have tripped!'

'You wouldn't have wanted me to ignore you?'

Kathryn stared at him. She wanted to say yes – yes, she would have very much preferred it if he had ignored her. He was impossible to be ignored. If it wasn't that she was madly, deeply, unaccountably in love with Louis Tumnal, then he would have been just the kind of person who would have turned her eye.

'No,' she said meekly. 'No, of course not.'

'Good.'

He smiled and offered her his hand again.

'Would you allow me to show you to your seat?'

Kathryn agreed, and allowed him to take her by the arm to lead her into the grand hallway of Wren House. Stairs swept upwards, with flowers and greenery woven around the newel post and between the bannisters. Looking up, she could see the enormous chandelier that hung down through the grand entranceway.

'This way,' Matthew said, as he led her down a side passage and stopped outside a small room.

'Why have...?'

'I thought you might like to leave your coat, and maybe freshen up?'

Kathryn hesitated for a moment, then agreed and entered the cloakroom. When she ventured back out into the passageway a few minutes later, she was half-hoping to have found Matthew gone. Not only did she find him waiting for her, but he was holding a small posy of white roses. He offered them to her graciously.

'For you,' he said humbly. 'I'm sorry I couldn't find red, but I thought these would match your dress.'

Kathryn took them with a mumbled thank you, turned, and returned to the cloakroom. A minute or so later she stepped back out, and seeing Matthew opposite, gave him a brief twirl.

'How do I look?'

'Beautiful,' he replied, and Kathryn blushed. He offered her his arm again.

'Shall we?'

Kathryn nodded, took his arm, and allowed him to walk her back down to the hallway and through into the great hall. It was a large, double-height room, with a stained glass of a woman who looked not unlike Miss Leroy at one end, and a gallery at the other. The room was set out with chairs facing the stained glass, and the bride and groom's chairs. To one side a string quartet was playing. The room was slowly filling, and Matthew led Kathryn to an empty row near the back.

'If you can excuse me, I should go and surprise – welcome – more guests.'

He grinned, and then grinned again as Kathryn laughed.

From her vantage point near the back of the room, Kathryn could watch the other guests arrive. There were a few she took to be family who took their seats near the front, and others who Kathryn guessed to be other friends, mostly teachers. A large number of guests were richer society people, and Kathryn was left to wonder exactly how many of them actually knew the bride and groom.

Kathryn looked down at the order of service and saw the music was being provided by The Dumas Quartet. She smiled as she remembered her recent re-reading of *Fire & Hemlock*, and the string quartet of which Tom Lynn was part of. She looked up to watch them, wondering who was taking the place of Tom on cello. As she sat and watched and listened, a brush of fabric and a rush of cold draught swept in next to her—

'Alright Kath?'

Kathryn jumped in her seat, and swung round to find Caz sitting next to her, grinning.

'You mind if I join you?' she said, already making herself comfortable. 'Don't know anyone else here otherwise – who are not teachers anyways. But I know you.'

'What are you doing here?'

Caz grinned mischievously.

'Don't really know; don't know the bride and groom really – apart from her being a teacher and all.'

Kathryn gaped at Caz's response.

'Don't worry, I ain't crashed it or anything. I'm here with Sarah. Her dad see, is friends with Miss Winters and with Miss Vernal – I'm here to keep her company later.'

'Louis *is* here, then?'

Caz nodded and pointed. Kathryn turned quickly to see him walking through the room, taking a seat in one of the rows close to the front. Next to him, she saw the unmistakable figure of her boss.

'And that's his wife? Sarah's mother?'

Caz shrugged.

'Guess so. Never actually met her before. It's always been him that I've seen around when I've been round Sarah's.'

Kathryn nodded, and looked again to the front.

'She works late I think.'

She remembered all those nights when she herself had pulled a late one at work and left eventually, while Amanda was still working away at her desk, talking to her colleagues in the US office. She sighed.

'I think she works too much.'

As she sat looking towards the front, wondering if she would get to talk to Louis today – daydreaming of getting a dance with him in the evening – he turned. He was pale, and looked tired. Where was the bounce and energy that he used to have? Her gaze met with his for a moment, and for an instant she thought there was no recognition as to who she was. As she watched, he held her in his gaze, and Kathryn thought there was a sense of pleading in his eyes.

'I think we are almost ready to begin.'

Kathryn jumped at the sound of Matthew's voice, as he eased into the seat next to her. She glanced back towards Louis but he had returned his attention to the front of the room, and there was a last minute jostling for places as people took their seats. The Dumas Quartet finished playing their last piece, and sifted through their music as they got ready for the entrance of the bride. Next to her, Kathryn felt Matthew's arm close over the top of hers as he tried to take her hand.

She pulled away from him sharply and rounded on him.

'What the hell do you think you're doing?'

Before Matthew had a chance to answer, the Dumas Quartet struck up the bridal entrance, and everyone turned to watch as the doors to the hall were pulled back and Polly entered, on the arm of a smaller, older man whom Kathryn assumed to be her father. Behind her, Beth and Sarah followed, and as they passed the end of their row, Kathryn felt sure that Sarah was looking – staring – imploring her to help.

For the rest of the service, Kathryn's mind spun with questions and thoughts. She couldn't stop thinking of Louis, and the way that both he and Sarah had been staring at her, like they hoped, and wanted, something to happen; or for Kathryn to do something. And then there was the presence of Miss Leroy herself at the service; her position opposite where the Dumas Quartet were placed, in a carved wooden throne. Kathryn tried, and succeeded, in not making eye contact with the Headmistress, and she wondered whether she had been spotted; then she remembered the presence of Matthew, and knew with certainty that of course Miss Leroy knew she was here.

Just as when Kathryn had attended Ben and Kirsten's wedding a couple of years back, the civil ceremony was not a long one. Bulked out with a couple of readings, and another musical interlude whilst the register was signed, suddenly it was all over, and Polly and Tom were leaving the hall, hand in hand. Leaving the great hall with everyone else, Kathryn received a glass of champagne before heading off to a quiet corner while photographs were taken. Thankfully, Matthew appeared to be otherwise occupied, although she did have to sidestep behind some other groups of important looking people on more than one occasion to avoid bumping into him.

Assuming she wasn't going to be needed for any of the photographs, Kathryn drifted off to explore some of the other rooms, finding a long gallery filled with pictures – some old paintings, and some modern photographs. She was drawn instinctively to one, recognising it immediately as herself, taken by Louis when they were up on White Horse Hill. *What*, she wondered, *was it doing here?*

She turned, and saw it, at the end of the long gallery – the other photograph – the companion piece to the picture of Louis. She started off, slowly at first, then faster, running to the end of the gallery. She stopped, and stared. Louis; and, like the picture of herself, it was taken up at the White Horse Hill, which meant that it was her own picture.

'How?' she gasped, staring at the picture that she had taken.

'He's a good man.'

Kathryn jumped and spun round at the sound of the lady's soft-spoken voice. It was the viola player from the quartet, a middle-height older lady with short dark hair.

'Ann,' the woman said, and greeted Kathryn warmly. Kathryn stuttered, hesitant and crumbling with uncertainness.

Ann smiled.

'It's okay, you're safe to say your name here, Kathryn. But you were right to be cautious, particularly when—'

She moved closer and lowered her voice.

'You don't know who, or what, might be listening.'

Kathryn stared at the woman, wanting to answer her, but finding herself unable to. Ann stepped closer to the picture, and seemed to stare into it.

'It's a good likeness.'

'I took it,' said Kathryn. 'I don't know how it comes to be here. I want to know...'

'They look very much alike, aside from the dark hair,' continued Ann. 'Louis and – and him...'

'Who?' asked Kathryn.

Ann turned away from the picture, and looked to Kathryn.

'We've been here before, you know,' said Ann. 'You have to save him, Kathryn. Get him away from here, tonight. Get him away from her.'

'From whom?' asked Kathryn.

Ann raised her finger to her mouth, and silenced them both. She nodded across the room to where, as Kathryn turned, she could see Matthew standing at the door, watching them. He announced it time for the wedding breakfast.

Kathryn found herself sitting at a table with what seemed to be a miscellaneous collection of friends and distant relations of Polly's. But, she considered, at least she was far away from the top table, and the prying eyes of Matthew and Miss Leroy. She was also in a prime location for watching Louis, sat at a table close to the top of the room with Amanda, Sarah, Caz, and another couple who she also assumed to be teachers.

Ann's words remained with Kathryn throughout the meal. She remembered how Miss Leroy had been determined that she would know nothing, and have nothing, to do with Louis. And she remembered the way that Louis had been looking at her with haunted, desperate eyes before the service. She looked at him now, and how he was quietly eating his food while Amanda did all the talking. Kathryn had her attention fixed so much on the joint preoccupations of Louis' table and her own thoughts and memories, that she missed so many conversations and questions that were directed at her from her own table. The multitude of conversations in the great hall was nothing but a cacophony of background noise and hubbub.

The wind whistled through the skeletal branches of the trees above, dark finger-like shapes that crawled across the sky to echo the shadows on the ground below. Lewis sat alone on a bench in the sunken Italian garden, staring at the pond in front of him. Ladies' footsteps echoed across the paving, and he looked up to see Amanda approaching, her auburn hair still radiant in the moonlight.

'Lewis, there you are,' said Amanda. 'I wondered where you had gone.'

Lewis smiled quietly and looked back towards the pond. Amanda took a seat next to her husband, and remained quietly companionable beside him. He looked up and round at her. She smiled, and he returned the gesture before returning his gaze to the pond, where the moonlight shimmered on the dark surface.

'You still love her, don't you?'

Lewis was startled, surprised, and confused by Amanda's words.

'I know about Kathryn.'

Lewis turned and stared, mouthing his confusion. Amanda reached out and took his hand.

'Break the chain, Lewis,' continued Amanda. 'If you love her, you should be with her.'

Lewis wavered. He lifted the hand that Amanda was holding, and felt the softness of her cheek. He shook his head.

'What the...?' Kathryn uttered uncontrollably, as she watched from the verandah outside the house. She could see

Louis halfway across the wide and open lawn, sitting alone in the Italian garden and looking for all the world like he was talking to someone.

'Louis, what are you doing?' she asked out loud, to no one in particular.

'He's not what he seems, you know that?' Matthew cautioned from behind her in his strong, confident voice.

Kathryn swung round to face him, angry at being overheard.

'How long...?' she began to ask.

Matthew shook his head.

'Not long. Only just found you again,' he said, as he passed her a glass of wine. Without thinking, she took it.

'He's different. He's not what he seems,' Matthew continued.

'I know,' said Kathryn. 'That's what I like about him.'

Matthew grinned, and nodded at Kathryn's words.

'He is very likeable,' he said. 'I know what you mean. He's infuriatingly odd, but impossible to hate.'

'That's it!' exclaimed Kathryn, as Matthew began to steer her away from the French windows towards one of the sofas that surrounded the dance floor.

'So have you known Louis for long?'

'All my life. Well, as long as I can remember... he's been around. He used to come here for flute lessons with my aunt.'

'Really?'

Kathryn's interest was raised at the mention of Louis' early life. Whether it was the marriage setting, or the wine, or Matthew's friendliness and more normal tone, Kathryn found herself warming to him. When he got going, he actually had quite a charming sense of humour. Kathryn listened to the tales of Louis as a small, shy, friendless boy, who would bring himself in school uniform and with a big leather satchel to flute lessons with Miss Leroy. She wondered from the description if it was the very same satchel that Louis now used for work; on learning that it was, the revelation made Kathryn smile.

Matthew admitted that Miss Leroy even scared himself at times, but he told Kathryn that she was different with children. She understood them, totally, especially if she recognised promise in them. Kathryn laughed at the way Matthew told his stories, and she drank more wine. She didn't even notice Matthew refilling her glass.

The music changed on the disco to a song that unconsciously, infectiously made Kathryn dance and jig in her seat. The folky-beat and tin whistle, the upbeat version of an Elvis classic.

'Love this song!' Kathryn beamed.

Matthew gazed back at her.

'I can tell.'

'Heard it on a film – was years later that I discovered their other music.' Kathryn said, dipping and jiving in her seat. 'Love it.'

On being told the band's name, Matthew laughed.

'Lick the Tins? Seriously? Sounds like it should be, well, punkier.'

Kathryn grinned.

'So go on, then, tell me. What music do you like?'

Matthew smiled, slowly, considering the question carefully.

'Pink Floyd, obviously,' he said eventually. 'Bit of Oasis, Pulp, then – Morrissey, and The Smiths. Going back, you can't beat a bit of Bob Dylan. And it has to be vinyl, I can't be doing with all this digital stuff. The sound has to be real.'

Walking back across the lawn towards the wedding, Lewis felt the cold of the mid-February evening. The lights from the wedding stretched out across the lawn as warm and welcoming, with the silhouettes of dancing beyond the windows. He walked up the steps to the terrace slowly, pausing for a moment outside the French windows. He looked around at Amanda, who was now standing alongside him. She nodded, and Lewis proceeded in, opening the door and allowing his wife to step through ahead.

Once in the room, Lewis steered Amanda through the room to a table not far away and otherwise empty. He helped Amanda into a seat, and then, as he stood by his chair, he looked up and saw her – Kathryn – across the room, laughing and joking with Matthew Leroy-Song. What, he wondered, was she doing with him?

Lewis glanced round at Amanda. He could tell she had seen Kathryn too.

'You should go to her. Explain...' encouraged Amanda.

Lewis shook his head dismissively, immediately. He sat down and pulled his chair closer to Amanda.

'I'd prefer to talk to you.'

'Who's he talking to?'

Kathryn's question came eventually, after a lapse in conversation in which Louis had re-entered the room, walked by her, and gone and sat on his own at a table further round the room.

'He's mad,' Kathryn said, shaking her head.

Next to her, as she watched Louis, she heard Matthew sit up and reposition himself closer to her. She felt his arm slip in around her, and his hand rested on her far shoulder.

'He is. Insane,' stated Matthew. 'Whereas you – and I—'

Kathryn turned her head to find Matthew's face right there, next to her.

'Are what?' she asked, her expression was filled with accusatory questions.

Matthew's response was to lunge forward and press his mouth to hers, in a warm, enveloping kiss. Kathryn pulled back, but not completely out of Matthew's grip.

'What do you think you're doing?'

'Showing you. He's not real.'

He kissed her again, and this time there was some reciprocation. Then Kathryn's gaze and temper flared.

'Matthew, no!'

She pulled away, and removed his hand from her. She gathered up her purse and left the sofa, glancing briefly back at where Matthew lounged across the sofa, already with his wine glass held for the drinking, and expectant of her return in his gaze. Kathryn looked away angrily and stormed across the room.

'Break the chain, Lewis. You have to.'

Lewis glanced round at Amanda. She nodded towards him. He turned again to where Kathryn was storming through the room towards him – past him. He stood up quickly, and almost tripped over himself, lunging to catch his own chair as it fell. Back on his feet, he stepped out into Kathryn's path. He reached out to catch her arm.

'Kathryn?'

His voice was hopeless and unconfident.

'Louis! Now you speak to me!' Kathryn's said, her temper still flared.

Louis stepped back, taken aback by Kathryn's reaction.

'I—' he stumbled over his words. 'I – Kathryn – I wanted to. I do want to...'

He stopped, finding his gaze drawn to the woven silverwork of plants and flowers that hung around her neck. He saw Kathryn's face turn towards him, and the scowl change to a wry grin.

Break the chain, Lewis.

'Louis? What is it?'

Louis stared at Kathryn's necklace, transfixed by the sparkle of silverwork that seemed to grow and entwine further around her neck. He reached out and fingered the chain carefully.

'It's beautiful, Kathryn.'

'It is, isn't it? Polly gave it to me.'

Louis smiled, as he turned the chain over in his fingers. He closed his hand around the chain.

'And I'm very sorry, but—'

He pulled the chain down, swiftly and sharply. Kathryn let out an involuntary yelp, as the chain broke around her neck. She protested at Louis' actions and reached for the necklace, as Louis tossed it away to where it slid off across the dance floor. The music had stopped. Conversations had ceased. People were looking. A silence drifted through the room.

'Louis, what have you done?' Kathryn said, her voice hushed.

Louis stuttered and faltered. He shook his head. Getting rid of the silver chain had seemed so easy, and yet he still didn't understand why he had had to do it. He stood in front of Kathryn, opening and closing his mouth like a goldfish, unable to speak. Kathryn looked from him to the guests beyond him, and to the guests on the other side. She swung round to see Miss Leroy standing, staring at her, and swung round again to see Matthew getting up, starting to push through the ranks of guests towards them.

Kathryn gulped, feeling her heart beating furiously beneath her dress. She glanced down at her side, and saw that Louis' hand was fidgeting. She grabbed it firmly, lifted her head, and looked directly into Louis' eyes.

'Louis. Run!'

She started off with Louis in tow, hands firmly clasped, through swathes of parting guests, and out of the ballroom into the long gallery again. From behind somewhere she heard Sarah's voice calling out to her dad, but they did not stop. Down the length of the gallery and through another set of doors, they took twists and turns through a seemingly ever-changing house in search of the main entrance.

Back in the ballroom, guests were murmuring as conversations resumed, and the disco continued. Beth sat at a table with Polly and Tom, who had now shed his jacket and cravat. She fingered the necklace around her neck as she considered what she had just seen.

'Beth?' Polly said, questioning her friend's quietness.

Beth looked up at her friend.

'I'm sorry Polly. It's beautiful, but—'

She reached round her neck and unfastened the necklace, letting it trickle through her fingers onto the table cloth.

'I've got to go.'

Kathryn and Louis skidded to a halt in the main hall. Matthew was advancing towards them from the door opposite. She glanced across at the main entrance between them, and back at Matthew. She tightened her grip on Louis' hand.

'Please, Matthew. Don't stop me.'

Matthew stopped still. He shrugged.

'You can go, that's fine. You were never supposed to be here anyway. But Louis, he stays.'

Kathryn shook her head defiantly.

'I don't know how you did it – making me think I was mad – that I had imagined Louis' existence, but it stops here. He's coming with me.'

Kathryn swung round, suddenly aware that they had been joined by more of Matthew's dark-suited friends behind them. She began to edge slowly towards the door with Louis.

'If you can run, run Katy,' said Matthew mockingly. 'It doesn't matter anymore. Louis still has his part to play.'

'No,' Kathryn replied, equally firm. 'It ends here.'

She glanced at Louis. He was still shuffling and uncertain, but going along with everything Kathryn said. From behind Matthew, a waiter darted out of the corridor and passed Matthew a flute. He smiled slyly, and lifted the instrument to his lips.

Louis felt his insides wrench. The tune hit him in the head, and he screamed out to Kathryn to run. They both dived through the doors and out into the cold February night, with the lilting flute music behind them. At the bottom of the steps Kathryn paused only to pull her shoes from her feet, and ran with Louis across the gravel and down the drive. Behind them a car roared to life, and the sound of wheels scrunching through gravel came up behind them. They were picked out against the wrought-iron gates by headlights; Louis and Kathryn ran faster, but were caught up as the car screeched to a halt alongside them. The passenger door was flung open, and Beth called out to them from the passenger seat.

'Get in!' shouted Beth. 'Both of you! Hurry!'

Kathryn bundled Louis into the back of the car, then landed herself in the front passenger seat; she slammed the door shut, and heard Beth click the central locking. They lunged forwards again as Beth turned out of the driveway and onto the road. Kathryn looked back to see all the figures up by the house.

Driving north out of town by the quickest most direct route, eventually Beth glanced across at Kathryn.

'So where are we headed?

Kathryn thought for a moment; Louis had no home now, and Matthew knew where she lived. She chewed on her lip.

'Bristol,' she said. 'They don't know about my folks. It's the only place they don't know.'

Beth nodded, as she steered the car across the ringroad and onto the dual carriageway south.

PART FOUR

Spring Birth

presto molto agitato

1

It was long past midnight when Beth finally pulled the car to a halt in the narrow country lane outside Kathryn's parents' stone cottage. Faint drifts of smoke floated upwards out of the chimney. Kathryn looked round cautiously as she helped Louis from the car, fearful that out there someone or something was watching them.

As the three of them approached the front door, Kathryn's father swung it open to greet them. Kathryn had phoned ahead and warned her parents of their arrival.

'Your mother has gone on to bed, I'm afraid,' Rupert told his daughter warmly.

Kathryn nodded, both unsurprised by her mother and relieved that she was spared the questions until tomorrow.

The three of them sat around the kitchen table in a state of stunned and exhausted silence, while Rupert made them all large steaming mugs of hot chocolate. Beth looked between Louis and Kathryn, and Kathryn sat and watched Louis' glazed and dazed expression.

'What a night!' exclaimed Kathryn finally.

Louis stared back at her, and eventually answered in a weak, nervous voice.

'It has been – weird – hasn't it?'

Rupert delivered the mugs of chocolate to the table, and pulled up a chair.

'So, what's the story?' he asked warmly.

One by one, Beth and Louis turned to look at him. Lastly, Kathryn turned to look at her father. She shook her head.

'I don't know. It doesn't make sense - when you try and say it out loud. Not even if you were there.'

'And believe us, we've been trying,' added Beth. 'The *whole* journey down here.'

Rupert nodded slowly, waiting for more explanation that didn't come.

'How about I start you off then?' suggested Rupert.

Kathryn, Beth, and Louis all turned and stared.

'Clearly you've had to save Louis from something - or someone. You've come from a wedding, and this together with what happened to you at Christmas—'

He looked at Kathryn as he said this.

'I'm guessing that whatever it was, it was magic.'

Kathryn gaped at her father.

'Not gangs of loan sharks, then?' Beth joked to Rupert.

Rupert turned towards her and smiled warmly, if somewhat knowingly.

'You and my daugh - Sarah would get on well together,' Louis said. 'She has a way of knowing what's what—'

'Louis!' hissed Beth.

Louis turned to look at her.

'You don't have a daughter,' Beth told him.

'I, err - umm - no—'

Louis fumbled and stumbled, glancing awkwardly between Beth and Kathryn.

'Louis,' Kathryn said, reaching across the table for his fidgeting hands. 'Who is Sarah?'

Louis looked up, glancing briefly at Beth before returning his gaze to Kathryn.

'She's my daughter.'

'And Amanda?'

'She's my...' He stopped. 'She's my imaginary friend.'

Kathryn nodded, Beth gaped, and Rupert looked from each of them to the next.

'You do realise how impossible this all sounds? If it didn't make so much sense.'

Louis frowned, fidgeting some more with his hands.

'In your... imagination,' Kathryn said hesitantly. 'When you live with your wife, and Sarah - do you live in the whole of your building?'

Louis nodded.

'I always used to. The whole place, it was owned by mummy and daddy - when they were alive.'

'Makes sense, I guess,' Kathryn said, reaching across the table to stop Louis' fidgeting.

'It does?' asked Louis. 'I felt sure you were going to say that I was a freaking weirdo, or a nutcase.'

Kathryn grinned.

'Oh, I already knew you were one of those.'

Beth stood up, slowly, and stepped across the kitchen with her empty mug. She stopped and turned, rolling the mug between her hands.

'I'm glad this makes sense to you two,' said Beth. 'Because I'm really confused.'

Kathryn and Louis both lifted their gaze to Beth from opposite sides of the table. Beth slapped the mug down into the sink, and approached Louis again.

'You don't have a daughter, you don't even have a wife,' reasoned Beth. 'I've known you since university days, Louis - I've never even known you to have a girlfriend!'

'I – I know...'

'So how is this possible?' asked Beth.

'Louis?'

Kathryn looked up at him, already guessing at the answer.

'How did you *meet* Amanda?'

'School orchestra. I remember it so clearly – it was after I started playing flute. Miss Leroy, she gave me the lessons. She got me to go along...'

Kathryn nodded.

'And did Miss Leroy help you with anything else?'

Louis nodded, nervously.

'She was brilliant,' he replied. 'I know what people say about her, and all the rumours, but she was never like that to me.'

For a moment Louis was back at school as a gangly, dark-haired boy, sitting on his own in the corner of the playground. He saw the advancing gang of older boys, and he ran – before they arrived – hiding in a quiet corridor at the back of the school.

Another vision crashed back into his mind, and he was sprawled across the playground, with his flannel trousers shredded at the knee with specks of red showing from the grazes, his battered flute lying next to him. There, behind him, was the click of stiletto heels, as Miss Leroy advanced towards him.

'They hated me, all of them; I don't know why. Because I was different? You don't know what it was like,' continued Louis. 'But Miss Leroy, she changed all that. Once I started having music lessons and joined the orchestra – and then Amanda. I had friends.'

'Friends,' repeated Kathryn.

Louis looked up.

'What do you mean?'

'You've only mentioned one – Amanda. And if she is...? Did you have any other friends?'

Louis stared back at her blankly.

'Amanda is the only friend you've talked about, and you never talked about her before now – before we…'

'Broke up?' said Louis. 'That was never meant to happen.'

Kathryn offered up a wry smile in return.

'I'm still not getting this,' interjected Beth. 'I've never heard of an Amanda either – or Sarah – and I've known you for, what, fourteen years?'

'You were talking *to* her tonight though,' Kathryn answered quickly.

Beth stopped. Consciously her hand went to her neck, and felt where there was no necklace.

'The necklace?' said Beth. The image of Louis tearing the necklace from Kathryn's neck flashed through her mind, and again she remembered the sense of release as she unfastened the silver chain from her own neck.

'It was trapping you both,' said Louis. He looked up at Kathryn. 'I'm sorry if I hurt you.'

'It's fine,' Kathryn told him. 'I know Polly gave the necklaces to us, but I think they were from Miss Leroy. I think she was using them to control us.'

Kathryn saw the confused stare that Beth was giving her.

'I know, it sounds impossible; but honestly, the relief when Louis ripped that thing from my neck,' continued Kathryn. 'It was like having a dead weight taken from me. And it kind of makes sense, with what Louis was telling us; if she's been controlling Louis all his life, it would make sense that she wanted to control his few friends too.'

'The witch!'

Kathryn frowned.

'Faery Queen, more like.'

At this, Louis, too, turned to look at Kathryn.

'How do you know?' asked Louis.

'I just know. It's in my books. But—'

Kathryn was up and out of her seat, halfway to the door before she addressed her father.

'Dad, can I borrow your laptop? Rawson – she has a blog – it should be on there—'

Rupert barely had time to nod before Kathryn was out the door, his directions to where in the study his computer was called after her.

Kathryn returned to the room, with the laptop resuming from hibernation. She set the computer down and began loading up browser windows, searching through pages; she quickly found Rawson's blog of writings about myth and legend, thanks to librarian-like cataloguing and classification. She leaned in closer to the screen to read off the details.

'Here it is,' said Kathryn. 'The Faery Queen is said to pay a tithe to Hell every seven years, and her mortal lovers often provide this sacrifice.'

Kathryn lifted her head and looked from face to face of her companions.

'Don't you see? Miss Leroy, she has a hold on all of us; but more than any on Louis...'

'I'm not her lover though,' protested Louis.

'No. And I don't think it's seven years either, but it's still similar. She's been controlling you though, that's clear.'

'But how?'

Louis' question fell into an uneasy silence, broken eventually by Rupert.

'She likes them musical,' Rupert said dispassionately. Slowly, heads turned and gazes fell upon him. He grinned.

'The Faery Queen. She likes them to be musical, the men that she preys on. And every seven years she takes their life and is reborn.'

'I thought it was nine?'

Rupert shook his head at Kathryn's interruption.

'In some stories, yes. Not in the original. In some versions she kills her lovers.'

Louis gulped loudly. Rupert nodded.

'Oh yes, kills. But in other tales it's done differently.'

'Miss Leroy has to take my life in some way,' said Louis. 'That's why she got me a sabbatical, so my absence from school wouldn't be noticed. I'm not going back.'

Louis' words were left lingering around the kitchen table, as a stillness surrounded them. Beyond the kitchen blinds, a car passed the house and a dog barked. Beth looked up at Louis.

'Eleven years,' said Beth. 'Eleven years ago we left university, and started working at the county school.'

Louis' surprise was tempered by a twisted, thwarted expression of calculation and mind-workings.

'That was when my dad died. Eleven years ago,' said Louis. 'When I – we – I'd known Amanda for eleven years by then.'

'Amanda's not real.'

'Back then she was, to me. And it's another thing – nine years.'

'She doesn't exist!' insisted Kathryn.

'Nor does the Faery Queen; she's a myth, but you are still determined to believe that she is going to take my life to further her own.'

Louis glared at Kathryn angrily, and with so much intensity that she had to look away. She picked herself up from the chair, and, shielding her face, she retreated to the sink, and filled her glass with cold water from the tap. She guzzled it down fast and refilled her glass, as Rupert comforted his daughter.

'Louis?' Beth began tentatively. 'I think you've made a mistake...'

Kathryn's attention was piqued, but she remained facing the sink, glass to her lips, and listened.

'How old is Sarah, Louis?' asked Beth.

Louis stared at her.

'She's year six, Louis,' Beth told him. 'How can she be eleven?'

Louis stuttered and stumbled over his words, tried to answer, and floundered. Kathryn turned around, nodding, and stepped forward again.

'Eleven years ago you *married* Amanda. At some point you imagined having a child, but you imagined her the wrong age.'

'You met her,' said Louis. 'She's real...'

'Seems like the Faery Queen is real,' countered Kathryn. 'Who's to say what is possible?'

Louis frowned, and the conversation fell silent. Beth yawned, and a collective decision was reached that it was time for bed.

2

Lewis woke just as the dawn light was creeping down the side of the valley towards the small stone cottage. Next to him, Amanda lay, still sleeping, in their bed. He pulled back the covers and got out, before replacing the covers over his wife. Lewis crossed the room and pulled on his corduroy trousers, retrieving his checked shirt from the chair by the window.

Moving quickly across the floor so as to not disturb Amanda, he winced as the latch to the door clunked loudly into the still morning, and again as the floorboards creaked and groaned. He pulled the door to behind him, and padded lightly downstairs.

Lewis had just made himself a cup of coffee when Amanda entered the kitchen in her nightie and dressing gown, still half asleep. Lewis looked up and smiled.

'You want one too?' he asked. 'I'm sorry if I woke you.'

He offered Amanda his own, as yet untouched coffee, and began again to make himself a new one.

'It's nice here,' said Amanda eventually, after they both were settled in the old Windsor chairs either side of the French doors in the kitchen. 'We should get away more often.'

Lewis looked up and nodded. He frowned.

'I wish I could be more spontaneous,' he said.

'You were pretty spontaneous last night, Lewis!' Amanda laughed.

Lewis looked down into his mug of coffee.

'I – I guess.'

'And we can be spontaneous now,' she continued. 'The sun is barely up yet. Let's grab the dog and head out for a walk. Now!'

Amanda sprung to her feet and reached out with warm hands to help up her husband. As Lewis stood to join her, he all but fell into Amanda's embrace, and couldn't help himself but laugh.

'You should probably get dressed first, though!' he joked.

Amanda took a step back, still holding her husband by the hands, and looked down at her nightie and open gown.

'It's not really in the spirit of impetuousness and spontaneity; but yes, I think you're right.'

A few minutes later and Amanda returned downstairs to the hall, having thrown on a pair of jeans, a thick, snuggly sweater and trainers. She had fixed her hair back into two girlish pig tails. A few minutes later and she, Lewis, and the dog then headed out into the back garden, and across the dewy, frozen lawn to the gate at the end of the lawn that led up into the woods.

The dog ran ahead, bounding through the woods; back and forth, and back and forth as he rounded up his human owners. Lewis and Amanda walked up through the woods, surrounded by the chorus of morning birdsong.

'We get too caught up in our Wren Hoe lives, don't we?' said Amanda, letting go of Lewis' hand briefly to duck forward through a narrow, overhanging section of path.

'I guess,' agreed Lewis. 'It's like at Christmas, when work stops and I have days to just be. I read so much – I always promise myself that I'll continue the practice once work starts up again, but I never do.'

Amanda waited for him, and they took each other's hands again to walk the next bit of path.

'Life gets in the way,' Amanda frowned.

'By the time we've gone through the post, got dinner, washed up, thought about the next day...'

'Kept on top of the washing and put the hoover round,' added Amanda.

'I only ever read before bed, and then it's the same two pages for three nights in the row because I'm so dog-tired.'

'You want to get the instruments out later? Play some duets – like we used to?'

Lewis turned towards Amanda and smiled.

Five bars rest, and Lewis and Amanda looked up at the same time, separated by three people, across the rows of the school orchestra. Lewis remembered it like yesterday; the joy as the music was carried along. Lewis remembered the two of them in the attic playroom at Bevington House; the duets, the sideways glances between bars, the laughter when it all went wrong.

They exchanged the memories, laughing and joking as they climbed up the hill through the woodland. A kissing gate at the edge of the woodland path loomed ahead, silhouetted against the morning sky. Above, a branch, stripped bare by the winter, rocked and jumped in the wind, like a conductor of the orchestra. Both Lewis and Amanda stopped short, both seeing in the branch the same thing – Miss Leroy – standing at the front of the orchestra, with eyes and ears tuned to every mistake. Lewis grabbed Amanda tightly and ran forward with her to the gate. Snatching a kiss across the bars, they rushed up through the grass—

Lewis' mind flashed back to school, and to running round the back of the school with Amanda, between the large shrubs that surrounded the boiler house that muffled the laughter and giggles as they heard the unmistakable clip-clip of heels on the path beyond, before relaxing into each other's embrace once they had passed.

At the top of the ridge Lewis looked down with Amanda at the lights of Bristol, and the docks beyond, spread out beneath them. Lewis reached out and took hold of Amanda's hand, feeling the warmth of her touch. And in his mind, Lewis saw the scene from behind, the two of them silhouetted at the top of the hill, against the early morning sky.

Louis woke with a crick in his neck, and a soreness running through his shoulder muscles where he lay half-curled on the sofa in the study of the unfamiliar room. He yawned, and bleary-eyed, pushed himself up onto a cushion as he eased himself into the day. Through a crack in the curtains he could see the day breaking outside.

A knock at the door, and Louis croaked an answer. The latch clattered, and the door to the study squeaked open. Kathryn slipped in from behind the door in her dressing gown, carrying a mug of tea.

'Morning,' she greeted him.

'Hi.'

Louis sat himself up, remembering now a little more of the reality of how he came to be here.

'Did you sleep well?'

Kathryn passed Louis the mug of tea, perching on the edge of the sofa next to him. Louis nodded.

'Weird dreams, though,' he said.

'Took me ages to get to sleep. It *was* quite a night, wasn't it?'

'Did that all happen?' asked Louis. 'The wedding? Miss Leroy...?'

'If it wasn't for Beth, I don't know where we would have ended up.'

'Beth, of course. Is she still...?'

Kathryn nodded.

'Still sleeping. Poor girl, she's shattered after driving half the night,' said Kathryn. She frowned. 'So, what were these weird dreams?'

Louis shook his head.

'I dreamt I was here,' he laughed. 'But it was different. Like I was on holiday.'

Kathryn laughed, stopping as the nervous awkwardness grew in Louis. She offered out a reassuring touch, and smiled.

'I feel like that too, when I come back here,' she explained. 'This is my home, but when I'm here - I guess it's not my working life - so it feels like a holiday.'

Louis nodded. What Kathryn said made sense, even if it's not really what *he had meant*. He wanted to tell her, to explain, but—

'I never wanted this,' he began. 'To hurt you, I mean. We were never meant to stop seeing each other.'

'I know.'

A little later, Louis joined Kathryn in the kitchen. Scruff bounded forwards to greet him enthusiastically, and Louis fussed over the dog like an old friend - like 'his' dog that he had greeted a few hours earlier in his dream. Looking up, he saw Kathryn looking back at him, enjoying seeing him get on so well with Scruff.

'He needs a walk actually,' said Kathryn. 'You want to go up the hill - see the lights of Bristol?'

After a few minutes Louis stood, with Scruff licking around his ankles, while Kathryn locked up. Then they were heading out across the garden, with Scruff bounding ahead and through the gap at the bottom of the gate that led into the woods. In the blue light after the dawn, a mist lingered on the dewy grass, and the silhouettes of the swaying branches above, set against the dark shadows, made them seem larger.

Louis looked across at the girl walking next to him - Kathryn. He smiled. This walk, it was so much like he had imagined, how he had dreamt; but he was with someone that he could look in the eye, and reach out and... touch. He reached out with his own hand to take Kathryn's, and snatched it back.

'This is where you grew up then?' asked Louis. 'I would have loved a woodland at the end of the garden.'

'It used to terrify me!' Kathryn laughed. 'It's the way the shadows move at dusk. I felt sure that there were pixies or fairies living out here.'

She ducked back, as one branch with long, pointed thorns reached out and grabbed hold of her. Louis unhooked her from the clawing arm.

'I can see how you would think that, with these bushes—'

Kathryn smiled and thanked him, as they moved on up along the woodland path. They walked on, passing through a kissing gate at the top of the woodland, for the last few steps up through the grassland to the top of the ridge.

Louis stopped, stunned by the view spread out before him. Across the flat land below, all the way to the dark stain that was the Channel, were the lights of Bristol.

Kathryn stepped up to him, and pushed her arm through his. 'You like it?'

'It's fantastic.'

They stood next to each other, neither speaking, both gazing out at the lights of Bristol. As they watched, dawn turned to day, and one by one the lights went out. Louis turned to face Kathryn.

'So...?' he said.

Kathryn looked back at him, happy to be with him, yet troubled by his uncertainty. She stared back at him with wide, loving eyes, and nodded to him to continue.

'Where now? Where are we safe?'

'Nowhere.'

3

Louis sat again in the back of Beth's car, holding Kathryn's hand tightly. He looked out the window at the country lanes as they blurred past, and the car lurched round corners. He'd never realised before, but Beth was quite the most erratically alarming driver. He wondered now if she had been to the same school of driving as Tom.

It took hardly any time to reach the market town of Middleton, where Louis and Kathryn were let out in the small market square under the shadow of the war memorial. There they thanked Beth again, and said their goodbyes. They refused Beth's offer of sticking around while they did their shopping and running them back to Kathryn's village, and so Beth headed off on the long drive to Wren Hoe. So, after repeated acknowledgements of thanks, all too soon Louis and Kathryn were standing on the pavement, watching Beth's car lurching away into the Monday morning traffic.

With the car gone, they turned to one another before making their way into the little pedestrianised street. As they walked, Kathryn couldn't stop herself looking; from herself in her dress from the wedding, her spare pair of boots, and an old, thick, woollen jumper she had found in the bottom of her wardrobe, to Louis in the suit that he had been wearing on Saturday night. She laughed repeatedly, explaining her amusement to Louis. It was just too funny to think what the two of them must look like: two waifs from a party who hadn't been home yet. Strictly speaking, Louis suggested, that was correct.

Half way up Sheep Street they arrived at McCreedy's. Possibly the smallest department store in the country, the store had been in Middleton since the Edwardian age, and was still run by third-generation McCreedys. Louis settled into browsing the store by heading for the back wall where, together with racks of double-breasted suits, tartan ties and dinner jackets, were shelf after shelf of neatly folded, pure cotton, checked shirts, and racks of corduroy trousers.

'Louis, what are you doing?' Kathryn laughed, intervening as Louis was about to slide another virtually identical shirt into the basket. Louis looked back at her with an expression of uncomprehending bewilderment.

'You don't have to buy up the whole shop. We're not starting a new life with none of our possessions. And my mum and dad do have a washing machine!'

Kathryn kept careful, compassionate watch over Louis as she returned all but one of the shirts to the shelves, and then steered him in the direction of the more casual, polyester mix shirts on hangers. When it came to herself, Kathryn was quick to find a couple of pretty blouses and a new pair of jeans that she needed anyway.

They paid for their purchases and headed out onto Sheep Street to stroll on up the road, criss-crossing between shops. Louis drew Kathryn towards the old-fashioned tobacconist and stationers. Inside, Louis cruised the racks of pens and artists materials, fingering them and cooing over them like an amazed child. Kathryn left him to coo and drifted away to browse the sweet aisle; and when Louis reappeared at Kathryn's side, it was with a paper bag clasped firmly in his hand.

'What have you got there?' Kathryn asked as they left the shop.

'Fountain pen. Remember the one I used to have?'

Kathryn nodded sadly.

'I feel lost without it, so—'

'It's a big bag for a pen!' Kathryn said, as she reached over and squeezed the brown paper.

Louis looked sheepish.

'There might also be some fudge…!' he relented.

At the top end of the street, Kathryn led Louis off down a narrow side street of stone buildings and passages between gardens. Cute cottage followed cute cottage as they wound their way round the backstreets of the town, and for every house that Louis cooed over, Kathryn enlightened him with stories of the building's history in mock guide book style. After about the fifth detailed explanation, Louis asked how she knew all of it, and Kathryn confessed to two summers during university working as a guide for the local tourist office.

'It's like those trips we took last summer,' Kathryn said, after they'd settled on a bench overlooking the fields at the edge of town. 'Do you remember that day up at the Uffington Horse?'

Louis grinned, and agreed enthusiastically. Of course he remembered that day – it was one of the best days of last summer – of his whole life! Next to him on the bench in the spring sunshine, he felt Kathryn wriggle closer. He glanced to his right and offered her his arm, and she slipped hers through.

On the edge of the village just down the road was a large house with two grand wings facing the view across the fields, the valley, and further still, the woodland. In its stately elegance it reminded Kathryn of the neglected grandeur of Bevington House.

'Louis?' began Kathryn eventually.

'Yeah?'

Kathryn glanced across again at the grand house, seeing for a moment herself in one of the upstairs windows looking out. She blinked, and she was gone. She turned back to Louis, where he was waiting for her question.

'There's one thing that I still don't understand. It's Bevington House - your home. How does that work?'

'I don't understand?' asked Louis. 'What are you asking?'

'When we were going out, you lived in a ground floor flat in that old house. I know you did, I was there - I slept there! But, after Christmas I went back there and it was up for sale, and so I broke in. I had to go back and see, to find out for myself...'

'And...?'

Kathryn pulled herself round to face Louis.

'The house, Louis. It was all one building. Where you had shallow cupboards, there were doors into other rooms, and the stairs were still there. How did it happen?'

'Developer, I guess? The new owners—'

'No, Louis,' Kathryn said. 'It was your house, but not your house. You had left Ardizzoni there.'

'Ardizzoni?' Louis said, looking up. 'You have Ardizzoni?'

Kathryn nodded.

'Yes! He's sitting on my pillow - on my bed - in Wren Hoe.

Louis gulped, and stared at Kathryn.

'Louis?' Kathryn prompted him.

'When my Mum died the house got sold for flats. I got to keep the ground floor. Sometimes I imagined that I still lived in the whole house—'

'With Amanda?'

Louis nodded.

'I loved growing up in that house. I really wanted my children to grow up in it too.'

'So you dreamed that that's what you did.'

Louis stared at Kathryn. She was right, but he couldn't admit it to her. And she sat and watched him; not judging him, just watching him. She jumped back in her seat, startled by the rustling in the air and the shadow across the sky. They both looked up in time to see a dove diving and swooping up into the sky.

'Dove from above,' Kathryn said, pointing across the field behind the big house. 'There's an old dovecote. Nice to see it still being used.

Back on the bus, Louis squeezed himself into the seat next to Kathryn. In one hand he clutched the dirty stub of a bus ticket, and with the other he reached out across Kathryn's lap for her hand. Their fingers closed around each other, and their bus set off out of town. Louis sat back and enjoyed having Kathryn's hand in his.

Helped along by the slow rocking passage of the bus on the slow country roads, Louis felt last night's absence of sleep catch up with him. His eyelids weighed heavy and—

Lewis looked to where Amanda sat next to him on the bus home from town. Her auburn hair was tucked back in a bob, and she wore the carefree smile of the fifteen-year old girl she was then. Lewis squeezed his girlfriend's hand gently, finding comfort in her closeness. She said something, and he turned his head towards her and laughed. She laughed. He loved the way she laughed.

A girl on the seat in from of them scrambled round and leaned over towards her parents, grinning and excited. Lewis was older now, as was Amanda next to him. He responded to Sarah's comment with the same enthusiasm that he used to have as a child with Amanda.

With a few, serious words, Amanda clipped Lewis' relaxed mood and told Sarah in no uncertain terms to turn around. Lewis watched, his gaze fixed on Amanda's straight mouth and pale complexion. Gone was the simple, natural makeup, and those little upturns at the corners of her mouth. Who, he suddenly though, was she? Where had the Amanda of his teenage years gone?

'Louis?' Kathryn repeated. 'We're here.'

Louis blinked. He was back. Next to him, getting out of her seat on the bus, was Kathryn, with warm, welcoming expression, bright eyes and, he noticed, an upwards turning at the corners of her smile. He gathered up his bags off the floor and followed her down the aisle, and off the bus to the small square of pavement beneath the bus stop on the county road opposite Kathryn's parents' house.

4

Kathryn finished making the bed in the small guestroom under the eaves at the back of the house. Classic FM drifting in from a distant radio as she moved around the room. She didn't notice Louis' footsteps on the stairs and as he crossed the landing, or the shadow that passed across the doorway.

'Can I help?'

Kathryn jumped at the sound of Louis' voice. She turned to face him.

'I think I'm done, thanks.'

Louis nodded.

'Thanks for doing this for me, and—'

'Why wouldn't I? I couldn't leave you there with that – whatever she is!' Kathryn said reassuringly, as she stooped to gather up the old sheets. 'How were my mum and dad?'

'Fine,' Louis said, with a shrug. 'They've taken Scruff for his walk now. I helped your mum with the vegetables for dinner.'

'She is warming to you then,' mused Kathryn. 'I was wondering.'

She stepped towards the door with her arms full of washing.

'Kathryn, wait.'

She stopped to turn and look at him.

'It's just that – I'm sorry. I've had the best day today, with you.'
Kathryn beamed.
'So have I. With you I mean.'
'And I should never – I mean – I really regret—'
Louis stopped again, struggling to find the words.
'Breaking up with you was a mistake. My biggest mistake.'
Kathryn took a step closer.
'Louis?' What are you trying to say?'
He hesitated for a moment.
'I'd like to, if it's okay, stop being broken up with you—'
She laughed with an infectious, playful laugh.
'I mean, I'd like it if you were my girlfriend again,' he said finally, and completely.

Kathryn stared at him, not with shock or surprise, but with joy. Slowly she shook her head and pulled him closer.

'You silly,' she told him, 'we already are together – again.'

She pecked a kiss on his lips. A , and a smile spread across his face, growing into a joyful grin. His hands moved out around her waist, as she dropped the ball of washing and stepped over it. His mouth found hers, and he kissed her. Kathryn slipped her hands across his shoulders, and cupping his neck, she kissed him back. Soon their tongues were exploring each other's mouths as if for the first time. Louis inhaled Kathryn's perfume, and felt the warmth of her breath. Their embrace tightened as time seemed to slow, and the sounds of the radio and a distant washing machine faded into the background.

Kathryn propped herself up on her side next to Louis where they had collapsed on her bed. She hooked his fringe out from his eyes and looked down into them, stroking the sides of his face with her fingers. He reached up and pulled her hand closer, kissing the fingertips.

Somewhere, away downstairs, pots and pans crashed and clattered in the kitchen. What would have happened, she wondered, had her parents not arrived home? Secretly she was relieved – better, she decided, to wait for an occasion when there was no chance of being interrupted. It was enough to know that it – that they were both – what each other wanted.

'Guess I didn't need to make up the other bed after all,' she smiled.

Louis shook his head. 'I don't mind. If you would prefer, we don't have to—'

Kathryn laughed and rolled back off the bed. She tossed a pillow in Louis' direction as she got up.

'Come on,' she said. 'I think dinner is nearly ready.

Downstairs in the kitchen, Louis and Kathryn sat opposite one another as Kathryn's mum ladled out platefuls of casserole. During dinner most of the talk revolved around the stresses and strains of Kathryn's Mother's Day. Giving up full-time teaching to work as a supply teacher was supposed to have made her life easier, but to hear her now, Kathryn was not so sure. Still, Kathryn felt relieved by this, as she spent the entire time exchanging what she hoped were secret looks with Louis, and wondering if either of her parents had noticed or realised.

Even after dinner, Kathryn and Louis were prevented from open talk while they cleared plates and washed up, as her mother continued to bustle and fuss over things that really didn't require bustling and fussing over. Eventually she headed off into the hall for the last time, and they heard her settle down in front of some mind-numbing soap opera in the lounge.

As Kathryn reached for the last bit of drying up, she tussled over how to explain her concerns to Louis. Yes, they were together again, but there was still so much left unexplained and unresolved. The mystery of Bevington House for one, and what part the evil – yes, she had decided that the headmistress was indeed evil – Miss Leroy was playing.

'Louis, we—'

But she got no further, for her father had now returned to the kitchen, carrying with him an old battered briefcase, and an equally tatty flute case.

'Louis, I remembered you saying you played,' he began, as Louis turned to respond, drying his hands.

'I did too, once … and badly,' continued Rupert. 'I've got no idea what state this is in, or if it's even playable – but you are welcome to try.'

Rupert fidgeted with the catches and opened the case, to reveal a silver, if dulled and tarnished flute.

'And I have bits of music here,' he said, slapping the leather briefcase reassuringly. 'I thought if you are here for a few days, you might find it amusing.'

At this point, Kathryn's dad gave his daughter a firm and lasting stare.

'And if Kathryn even gets her oboe out, I think we have some ducks.'

'It would be amusing,' Kathryn added hastily. 'But I think my oboe is in my room back in Wren Hoe.'

Rupert shook his head.

'No, it's in the cupboard in my study. I checked.'

Kathryn rolled her eyes at the news. Louis nodded and accepted the flute gratefully.

'It could be fun; thank you, Mr Summers.'

'Rupert, please.'

'Thank you, Rupert,' Louis added politely. He stood and stared at the three segments of instrument in their case.

Rupert hovered at the island unit, idling from foot to foot, waiting. Louis glanced up from the instrument case at Kathryn, and with a look of despair asked her silently why her Dad was still here. Kathryn smiled, and reached out a comforting hand to Louis.

'Louis,' she said softly, 'are you not going to try it?'

She glanced across at her dad, and the look of hope that crossed his face at the suggestion.

'Oh, right. Of course,' said Louis.

He placed the case down on the granite worktop, and carefully picked out each segment of flute to slot them into one another. The joints were a little stiff, but nothing that a bit of cleaning wouldn't fix. He lifted it up in both hands, and let his fingers find their places on the keys. He peered close, and tried each one. Some were stiff and some loose, and the pads were worn and sticky.

'Need some Rizlas,' Louis said, and waggled one of the keys some more.

And then he saw her. At first he saw just her fingers on the keys, playing the tune as a duet, but then her face at the flute. His tune faltered and broke, and she stopped playing too, but told him where he went wrong, and how he must play it right. Her voice was just how it had always been when he was younger, clipped and shrill. Obediently he put the flute to his lips and played again, this time finding the tune immediately. In front of him, in another hall, Miss Leroy spoke to him, congratulating him and encouraging him. She praised his playing, and pushed him to carry on.

Louis felt the rhythm flow through him as he felt himself become at one with it, and he began to move more fluidly and expressively. Through the open kitchen door he could see her – Miss Leroy – at the end of the hallway. Clip, clip, clip, the stiletto heels advanced towards him. All the while she encouraged him, speaking to him like she was in his head, and he carried on playing obediently.

'Louis, stop!'

Louis heard Kathryn's voice, saw her standing next to him in the kitchen. For a moment his playing wavered. Miss Leroy stopped walking, but encouraged him to carry on playing. He found the tune again and continued the rhythm.

'Louis! Please—'

Louis turned to face Kathryn and saw her pleading desperation for him to listen, but continued playing; Miss Leroy was there in his head, encouraging him to continue. His fingers slipped and slithered over the keys, and the notes jumbled out of the instrument as he struggled to keep to the tune.

'Louis!'

Kathryn grabbed the flute from him, and Miss Leroy was gone. She stared at him.

'Louis, what happened? It was like you were possessed.'

Louis panted breathlessly and sank into a chair.

'I think I was,' he said. 'She was here.'

Kathryn stared at him.

'Who?' she asked. 'Who was here?'

Kathryn knew the answer even before Louis said it.

'Miss Leroy.'

Louis and Kathryn sat opposite one another in the kitchen, with the old flute lying between them on the oiled pine table.

'How?' Kathryn asked eventually.

Louis didn't answer; couldn't answer. He just sat staring at the keys of the instrument, and remembering how the old woman told him what to play.

'What was the tune?' asked Kathryn persistently.

Again Louis didn't answer, but nor did Kathryn rush him. She could see that he was thinking things over – working through his thoughts in his brain, much as a cow grazed the nutrients from its fodder.

'It was the first thing I learnt to play,' he said eventually, offering Kathryn a weak and troubled smile. 'Miss Leroy, she taught me.'

Kathryn rolled her eyes.

'It explains why it brought her to mind. Why you thought you saw her.'

'I didn't *think* I saw her!' Louis snapped. 'I *did* see her. She was here, telling me what to play!'

Kathryn shook her head.

'I accept that you thought you saw her, but she wasn't actually here. She was in your head.'

'If you hadn't stopped me when you did, I think she might have got through.'

Kathryn narrowed her gaze with confusion.

'Louis, you're really not making any sense.'

'She was there, walking down your own hall. Except she wasn't. She was in my head, but—'

Louis stumbled over the words.

'If I'd carried on, she would have found some way of getting out of my head and being here.'

'Do you think she knows where we are?' asked Kathryn.

'She knows that I'm in this room, or *was* earlier. I don't think she knows where this room is, yet.'

Kathryn shook her head sadly. She remembered the wedding necklace, and the way that having it torn from here neck broke the chains that bound her obedience.

'It's not possible,' she said defiantly. Glancing up and away from the flute on the table, Kathryn saw the look from Louis' eyes, and in it his desperation.

5

Kathryn lay in the bed in which she had grown up, in the room that had always been hers, staring up at the shadows on the ceiling from where the moonlight filtered in through the curtains. It felt weird lying in this bed with Louis beside her. She glanced over at his sleeping body, gently rising and falling with each breath.

'Louis, are you awake?' she whispered.

Louis responded with a groggy murmur. Kathryn turned over to face him, and saw the dark outline of his face squished into the pillow.

'I've been thinking about this – us – and Miss Leroy.'

'Kathryn – sleep,' groaned Louis.

Kathryn reached out defiantly and pushed and pulled him awake.

'No, listen, we have to talk about it.'

'Agreed,' said Louis. 'But now?'

He tried to pull the covers back up around his shoulders.

'Yes, we have to decide what we're going to do,' Kathryn persevered, wide-awake now. 'I thought I just had to tell you, talk to you, to get you back – get you away from that woman; but it's not that simple, is it?'

Louis stared at the girl next to him.

'I used to think I overanalysed things.'

'This is serious, Louis!' Kathryn reprimanded him. 'She's the Faery Queen, right. So it's not just a matter of us escaping from her. We have to defeat her too.'

'I guess,' Louis agreed.

'That's the question then. How do we defeat her?'

'How does one normally go about defeating the Faery Queen?'

Louis' question was as simple as it was obvious. The answer was, sadly, less obvious. Kathryn lay there, staring almost without knowing at Louis, as a thousand different ways of killing a fairy queen flitted through her mind like butterflies on a rose bush, or the fanned pages of a book. She lay there next to Louis, and wished that they were back in Wren Hoe with her books. She could visualise the volumes she wanted to consult, and she knew exactly where they were. They were all miles upon miles out of reach from where she currently was.

'Kathryn?'

She heard Louis' voice, but her mind was already elsewhere. Remembering the stories she knew, from the ones she loved and could recite backwards, to others that she had read but whose stories were mixed up with other plots. Kathryn looked up at Louis, where he lay just next to her. She reached out and stroked the side of his face, and smiled.

'I'm trying to remember,' she said. 'Night night, Louis.'

'Night night, sleep well.'

Kathryn turned over and tucked herself up, her mind still pouring through memories and half-remembered stories. In time, tiredness overtook her, and she fell asleep.

A chorus of birdsong woke Kathryn. Louis was still fast asleep, so she eased herself out of bed and dressed quickly, before creeping out of the house and collecting Scruff as she made her way out into the early morning.

She took the lower path through the woods that worked its way up gradually to the ridge, rather than the straight and direct route which she had taken Louis on. In the early morning light, the woods were beautiful with the soft colours of light behind the lush growth of young leaves. Kathryn still felt the aches of a disturbed sleep; she was still not properly used to sharing a bed with someone else, or the subconscious awareness that she could not move across the mattress and wrap herself in the duvet as she had grown used to. She stopped and stretched, rubbing the soreness from her limbs.

As she had drifted from midnight darkness to sleep, she had wondered whether she would remember what she had decided come morning. She had; and she was every bit as certain it was what she had to do. The only difficulty was how to break the suggestion to Louis. He was not going to like the idea.

When Kathryn reached the top of the hill, she walked the ridgeway back past the exposed outcrops of limestone above the heathland to the far side of the hill. Scruff bounded off ahead of her, picking at various interesting scents, before dropping them equally quickly in favour of something new. Returning to her briefly, he circled her legs and ran on again, this time much further towards another early morning walker.

Who the...? Kathryn knew every one of the regulars who came up here, and without exception every one of them, at this time in the morning, were dog walkers. She couldn't help but stare at the man as she approached, wondering who he was. He seemed familiar, but from where...? And then it hit her. Matthew. What was he doing here, and how did he find her?

The man stopped on an exposed promontory of rock overlooking Bristol, like he was waiting for her. She stopped and called Scruff back. At first Scruff obeyed and began bounding through the grass until the next distraction, and then he ran forward, and no amount of Kathryn calling him back could stop him running off and leaping around the man enthusiastically.

Matthew was crouching low now, fussing and petting Scruff, and Kathryn didn't like it. She called her dog again, shouted her commands, but still Matthew fussed and stroked the dog. Kathryn gritted her teeth, sped up to a marching pace, and stormed towards the outcrop of rock. Her fingers readied themselves on the dog's lead, as ahead of her Matthew seemed to be waiting for her approach. He was grinning.

How dare he grin at her! Kathryn seethed inside with anger and stomped closer. She ran through in her head the words that she was going to tell him. She was ready to let rip and her anger fly as she stomped up to him and—

'Katy, Scruff's looking well—'

Kathryn stopped and stared back. Standing up in front of her was not the young, dark-haired Matthew, but the greying, fifty-something Mr Pullen, local vet and friend of her father's.

'Oh, hi, Mr Pullen.'

Kathryn winced a smile, hoping that he had not seen any of her temper.

Kathryn was still brooding as she sat at the kitchen table eating her cereal, Louis sitting opposite with Rupert's newspaper. She stared blankly into space and wondered how Matthew did it, working work his way into her thoughts so convincingly.

'You okay?'

Kathryn started, woken from her dream by Louis' opener. He had let the newspaper slide to the table next to him, and was looking at her with some concern.

'Yeah fine, just thinking.'

To anyone other than Louis, Kathryn decided, it would be self-evident that she wasn't fine; but Louis might buy it.

'Did you have a nice walk?'

Kathryn nodded.

At that moment the letterbox clattered, followed by the slap of the post landing on the tiled hallway. Kathryn stood, sensing that Louis was expecting a reply, but the only thing she could think of to say was something she couldn't tell him. She was sure the man on the hillside had been Matthew, but he hadn't been. She couldn't mention this to Louis. What she could do, she was now totally decided on, was get her books, and that meant leaving Louis and going back to Wren Hoe.

She looked up and was about to speak, when the clatter of a door latch was heard and Rupert stepped into the kitchen with a puzzled expression on his face, clutching a small buff-coloured envelope.

'Problem, Dad?'

Rupert shrugged and shook his head. He held out one envelope so that Kathryn and Louis could see what was written on it.

'The Occupier?'

Kathryn looked at Louis with wide eyes. Louis shrugged.

'Well, you going to open it?' asked Kathryn, as she looked now to her father.

Rupert slipped his finger beneath the flap and tore it back along the fold. Inside was one small sheet of glossy paper, which once unfolded revealed itself to be a concert poster.

'The Dumas Quartet? Some church in Bristol. Odd.'

Rupert was about to scrunch up the paper, before Kathryn reached out and snatched it safely away.

'We'll be there,' she read, screwing up her face in confusion. 'What does that mean?'

Eventually Louis answered: 'The Dumas Quartet; that's Tom's group. And that's Polly's handwriting.'

Kathryn narrowed her gaze, and turned over the flyer again to look more closely at the concert details.

'It's tomorrow. They must need to tell us something - about Leroy maybe? But they're too scared to put anything in writing.'

'Guess we're off to Bristol tomorrow, then,' said Louis.

Kathryn nodded. She guessed then, that she would not be getting back to Wren Hoe tomorrow, which meant two more days at least before she could get to her books.

6

The train slid gracefully into the long, curved platform of Bristol Temple Meads, beneath the cathedral-like vaulted ceiling of Isambard Kingdom Brunel's station. Louis and Kathryn alighted from the train and made their way up the stairs, across the bridge, and down to the grand main entrance. The next bus was already waiting in the forecourt and they boarded it quickly, making their way to the very back seats from where they could watch everyone else boarding. Neither of them mentioned it, but both were sure that they had to be on guard not to be seen.

Kathryn had never been to the church in question, but she had checked it out on the internet before they had left, and had a pretty good idea how to find it. It was in a bohemian part of town, about a mile or so's walk from the city centre, and reminded Kathryn of her own dear Jericho with its network of tiny streets. The church itself was situated just off a small tree-lined square. They knew they were in the right place straight away though, because of the mustard-yellow car, parked two streets away, at a jaunty angle.

'Tom,' muttered Louis as they passed.

Right outside the church they discovered Beth's car, neatly parked in a space next to a kerbside metre.

'They really are *all* here,' Kathryn said, and grinned.

Outside the entrance to the church was an A-board displaying a larger version of the poster that was in Kathryn's hand, and a strip of paper across the middle of it advertising that tickets were still available. Louis laughed, commenting to Kathryn how absurd it was to imagine that a weekday afternoon concert by an unknown string quartet in an obscure church in the middle of Bristol could possibly be sold out.

Inside they were greeted by the 'Box Office', which consisted of a round-faced old woman with a propensity to chat. Eventually they managed to pay the token entrance fee; being given an A4-folded, hand-typed and photocopied programme, they were then allowed to enter the nave of the church to find some seats.

Despite Louis' earlier scoffing, there were a number of people – possibly as many as twenty-five – already there, spaced out around the church. Louis picked out Tom straight away, hunched over his cello, tuning it; and Kathryn recognised Ed, Sam, and Ann from when she had met them at the wedding.

Next, Kathryn began scanning the audience, and sure enough picked out Polly and Beth amongst others, in the middle of a row half a dozen or so from the front. She pointed and they both headed off to join them, filing into the row behind them. As they took their seats Louis was about to greet his friends before Kathryn stayed him with a firm grip to his arm. He spun round, and stared at Kathryn with confusion.

Kathryn pulled him closer and whispered, 'Isn't that…?'

She pointed to the girl seated next to Beth, with the ponytail of fair hair; and next to her another girl of about the same size.

Louis glanced around, then back with equal confusion. Kathryn all but mouthed the word: 'Sarah?'

'And her friend,' hissed Louis. 'Caz.'

'What are they doing here?'

Louis shrugged, his face twisted with uncertainty. At that moment Beth noticed them – and Polly shortly after – and realised that they had arrived and were leaning across the pews to greet them warmly and ask them how the last couple of days had been.

'And guess who else we've brought with us,' said Beth in a brief lull to the conversation, nudging Sarah and Caz into greeting. 'You remember Sarah, don't you? We bumped into her and Caroline. It's half term and they were at a loose end – and you know how much Sarah loves her music. Thought it would be nice—'

Louis smiled, if weakly, and acknowledged Sarah, unsure whether he should be greeting her as teacher or father.

'Hey, Mr Tumnal.'

It was Caz who spoke first.

'Where have you been?'

'Bit of a break. Things, you know.'

Louis felt his face twitch in a wincing kind of way, and hoped it wasn't too obvious.

'Sarah, how are you?'

'I'm good,' began Sarah.

Louis breathed with relief.

'Apart from dealing with my Dad. He's walked out on Mum and me.'

'Oh...'

'But what would you know about *that?*'

'No, I mean,' Louis hesitated. 'It's terrible.'

Louis felt Kathryn's elbow dig into his ribs. He glanced sideways, and knew from her expression that he had already said too much. Sarah remained where she was, staring at him with her big, wide, searching eyes that seemed to be able to get to the bottom of whatever you were thinking. Louis looked back at her; emptily, hopelessly trying to figure out what to say next.

'How – how's school?' he asked eventually.

Sarah rolled her eyes and turned away from Louis to face the stage again. Louis sat and stared at the blond ponytail, and the wisps of stray hairs around her neck and the hem of her T-shirt. His fingers fidgeted as if with a mind of their own.

Kathryn reached over and stayed his hands. She pulled him closer and whispered: 'So? Does she know who you are? I mean, *which* you are?'

Louis shook his head.

'I can't tell, can you?'

Any forthcoming answer was hushed by the last strains of tuning notes drawn out over strings, and the expectant silence throughout the church that followed them. A short piece by Haydn was followed by an altogether more challenging Bartok composition, during which Louis' mind wandered – partly allowing his gaze to take in the architecture of the Saxon church, but mostly for his brain to agitate over who the Sarah was who was sat in the row in front of him, and what she knew.

Suddenly the music was over, and the audience was applauding; some on the far side of the nave were even standing in appreciation of what they had heard. Louis and Kathryn glanced at one another—

'So, what did you make of that?' asked Kathryn.

Damn, reasoned Louis, she had got in before him with the easy question.

'Um...' began Louis. 'That first piece was amazing. Really, I loved it.'

Kathryn nodded towards the people presenting the quartet with a lengthy standing ovation.

'And the Bartok?'

Louis glanced around, almost guiltily, and ducked closer to Kathryn. He whispered: 'I – it wasn't really my kind of thing.'

'Me neither!' exclaimed Kathryn with relief.

By now the applause had ebbed away, and the audience were beginning to mingle and stretch their legs. Tom laid down his cello and made his way over towards Louis and the others.

Kathryn and Louis shuffled out of their row, joining the others in a group. As Polly and Tom raved about what they had just heard and played, there were varying degrees of agreement and perplexity from the others.

'I didn't like it,' Beth said quietly to Louis, while Polly was hugging Tom with enthusiasm for his performance.

Louis shook his head.

'Nor did I. Neither of us much liked it,' he added, with a glance across at Kathryn.

'It wasn't that bad,' said Kathryn. 'I mean I appreciated it, kind of...'

And then Tom and Polly were joining the conversation, and they were feigning their responses and remarking on how good the playing was; Louis found himself trapped by Tom's knowledgeable and enthusiastic deconstruction. At this point, Kathryn started to ease herself away from the group, signalling to Louis that she was in search of drinks. Louis excused himself to step towards Kathryn.

'No Louis, you stay with your friends,' she told him. 'I'm fine.'

She turned and headed off towards where she could see a queue forming. Louis watched Kathryn go, before treturning to Tom's energetic, animated deconstruction of the music.

'I'm glad you came.'

Louis smiled, if awkwardly, at Beth's words.

'We had to, really – the cryptic note – we didn't know what to expect.'

'Yeah, sorry about that; we didn't think it was safe to say any more. Well, we didn't want to say anything. When you left the wedding reception, Kathryn was so scared. We knew she wanted to keep you where you were secret.'

'So why did you bring *her*?' he hissed, pointing at Sarah.

Beth returned Louis' gaze with amused frustration. She shook her head with a frown.

'Truth is, Louis, she wanted to come.'

Louis gaped.

'How? Why? Beth, outside of school you don't even see her? How did she even know about today?'

Beth shook her head as she tried to work out if Louis' reaction was for real.

'When I left you the other morning I had to see Tom and Polly, and they were, of course, still at *that* house. And Sarah was with them.'

'Did you see *her*?'

Beth shook her head.

'The place was a mess.'

She frowned and moved closer to Louis, lowering her voice like she was concerned that she would be overheard.

'She was still in residence, I could tell that. Everyone had that on-edginess that she made you have. But she had taken to her rooms.'

Louis nodded. He knew that feeling completely, or at least recognised it. He remembered simpler times, when it had seemed Miss Leroy was his only friend and the only one who didn't have *the fear*. He certainly feared her now, and that all too familiar sound of stiletto heels clicking down a polished school floor sent shivers running down his spine as he heard it inside his head now.

'I managed to gather up most of your belongings.'

Louis started back to the here and now, looking up as Beth spoke.

'Polly helped me. Took us ages as we had to do it little by little—'

Her voice trailed off, as both she and Louis saw Sarah approach. Beth saw the awkwardness and diffidence in Louis' posture. She turned and welcomed Sarah warmly.

'Miss Vernal,' Sarah said brightly.

'Sarah,' Beth said with a smile.

Sarah stepped on, looking up at Louis with her big, wide, searching eyes. She waited.

'Sarah,' Louis said eventually.

Sarah nodded, presenting him with confidence and firmness.

'Sarah, what are you doing here?'

Sarah shook her head briskly and hissed her disbelief.

'Dad! Why are you being so - *weird?*'

Louis was stumped, in any response he had been preparing himself to give. He looked to Beth for support, but she was already edging away to meet Kathryn on her return with the drinks. He looked again to Sarah, fired up with months-worth of determination to have answers.

'I get that you and mum have split up, and you've found someone else. What I don't get, what I'm fed up with, is why you keep treating me like I don't exist!'

'You don't,' Louis said too quickly. 'I mean, you shouldn't—'

He stumbled over the awkwardness of the words. Sarah's only response was a defiant crossing of her arms, and a resigned stare.

'I mean, obviously you do - you're living proof that you do exist - as sure as you're standing in front of me, having a go at me—'

He tried a laugh, which faltered into a wince.

'And I love you like you were my own, but—'

'What are you saying? That I'm not...?'

Louis shook his head urgently.

'No, no. You're all mine – I see that now. But… it's not like you think. It's complicated.

'Go on.'

'It goes back to how I met your Mum.'

'You were school friends. First loves or something.'

'Yes, but…'

Louis never got a chance to explain further. Kathryn and Beth were hovering nearby, as around them the audience were beginning to take their seats again for the second half.

Back in his seat he was tense and on edge, staring at Sarah – his somehow daughter – in front of him. Next to him, Kathryn reached across and took his hand, just as the vibrant, rasping notes from Tom's cello sounded the opening, powerful bars of the string quartet version of Elgar's Cello Concerto.

For Louis, time slowed as the long, bowed notes reverberated around the stone arches of the church, and he found himself lost in the music. He allowed his gaze to drift to the altar, and the stained-glass window with the afternoon sun picking out the myriad of colours. His gaze defocussed, and his mind drifted.

The long-bowed chords of the music reached out across the church and bound Louis to his chair. They drew him back to the music, and seemed to strike him back to attention if ever his concentration was about to slip. Far from calling in people to face him, the music banished everyone; so that there was only the one thing: the music.

7

Applause ricocheted around the walls of the church. Louis started, suddenly aware that the music had finished, and the Dumas Quartet were taking their bows. All around him people were standing, clapping, and Louis leapt to his feet too to join in the applause.

Eventually the ovation subsided, and the audience began to drift away, milling about for a bit in the aisles and around the doors. On stage, the quartet began packing up their instruments and dismantling music stands. Louis and his friends found themselves helping with the stacking of chairs and putting the church back to rights.

He found himself next to Sarah at the back of the church. With the look she passed him, she didn't have to say anything. Louis frowned and drew her to one side.

'I'm jealous of you, Sarah.'

She looked back at him quizzically.

'Your friends, your confidence, your surety. Growing up, I never had any of that.'

They found a quiet corner in the vestry, and a couple of chairs on which to sit.

'You know when you change schools, join a group – even just go up a year? Every time I told myself it was going to be different, that this time I would have friends – be part of that wider social group…'

'Dad? What are you trying to say?'

Louis shook his head, more at his own character than Sarah's question.

'I'd go to all the sessions, be at every class, have a group of people I thought I was close to; and then I would discover that they'd be going out socially and I wasn't included.'

'Everyone gets that.'

'Do they? I've never seen you and Caz pre-arrange anything. You just instinctively, automatically, *do*.'

Sarah stared at her father, at his previously unseen passion and openness.

'If I went out after school it was to a club or a class, or something arranged days – weeks beforehand. You know what it feels like, to find out the next day the films that your so-called friends have been to see?'

Louis was impassioned now, fired with the realisation of his past.

'What about *me*? I was always mad to ask that. Why was *I* never invited? When were these plans made, because I never heard about them!'

'Maybe they didn't think you'd want to?' offered Sarah.

Louis shook his head.

'Amanda – she was the first person to be that close friend I'd always wanted. Of course I was going to fall in love with her.'

Sarah's expression twisted with disbelief at hearing this.

'And you think that makes it alright? Because you've only ever loved one person, it somehow makes it okay to cheat on them?'

'No!' Louis said, shaking his head ferociously. 'Amanda, she was perfect. Everything I loved, she loved. Everything I did, she did too. It was like she was made for me. I could never cheat on a person like Amanda.'

'Dad! You have!'

'Sarah, you're not understanding me. She was perfect for me in every way, because she *was* made for me – by me – she was my imaginary friend.'

Silence. Louis' breath-catching the only punctuation as Sarah took in his admission, Slowly, tentatively, she put her next question to him—

'So what does that make me? Am I an imaginary daughter?'

'No. I don't know. Maybe, once?'

Louis shrugged.

'I think you, Sarah, are one of the most real things in my life. Next to Kathryn.'

Sarah straightened up in front of Louis and stared at him. She lifted her hand up slowly, and slapped her father's face.

'Sarah!'

'What? Did that hurt, *Dad?* If I am as imaginary a daughter as your wife is, then how can me slapping you hurt? How can an imaginary person hurt anyone? How am I here? Who am I?'

Louis shook his head.

'I don't know. It's something to do with Miss Leroy. She has some control over my life that I'm only now figuring out.'

Silence lingered in the void that followed Louis' words. Louis looked to Sarah, and she couldn't stop staring at him. Inside, Louis felt that for the first time, in a strange, mixed up way, it all made sense. He offered his hand to Sarah.

'Friends?'

Sarah shook her head.

'No, Dad, it doesn't work like that! You don't just get to tell me that I am some imaginative figment of your loopy mind, and then expect everything to go back to—'

She stopped, and considered what she had just begun to say. 'How things might have been.'

Louis stared. His daughter's self-confidence was everything he could have hoped, or dreamed – for her to have. She had everything that he had never had as a child. If she really was some creation of his imagination, he now wished that he hadn't given her quite so much confidence.

'No Dad, not friends.'

Sarah chewed on her lip and grinned. She took his hand.

'But you are still my dad, *Dad.*'

She grinned, if wryly, and Louis smiled weakly.

'Come on. The others will be waiting.'

Venturing out of the tiny vestry, they found that indeed the others were waiting; in fact, the nave of the church was deserted, apart from Ed and Sam in earnest discussion over some music, and Polly dashing back in to fetch banners. She called out to tell them that the other others were by the cars.

It was lucky that the church was in a quiet side-street, because Tom's car had by now been moved closer to the church, parked up alongside Beth's car and Anne's camper van, with its doors flung open and the interior packed with boxes and cases. Kathryn was in conversation with Beth and Caz, and all three looked up as Louis and Sarah emerged into the daylight and descended the steps to the pavement. Kathryn looked searchingly towards Louis, glancing occasionally to Sarah.

'Is everything...? Are you both okay?' Kathryn asked tentatively.

'I'm fine,' answered Louis. He glanced round to Sarah and saw her nod. 'We're good.'

'Head's going to explode, but yeah,' added Sarah.

Louis stepped towards Kathryn and pushed his hand into hers.

'I guess we ought to go then, find the bus—'

Kathryn turned to Louis and stopped him. She stared widely at him.

'Actually, we're not getting the bus. I was talking it over with Beth and Polly – Beth's going to drive you back to Dad's.'

'What about you?' asked Louis suddenly, in a faltering, panicked voice.

'There's some stuff I need to do – things I need to get – Polly's agreed that she and Tom will take me back to Wren Hoe...'

'You're going home? When...?'

Kathryn hugged Louis closer.

'Don't fret. I'm just going to grab some stuff and sling it in the bag. If we leave now I should be able to make the last train. If you can, ask Dad to pick me up at Middleton.'

'I – I don't know.'

Louis glanced round at Sarah, then back to Kathryn

'Is it safe? What if Miss Leroy – well, either of us...?'

'Relax. I'll be in and out, she won't even know I've been back to town. And Beth's your friend, she has no hold there. You'll be fine.'

She reaffirmed her words with a warm, rich, smile.

'What about me? Where do I belong now?' added Sarah, as she turned her attention between Louis and Kathryn.

Louis looked to Kathryn. She hesitated.

'I think you need to go back to Wren Hoe too, for now – at least to... Beth, can Sarah stay with you?'

Beth shrugged a 'yes'.

'I'm beginning to understand all of this,' Kathryn said. 'I think. I need to check a few things. Miss Leroy knows about you – but there's something I'm still not sure about.'

'Kathryn. You're scaring me,' said Louis.

'Sorry, I'm rambling.'

She grinned, nervous a little from the silence that followed, until everyone was finally on the pavement and ready to go.

From the back seat of Tom's old car, as it lurched to a start and circumnavigated the little square, Kathryn watched Louis. For a moment she felt like calling out for the car to stop and going back to him, now. It would be easy. Yes, she needed to go home, get the books that she needed; but they were good to go up to Wren Hoe tomorrow – or she could go alone, like she had planned to today. She felt an urgency though, that she needed to find out sooner rather than later. She felt things were coming to a close, and she *had* to be ready. Turning in her seat, she leant her chin on the back seat of the car and watched Louis, Beth, Sarah, and Caz get smaller and smaller in the distance, until Tom swung the car round the corner and she was flung back into her seat.

Kathryn found herself gripping the seats until her muscles ached, as she tried to decide whether it was better to shut her eyes or keep her gaze fixed on the road ahead. Alarmingly soon, they hit the motorway bound for Wren Hoe.

Most of the way back, Tom was enthusiastically deconstructing the concert, going over the bits that went well and castigating himself – or a fellow member of the quartet – for the bits that hadn't. It was the kind of conversation where neither Polly nor Kathryn contributed to it, and Kathryn drifted away from it, letting it fade into the engine noise of the car, the road around them, the blast of horns and screeching of brakes from surrounding vehicles as Tom lurched and weaved through the lanes.

I'm going to die, I'm going to die, Kathryn found herself thinking; it didn't help with taking her mind off the journey. It was a relief when she saw the dark towers of Didcot power station, and they passed the turning to Abingdon. It was when they were taking the road across the top of Port Meadow that Kathryn made her next decision. She leaned forward across the front seats and asked for them to pull in at the next layby.

Tom swerved in at breakneck speed, and lurched to a halt so abruptly that Kathryn had to grip the seat so tightly her arms ached, in order to stop herself flying forward into Polly's headrest.

'Are you really sure about this?' asked Polly, leaning round to the back of the car. 'It's really no trouble to take you to the door. Is it Tom?'

Tom shook his head.

'It's fine. I need to clear my head, and the walk will be good. It's such a gorgeous evening for it anyway.'

Polly nodded. She couldn't disagree there. After the clear skies of a spring day, the setting sun was casting the most beautiful light over the fresh new growth in the fields and the hedgerows.

Kathryn closed the car door with a persuasive shove and stepped clear, climbing over the stile onto the footpath. She turned and watched as Tom pulled out of the layby, swerving out into the road in front of a large lorry with the accompanying noise of horns and brakes. The little yellow car sped away through the traffic, with the unpredictability of a wild and untamed horse.

Kathryn turned and made her way down the steep embankment to the Thames path, turning right under the flyover towards the spires of Wren Hoe, where they seemed to rise out over the flat plain of Port Meadow.

8

Away from the woods of her youth, the meadows that stretched from the railway and the canal to the east and the meandering river to the west were some of her most favourite places in the world. Port Meadow was a suitable replacement for those woods, and Kathryn often came for walks down here. In the summer months, there would be barbecues with her friends, or the big summer party to which everyone who lived in Jericho was invited, beginning in the afternoon with sports and games for the children while the hog roast was cooked, before the drinking and the dancing would begin; culminating after dark with fireworks, and more drinking. Sometimes she couldn't come down here because it was too wet, and one summer recently the big party had to be cancelled due to floods that submerged all the land from river to railway, and closed the Seacourt Metro for a time.

This spring had been much drier though, and today the ground was firm underfoot. She made quick progress, soon reaching Wolvercote where she crossed the river by the old Wytham toll bridge. She stopped at The Trout Inn to buy a bottle of water, a packet of crisps, and a bar of chocolate – realising only now how hungry and thirsty she was after a full six or seven hours since her last meal.

From The Trout, Kathryn took the direct route home through the allotments. The sun was beginning to sink low in the sky, but there were still people out working their crops. She knew some of them by sight, including an old couple whose plot bordered the footpath, and who often loaded her up with bags of vegetables. The man was there today, and greeted her as he straightened up from being bent double over his potatoes. She replied, but was careful to keep moving. She didn't have time to stop. Not today.

Eventually she arrived back at the canal, and ventured up the bank and through the gate in the fence to stand once more on the tow path. Immediately she turned for home, making her way along the canal past the boats; a mixture of working barges, holiday lets, and loved and cared for homes. Between the tall tenement blocks and old industrial buildings, and the mature trees that lined the waterway, the tow path was a dark place of shadows, even with the sun as it was today.

Past the distinctive tower of St Barnabas' Church, with its little canal-side plaza of cafés and restaurants on the opposite side of the water, Kathryn felt a feeling of comfort and safety wash over her to be back in civilisation. It was a feeling that was short-lived, for further up the tow path was the canal basin and service-yard, an altogether more shadowy place not helped by the group of young men gathered around the boats, laughing and drinking. She could see the smoke from their cigarettes rising as she approached, and heard their voices. One voice in particular carried far, clear and clipped, which she remembered from having heard it at the wedding ceremony.

Kathryn stopped. She could see the red brick bridge she needed to take, and the way to it just before the group of youths. She remained firm and resolute, continuing her walk with all the confidence she could muster. At the bridge, she turned sharply off the path to cross, accompanied by some shouts and jeers and lewd comments from the gang. As she passed above them on the bridge, she noticed, from the corner of her eye, Matthew with his clipped-voice. In sharp suit and polished shoes, he looked at odds with what she could only call ruffians.

Kathryn carried on walking across the bridge, around the corner into the bottom end of Juxon Street, and then ran. She ran without stopping, over the crossroads by the school, all the way up the street until she reached her own front gate.

It was like coming home. She stopped with her hand on the front gate and looked up at the little terraced house. She loved the fact that she worked down the road at The Press, and that she lived in one of the old printers' cottages. She stepped up the short front path past the tangled rose bushes, and pushed the key into the lock.

Once inside, she dropped her bag on the sofa and slipped off her coat. What she had to do wouldn't take long, but it would take long enough. On the side by the phone there was a stack of mail for her – she leafed through it casually, dropping them unopened into her bag to look at later. On the coffee table, where she had left them, were the stack of books she got for Christmas. She gathered these up first, and put them alongside her coat.

Kathryn stopped. Footsteps sounded on the landing above as the old floorboards creaked. She looked up as Nina padded down the stairs in her silk dressing gown, loosely closed with a lacy night dress on beneath.

'Nina,' Kathryn greeted her housemate.

'Kathy, hi,' said Nina. 'Didn't know you were back. You okay?'

'Yeah, I'm good.'

Nina reached to retrieve a bottle of wine and corkscrew.

'You?'

Nina nodded. Kathryn would say more, but found herself preoccupied with the bottle of wine in Nina's hands as she uncorked it. Her gaze was drawn to the two glasses standing nearby.

'Jonathan?'

Kathryn smiled, pleased to have remembered the name of Nina's latest boyfriend.

Nina grinned sheepishly.

'I've not been with Jon for *ages*, Kathy. It's Matt, now. And I promise we'll try and keep the noise down. See you, Kath,' she added, gathering up the glasses in one hand, and heading back upstairs with the bottle of wine in the other.

Kathryn sighed quietly, before gathering up her collection of belongings and carrying them upstairs to her room. The room was just as she had left it, and as soon as she entered, she remembered how much she loved her little home. Reaching first for the top of the wardrobe, she pulled down the old, battered sports bag that she had bought during her first year at university, purely for the end of term commutes home. She stood over it for a moment, as she pondered where to begin.

First, Kathryn retrieved her laptop and stowed it in the bottom of her bag with the charging leads. Then she began stowing her other books around it. Lastly, she filled out the space with some clean underwear and some changes of clothes. Her eyes fell to the bear who sat on her pillow watching over her. Ardizzoni. She tipped her head to one side and smiled at him. He appeared to smile back.

'Come on then, old thing.'

She lifted Ardizzoni up with the same care that she would a cat, and held him in front of her. She gave the old bear a cuddle, and pressed her face into his old fur. She was sure she could smell Louis on him.

'Time to go and see your daddy again, old man.'

Kathryn tucked him into the top of the sports bag, rearranging a fleecy jumper under him as a pillow before zipping the bag shut. Glancing across the room, she saw the time change on her clock radio.

The time. Her brain processed the information. *Christ, was it that late already?* She flung herself out of her room, across the landing and into the bathroom. While sitting on the toilet she thumbed through the internet on her phone, checking the train times; soon she was drawn into Facebook, the lure of one-liners from her friends, and then a relationship status. Even before she saw Nina's new relationship, the picture hit he between the eyes like a brick.

Matthew Leroy-Song. *Matthew? Matty...?* She had to get out of here.

Quickly, Kathryn pushed her phone back into her pocket and finished up in the bathroom. As she stood drying her hands, she heard voices on the landing: Nina's, and a man. Matthew. Kathryn slowed her own breathing, trying to listen through the door, to the footsteps on the stairs. She flicked the lock and flung open the door, in time to see Matthew leave through the front door. She caught Nina on the landing, still in her nightie and dressing gown.

'Kathryn?'

'What happened to your night in?'

Kathryn watched Nina carefully. She liked Nina, trusted her; but the rate with which she went through an odd selection of men gave her concern.

'The poor lamb, remembered he had to meet someone,' Nina said with soppiness. 'Business, you know.'

'At this time?' Kathryn said, feigning surprise.

'He runs his own business – property and the like. He's very good at it. At the moment he's sorting out the Canal Street development.'

Kathryn nodded. It made sense. Between the Leroys and the university, they had most of Wren Hoe signed up.

'So, how's your man?' Nina asked to break the silence.

Kathryn paused for a moment.

'Good thanks. Actually I need to – this was only a passing visit – needed to collect some things.'

Nina nodded.

'I was going to call a taxi, but since Matt – your boyfriend – has left, you couldn't give me a lift to the station, could you?'

'How do you know...?'

Nina saw the look coming from Kathryn and gave up her question.

'When do you need to go?'

'Umm, now?'

Nina rolled her eyes, and returned to her room.

Downstairs, Kathryn sat in the lounge, all set to go with her bag packed in front of her on the floor. She fidgeted impatiently with her fingers, as above her Nina could be heard creaking across the floor. She checked her watch, and fidgeted again as she watched the ticking hands.

Eventually Nina stomped downstairs in her long coat and black boots, brandishing her phone and her car keys.

For the journey across town, Kathryn wanted to talk to Nina, to ask her about Matthew; she couldn't find the words, and she was scared for the answer. The journey itself was scary enough, as Nina lurched around corners, jolting forwards and back. Nina, Kathryn realised, must have been to the same school of driving as Tom.

Outside the station, Nina parked half on the kerb in a bus stop despite Kathryn's protestations. She pulled her bags from the backseat, stepped back, and gestured at Nina to be gone as uniformed attendants closed in. Kathryn fled up the steps and into the station.

All the ticket machines were out of order, and with the large station clock ticking, Kathryn was forced to wait in the longest, most snake-like queue since her childhood. The queue was, at last, moving and she shuffled forwards quite quickly, if tediously. As she neared the booths, and while she was glancing around the cavernous hall, she saw him. She stopped and stared. Matthew. *Here?*

Dimly, Kathyrn heard the mechanical voice summon the next customer, but she couldn't move or take her eyes off Matthew. How did he do it? How did he always manage to be where she was?

She was prodded and poked back into the present by an old, impatient man bent double over a stick behind her. She garbled an apology, and moved to the hatch to request her single fare to Middleton. Between every stage of buying her ticket, she kept glancing back over her shoulder. Matthew was still there, now talking with some friends by the turnstiles.

With her ticket bought, Kathryn moved to the side, and from there slipped quietly out a side entrance back to the forecourt. She made her way round the side of the building, to a smaller entrance that led directly onto the platform. Looking both ways, she made her way over the footbridge to the Bristol-bound platform.

9

Kathryn's heart pounded inside her, and t. The ticking of the station clock seemed to echo loudly around her. More than ever she fidgeted with the ticket in her hands and the watch on her wrist, praying that the train arrived quickly and she could be boarded and on her way before—

'Kathryn?'

Kathryn jumped back and almost fell over her own bag. As she steadied herself, she looked up to find the tall figure of Matthew standing over her.

'Sorry. I hope I didn't scare you.'

He reached out a hand to steady her. Kathryn snatched her arm away and took a step back, pushing her bag at her feet with her.

'You just startled me,' she said. 'You shouldn't creep up on people like that.'

'I was just saying hello, Kathy.'

'It's Kathryn,' she replied. 'And what are you doing here?'

'Saw you in the ticket hall. Thought I should say hello.'

He grinned at her. Kathryn stared at him, finding it hard to comprehend his nerve.

'And you just happened to be here? Don't you have people – someone – that you should be with?' demanded Kathryn.

'Just seen them off,' Matthew said, gesturing to the train now departing from the opposite platform. 'Business contacts, you know?'

'Really?' Kathryn said brusquely.

'You don't believe me?'

Kathryn frowned and shook her head.

'I know about Nina.'

Matthew responded blankly.

'Nina. Your girlfriend.'

'Oh, that was you...'

'Please, you know it was! It's probably why you started seeing her,' Kathryn said, her heart beating faster. 'I bet you had a proper snoop around my room, too.'

Matthew laughed.

'Didn't have time for that. You know Nina.'

Kathryn stared at him. Slowly she shook her head.

'I don't know why you sound surprised. You know we share a house.'

Matthew gasped.

'And don't look surprised. I know you know.'

Kathryn fixed him with an angry stare, before grabbing her bag and moving off down the platform. She didn't turn back once, although she felt Matthew's gaze on her all the time.

An announcer read out the next departure in a mechanical intonation as the train drew into the station. The doors slid open, and she boarded hastily. Finding a table seat, she stowed her bag on the seats opposite and settled down; only then did she look out the window, and back down the platform to where she had left Matthew. He was still there, just where she had left him.

Damn it, she cursed, he will have seen me get on the train. He will know that I am bound for Bristol.

The train lurched to a start, and began sloping out of the station. Looking up again, she saw Matthew was nowhere on the platform. *Good,* she decided, and settled back with her phone and book for the journey.

The train accelerated out through sidings and jostling trams; through the downtown West End of the city, across the latticework of river, canals, and tramlines. Kathryn soon lost herself in the pages of her book – *The Albion Book of Ballads.* She flicked through the pages quickly to find the story of *Thomas the Rhymer.* A few verses in, and she thumbed through to the story of *Tam Lin.* The more she read it, the more she found herself thinking of Bevington House and its modest grandeur, and of Louis inheriting it from his father, just as Tam Lin was the grandson of minor aristocracy. Tam Lin, bewitched by the Queen of the Fairies and given various gifts in recompense for—

'No,' Kathryn exclaimed loudly, to the surprise of those sitting near her. 'That's not it,' she muttered under her breath, as she paged back to the story of *Thomas the Rhymer.* She always got them muddled in her head.

'Problem?'

Kathryn jumped at the sound of that voice – Matthew's voice. Kathryn looked up to see Matthew easing himself into the seat opposite. She glared at him.

'You don't mind? The seat's not taken?'

His voice was too friendly in tone. She found herself caught unawares, shaking her head and unwittingly inviting him to sit with her. Quickly regretting her friendliness, she shifted her position, re-angled her book, and returned to her reading. She found herself unable to concentrate on the words, distracted as she was by the knowledge of Matthew's stare upon her. With an audible sigh she snapped the book closed, set it down on the table in front of her, and looked up crossly.

She waited for Matthew to speak, but he remained defiantly silent. She continued to glare at him.

'What is it with you? Are you stalking me?'

Matthew shrugged.

'There's no law saying what trains I can get on.'

'Really?'

'I've got a friend to visit, and – train journeys can be so tiresome and boring–' Matthew explained, with a mischievous grin. 'I thought I may as well sit with a friend.'

'We're *not* friends.'

Matthew laughed, but jokingly and not out of menace.

'Seeing as I'm with Nina, we may as well get used to being so.'

Kathryn rolled her eyes and returned to her book. She couldn't focus though, aware as she was of Matthew's continued gaze.

'What do you want?' Kathryn said, suddenly and abruptly.

'You really need to ask?'

'Yes. I have no idea.'

'You.'

Kathryn gaped.

'Don't tell me you are surprised.'

'I am!' Kathryn exclaimed. 'And what about Nina?'

Matthew shrugged.

'How else could I get close to you?'

Kathryn shook her head vehemently.

'Why would you need to?'

Matthew leaned forward, maintaining his gaze on her as he reached for her book.

'Because I can help you.'

Kathryn too, sat forward. She shifted her book away.

'I don't need your help.'

Matthew grinned, almost laughing.

'They're good stories,' he said, nodding towards the book. 'But they need interpreting. Tam Lin, always the hero and never the villain. Why is that, Kathryn?'

'Maybe because he was wronged by the Faery Queen?'

Matthew shrugged.

'I always thought it was Tam who did all the wronging. What of poor, wronged Janet? Fair, innocent Janet?'

He reached out towards Kathryn, but she knocked him back. 'She saved him!'

'And the Faery Queen didn't? He fell from his horse. He was dead if she had not saved him. He was happy with the life she gave him.'

'She bewitched him. Of course he was happy – he had no other choice.'

'And is he happy now?'

Kathryn was about to retort, when she realised where he was leading her. She jammed her mouth shut, and pulled her book away from him before stowing it defiantly into her bag.

'I can't believe I'm arguing the merits of fairy tales with an arrogant – with *you!*'

Matthew didn't answer, just continued to stare at Kathryn with those dark seductive eyes. Kathryn shook her head, before grabbing her coat and bags and squeezing out of her seat.

'Excuse me,' she said firmly, and jostled her way down to the next carriage. For the rest of the journey she perched on the pull-down seat by the doors between compartments, hoping that Matthew had finally got the message.

At the same time, her mind buzzed with new information. Matthew had clearly been talking about Louis, which meant she had been right about Mrs Leroy. Why was she so keen to paint herself as the evil avenger? And why was he giving her the answer? If Louis was Tam, and she was some modern-day Janet, then she was right that she had to save Louis - so why tell her?

As the train neared its destination, with the announcer reading out the familiar next station stops of the last train, Kathryn's thoughts turned to how she was going to give Matthew the slip. He was going to know she was somewhere in or near Bristol, but she would really prefer if that was all he knew.

To Kathryn's relief a lot of people alighted from the train, and she was able to leave the station surrounded by a small throng of people. Kathryn headed straight for the opposite exit that she needed, and as she headed down the steps she turned to see Matthew watching her. She turned away again and smiled, pleased at least that her plan of deception was working. Out of the station, Kathryn hailed the last taxi in the rank, bundling herself into the back with garbled instructions.

A few moments after the taxi pulled away, Kathryn was lurched sideways across the back seat, to the company of much horn blasting and driver swearing, as he swerved to miss a man in the road. Kathryn turned and peered out the back window, to see Matthew looking back at her.

'Damn idiot,' muttered the driver.

10

It was gone midnight by the time Kathryn arrived back at her parents' house. She let herself in, surprised by the sounds of laughing and joking coming from the lounge. Her face twitched with curiosity as she went to investigate. She found Louis playing scrabble with Beth, Sarah, and Caz.

'Dad, that's not how you spell it.'

'Trust an English teacher not being able to spell.'

Beth and Sarah were joking, as they came to realise Kathryn was stood in the doorway. Louis started, and got up hastily, knocking over his rack of scrabble tiles in the process.

'Kathryn, you're back.'

He hugged her, and she responded diffidently.

'What are *they* still doing here?'

Louis looked down, and remained silent to the question.

'It was your Dad,' Beth spoke up. 'We were going to head straight off, but he insisted we stay for dinner, and then—'

'You shouldn't be here,' said Kathryn, looking at Sarah. 'It's not safe for you.'

Kathryn felt everyone's gaze turn towards her, but she chose not to elaborate.

*

Later on, Louis and Kathryn were alone in her bedroom and pulling back the bedspread. Every few moments Kathryn looked up at Louis, and then Louis would look up at Kathryn. Neither spoke, unsure of what to say or how to begin. They went through the actions of getting ready for bed in silence.

Kathryn felt bad for breaking up the party. She should not have been cross to find Sarah, Caz, and Beth still here. Indeed, after the things she had discovered earlier that very evening, it was probably best that they were all still here. She should still not have shown her annoyance as vehemently as she had, but their presence had just been a shock. They had thrown her plans of what she was going to say, discuss, and do. She looked up again at Louis now as he stood, back to her, peeling off his shirt, and wanted to apologise to him so much.

For Louis, he was trying to figure out what he had done wrong? How had he upset Kathryn so badly? What could he do to rebuild the bridges? He folded his shirt carefully and lay it down on the chair. Kathryn was looking at him, he could tell. Dare he turn around? It was like confronting his fears all over again. Elsewhere in the house he could hear footsteps, doors opening and closing, Sarah and Caz's voices, and he was reminded why he was here.

'We have to talk.'

Kathryn's words cut through the silence, and stopped Louis' thoughts in their tracks.

'We have to decide what we are going to do, Louis.'

Slowly, and with trepidation, Louis turned around.

'Sounds ominous,' he said hesitantly.

Kathryn beckoned Louis to come over, and they both sat on the edge of the bed. Kathryn turned to face him.

'I knew I had to save you from Miss Leroy, that things would be okay once I got you away from her,' Kathryn started to explain.

'I sense a *but*...'

Kathryn frowned.

'It's far from that simple.'

Louis nodded, and in the simplicity of a look, urged her to continue.

'She knows. Miss Leroy knows where we are.'

Louis gasped.

'Relax, we're safe tonight, but it's my guess she'll know about this house, and my parents – everything.'

She went on to explain how the gang of youths had been waiting for her at the canal, and of how it was no coincidence that Matthew had been in her house; and then how he had followed her all the way to Bristol, and of how he would have been sure to have tracked down the taxi driver. The more she told Louis, the more Kathryn felt she had been stupid to think she could have gone all the way to Wren Hoe and back undiscovered.

'So how do I escape her?' asked Louis.

Kathryn drew a half-smile across her face.

'What do you know about Tam Lin?'

Louis shrugged, offering up a blank expression.

'It's a fable. A myth, a legend.'

Kathryn continued to explain her thoughts, and how Matthew had hijacked her reading on the train; intent, she supposed, on putting her off the scent, but only convincing her of the truth.

'He must have known he was telling you how to defeat his mother,' countered Louis.

Kathryn shrugged.

'I don't know. Maybe he just hoped to convince me that it was useless – any attempts to save you.'

'Makes sense, I guess.'

Louis fell to thinking, trying to remember the details of the story.

'Do you have it, the story?' he asked.

Kathryn fetched her copy of *The Albion Book of Ballads*, opening it instinctively at the right page, and passed it to him. Louis took it and began to read, scanning across some of the verses.

'I thought it was seven years?'

Kathryn nodded.

'In the original yes, but not. It seems to change with every retelling. It's usually seven, sometimes nine. There's one that's only five years. But the pattern's always the same; and with you, I think it's eleven.'

'Sarah's eleven.'

'It was your eleventh birthday when you were given the flute, and Miss Leroy claimed to have saved you.'

Louis was left silenced by this. His brain fought hard to process the intelligence, to the point that his head actually hurt. He stared at the ballad on the pages in his hands.

'But if you're right about this, and I am...'

He faltered, unable to say the name.

'And Miss Leroy, she's the Faery Queen, then that must make you Janet, and I've not – you aren't...?'

Kathryn shook her head and grinned, hoping to reassure him.

'It's a fable,' she said. 'It's got many retellings, and many more interpretations.'

She laughed.

'You should know this Louis, you teach this stuff.'

Louis shrugged and, frowned. 'So how do I free myself from her? Be rid of her for once for all?'

Kathryn lifted herself up from her perch on the end of the bed, and crossed the room to her bag. She folded back some clothes to reveal Ardizzoni's face. She smiled.

'I brought you something else back from Wren Hoe.'

Louis looked up, expectant and curious. Kathryn lifted the old bear out of the bag, and turned to present it to Louis. His eyes lit up brightly.

'Ardizzonni,' he exclaimed breathlessly. 'I'd forgotten that you had him.'

He took the bear gladly, and hugged him to his chest. His eyes began to fill with tears of joy.

'You have to have him back,' said Kathryn. She could feel her own eyes swelling with tears.

'I couldn't keep him, not if...'

Louis looked up, his bottom lip quivering.

'The only way to save you is to let you go.'

Kathryn's eyes were by now bloodshot and wet.

'I have to go back, don't I?'

Kathryn choked over the words.

'It's the only way.'

'I – I can't...' Louis stammered, his grip tightening on Ardizzonni as he pulled him closer to his chest. 'You've been the most real thing in my life. I can't give you up.'

'You have to.'

Kathryn couldn't help herself but sob.

'I have to. It's the only way.'

Louis shook his head defiantly; hugging his bear tighter, he turned and stepped aimlessly away, shuffling around the room. Kathryn stood staring, with tears streaming down her cheeks; she tried to speak, but at every attempt the words got caught in her throat, and all that she could utter were small, pathetic gulps. She took a deep breath, but it didn't really help.

'Can't we just go away? Go somewhere where she'll never find us?'

Kathryn shook her head.

'No. She'll find a way – *they'll* find a way.'

When Louis turned towards her, albeit with his head bowed, she knew he did understand.

'I thought here would be safe; but tomorrow Leroy will know we are here, if she doesn't already. They would find us wherever we go. We can't run. We can never run.'

Louis crumpled to the floor, hunched up at the foot of the bed with his face pressed into his old bear. Kathryn slid down onto the floor next to him, slipped her arm round him and hugged him tightly.

'If there was another way,' she said.

Louis tucked his head into the curve of her neck. He could hear the thump of her beating heart. Kathryn kissed the back of his head and stayed with him, sitting in silence.

11

By the time Kathryn woke the following morning, the rest of the house was already awake. She showered and dressed and went downstairs, to find the others had already finished breakfast, and were just sitting with the last of their coffees in a subdued room of muted conversation.

Louis jumped up and ushered Kathryn to a seat, then went to fetch her breakfast.

'Coffee?' Beth asked, as she too got up.

Kathryn smiled weakly, and thanked Beth.

'Louis told us what happened,' said Sarah. 'It doesn't seem fair.'

Kathryn frowned.

'Janet wins out in the end though,' continued Sarah.

Kathryn looked up, at first surprised by what she heard Sarah say. She lifted a finger to her mouth, and fixed Sarah with a stern, silencing gaze.

Louis deposited a bowl of muesli, topped with fruit, yoghurt, and a drenching of milk in front of Kathryn. She looked up, and smiled a thank you.

Later, Kathryn was helping clear the table. She sidled up to Sarah and pulled her close, locking her gaze onto hers.

'Don't ever tell him. He can't know.'

Sarah looked puzzled, but nodded confirmation of Kathryn's request.

The day drifted on, listlessly. Following breakfast, Kathryn repacked her bags and looked to squeeze them into the boot of Beth's car.

'It's not even twenty-four hours, and yet I'm taking them off again across the county.'

'You think that's weird?'

Louis nodded to the heap of cardboard boxes and battered cases.

'That's my life in those boxes, in the back of a car.'

Kathryn turned towards Louis. She wanted to say something – anything – that would help. Her mouth twisted with a hopeless smile that was half frown.

The journey back to Wren Hoe was an awkward two hours' drive, on seemingly endless roads. Spring sunshine gave way to heavy clouds and sharp showers, until Beth entered the city in a non-descript grey mizzle that dampened the already suppressed mood. Beth turned off the Banbury Road into the leafy Park Town, and parked up at the end of the drive to Hunsdon House.

They fell out of the car onto the street, and Louis retrieved one small suitcase and a canvas bag from the boot.

'It is okay, isn't it?' Louis asked Beth for the Nth time. 'Just until I know what's happening.'

'Sure. My spare room is a dumping ground anyway.'

Beth slammed shut the boot.

'So this is it, then?'

Louis turned now to Kathryn.

'It's the only way.'

Kathryn kicked at the cobbled gutter with the toe of her shoe. She put her arms out for a last embrace.

'Thank you.'

Kathryn frowned, followed by a sigh. She kissed him on each cheek, and lingered to whisper. 'I won't forget you.'

Kathryn stepped back, and turned now to Sarah.

'Look after your dad, Sarah.'

They hugged briefly, before Kathryn stepped back alongside Beth and Caz to watch, as Louis Tumnal and his daughter Sarah began their walk up the curving drive of Hunsdon House. Somewhere in the distance sirens echoed across the city, either police or ambulance, racing to an emergency.

'You sure I can't give you a lift?' asked Beth.

Kathryn looked at the two bags on the pavement and shook her head.

'I'll be fine,' answered Kathryn. 'It's not far, and I quite like the metro and tram. Might pick up something to eat in town, too.'

'If you're sure. It's no trouble.'

Kathryn nodded.

'And keep in touch. You've got my number if you need me.'

Again, Kathryn nodded, and this time managed a smile.

Beth and Caz headed back to the car, and soon they were off. Kathryn remained for a moment at the end of the driveway, watching Louis and Sarah. A blast from a car horn behind her, and she turned to see Beth heading back to the end of the road. She sighed, took up her bags, and began her own way home. The distant wail of sirens grew louder, and louder still. She was half-way to the junction when an ambulance screeched round the corner and passed her. Kathryn turned and watched as the ambulance slowed and turned into the drive to Hunsdon House. For a moment she considered going back to investigate, before she remembered she had to give up Louis, and that meant passing up her natural instinct toward curiosity.

The tram deposited Kathryn outside the Phoenix Picture House on Walton Street. She stopped to pick up a copy of the programme from the slot in the wall, and walked the last bit round the corner to the little house on Juxon Street. It being a weekday, the house was her own for the rest of the afternoon, and Kathryn took her time unpacking, as well as tidying up after an always annoyingly untidy Nina. She ran a bath, put on some music, and luxuriated in having a house to herself. By the time she dragged herself from the bath, she felt pleasantly prune-like at the extremities, and relaxed. She dried herself, put her hair in a towel, and slipped into her nightie and fleecy dressing gown before booting up her computer. Her inbox quickly filled up with unread messages, mostly junk or the latest offers and recommendations from Amazon.

After two pages of deleting, and only two brief emails from friends she couldn't be bothered replying to, Kathryn tired of the computer and closed the lid, heading downstairs instead to make dinner to the accompaniment of whatever filled the Radio 4 schedules on a Wednesday evening in May. She laughed along with a surprisingly funny comedy, and caught up with the goings on in Ambridge, not that she really followed them. She sat at the small dining table and ate her dinner with a book for company, and after she finished she took the book with her through into the lounge and tucked herself up in the armchair. She kept on meaning to put a CD on, but carried on reading until it was suddenly too late, and she made her way up to bed.

The following morning, Kathryn woke with her alarm and got up. The house was eerily quiet, with no sign of Nina around, and Kathryn supposed that she must be with Matthew, wherever he now was.

At quarter to nine she made the short walk down Walton Street. She greeted the friendly porter as always, and climbed the three flights of stairs to the attic office in B Wing where journal production could be found. Walking into the office, Kathryn felt like she was returning from holiday, but with no stories that she could tell. She snuck into her pod and booted up her computer. Charlotte and Eleanor, both early-starters, greeted her.

'You feeling better?' Charlotte asked.

Kathryn looked up with surprise. *Better?*

Charlotte concentrated her gaze, nodding her meaning firmly across the divide.

'Oh yes,' muttered Kathryn. 'Mostly, thanks. I've felt better.' That last addition was not, at least, a complete lie.

'Has anyone said anything?' Kathryn asked, looking, as she spoke, at Amanda's office, which was currently closed up.

'Not really.'

'And Amanda, she's...?'

'Dreadful.'

Eleanor leaned closer across her desk.

'She's been in a foul mood pretty much since you've been off. Real stinker, I'm telling you.'

'Sorry about that.'

Eleanor started with surprise, but moved past it. She got up and walked round to Kathryn's desk with a page of notes.

'Anyway, Charlotte and I have been keeping an eye on things. You owe Charlotte a makeup big time – your monster issue – and I'm afraid you've got one today, but I think you're all square with it.'

Kathryn garbled her humbled thanks, as Eleanor continued to brief her with the state of her work. When she got into her emails, she discovered that Eleanor and Charlotte had not been kidding about keeping on top of things, and within the hour she was able to get stuck into the issue makeup. After the last week, it was good to get stuck back into the world of author corrections, proofreading symbols, and even workings.

Kathryn and Charlotte laughed in a shrill and girlish tone to Eleanor's joke, a dry sardonic commentary to something on the news. They fell out of the kitchen with a giddy swagger, clutching their mugs of tea and coffee and chatting as they weaved their way at a stop-start pace down the corridor, ducking around a neglected post trolley and sidestepping around colleagues. As they approached their open plan office, their conversation was silenced by a frantically gesticulating Lucy, who then proceeded to dart forward to greet them and explain in hushed whispers how the boss was in, and in an unforgiving and foul mood.

The three girls returned swiftly and silently back to their desks, and back immediately to their manuscripts and the production management system. Behind her, Kathryn could hear the furious bashing out of emails from Amanda's office, and the sharp sound of her voice as she castigated another typesetter. Kathryn's own poise tensioned to the point that an hour and a half later she had a sore neck, aches running from wrist to fingers, and a pain running down her whole left side.

'Lunch?' Charlotte said quietly across the divide.

Kathryn looked up and nodded. She flicked the computer into locked mode, stretched, and reached down to retrieve her bag. Gathering up a few more surrounding production editors, they began to make their way through the office.

'Where do you think you're all going?'

Amanda was stood glaring from her open office doorway.

'Just... lunch?'

Even as she answered, Kathryn knew that it was a mistake.

'You can't all go,' said Amanda. 'Someone needs to man the office.'

Eleanor returned to join Kathryn, with Charlotte just behind.

'We always have. It's fine.'

'It is *not* fine,' said Amanda sharply. 'One of you at least needs to stay until the others are back.'

She looked at each of the girls, but settled again upon Kathryn.

'It's really not...'

'It is, really,' repeated Amanda.

Kathryn relented and waved the others on.

'It's fine. You go on. I'll stay.'

'You sure?' offered Charlotte.

Go, mouthed Kathryn. After a moment of hesitation, Charlotte and Eleanor headed off, and Kathryn returned to her desk, keying past the log-on screen and returning to the spreadsheet that ached ahead of her.

Glancing around, Kathryn saw Amanda turn away from watching her and go back to her desk. Kathryn returned to her work, referencing her piles of manuscripts with her scrawled notes and the spreadsheet open on her computer; her fingers tabbed awkwardly between the spreadsheet and the web-based production management system, making what was normally the kind of task she could do in her sleep clumsily long-winded.

'Kathryn!'

It was Amanda's sharp tone. Kathryn turned guardedly to the direction of Amanda's approach.

'What can I do for you?'

She hoped it didn't sound too sarcastic.

'A word,' replied Amanda curtly. 'In my office.

Kathryn sighed and picked herself up from her desk with a concealed frown, before trailing after her boss with the enthusiasm of someone entering a dragon's lair.

Amanda gestured her employee into a seat at the meeting table, joining her with a file full of print-outs. Kathryn sat and stared stoicly at the table in front of her, and waited.

'I've been reviewing your journal schedules...'

Kathryn looked up. She nodded.

'There are a few irregularities that I've noticed.'

'Really? I know a couple are overdue but that's because—'

Kathryn saw Amanda's mouth curl.

'They are because of authors I'm in daily contact with...'

Amanda turned her head to one side, and raised an eyebrow. Kathryn shook her head furiously.

'This isn't to do with schedules, is it?'

Amanda looked up, and back at Kathryn with a calm curiosity.

'It's Louis, isn't? You can't face that it's over between you...'

As soon as Kathryn spoke, she knew that she had said too much. She readied herself for the explosion that would surely follow.

'You can go for your lunch now,' Charlotte said gaily, as she returned to her desk with Eleanor. She followed her words with a gaze across the divide at her friend. Kathryn remained at her seat, almost fixed in stone at her work with a look of sheer concentration.

'Kathryn?' Charlotte tried again. 'Lunch?'

This time Kathryn shook her head briskly, but didn't answer until a few moments later.

'Can't,' she said. 'No time.'

Both Charlotte and Eleanor followed up with concerned gazes.

'Apparently it is absolutely imperative for me to create the schedules for every issue of every one of my journals for the year ahead.'

Charlotte shuddered, her mouth gaped.

'The year ahead?' Eleanor said. 'Like to the end of next year?'

Kathryn nodded, fuming.

'I hope that's not going to be something for all of us...'

Kathryn shook her head.

'Just me, I think.'

12

In the late afternoon sunshine Lewis sat on the terrace at the back of Laurel Place. A book lay notionally in front of him, but his eyes were closed and his head was back. Nearby, Sarah sat reading too, voraciously devouring page after page of a story.

A shadow descended across Lewis' face, as Amanda leant over him and kissed his lips. He blinked his eyes open and smiled.

'Good day?'

'Shattered.'

She sighed and threw her bag down on the table.

'Busy doesn't even cover today.'

'Sherry?' Louis asked, sitting up.

'I'll get it. You want one too?'

Minutes later, they were both sat on the terrace enjoying a glass of sherry in the evening light. They said little, not needing to, and looked up across the lawn as they heard the crunch of gravel under a car, as it made its way up the drive to the house.

'Suppose we ought to make ourselves sociable,' Lewis said. 'Come on.'

He got up from the seat and moved to offer Amanda a hand. As they were about to go in, she stopped and called Lewis back. He turned and looked.

'I just wanted to say,' she began. 'It's good to have you back, Lewis.'

Lewis and Amanda stepped through the conservatory, and from there into the drawing room, arriving in the hall in time to see Miss Leroy disappear upstairs, surrounded by uniformed attendants. Matthew stood at the foot of the stairs with slumped shoulders, staring vacantly out of sunken eyes.

'You look awful.'

Matthew stared back at Lewis. Amanda ducked round to his side, trailing a hand around his waist as she went.

'I must apologise for my Lewis,' she said. 'He has all the tact of the central bus station.'

'How is she?'

'Fading.'

Matthew's reply was muted. He shrugged his shoulders.

'She shouldn't be here,' said Lewis. 'She shouldn't have left hospital.'

Amanda elbowed Lewis in the ribs, and he stopped speaking, albeit with a turn of the head and a face twisted with confusion.

'Ignore my husband.'

Matthew smiled thinly. For a few moments longer, Lewis stood a few steps beneath Matthew at the bottom of the stairs, both looking at the other, and both remaining silent. Lewis opened his mouth to speak, and. He saw Matthew was about to as well. Both stopped, and silence endured.

'We'll leave you to it,' said Lewis. 'Give our regards to your aunt.'

Matthew nodded. He turned and made his way slowly up the grand staircase. The last of the setting sun shone through the stained glass at the top of the stairs, where it illuminated the face of one of the Leroy ancestors. The light sunk lower, picking out the starkly recognisable face of Miss Leroy, and then as it sunk lower it shone more brightly through clear glass. The light picked out particles of dust, rising and swirling in the air. A dove seemed to descend through the house interior, breaking as the sun finally sunk too low.

Sarah sat, feet tucked up on the day-bed in the conservatory, reading. Behind her, in the house, music filtered out to her. In the sitting room Lewis sat in front of the hearth, playing duets on his flute, with Amanda next to him on oboe.

The music was comforting for her. It was the soundtrack to her childhood, and a reminder of simpler times when her life was contained to her relationship with her mother and father within the walls of Bevington House. It was a reminder of a time before things got complicated. Sarah turned her head and looked through the French windows at Lewis, pursed lips to his flute, and Amanda with her radiant, almost glowing red hair. Was this how they had been at school? At the orchestra where they had met, when her mum had been Miss Amanda Jones?

Lewis sat in an upright chair net to Miss Leroy, where she lay propped up on pillows.

'Thank you.'

Lewis looked up, and saw that there was a sparkle back in Miss Leroy's eyes.

'I heard you playing music again earlier.'

Lewis shrugged.

'I don't think I realised how long I had stopped for.'

'Will you get your flute now?' Miss Leroy asked, in a kindly but still authoritative voice.

Lewis returned to Miss Leroy's room a few minutes later carrying his flute, wondering why he was doing this. Taking a seat beside his old headmistress, he sat for a moment with the flute.

Miss Leroy nodded.

'Play it. You remember, don't you?'

As Lewis lifted the instrument to his lips, he felt like that little boy of eleven all over again. Without really thinking about what he was doing, he arranged his fingers on the keys, pursed his lips to the head joint, and played. The song, his song, sounded. He stopped; the note-

perfect rendition had surprised himself. He saw Miss Leroy smile, and he began again. This time, the song sang out strongly and lilting.

He surprised himself at how the notes sprang and danced from his fingers; t. The song of his childhood sung from him like it was yesterday, like it had been woken from some eleven-year coma. He played every dynamic and repeat, every dal segno and tempo change.

Miss Leroy relaxed in her bed, closed her eyes, and let her breathing settle into a slow, gentle rhythm. Lewis played on, and at the open door Amanda stood. She beamed at what she saw, lifted by Lewis' song.

Across the room, Miss Leroy drifted into sleep, and eventually Lewis finished playing, moved his chair back to the wall, and left the room quietly with Amanda.

Over the next ten nights, Lewis repeated his playing. In the mid-evening he would go to the old lady's room, sit by her bed, and play. Every night Amanda would come and watch from the door, listening, and every day her face seemed younger and fresher, her hair more radiant. Every day, after another rendition of Lewis' song, Amanda was more like the girl that Lewis had fallen in love with.

On the eleventh night, Lewis went to Miss Leroy's room and sat by her bed with his flute. In the beginning he had tried conversation, but she was not interested in talking, and he didn't know what to say. With a look, she could command him to play, and play is what he did.

Now Miss Leroy looked tired. So tired that Lewis was almost scared to do anything at all. Miss Leroy opened her eyes far enough that he could see her expectation. He put the flute to his lips again and played. Some time during that eleventh song, it finally happened. Miss Leroy died.

13

Kathryn finished the schedules as had been requested, but only by working through to gone seven o'clock. She sent them off to Amanda by email, closed down her computer, and left work as the cleaners worked the deserted corridors.

Waving goodnight to the porter at the gate, Kathryn headed round the corner to join her friends at The Duke for cocktails. Rarely had a long Bloody Mary been so welcome, and she downed it gladly. A couple of Lemon Meringues later, and a glass or two of prosecco, and she made her way back up through Jericho to her little house, and slumped into bed. She lay there staring at the ceiling, thinking now that two Ginger Toms might have been two too many to end the night.

The next thing Kathryn remembered was the chorus of birdsong in the dawn light – and half an hour of dozing later, the crashing and clanking of the refuse collectors on the street beneath her window. She clutched her throbbing head and groaned.

She washed and dressed, and made her way downstairs to force a large mug of coffee down her with a slice of buttered toast, before heading out to work.

The same porter as last night was on duty in the lodge, as she pushed through the turnstiles to the quad within, and he remarked to her on how few hours it had been. She laughed the comment away, but it only served to remind her of the hideousness of yesterday. Her feet turned to lead weights of reluctance as she climbed the two flights of stairs. Her stomach churned with the thought of what might await her at her desk. What response will she have had from Amanda, and what other follow-up tasks of agony had she in store for her?

When she did arrive at her desk she was the first of her pod to arrive, and Amanda's office was still dark. Kathryn sighed all too audibly, slung down her bag, shed her cardigan and fired up her computer, before heading off to get a second cup of strong, black coffee.

Back at her desk, and with her hand clasping the body of the steaming mug, Kathryn opened up her emails. Scanning through the arriving fury of emails from Singapore printers and Indian typesetters, and a couple of long-awaited author replies, there was no email from Amanda. Kathryn perked up at this, and set to prioritising the day's actions. Not long after Charlotte and Eleanor arrived, in a state of equal fragility to that of Kathryn, and the morning passed mercifully quickly. Back from lunch, and Amanda was once more occupying her office. The afternoon however, passed similarly and mercifully quietly.

When it came to home time, Kathryn did not delay in escaping the office and heading down to the canal, partly to put behind her the lurking fear in her mind from her encounter with Matthew a week earlier, and partly because it was such a nice walk into town down by the water. She picked up a few groceries from the covered market, and then headed to her favourite record store. Tucked away down one of the narrow lanes that ventured off the main Cornmarket, it was a proper indie store that still stocked and smelt of vinyl. In a nod to modern times, there was an eclectic selection of CDs, and a range of accessories for MP3 players. Kathryn found a new album by a favourite artist that she was previously unaware of, and paid for it without a second thought, looking forward to sitting down with it that evening.

Back outside she made her way onto the busy main street, to be swept down into the flow of a tide of commuters finishing their day at the office. She allowed herself to be buffeted left and right, until at the corner of St Giles and The Broad she headed in the direction of the tram stop. A surge of people going against her pushed her around, and jostled her round the corner. As she ducked round the people and squeezed through gaps, she came face-to-face with a girl; Caz. Then, as quickly as they had met, Caz was on her way through the crowd with a friend.

'Caz!' Kathryn called. 'Caz!'

Caz pushed on through the crowd, without anything so much as an acknowledgement. Kathryn didn't know why but she followed, pushing through the crowd that seemed to be letting Caz and her friends through, while intent on jostling Kathryn out of step.

Through the crowd, Kathryn saw Caz head down the steps to the metro station, and she followed. The train was waiting at the platform, and Kathryn saw the back of the head and the figure she recognised as Caz's board a further carriage. She threw herself down the rest of the steps and across the platform, to dive into the nearest carriage just as the doors slid shut.

The metro jolted to a hesitant, rattling start, as it shifted out of the station into the tunnel. Kathryn moved through the carriage, weaving in and out of other passengers to reach the connecting door towards the front of the carriage. Grasping at the handle, she found the metalwork jammed and no amount of forcing and coercion could shift it. Through the small, grubby window, Kathryn could see Caz in the next carriage. Just a few feet away, but separated by two panes of diesel-fume stained windows. Kathryn banged on the window with the flat of her hand, and stared. For a moment Kathryn thought that Caz had heard – had seen here – certainly the girl looked up, and seemed to stare directly at Kathryn. But no, nothing.

Kathryn stood by her window and watched. At the next station, she followed Caz off the train in a throng of other passengers. Across the platform and up the stops to the street above, and – she was gone. Kathryn looked up and down the street, but could see no sign of Caz. She threw up her gaze to the heavens in despair, and let out a silent scream.

She was in Park Town, and found herself drawn down the leafy street of detached houses to the driveway of Laurel Place. Kathryn could have been standing at the end of the driveway, for just a few seconds, or many more minutes, she couldn't tell. Every little while she looked up at the house at the end of the drive, until finally she began to walk purposely towards it. Her feet crunched on the gravel, and she skipped sideways to the grass instead, taking the verge beside the drive with her eyes fixed all the time on the house ahead.

As she neared, she found that she could hear music drifting out into the still evening light, duets of flute and clarinet that sang out strongly. Kathryn stepped quietly around the side of the house, to where French windows to a room stood open, and it was through these that the music leapt out. Kathryn stayed just long enough to see Lewis and Amanda together, playing their duets. She saw Sarah too, sitting in an armchair opposite and reading, and she ducked back out of sight as Sarah looked up.

Kathryn fled quickly across the lawn to join the drive further down, and out the gate to the end of the hedge. She panted breathlessly and continued walking, back down the street towards the metro station.

Alighting from the tram in Jericho, Kathryn came face to face with a newspaper street vendor, and the headline on the local paper impossible to miss.

MOTHER OF CITY DIES

Alongside the headline was a picture of Miss Leroy at some civil engagement. Kathryn thrust her pennies at the vendor and grabbed a copy from the pile. Kathryn took her newspaper, and without further delay made straight for home. Once inside she slung down her bag, kicked off her shoes, and hit the sofa to read the newspaper through.

It was breaking news. It had happened that afternoon, but even so there were pages of obituaries and reflection already, and a timeline of when the funeral would be and whom would be invited. She continued to stare at the printed article until her eyes hurt. She continued to remember that afternoon – just a few hours earlier – and the music that she had heard. She continued to hear the music in her head now, over and over on a constant loop.

As she listened to the music from earlier endlessly playing in her head, her eyes focused on the words in the article. After a few minutes, her brain finally recognised the words as the name of the pieces Lewis and Amanda had been playing. Of course, she realised, they had been rehearsing for the funeral.

Her funeral.

14

'Bored yet?' asked Charlotte the following morning when Kathryn arrived at work.

'Huh?'

'The news,' said Charlotte. 'I had to switch off the local radio this morning. They just kept going on and on about *that* woman.'

And by *that woman*, Kathryn knew Charlotte was referring to the late Miss Leroy. Kathryn frowned and fired up her computer for the day, to lose herself in another day of editorial queries, typesetter battles, and author corrections. At some point Eleanor arrived, a little sore after a dental appointment, and later still they all took themselves off for coffee, only realising then that Amanda was still strangely absent.

'She's connected somehow to The Family, isn't she?' Eleanor said.

'It explains why she is always holier-than-thou when conversing with us mere mortals,' agreed Charlotte.

Kathryn kept quiet. She remembered what she had seen last night, of Amanda playing music with Louis in the drawing room of Laurel Place.

By noon they were all long past ready for lunch, but when Charlotte first broached the question, Kathryn was hesitant over her response.

'Kathryn?' Charlotte prompted.

Kathryn shook her head.

'Think I might go home for lunch, actually.'

'Everything okay?'

Kathryn nodded, if unconvincingly.

Leaving The Press in the warm spring sunshine, she walked the three blocks to her house. She grabbed a drink from the fridge and a packet of crisps, and retrieved her copy of *The Albion Book of Ballads*.

The Faery Queen was dead, which meant that she had to take a life to be reborn. So, she reasoned, all she had to do to save Louis now, was to make sure that Miss Leroy stayed dead. Kathryn swigged down more juice and crunched on her crisps as she stared at the verses of the ballad again. She turned to the beginning, and read the whole thing through to the end again to make sure.

The whole of the rest of the afternoon, Kathryn found it hard to concentrate on work. The accuracy of scientific and technical data in articles selected for publication in journals of questionable impact factor seemed somehow unimportant when it came to a man's life.

Eleanor shut down her computer with a massive sigh.

'Anyone for The Duke?' she asked.

'Two nights in a row?'

Charlotte cleared her desk and began to gather her belongings.

'Too right,' agreed Kathryn.

They voiced their intentions to some further friends then headed out, and were standing at the bar before five o'clock, pointlessly holding the cocktail menus.

'Ginger Tom, please,' Kathryn asked the barman, and pulled out a grubby tenner from her purse.

The three friends took their drinks and made their way to their traditional table at the back beneath the glazed conservatory roof.

'This week just does not get any better.'

Charlotte sat down with her Raspberry Martini in front of her.

'It really doesn't,' said Kathryn. 'Of course, it does give us the perfect excuse to—'

She sipped from her glass, and almost instantaneously beamed. Eleanor laughed.

'Have we ever come to The Duke three nights in a row on school nights?'

Kathryn shook her head.

'Good, isn't it?'

They settled round the table with their drinks, picking out the soundtrack of classic pop and rock from the snatches of neighbouring conversation; an older group sharing a bottle of Prosecco between them are talking about the death of Miss Leroy, and her contribution to the university and to the city orchestra.

Charlotte leant closer across the table, fixing her friend in her sight.

'You have a plan, don't you.'

Kathryn shrugged innocently. After a few minutes she relented, and pulled some folded sheets of paper from her bag.

'I don't know why they keep on going on about it. We all know precisely what's going to happen.'

Charlotte and Eleanor both stared. Kathryn unfolded the paper, and smoothed out the creases.

'Eleven years ago. And eleven years before that.'

Kathryn pointed to her notes.

'How old is – was – Miss Leroy?'

'Got to be pushing eighty.'

'Seventy-seven.'

'Seven elevens?'

Kathryn nodded.

'So what's your plan?'

Kathryn sat staring into her drink, watching the lights dance through the fractured, twisted shapes of ice cubes. She heard Charlotte's question and the subsequent revised repeat of it, but only in so far as she heard Charlotte's voice, and knew the words were directed at her.

'Kathryn?'

Kathryn looked up, and slowly shook her head.

'You're going to go, aren't you?'

'I thought I could let him go. That it would work.'

'Not that simple,' said Charlotte.

Kathryn shook her head.

'So...' Charlotte continued to probe Kathryn.

'Miss Leroy has – had – still has – a hold over Louis. She needs him because every eleven years she needs to take a life to continue her own.'

'But she's died.'

'Every seven cycles she has to be reborn, and that means she has to die. I think, I'm hoping, that now is her weakest point. I have to stop her.'

'When?'

'Her funeral, I think.'

Kathryn retrieved a discarded newspaper from the seat next to her, and pulled it open at the story about her death.

'It's the twenty-first. The solstice.'

Charlotte frowned.

'The end of spring. The centre of new life. Guess it makes sense.'

Kathryn sat with her cocktail, thinking – obsessing – stressing – over what she had to do. She flicked through the pages of her notebook, at the notes that she had made.

'What's the plan?'

Kathryn looked up in answer to Charlotte's question.

'Turn up. Hope something comes to me...'

Kathryn frowned, and knocked back more of her Ginger Tom.

Kathryn left The Duke at eight-thirty, going her separate way from Charlotte and Eleanor, and it was still light. She made her way home and cooked herself dinner, then read some more from her books. By ten o'clock she was feeling the pull of her bed, and headed upstairs to snuggle down and read some more.

Eventually tiredness overcame her, and she put her book to one side, slid down in her bed, and switched out the light. She laid there for an undetermined amount of time, listening to the sounds from the street and gazing imaginatively into the shadows and shapes thrown across the ceiling and the wall by the blue light of a spring night.

She was just dozing off, or in some other place similarly between awake and asleep, when she was started from her slumber by the sound of a car pulling up outside, and of voices on the doorstep. Kathryn lay there, straining hard to hear what was being said between Nina and Matthew. Just as Kathryn was tuning her ear into the conversation, the wind would change to carry their voices somewhere else, or there would be some other background noise and she missed the critical words, and had to begin again the process of tuning in her ear. Then it went quiet again, followed shortly after by the sounds of a key turning, the latch of the door opening and closing again, and then a little later a car driving off.

Nina's footsteps climbed the stairs of the house, alone. Kathryn laid in her bed listening, and then—

Kathryn woke with the morning sun streaming in through the window. She got up, washed and dressed, and headed out into the early morning. She jumped the next tram to rattle down Walton Street and rode it all the way to the city centre, changing to head up to East Oxford with its streets of red brick and industrial history. Alighting from the tram at the top of The Hill, she crossed the road and rounded the corner to the long, low wall in front of Wren Hoe County School.

She was passed by an old, dirt-stained car as it grumbled and wheezed past her and turned into the car park; Beth. Kathryn broke into a run to catch up.

'Beth! Wait up!' Kathryn called out, as she crossed the car park.

Beth was already locking up her car, with her arms full of exercise books and bags. She hardly seemed to recognise Kathryn, as she slowed in her final approach.

'I'm glad I caught you—' Kathryn panted.

Beth stared at Kathryn.

'Kathryn,' said Kathryn. 'You remember. I'm...'

She hesitated.

'A friend of Louis' – Lewis'. Louis'.'

Beth stared back at Kathryn, with maybe a vague sense of recognition in her hazel eyes.

'You don't remember me, do you?'

Kathryn could tell that Beth was trying to remember.

'Louis Tumnal. You brought Sarah and Caz down to Bristol to see us – the concert. You must remember.'

Beth shook her head.

'She's made you forget, hasn't she? Miss Leroy; somehow she's made you all forget me.'

Kathryn took a step back. When she woke this morning, she had felt an overwhelming need to see Beth; because she had feared that something like this would happen, and she wanted to allay those fears. Now her hopes were quashed, and all her fears realised. She backed away from Beth's car.

A car horn blasted behind her, and she had to jump clear as Tom's mustard-yellow car swerved into the car park and screeched to a halt.

'Polly!' Kathryn greeted her friend, as she got out the passenger side door.

Polly looked straight through her, and Kathryn noticed a glint of sunlight from something around her neck. She looked closer; it was the wedding necklace – a pattern work of silver flowers to bind around her neck. Now she looked more closely, she could see the same gleam of silver beneath the neckline of Beth's shirt.

'Take them off!' Kathryn shouted to Beth, and again to Polly. 'Those necklaces, they're controlling you!'

Polly stared back at Kathryn like she was some mad old crone. Beth was equally perplexed, but put her hand to her neck to feel the necklace that hung around her.

Kathryn stared. She shook her head, and stared again from one to the other.

'You really don't remember, do you?'

Tom blasted on his car horn behind Polly, and she stopped to say goodbye before he drove off, lurching and screeching away in his usual manner. Polly turned back again towards Kathryn, but with no further increase in recognition.

'Excuse me,' Polly said, as she stepped past Kathryn towards the main school entrance. Beth began crossing the playground after Polly. She kept looking across at Kathryn as she walked. Kathryn looked back, now imploringly and almost begging.

Kathryn sighed at last, as her shoulders slumped forwards and her face dropped. Beth stopped, and turned, her hand once more resting on the necklace. She took a few steps back towards Kathryn.

'Forget us,' Beth said, 'Go. Go now, and forget we ever existed.'

Beth turned again, and crossed the playground to follow Polly inside.

15

The disappearance from her life of everyone who had known of her relationship with Louis bothered Kathryn intensely. When she arrived at work later that morning, she was half expecting Charlotte and Eleanor to not recognise her; but no, they greeted her just as warmly as usual. And again, Amanda was absent for the day, so the office took on a relaxed attitude, with the whole department decamping at lunchtime for a thick, meaty burger and chips at the Old Bookbinders.

For a while, life almost felt normal. Sitting in a sunny beer garden with her friends and co-workers was something they did at lunchtimes every year, when the days were warm and sunny. The light was perfect today. It filtered down onto the tables –

large slabs of rustic oak perched on old saddle stones – through the fresh lime green of new leaves of wisteria. Kathryn stared up at it, finding the colours and patterns hypnotic. She reached for the compact digital camera she always kept with her in her bag, and composed the shot in the frame of a photograph. Playing with the settings and the focusing, she snapped a series of near identical yet completely different pictures, enjoying the moment of spontaneous creativity until – she stopped.

Kathryn put down her camera, but her gaze remained aloft, her eyes unable to blink.

'Kathryn?'

Kathryn heard her friend and turned to face her, but she said nothing. A year ago, she had been eagerly looking forward to starting her photography summer classes. A year ago, her Mr Tumnal had stepped tentatively into her life from the other end of a camera lens. She put her camera back in her bag and turned back to her friends, forcing her mind to tune back into the conversation.

Pushing thoughts of Louis and photography to the back of her mind, Kathryn tried to get on with the day; but her mind was an engine of creativity. Even on the walk back to work, Kathryn found with every turn of the head or snatched glance, the ordinary detail of some street-side object brought to mind a photograph; and in the photograph, the thought of Louis.

An afternoon of proof corrections did at least present Kathryn with no new photographic vistas, and so, for the duration, she was able to return again to some kind of normality.

Come the end of the day, Kathryn headed straight home in preparation for tomorrow. As her evening meal cooked, she ironed a smart blouse and got ready the sombre trouser-suit she reserved for editorial society meetings. After dinner she read, poring backwards and forwards through *The Albion Book of*

Ballads. She read both *Tam Lin* and *Thomas the Rhymer*, until she could most-likely read them back from memory. Eventually she woke, a little after midnight, still on the sofa with her books scattered about her. She gathered them up, fetched a glass of water, and headed for bed.

Kathryn read some more in bed, then fell asleep suddenly with the light on. At some point she woke briefly with a crick in her neck, turned off the light and pushed herself down in her bed. She soon drifted back off to sleep - a sleep that found her searching through some woods.

They were the woods at the back of mum and dad's garden, except that they weren't. There was a river running through it; wide and snaking through the woods, and impossible to cross; Louis was at the far side, looking at her - no, he was walking, slowly and calmly downstream. She chased up and down stream, forcing her way through the trees that seemed to be ever denser the more that she went through them, with brambles that reached out and clung to her as if trying to hold her back. Her heart raced as she looked for a way to cross, but she couldn't find one. In her mind there was a bridge downstream, but every time she thought it was almost there, she found that she was wrong.

Kathryn tripped and stumbled her way through reaching vines and over twisted roots, on a path that took her away from the river and further into the dark forest. She fought her way to get back to the river, but the forest closed in around her; paths that used to be paths were no more. She turned and turned again searching frantically for the path, only to have to resign herself to going on.

And then she heard it; the music. Pipers, somewhere near in the forest. Having given up on the river, she followed the sound of the music through the forest, before finally emerging out into a meadow in the strange, ethereal light of an Arctic midnight. It looked like Port Meadow though – and actually, she could see the front of her own house overlooking the lock. Her brain didn't question the fact that her house didn't face a lock, nor was it in sight of the canal.

The fair was in progress. Kathryn kept on bumping into friends and colleagues, and not one of them questioned that she was wearing her pyjamas. She looked for the pipers, but couldn't hear anything for the blaring of the fairground stalls. Kathryn continued on, weaving through the stalls, past the hog roast and the beer tent, and – she stopped and listened – there – there it was again, the music. She recognised the tune, but realised that it wasn't pipers but strings; a fiddle maybe, and a cello, and...

Kathryn broke into a run, until there in a clearing in the trees – she spun round again to find the fair gone – the Dumas Quartet were playing. Who were they playing to? Kathryn screamed the question at them, but they ignored her and carried on playing. And then she saw him; Louis. She could see why she had almost missed him. Now she looked more carefully, she saw that he was enthroned in a kind of wicker chair. She wondered about the word 'enthroned', as it was more like he was 'bound' by a thick vine. Tendrils on its branches and sticky suckers crawled across his body, and over his face.

Kathryn set to pulling the vines from him, but the more she ripped them away, the faster they grew back. Where the sticky suckers had rooted themselves to Louis' face, they left scars and red rashes on his skin. He didn't scream out or protest at all; he didn't seem to react to the voracious attack of the creepers.

There was laughter, too. Kathryn spun round to see Nina and Matthew laughing at her; full and hearty, guffawing laughter from their bellies. In the closing darkness, only their faces were visible; menacing faces in the gloom. Matthew reached out to her from the shadows, with a hand composed entirely of dry autumn leaves. Kathryn pulled herself from him and fought to keep him off as the hand of leaves reached closer. She felt the leaves crumble and flake in her own hands.

And then she saw him – it – the leaf monster, rearing up behind her, looming over her as the wind whipped fallen leaves back into its body. Its eyes burned brightly beneath the darkly featured face. They were twinkling eyes, the icy gaze of Miss Leroy. Kathryn stepped back.

Alone on a far-off hillside, surrounded by a pool of light, a lone-piper played – a young boy – of eleven years. Kathryn stared as the piper played. He was Louis as a young boy with his flute. He was playing his song on a distant hillside, and Kathryn realised there and then, somehow, that it was the song that belonged to Louis; that the song owned him, and that was how Miss Leroy did it. It was how she controlled Louis, and through him, everybody.

'You can't stop it.'

Kathryn spun round, to where the leaf monster had spoken with Miss Leroy's distinctive voice.

'It's useless to try. Pointless to even think of it.'

Kathryn shook her head defiantly, turned, and ran. Across Port Meadow she ran through tall grass and buttercups to the mound where Louis played. He had his back to her as she approached, playing his flute, with a small mane of infant's fair hair tumbling around his shoulders. She approached him, and as she took the final few steps, he turned towards her.

She stopped and stared. Her mouth gaped.

16

Traffic was at a standstill in the centre of Wren Hoe on the morning of the funeral. Kathryn found it easy to slip in with the crowds near Christ Church College, and made her way round the quad with university fellows, city dignitaries and townsfolk to the small college chapel. By the time she had queued through the cloisters the chapel was packed, from the main knave to the side aisles. Kathryn made her way down the main aisle, until she found space on a pew to slip into.

She found, from her vantage point, that she could see the choir stalls, at the front of which she could see Louis. Was that Louis, she wondered, or Lewis? Her mind ached at the thought. She had thought she'd got it straight, but then... seeing him there, now, and next to Amanda? She doubted her decisions. The other side of Amanda was Matthew; and next to him, in the closest thing she owned to sombre black, was Nina. Kathryn stared. From the top half of Nina's dress she could recognise it from many a Friday night and Saturday morning, and knew how inappropriately short it was behind the pew.

If only she was this popular in the staffroom.
Maybe that's why. They're all here – to make sure.
Ss-shh!

Just saying.

Kathryn found herself turning into the conversation from the row behind. She heard the words, and smiled at the wry, inappropriateness of the humour long before she recognised the voices.

I guess a lot of these people are here out of duty.

Because of who she was, not the person she was.

'Beth!'

Kathryn swung round in the pew to see Beth sitting immediately behind her, with Caz to one side and Polly to the other, and Tom beyond that.

'Hello, Kathryn.'

Kathryn gaped.

'You're talking to me – *now?*'

Kathryn scowled, mainly at Beth, but also, in passing, to the others.

'I thought you'd forgotten me.'

Beth shook her head.

'Not at all. You gave Louis up, so his friends disappeared with him. But you're here now – so—'

'You have us back,' added Caz.

Kathryn frowned. She was doubtful on the one hand, but – and here she looked over her shoulder again, at the four of them sitting together in a pew – it *was* good to be able to talk to someone about things. About Louis.

Someone brushed past Kathryn as they – *she* – took a seat next to her at the end of the pew. It was a girl; slight, and with fair hair tucked back in a ponytail.

'Sarah?'

Sarah turned her head with a smile towards Kathryn. She turned back to face the front as the organ processional began; the background hum of conversation died away, and the last few of the congregation took their seats.

The priest of the chapel stepped forward, and announced the occasion to the assembled mass, on what sad occasion they were gathered together to commemorate. As he spoke, Sarah silently reached across to Kathryn to hold her hand; Kathryn allowed her to take it, and she herself felt comfort in the closeness.

A hymn followed, wherein the cathedral was roused in celebration of Miss Leroy's life. Kathryn found herself awkwardly joining in with the song, but her voice faltered, distracted by Louis in her line of sight. She forced herself to look away, and instead reflected on the architecture of the chapel – a cathedral in all but name – and at the saints that looked down on the congregation. The bust of St Eldridge looked down on all in the church, clothed in vines of stone with the small chiming bell hung beneath.

Eldridge. He seemed to be speaking now, extolling the virtues of the dearly departed Miss Leroy. It was not Eldridge speaking, though; Matthew had stepped up to the pulpit, and was eulogising his aunt. Kathryn saw the television cameras pan round and tighten on their subject. She drifted in and out of the words, hearing some, and zoning out from others. It was standard for a public funeral. All the respect that was necessary but nothing of the personal relationships. Matthew was stoic in his words.

Eventually he concluded the eulogy, and the congregation were brought to their feet by another hymn. Kathryn watched as Matthew stepped back alongside Nina, who offered her boyfriend a supportive arm. It was then Kathryn noticed that Louis and Amanda were no longer in their places in the choir stalls. Her gaze darted this way and that across the church as she mouthed – badly – the words of the hymn. She didn't have to wait long to find out what happened to Louis though, for following the hymn, he and Amanda came forward with flute and oboe to play a duet for the deceased, a series of movements during, and between, the final moments of the blessing. And then it was over. The pall bearers took their positions again alongside the ash coffin and formed the head of the procession out of the church.

Louis and Amanda put down their instruments, and stepped in behind Matthew and Nina. Kathryn watched them go, with the yearning to snatch Louis away pulling strongly at her. She felt Sarah's hand hold her back as she readied herself to leave, and follow the procession.

'Sarah, I have to.'

'I know, but—'

Sarah seemed to just not finish her sentence.

Kathryn watched the church begin to clear. She wanted to leave. She needed to get going. Eventually Sarah began to move, and they stepped out into the aisle; Kathryn rushed out of the church like a stopper released from a bottle. She made to follow everyone else to the door, only to stop a few steps on. She looked back at the stationary Sarah.

'What?' she hissed.

Sarah said nothing, merely turned in the opposite direction and began heading towards the choir stalls. Kathryn shook her head, but followed. Sarah stood near the foot of the pulpit where Louis and Amanda's music stands remained, and on their stands, the flute and oboe.

Kathryn slowed her approach.

'Sarah, you're a genius.'

She saw Sarah grin. Kathryn stepped forward and grabbed the oboe. She took the flute too, and offered it to Sarah.

'You can play too, can't you?'

Sarah took her father's flute.

Emerging out of the front of the abbey into the garden of Christ Church, Kathryn and Sarah followed the throng around the quad and out onto the street beneath the Tom Tower. A solemn, stately bell chimed a mournful beat across the roofs of the city.

The procession had already made off towards the city centre in a black hearse, followed on foot first by the family, and then by the city dignitaries. Some of the congregation followed at the rear, only to filter off into the other city streets. Kathryn and Sarah met up again with Beth, Tom, and Polly, and together they were amongst the last of the public to follow the funeral procession. Expecting the long walk to either the City Cemetery at Cuttleslow or the private ground in Jericho, Kathryn was surprised to find the procession turning off the Banbury Road into Park Town, and back to the foreboding presence of Laurel Place in its sweeping grounds.

By the time Kathryn and Sarah arrived at the gates, the procession had already disappeared around the side of the house, and security were closing the tall wrought-iron gates. Kathryn recognised a couple of the suited men from that evening down by the canal, and tried to push her way through the gates with Sarah.

The man shook his head and shoved her back. Kathryn turned, and ushered Sarah forward in front of her.

'You have to let us through,' said Kathryn. 'Her dad's inside.'

The man on the far side of the gate shook his head in silent response. Beth pushed forward from behind Kathryn, with Polly and Tom.

'You have to let us through,' Kathryn persevered.

'You've had the public service. This is just family.'

'We worked for her. She used to call us her family,' Beth interjected. 'Tom virtually is–'

'I'm sorry. Those are my orders.'

The man closed the gate, slipped the bolt, and fastened the padlock.

Kathryn still had her hand on the ironwork. She cussed the man, lashing out at the gate before stepping away with Sarah and her three friends.

'We have to get in there!'

Kathryn stood on the pavement and stared back towards the gate, feeling the dejection of failure. She turned to her side, to see Sarah staring back at her.

'We can still get in,' said Sarah. 'Look, I'll show you.'

Sarah turned and headed back down the road, and into the garden of the neighbouring house. Sarah led them through a herbaceous border into the gloom at the side of house. Eventually, the path ended at an old brick shed.

'Really, Sarah?'

Sarah turned and grinned.

'You can get through all the gardens from here down to the river, without ever going on any roads. Dad showed me years back.'

Sarah carried on, squeezing between the bushes and brick wall. Kathryn followed, only to find Sarah gone. She stood, staring at a stack of old bricks and rusty watering cans and overflowing compost heaps.

'Sarah?'

Beth, Tom, and Polly joined her. A little voice spoke as if out of nowhere.

'Over here,' the compost heap appeared to say.

Tom pointed to fresh footprints going up through the compost heap. Kathryn nodded, and picked her way up, to peer over the wall and down on Sarah. Sarah encouraged Kathryn from below, and Kathryn eased herself down onto the top of the wall, and from there jumped down. The others followed quickly, and Sarah led them on through the thick maze of shrubs and tunnels beneath the dark shrouds of yew trees.

Eventually they slowed in their approach, creeping forward to peer through the bushes into the rose garden with the sunken Italian pool. The family stood nearby, gathered around the coffin and surrounded by the faceless city dignitaries.

'It's like an army.'

Kathryn looked at Sarah.

'It *is* an army – *her* army.'

She turned and looked again at the dignitaries, still and silent, with uniform expressions that made them seem almost featureless.

'What happens now?' asked Beth, as she stepped up next to Kathryn.

'I'm – I'm not sure.'

Kathryn's hand tightened around the clarinet. Over in the rose garden Amanda and Louis stood, hands held, facing each other; she seemed to be telling him something, and he seemed upset.

'Mum – she's ending it.'

Kathryn shook her head, unable to take her eyes off the scene.

'She's taking him.'

Amanda snapped her fingers, and two men, dark-haired and slight of figure in sharp suits, were at her side within an instant. She glanced from one to the other, and nodded her head towards Louis. Immediately they set about stripping the clothes from him, until he stood in front of Amanda as naked as the day he was born.

Kathryn watched helpless from the shrubbery as the men tore at Louis' clothes, like hyenas pulling the flesh from their prey. All the time Amanda stood watching, like she was the pack leader waiting to be fed.

'You understand, don't you?'

Louis bowed his head subserviently, and nodded.

Amanda waved her hand, summoning another sharp-suited assistant who was swiftly at her side brandishing a flute – Miss Leroy's flute. Amanda took it and brandished it before Louis.

'Can you remember?'

Amanda offered the flute to Louis. Again he nodded, and took the flute. He handled it slowly and carefully, taking his time to try every single key, and size up the weight and feel of it. He lifted it to his mouth but didn't play, just felt it in his hands.

'Play,' Amanda said, with careful and pronounced intonation. 'Play it for me.'

Louis looked uncertain, but pursed his lips to the head joint and readied his fingers on the keys. He blew air softly through the instrument; a single, continuous note.

Don't do it, don't do it – don't do it, Kathryn found herself hissing under her breath—

—and the tune sung out, springing from Louis' lips into the garden. It was *that* tune, in what Kathryn feared was a last reprise.

Kathryn watched and stared as Louis played. She couldn't tell if it was the changing shadows or the way she was looking down on the rose garden, but it seemed to her that as Louis shrunk back and all but sank slowly into the water, Amanda rose up. Kathryn found herself fingering the oboe in front of her. She lifted the instrument up and closed her mouth over the dry reed to soften it, feeling the rice-starchiness on her taste buds. She tucked her bottom lip over her teeth, filled her diaphragm, and blew. An odd, breathy sort of non-note resonated from the instrument, which Kathryn silenced as quickly as she created it.

A quick glance round, and it seemed that neither Louis and Amanda, nor the shadowy men surrounding the rose garden, had noticed. Kathryn began again this time, listening carefully to Louis' tune and coming in with him.

Louis' playing waned.

'No!' Amanda said sharply. 'Don't stop now.'

Louis began again, as did Kathryn. Kathryn watched Amanda keenly, observant of her every expression. As she played a counter line to Louis' melody, she also saw Amanda looking taller, straighter, her hair more greyish, and a glassy glint to her eyes. She was beginning to look more and more like a younger Miss Leroy, while Louis stood opposite her, sinking lower in the pool of water.

Kathryn now saw what was happening, how the tune was taking something from the man and feeding the woman. She could see it was the song that was orchestrating it, and that somehow she had to reverse the change.

Sarah rushed forward to stand alongside Kathryn, and joined the song. She looked up at Kathryn; with her wide searching eyes she seemed to be telling her something. With tongued inflections and nimble fingering, she added glyphs and trills to embellish the simple song. Sarah nodded her head to Kathryn encouragingly.

Kathryn followed Sarah's lead, feeling the flow of the music and adding her own embellishments; in doing so she fumbled some notes and slipped some keys. She kept her eyes fixed on Amanda, smiling inside as she saw the panic on the face of the Amanda-Miss Leroy figure.

For a moment, Louis stopped playing. He had heard Kathryn and Sarah's playing, and was now looking down the length of the pool at Amanda for guidance.

'Play on,' encouraged Amanda. She signalled to a couple more of her suited men, and instructed them to search for the source of the music.

Kathryn and Amanda began another round of the song, with ever more defined intonation. Louis played again as he drifted further in the pool from Amanda, the level of which now came halfway up his chest. Kathryn and Sarah played on, louder now; more deliberately louder and with defined variations, as around them the sprites and dark-fairies searched through thicket and shrubbery.

Amanda stood tall, less and less the girl with auburn hair that Louis had sat next to in band, and more the image of the headmistress who taught him to play.

And then he did it. Louis played a variation – a snatch of Kathryn's own tune.

'No!' Amanda shrieked.

Louis couldn't stop now. Once deviated from the notes that were learnt by rote, his interpretation was unstoppable and unpredictable in his choice of direction.

As far as she might while playing the oboe, Kathryn smiled at the result. The Amanda-Leroy *thing* seemed pained by the developments, and already her presence was less. The level of the water that surrounded him seemed to be lower too.

A rustling in the bushes behind them, voices too, and her oboe was being pulled from her hands. Firm hands grasped Kathryn's arms, and pulled her forcibly away. She could still hear Louis and Sarah's music continuing strongly as she was bundled through the shrubbery, down twisting paths of dark shadows until she was delivered to the rose garden, and to Amanda; Amanda, who now knelt, broken, on the grass.

'Lewis! Lewis! Don't fail me now...'

The man holding Kathryn now released her, but pushed her forward in front of Amanda. Looking round, Kathryn saw that he was Matthew.

Amanda looked up and saw Kathryn.

'Thank you, Eldridge,' she said to Matthew. 'You've brought me the girl.'

'For all the good it will do you,' added Kathryn immediately. 'It's over. He's not yours.'

Kathryn looked towards Louis, still playing the flute, still naked in the pool of water that now ebbed and flowed, higher and lower. She looked back to Amanda for her response.

'You can't seriously think you can defeat me?'

'I don't have to,' Kathryn said simply. 'You've defeated yourself. When you gave Louis his creativity, his gift.'

'You have no idea what you're talking about.'

Kathryn shrugged away Amanda's reply.

'When did you change it from seven years?' asked Kathryn, though not waiting for any reply. '*You pays the tythe to hell; He so fair and full of flesh; He fear it be himself.*'

'Then you should know you can't stop it. *If* you're right, that is.'

'Oh, I'm right. Eleven years, isn't it; father and son, over and over again. Time after time.'

Amanda laughed, a sly, menacing laugh as she listened to Kathryn's explanation. And all the time Louis played on his flute, and the water that surrounded him filled and emptied in some endless struggle. Somewhere in the bushes, Sarah still played her accompaniment while dark-elf foot soldiers searched the thicket.

'Except Louis is different, isn't he?

'He should have gone last time. What happened? You take the child when the child becomes the man, and in his place another child waits. You've always been so careful to observe your own rules.'

Amanda stayed silent, watching the level of the pool slowly rise over the height of Louis' chest. Kathryn glanced round, and her heart quickened its beat.

'Why didn't you take him eleven years ago?' demanded Kathryn.

Amanda turned and looked down on the girl who was staring down at her. She had a look of pity in her eyes.

'Pity.'

She almost spat out the words.

'His mother grovelled and snivelled and begged at my feet, and I took pity on her. I took her instead.'

'She wasn't the same though, was she? You don't just take anyone though, do you? You're always so careful. You *like* them kind, you *like* them creative. But you also *need* them to be strong.'

As Kathryn spoke those last words, she realised that the rose garden was silent; the music was gone. Spinning round on her heels, she saw Louis up to his neck in water, his flute still in one hand, but floundering. She turned back to Amanda.

'Stop this!'

Amanda turned and smiled, slyly.

'I won't be taking anyone's pity again.'

She snapped her fingers in the air, and Matthew was at her side again; this time he was holding a struggling Sarah.

'Lewis' mother might have been weak and foolish, but he has played his part well. This girl will more than make up for any earlier shortcomings.'

Amanda stepped down now to the edge of the pool. Barefoot, she stepped into the pool, and reached out to Louis.

'Come. Take my hand. It's time.'

They'll shape me in your arms, Janet.
A mother-naked man.
Cast your green mantle over me
And sae I will be won.

Kathryn heard the words like they were her own, but she hadn't said anything. She heard Sarah scream her name, and she saw Amanda reaching out through the water for Louis.

She felt her own necklace round her neck – the Maori Greenstone that her father had given her. It wasn't a cloak of any kind, but – her fingers slipped the knots on the cord, and pulled it over her head.

'No!'

Kathryn threw herself into the pool, and, fighting her way through an improbable current, she reached out and threw the pendant over Louis' head.

'You won't have him. Louis, you're mine!'

What happened next all happened at the same time. Amanda screamed; Louis dropped back in the water, released at last from her hold; and Kathryn pulled her man into a tight embrace. The current in the sunken pond in the rose garden turned. The water drained away from Louis and Kathryn, and swept Amanda out of the garden.

Louis and Kathryn looked down at their feet where they stood halfway up to their shins in pond water amongst lilies and irises. Trapped beneath the surface was the ghostly shape of a grey-haired old woman.

'It's over,' said Louis.

He hugged Kathryn tightly, and they turned and stepped out of the pool and began to walk out of the rose garden.

'Dad!' Sarah called as she ran towards him, and threw her arms around both Louis and Kathryn. As Louis fiddled with the hair at the top of Sarah's head, he turned and looked to Kathryn.

'You don't mind, do you?'

Kathryn shook her head and smiled. The three now continued on up the steps out of the Italian sunken garden and through the roses. The council members and city dignitaries had gone. Far off across the lawn, Matthew and Nina stood and watched, until they, too, turned and left.

Nearby, a young woman with beautiful auburn hair sat on a bank of grass, with her head in her hands.

'Is that...?'

Louis nodded.

'My imaginary friend. It used to be so simple.'

CODA

neue tempore

It was two weeks later that Louis and Kathryn found themselves back at the city cemetery. They left the chapel where it stood in the centre of the parkland, with Sarah at their side; they made their way to an empty grave, to where Matthew and Nina were already stood waiting. Matthew was holding a small, plain wooden casket.

They exchanged cursory greetings, and after a few minutes they were joined at the graveside by Beth, arriving with Polly and Tom. No words were spoken as Matthew placed the casket into the grave and took a step back. Nina passed him a shovel. Slowly and deliberately, he shovelled soil from the pile into the grave until it covered the casket.

'Now it's over,' Louis said in a hushed aside to Kathryn and Sarah.

'Is she really gone?' asked Sarah.

'She is, yes,' Kathryn said. 'For as long as there are fairies though, they will always have a Queen.'

All three looked down at where a stone already marked the head of the grave. It was a simple slab of granite with no name, just a simple inscription:

CHILD OF CARTERHAUGH

Louis turned away from the grave with Kathryn and Sarah, and stepped away from the others. Away across the cemetery stood another woman with auburn hair.

'How is she?'

Sarah looked up at her father with a slight frown.

'Free. I think,' said Sarah. 'Does that make sense?'

Louis nodded.

'She was *my* creation, my escape, *my* happiness; and then *her* plaything. *She* never had a chance to be real.'

Sarah shook her head.

Kathryn stepped forward, staring across the cemetery.

'I feel like I should feel guilty, Sarah. I didn't know what would happen to her – your mum – I didn't consider...'

Her voice trailed off as Sarah's gaze intensified on her.

'I... we did what we had to do.'

Kathryn's hand closed around Louis'.

'Will you ever see her again?'

Louis shook his head.

'I don't think so.'

'What will happen to her?'

'I dreamt her up, with all the skills and qualifications she possesses. She has the confidence that I never did.'

'She'll be fine, Dad.'

Kathryn turned again to Sarah.

'And how about you, Sarah?'

Sarah didn't answer, except that she walked back with them across the cemetery. When they turned for a last look, Amanda was gone.

*

A month later, and it was a hot, sunny day in early August when Louis and Kathryn headed down to Port Meadow for the big summer party. They met up with Sarah outside the distinctive tower of St Barnabas.

Both Kathryn and Louis had their cameras with them, and Louis had his leather satchel slung over his shoulder. He had relinquished his cords for chinos and a linen shirt, and he still wore Kathryn's greenstone around his neck. Splitting up at the stalls, Kathryn to find cider, and Louis and Sarah the juiciest, most succulent smelling hog roast they could find. They regrouped by the river to eat and drink; and afterwards, as Kathryn and Louis set about a series of self-set photography challenges, Sarah tucked herself up to write.

ACKNOWLEDGEMENTS

If ever there was a reason to car share to the day job, this book is it. Thank you to Caroline Simms on that day, a little after 7.30am on Wednesday 9 August 2006, for mishearing me when I said, 'It's a bit autumnal today'. If you had heard me correctly then we may never have spent the next 45-minute commute discovering who Mr Tumnal was... and then, a further 45 minutes in the afternoon working out what his story is. Thank you.

Thank you too, to my brain, for being the weird and wonderful thing that it is, that let me come up with such a completely, delightfully wonky story as you will find this to be.

Talk about this book with the hashtag #MrTumnal @ shepline

ABOUT THE AUTHOR

T E Shepherd was born in Derbyshire but grew up in Lowestoft, Suffolk before moving to Cheshire to study a degree in Creative Arts. He lives in Oxfordshire with his wife Emma and their seven cats, four chickens, two bunnies and some fish.

For more information on future works visit journal.shepline.com or www.facebook.com/teshepherd

Talk about this book on Twitter with the hashtag #MrTumnal @shepline